Paint
a Picture

by
Patsy Collins

Lovely to meet you

Paint Me a Picture is dedicated to all those who've helped or encouraged me in my writing. There are many such people; my family, teachers and workshop leaders, members of the writing groups and forums to which I belong, my blog followers, those who read my tweets or have liked my facebook author page, everyone who read or helped promote *Escape to the Country,* authors whose work I've enjoyed or which has inspired me and, of course, to **you**.

Chapter 1

Above her, a seagull screamed.

Mavis looked up, beyond the huge stone permanence of Portsmouth's sea wall, to the heavy bulk of the dark, menacing sky. The icy blasts from the Solent taunted and threatened, first pushing her forward and then buffeting her back. The seagull screamed again; its cry echoing her misery. Mavis shivered and strode towards the Round Tower. There was a week before she would die; she needed the comfort of looking down into the lichen grey waters.

"Spare some change, love?"

Mavis stopped walking and looked back. A man, huddled in an anorak, sat with his back to the rampart.

"Were you speaking to me?" she asked.

"Anyone who'll listen really," he answered, without lifting his head.

Other people hurried by, turning their collars up against the biting wind and their faces away from Mavis and the beggar.

"I'm listening."

He glanced up, but didn't make eye contact. "I'm hungry and I've got no money, no job, nothing. I asked if you could spare some change."

Mavis shook her head. The man was just a filthy layabout. He would probably spend any money she gave him on drink and drugs. Mavis didn't have time to worry about the problems of a down and out.

She walked on.

It was cold, too cold to be hungry. Mavis had eaten her sandwiches before leaving the office. She fed the birds every day, though they did no work. She'd judged the man by his appearance and her own prejudices. Perhaps he truly did need food. She went back.

"Are you actually hungry, or do you want the money for drink?"

The man looked up again; he stared at her for a moment before replying. "A woman gave me a sandwich yesterday afternoon. I've not eaten since then."

"Come with me." Mavis waited for him to rise, before leading the way to White Hart Road.

"Where are we going?" the man asked as he hurried after her.

"To the chip shop."

"Nice one. Cheers."

"I shall buy you one meal; that is all."

"That's good of you. Thanks."

"Do you have nowhere to live, no family?"

"No."

"Then you should go to social services or a church and ask them for help. You can't rely on the compassion of strangers; that won't get you far. If you wish to change your life, you must do it yourself."

The man looked at her for a moment and then half nodded, half shrugged.

"What would you like?" she asked as she walked through the open doorway of the chip shop.

He looked as though he didn't understand the question.

Mavis pointed at the large price list, high on the chip shop wall.

"What would you like?" she repeated.

"Oh, right. A hot pie would be nice, if that's all right?"

"A pie, portion of chips and a soft drink, please," she said to the boy behind the counter.

"What kind?"

Mavis looked at the hungry man.

"Steak and kidney, and a Coke?" he said.

"Steak and kidney, and a strawberry milkshake, please," Mavis said. She turned to the man. "The milkshake will be more nourishing than a can of fizzy drink."

He nodded.

"The pie'll be a couple of minutes. Is that OK?"

"Yes," Mavis answered. She took a ten pound note from her purse, accepted her change and turned to the hungry man.

"Enjoy your meal."

"I will."

Mavis left him to wait for his food and walked briskly towards the stone steps.

"Thanks very much," the man called after her. She didn't look back.

Mavis climbed the steep granite steps. High above the busy street and the narrow pebble beach she was exposed to the full force of the salt-laden wind. She hurried along the uneven walkway, towards the dank shelter of the fortifications. The stench of stale urine ensured she didn't stop to catch her breath before she'd climbed the final steps and reached her destination. Her heart thumped from the exertion. Mavis's kindness towards the stranger had delayed her, but not for long. She clutched the stone perimeter for support and looked out to sea only a few minutes later than she'd expected.

She stepped back from the edge and gazed around her. The short rows of wooden benches were as empty as her life. She approached the concrete plinth topped with its bronze coloured plaque. 'A picture paints a thousand words' had been the quote on her calendar that morning. The raised images of the plaque could tell visitors a great deal about the local attractions, but there was no one to show an interest in the information. She removed a suede glove and ran her chapped hand over the chilled surface, touching the raised shapes of the landmarks: sea forts and the Anglican cathedral; the Isle of Wight she'd not visited since her schooldays; the Spinnaker Tower she'd not seen the view from. So many places she'd never visited; so many things she would never do.

Mavis turned her back to the sea; she knew it needn't be that way. Tomorrow, in her lunch break, she could walk to the cathedral and admire the stained glass windows. She could go to

Portsmouth at the weekend, have a drink in one of the Gunwharf bars or coffee shops and then ride in the lift to the top of the Spinnaker Tower. She could look out at the sea, the ferries and the Isle of Wight or over to the masts of HMS Victory and Warrior in the historic dockyard. Standing on the glass floor, she could marvel at how small the people appeared as they queued for their turn to witness the same sights.

Mavis faced the sea again. She knew she wouldn't do any of those things. She'd work another week; spend another weekend alone and then climb the grey stone steps for the final time. She'd climb up slowly, and descend quickly.

Mavis had not lived well; her death must be more successful. She must be careful about any clues she left. There would be an investigation into her death. In her mind, a dashing detective and his side-kick knocked on doors, made enquiries. A fluffy looking sharp-witted old lady read her obituary in the paper and provided fascinating revelations about Mavis's past. A wigged judge asked uncomfortable questions in court.

It would be easiest and simplest to leave a statement. That solution wasn't without disadvantages. There was Cousin Linda to think of; she would be hurt to learn the life she'd helped Mavis to create had proved unbearable. There were the birds too; she was sorry she couldn't continue to feed them. She'd enjoyed watching them and feeling they depended on her. Soon, there would be no one to chase away her neighbour's cat. The birds would still be fed though; she'd made sure of that. Her estate was willed to the RSPB. The house could be sold to raise money, provided an arrangement was made to ensure suitable food and clean water were always supplied in the garden. She'd wondered about her life assurance. If suicide was suspected, the company might not pay. With that in mind, her explanatory note never progressed beyond a rough draft. She read it. Just a list really, of disappointments; a description of loneliness. After tearing it into thin strips, she balled it in her hand and held it over the drop, from tower's edge, to the ebbing sea. Her fingers didn't release her unhappy thoughts. The wind didn't blow her troubles away. Mavis held them tight. She would take her litter away with her.

Her heavy coat shielded her body from the worst of the wind, but not her stocking clad legs and bare head. She would have been far more comfortable in her lined suede boots. Boots were unsuitable for the office; she wore low-heeled court shoes in the same deep blue as her coat. She hunched her shoulders, raising the collar to protect the back of her neck. Still the cold, sharp gusts tugged at her greying hair and numbed her ears.

Mavis fumbled in her shoulder bag for a handkerchief. The cold wind made her eyes run. Returning the damp cotton to her bag, she saw the tube of E45 cream. She might as well use some; it would be wasted otherwise. Sitting on a backless wooden bench, she unscrewed the cap. After squeezing cream onto her palm, she ran a finger around the thread to clean it and replaced the cap, taking care no trace of cream soiled the outside of the tube. Using her right index finger, she dabbed cream on each nail of her left hand. She repeated this in mirror image, until each nail was topped with a wisp of cream. She held her hands flat in front of her to ensure the distribution was even. On her rounded nails, the effect looked like the tiny iced biscuits she'd enjoyed as a child. She massaged the cream into her cuticles and then rubbed her hands together until the cream was absorbed. She did so almost every day, yet her hands were rough and sore. Still cracks appeared in her cuticles and the sides of her nails. Cleaning fluids stung and clothes and paper snagged at her skin.

A large ferry went by; a passenger waved. Mavis didn't know who they were waving at; there was no one there but her. She wondered where the ferry was headed; not to the Isle of Wight, it wasn't a Wightlink boat. Not a boat at all, but a ship. Sailing to France or, possibly, Spain.

Mavis knew where she was going.

Next week, she would get the bus as usual from Lee-on-the-Solent into Gosport. Her ferry ticket would be punched for the harbour crossing. Once in Portsmouth, she would walk down past Gunwharf Quays. The bars and shops would be closed; the first members of staff arriving to unlock the doors and switch on the lights. Perhaps cleaners would be there dusting and sweeping. There would be security staff too, but no one would notice her walk by. No one ever did.

She would walk on, past the café and tattoo parlour, under the railway bridge but not turn left as had become her routine. Instead, she would go right and follow the old harbour wall. Passing through the fortifications, she would hold her breath to avoid the smell. No one would hear the echo of her footsteps. She would sit on this bench at the top and have a last drink to wash down the pills. The fall alone was unlikely to kill her. She'd seen children diving off the tower for fun on summer days.

There would be no children and no tourists. Mavis had visited the tourist information office to enquire after shipping movements. When a visiting warship or a new ferry was expected, the tower filled with amateur photographers. They gathered together with their uniform anoraks and radio scanners. Strange hobby.

Other than the regular ferries to the Isle of Wight and the continent, no ships were forecast to pass through the harbour entrance during the third week of January. Mavis would be alone.

Her death would not look accidental if she were to leave work at an unusual hour, or make a special journey to Portsmouth. Tide times had been carefully checked to ensure a high tide coincided with her lunch break. She wished to be washed out to sea, not smashed on the tower's foundations. She would drink the gin and swallow the sleeping tablets. There would be no pain. All she would feel was cold, empty numbness. Death would echo life. After, there would be no more loneliness. The water would cover her, the ripples cease, and it will be as if she'd never existed.

First though, would come the climb, onto the wall and over the dull silver safety rail. Once there, the worst would be over. She would choose a position where the outer rail was missing; very little remained of the rust pitted, blue painted metal. Mavis stood and walked to the wall. She imagined grasping the railing and hauling herself up. It would require effort, but she could manage. She could sit for a moment, longer if she wished, to compose herself. Then, she would slide forward, keep sliding forward until the solid grey stone, with its saggy wrapping of tarmac, was no longer beneath her. There would be the air and then the water and then nothing.

Or perhaps she would stand? That might be better. She could stand right on the edge, poised neatly between life and death. She could stand, calmly waiting for the right moment and then step forward. Just one small step to the end she longed for. Or she could jump. She did not think she would jump. It did not matter; all that mattered was she climb and then fall. Then nothing would matter.

Mavis backed away from the wall; she wasn't quite ready. The tide was not high enough; she did not have the tablets. It was not time yet. She glanced at her watch; not time to return to the office either. She planned to walk in just as work resumed. There would be no chance for one of the girls to ask if she'd enjoyed her lunch break. Such questions were, for Mavis, always difficult to answer. That day there could be no answer at all.

Mavis heard a child's squeal of excitement and quick light footsteps. A small girl, wrapped in quilted pink, raced around the perimeter wall. She screeched and whooped, running with outstretched arms. Her fingers, protected by knitted gloves, were held wide apart like woollen shooting stars. A woman arrived in the child's wake.

"Look at me, Mummy," the child called as she climbed onto a bench. She skipped along it and jumped off the end, darted up the steps and behind the seating area. Around and around she ran. Each time she passed the telescope she hooked her elbow around it and swung twice about, before ducking under the railing and continuing her lap. Blonde hair and ribbons streamed behind her. Her feet moved swiftly over the tarmac surface. Mavis could not distinguish each separate step; they merged into a flutter of sound. On the third circuit, the girl's mother caught her.

"Come on love. It's cold."

"It's not cold if you run."

"I'm too old to run," the woman said with a laugh.

The child's mother didn't look too old. Mavis was too old for running; she didn't believe she'd ever been the right age. She'd moved quickly when late for school and when her class had a sports lesson. She'd never run as this child had, for the fun of seeing how fast she could go. Mavis had never done anything just for fun. Mother wouldn't have allowed her to behave in such a wild, abandoned manner. Daddy would have done, he would have encouraged her to run far. He'd have told her to run fast, to leave before it was too late.

Mavis's mother was gone now; her suffering ended. It hurt to remember Mother harsh, demanding, and in pain. It hurt more to recall Mother softened into gratitude and fond recollections. Mavis pushed those memories away.

Mavis blew her nose and wiped her streaming eyes. She must not think of Mother. She hadn't realised how much she would miss her; she'd expected only freedom from the burden of caring, the impossibility of pleasing her.

She'd forgotten, or perhaps never appreciated, that while Mother was alive, there had been another person interested in her. Mother had always wanted to know where she'd been and every detail of anything Mavis had done. Maybe it had been to relieve the tedium of doing nothing except gaze at a television her eyes could no longer focus on. Maybe it had only been to criticise but, whatever Mavis had done, she could talk about it, assured her words were welcome. If the Hellebores had set seed or the robin had stopped visiting, those things were discussed. If a neighbour had bought a new car, or had a visitor, that was discussed. If the cost of a loaf of bread had increased or there was an offer on digestive biscuits ... now there was no one to tell. The house felt empty. Mavis didn't speak from saying, 'thank you' and stepping off the bus after work, until the following morning when she said, 'a return to the ferry please'.

Mavis spoke to people at work, of course. She must return there at once or risk arriving late. If she returned late, she would have to provide an explanation and she had none.

As she passed the place where the beggar had sat, Mavis wondered about him. She hoped he'd heeded her advice and gone in search of help. It was wrong for a man to have no home, no purpose, nothing that mattered to him. Maybe he would find a way out of his present difficulties. Perhaps the food she had bought him had given him the strength to take his first few steps toward a new life.

Chapter 2

A week later, Mavis awoke to the sound of rain on her windows and the knowledge that, at lunchtime, the tower would be deserted and the tide high. She opened her curtains, but made no attempt to look out into the darkness. She would have seen nothing but her own reflection. Mavis had no wish to look at her mousey hair, with the tight curls grown out. Since Mother's death, Mavis had not booked an appointment with the hairdresser who used to visit to trim and perm their hair.

Mavis removed yesterday's tiny paper sheet from her quotation calendar, a gift from someone at work. Mavis didn't know who. They had each drawn a slip of paper from an envelope and bought a small gift for the person whose name was revealed. Mavis thought the idea silly until the day they finished work for the Christmas break. She was handed a brightly wrapped package. She'd enjoyed seeing it sitting under her potted tree, awaiting the time for it to be opened.

It had been pleasant to have a gift to open on Christmas Day, after eating her chicken portion, Brussels sprouts and cranberry sauce. After the Queen's speech, Mavis had opened the card from Cousin Linda and removed the expected garden centre vouchers. They were welcome and would, she'd thought at the time, provide happy hours of deliberation over the plants she would exchange them for. Mavis had put them safely away, before picking up her gift. She removed all of the sellotape, rolled it into a ball and put it in the rubbish bin. Next, she removed the paper and, after folding it neatly, she put it in the recycling bin. Then she'd looked at her Christmas present.

The gift had not been a good choice. It was not practical; no room to write in any appointments she might have. Instead, each day was represented by a separate square of paper, bearing the date, details of a public holiday where appropriate, the phase of the moon and a trite saying. Most were not real quotations at all, just meaningless platitudes. The paper was good quality, the calendar sturdily made, obviously expensive. Whoever had bought it would have done well to speak to Janice. The girl had asked if Mavis ever used a calendar and learnt she purchased one early in January; they were cheaper then. She hoped Sandra had been better pleased with the pocket dictionary Mavis thoughtfully selected for her. The young woman's spelling ability was sadly lacking. There should now be an improvement.

Mavis folded yesterday's sheet of paper neatly in quarters and placed it in the recycling bin. As usual, another pathetic cliché was revealed. 'Today is the first day of the rest of your life' was the day's offering. Technically, that was true, she conceded; but it would be a short new beginning. After fifteen days use from her gift, Mavis intended to jump.

Breakfast eaten, Mavis drained the teapot and emptied the leaves into a plastic bag which she knotted securely. To many people, it wouldn't have mattered if she'd not washed her cereal bowl or wiped the sink. It mattered to Mavis. Even in death, she would be tidy.

Mavis unlocked and unbolted the kitchen door and switched on the outside light to illuminate the garden. She emptied her bread bin onto a clean tea-towel and took the bread and some biscuits outside and crumbled them on the bird table. She filled the peanut and seed feeders, scattering the remaining food over the lawn. Inside, she placed the crumb covered tea-towel in the laundry basket. Next, she opened the fridge and removed a block of cheese, half a pound of lard and a single slice of ham. Mavis opened the kitchen cupboards and took out plastic containers holding her branflakes, raisins, pearl barley and rice. Uncooked rice was an unsuitable food for birds she remembered; so returned it to its proper place. The other items were heaped on the bird table, covering the bread. There was too much and some fell, making a mess. There was no time for her to remedy the situation, she had a bus to catch, a life to end. She must try not to let the untidily heaped food bother her on her final journey. The birds would eat it; the mess would soon be gone. Back in the house, Mavis dispensed antibacterial cleanser onto her hands and washed them thoroughly. She dried them, put the used towel in the laundry basket and then applied cream to her cracked skin.

After a final check that everything she would need was in her shoulder bag, Mavis was ready to leave. Before opening the front door, Mavis glanced in the hallway mirror to check her hair was tidy and that no trace of breakfast or toothpaste showed on her face. Use of the mirror was unpleasant, but necessary. Her green eyes reflected her continued disappointment in her appearance. Despite care to keep her weight correct, her skin and hair clean and her clothes neat, she had never been attractive. Her hair was neither sleek straight black, nor wavy blonde, but an indifferent brownish colour. It wasn't even the same shade all over, but threaded through with streaks of the red and the pale gold she longed for. Her eyes were neither deep wells of liquid brown, nor sparkling pools of crystal blue; instead, they were the colour of duckweed. After ensuring her hair was tidy, she went out, locking the front door. She stood for a moment looking at the key. The solicitor kept a copy. She considered posting the one she held through the letter box. That would be the tidy thing to do. No; not for an accidental death. It would be something out of place, a clue to her intent. She slipped the key into the zipped compartment in her bag, just as usual.

Mavis walked to the bus stop and stood in her customary position behind the shelter. The group of people who caught her bus all had their regular spot to wait. The middle-aged couple, married, she supposed, sat together on the bench. The woman's large navy blue bag bulged between them. One of her chubby hands rested on the bag, the fingers constantly flexed and then curled as if to pounce for the handles should the bag decide to make an impulsive bid for freedom. Her husband sat very still, his hands thrust into his coat pockets, his head down, feet tight together. He would neither act impulsively, nor react if others did so, Mavis felt sure.

The pale girl stood in the far corner, lost in the exclusive world created by her headphones. At least she had her back to Mavis. Whenever she faced Mavis, the girl's unblinking stare was unsettling. Mavis couldn't tell if the girl was staring rudely at her, or if she looked right through. In either case, there was no way of guessing what she was thinking.

The fat woman, with her even fatter son usually arrived breathlessly as the rest were boarding. One fewer piece of toast in the mornings would have been advisable. Mavis had often wished

14

to tell them that would improve their waistlines and time keeping. She never did, of course. Mavis never spoke to any of them.

A gang of school children loitered to the left. They bickered and squabbled like a flock of good-natured starlings. They were not dressed in a proper uniform; sweatshirts embroidered in red with the school's crest, were worn above dark trousers or skirts. The skirt lengths varied with the seasons, either brazenly short or so long they were stepped on as the girls sauntered onto the bus. The skirts were usually straight but, for a time, had been very full; this style was quickly replaced by precise pleats. However much they varied from term to term they varied little from girl to girl. The tall blonde girl arrived on Monday with a new variation; by the following Monday, the others would be similarly attired. Theirs might not be quite so short or tight or frilled, but there was no doubting the inspiration behind the change of look.

The boy was there again. He didn't catch the bus every day. She could detect no pattern in his choice of days. She knew he lived close to her. She'd seen him walk past the house as she locked her own front door. One morning he'd still had his arm raised in farewell, to whoever he left at home, as Mavis stepped over the threshold into the cold morning. He'd lifted his hand again to her as he passed. She'd felt the corners of her mouth rise in response.

He always nodded in recognition now, as he reached the bus stop. Sometimes, that formed the only voluntary contact she experienced all day. People spoke to her: the bus driver told her the new price of the fare when it changed; the Gosport ferryman told her to watch the step as she disembarked on windy days. At work, the others in her office greeted her and occasionally asked if she would like a cup of coffee; just what they'd say to anyone though. They didn't notice her as a person. They didn't know her at all.

"There's room inside," the boy said. Very polite for a youngster, must have good parents. He beckoned Mavis in out of the rain she hadn't realised was falling. He moved his bag from the entrance and gently nudged another schoolboy off the seat.

"Thank you," Mavis said as she stepped past him into the shelter.

He smiled. "No problem. Left in a rush this morning I expect."

Unused to being spoken to before work, she stared at him.

"You forgot your brolly," the boy pointed out. "You've usually got one. I'm always doing that. Rush out at the last minute and forget things."

"Yeah like your brain." This was from the boy who'd been moved to allow her to sit. They pretended to fight, pulling faces at her as they dodged about, including Mavis in the game. She smiled; another thing she was not used to doing. The couple spoke to her too; general remarks regarding the weather and lateness of buses. They'd never acknowledged her presence before. Once the boy had spoken to her, Mavis became visible.

The schoolchildren, as sometimes happened, stood aside to let Mavis and the older couple get on. The pale girl didn't wait. The moment the bus stopped, she stepped forward, knocking into Mavis and catching her trailing belt buckle in the strap of Mavis's bag. The girl glared and then wrenched it free as though Mavis had deliberately impeded her progress. Mavis saw the girl's nails were long and sharp. Characters in books were sometimes portrayed as having vicious talons; never before had Mavis seen fingernails that made such a description accurate.

During the bus journey and short ferry crossing, Mavis thought of the boy. Would it worry him if he was the last person to speak to her before she jumped to her death? He'd been kind to Mavis. She would not like him to be afraid of sleeping, to dream of her body falling. A silly thought. Why should he mourn her death? Still she thought of the boy; Mavis didn't want to hurt him, even for a short while.

As she strode away from the ferry, a gust of wind threw chill rain on her face and wafted the smell of cooked bacon to her nose. She'd often seen bus drivers clutching a bacon sandwich and plastic mug of coffee. What a treat that would be; such a change from her usual cup of tea and bowl of bran cereal. The time for Mavis to avoid unhealthy foods had passed; she could eat what she wished. It wouldn't have time to clog her arteries. The salt would return to the sea without any effect on her blood pressure. She was not hungry, but could delay her death until after eating a bacon sandwich at lunchtime.

She would go to work for the morning, and leave the office at lunchtime, buy a sandwich and carry it to the top of the tower. After eating it, she would drink the gin, take the tablets and

16

jump. The tide might be too low then. If that was the case, she would return to the office and continue with her plan after work.

Perhaps early evening would be preferable? She wouldn't be missed until the following evening. If her body stayed submerged long enough, it might look like an accident. That would be better for the boy and the insurance claim. How long would it take for the sea to wash away proof of her actions?

Her route then did not deviate from the one she'd followed every week-day for the last four months. Both Nicola, her boss, and Janice, the office junior, were there before her. They greeted her as usual. Would they have done anything differently if they'd known this was to be the last time? Mavis replied to their cheery calls as she took off her wet coat. Reaching to hang it, she noticed how red and rough her hands were. They would become pale and wrinkled as a result of immersion in the cold brine, but that was still several hours away. She reached into her bag and brought out her tube of cream. She squeezed some into her palm and proceeded to work it into her finger tips, soothing the ragged cuticles, reducing the scaly appearance of the dry flakes on the backs of her hands.

Janice waved a mug enquiringly at her and Mavis nodded acceptance of coffee. Her supervisor, Nicola, offered commiseration for the soaking Mavis had received.

"It is warm in here. I shall soon dry out," Mavis said.

Janice carried in a tray with their mugs on. Mavis curled her cold fingers around the hot china. Janice did the same.

"Oooh, taters out there today innit? I know they reckon it's not so cold when it rains, but it feels like it is. Did you get cold on the ferry, Mavis? The wind off the sea can be fierce."

"No, not on the ferry particularly, but I did get cold as I waited for the bus."

"Yeah, it's worse when you're stood still. It's OK walking like. That warms you up, except your hands."

Mavis looked at Janice's hands; they didn't look particularly cold. The skin, unlike the nails, was not red. Nor was it rough, like Mavis's. It was smooth, as smooth as the girl's face. The short neat nails looked bright and cheerful. A sign that Janice took care over her appearance. Her eye lashes were enhanced with generously applied mascara and her lips slightly glossed. Today, she had chosen not to colour over the white streak in her right eyebrow.

As she watched Janice, Mavis lowered her own hands below the desk. Each time she lifted her mug to take a sip of tea, she first ensured the back of her hand, not her rough cuticles and blunt cut nails, were facing the other women. She knew her colleagues were more attractive than her; most women were. She hadn't before realised that was due partly to their own efforts. Perhaps some people created advantages for themselves where none existed naturally.

Nicola's make-up was both more comprehensive and more subtle than Janice's look. The neat ovals of her fingernails were polished but not coloured. Her complexion was clear and even. Too perfect for her age and the harsh weather; yet there was no obvious sign of cream or powder. She smelt of distant summer flowers.

Mavis wore no lipstick, no powder, and no scent. People might try to gild lilies, but none would trouble with a shrivelled potato.

When Lucy arrived, she offered to refill their mugs as she made her own drink. Janice accepted; the other two declined. When Sandra arrived, she too made herself a drink and carried it to her desk. The chipped cerise varnish of her finger nails didn't match the chipped exterior of her red and white mug. The dark smudges under her eyes however, were a perfect match for its tea-stained interior.

At nine precisely, the computers were switched on and work began. Mavis typed as accurately and as indifferently as usual. No one watching her would have guessed this was to be her last day. They could not have known she would be absent from her desk, floating cold and dead that afternoon.

Returning to her desk from a trip to the toilet, she heard her colleagues chattering.

"Old sourpuss seems almost human today," Sandra said.

"She actually smiled when I made her coffee. Wonder what's got into her?" asked Janice.

Mavis didn't mind that they thought her miserable; all they were doing was observing the truth. Only she knew that she'd finally found a solution to the misery.

"Mavis, you've got to switch off now like. Had you forgotten?" Janice said.

"Switch off? But I have work to do."

"Well, save it. It's only for, like, half an hour they reckon. Don't you remember? They're upgrading the server."

"Oh, of course! I had forgotten."

In truth, she'd not registered the details of the memo issued on Friday. As she hadn't expected to still be alive that morning, the workings of computer technicians were of no interest. It was a break in her normal pattern though. Mavis did not forget things. She did not work when she should stop any more than she would stop when she should have been working. She was more reliable than the machines they worked on. She did not shut down without reason; did not get viruses or run slowly or blow a fuse.

As they couldn't work, they drank coffee. It was Mavis's turn to make it, she decided. She preferred to do it while the others chatted. She did not understand their discussions. She didn't listen to the same music, read the same celebrity worshipping magazines, watch television soap operas or go to the same places they did. Mavis didn't listen to any music. Her usual reason for switching on the television was to watch the gardening programmes. When she felt she should be aware of world events, she sat through the depressing news items. The only places she went were to work, food shops and the library. She did read, of course. She read all kinds of books; read them alone and discussed them with no one.

In the kitchen, Mavis washed her hands. The company provided a proper soap dispenser. It contained only ordinary cleanser, but at least the staff were not expected to share a bar that was left exposed to dusty air and dirty water between uses. The roller towel was less satisfactory. It was not hygienic; instead, Mavis used the rough paper towels provided for mopping up spills.

She emptied the stale water from the kettle and refilled it. She wiped clean the sticky tray and moved the mugs which were upside down on the draining board, and cleaned that. Mavis often volunteered to make the drinks; at least then, she knew her mug would be clean.

The cat one was Lucy's, still heavily marked with her vibrant lipstick. Mavis washed the mugs then dropped a de-caffeinated teabag into Lucy's. Nicola had a gaudy mug emblazoned, 'Worlds Best Mum'. That was appropriate as Nicola treated them more like family than subordinate staff. She drank her coffee strong and black. Sandra's choice implied she supported Liverpool football club. Because of the strong tea Sandra regularly left sitting in it, the base was stained with tannin. Mavis sometimes squirted bleach into the mug and let it stand for a while before scouring it clean. Sandra was never grateful; instead she complained the mug smelt funny.

Mavis's mug was decorated with a pattern of brightly coloured tulips. It tapered at the bottom and curved in at the top, the shape representing the flower beginning to open in the sun. She bought it on the way home from her first day there; pure indulgence of course. Instead, she could have used one of the corporate ones kept for visitors. She could have brought in a cup and saucer from Mother's set. There were eight of them; she did not need them all for her solitary drinks. In this new job, this new phase of her life, she'd wanted something that wasn't Mother's. She wanted something of her own. Something that was not just practical; but bright, pleasant and cheerful. Mavis was not sorry she'd bought a mug she didn't need; she was pleased. Mother hadn't allowed coffee in the house and in the months since her death, it had never occurred to Mavis to buy it and carry it home to the house that was once hers. Mavis drank coffee, at work, from the tulip mug.

When she came in with the tray, her colleagues were working on a crossword puzzle. Mavis passed out the drinks.

"Mr Orwell. Creator of the original Big Brother. Six letters," Sandra read.

Sandra always read the questions, possibly to disguise the fact she rarely knew the answers.

"When was the original Big Brother?" asked Nicola.

"Dunno," Lucy replied. "Been going for years now."

"1984," Mavis answered.

They all turned to look at her.

"Well, before that really, I suppose."

"Blimey, didn't know it was that long," said Janice. "Fancy you knowing that, Mavis. I didn't think you ever watched it."

"I don't. I read the book."

20

"There's never a book about Big Brother. It's not that sort of programme," said Janice.

"Anyway, it don't answer the question. What was it again, Saz?" asked Lucy.

Sandra repeated the question.

"So what's the answer then? Seeing as how you read the book," Janice said.

"Don't be nasty, Janice," said Nicola.

"George," Mavis answered.

"It fits," Sandra said and wrote it in.

The crossword continued without further input from Mavis.

Later, Janice apologised for her remark.

"I've not read many books. Mum thinks it's a waste of time and money like, so I don't buy any. Saves on arguments. Is there really a book about Big Brother? Or were you having me on?"

"The book is called *1984*. It was written by George Orwell. It is about people being watched all the time, by Big Brother."

"So is it like the telly programme?"

"I don't know, Janice. I have never watched the programme."

"But you said it was rubbish once. I'm sure you did."

"Yes. That is why I don't watch it."

"How do you know it's rubbish then?"

Janice was right; Mavis had simply dismissed the programme without ever watching it. She'd dismissed Janice too. When the girl had admitted she never read books, Mavis had thought her shallow and unintelligent. It had never occurred to her that Janice might possess an inquiring mind, thwarted by a difficult parent. She'd thought badly of her, as Janice probably did of Mavis. Perhaps Mavis could change the girl's opinion, maybe help her before she finished with her own life.

"Janice, I have an idea. You could read the book and compare it with the television programme."

"Maybe." Janice sounded uncertain.

21

"I have a copy of the book. I could lend it to you. You could read it on the bus whilst travelling to work, and in your lunch break. That wouldn't worry your mother. You'd be wasting neither time nor money."

"You'd lend it to me?"

"I will bring it tomorrow."

"Thanks, Mavis."

To keep her promise, Mavis would have to delay her suicide plan by a day. She decided, due to the unpleasant weather, to delay her trip to the café too. It was nice to have something to look forward to until the time when she would have no future.

Monday the twelfth of January had indeed been the first day of the rest of her life. It was to have been the last day too, but that day would come tomorrow. That thought comforted her as she closed her eyes and waited for sleep.

Chapter 3

Reluctantly, Mavis opened the curtains on a day she'd not expected to have to face. The dark sky echoed her mood; the falling rain foreshadowed her future.

"Happy birthday, Daddy," she whispered to his memory, before splashing clean water onto her tear-stained face. She blew her nose and took a long, deep breath. It wasn't a day for tears.

Mavis was pleased her attempt to make her death look accidental meant the half empty bottle of milk was still in the fridge. Black tea was really not civilised, and a proper breakfast was essential every day. Perhaps even more important on one's final day? As she waited for the kettle to boil, Mavis tore Monday's quotation from the calendar and folded it in half, then in half again. After disposing of it, she read the current day's entry; 'Life is not a dress rehearsal'. Mavis hoped that was true; once she brought the final curtain down, she had no plans for an encore.

Her copy of *1984* had been a Christmas gift from Cousin Linda. Mavis re-read the inscription, 'Happy Christmas Mavis, try to escape from the Thought Police every now and then, best wishes, Linda'. Only then did Mavis realise Linda meant for her to get away from Mother occasionally.

Mavis opened her shoulder bag and found, under the pills and gin, a pen. She wanted Janice to know the book was hers, not to feel after today's 'tragic event', she'd no right to keep it. 'Janice,' she wrote and then wished she hadn't. The writing of the name created the need for a comment and Mavis could think of nothing meaningful. She leafed through the book, hoping for inspiration. 'Hope you find this doubleplusgood,' she wrote and added her signature. Janice would know she was intended to enjoy the book; that was all the message need convey. Mavis decided wrapping the gift was unnecessary. She protected it with a plastic carrier, before adding it to her already heavy bag. After checking the kitchen was immaculate, she buttoned her coat, checked her hair and face in the mirror and undid the bolts on the front door.

As she opened the door, a gust of wind caught her umbrella, jerking her arm up. An image of Mary Poppins flashed into her head. She could not jump with an umbrella and, if the rain continued, she could not leave the office without it at lunchtime. After shaking off as much water as she could, she propped it up in the garage with sheets of newspaper beneath to absorb the drips.

Mavis walked quickly through the cold rain towards the protection of the bus stop. As she waited to cross the road, a car drove at speed through a puddle, sloshing filthy water over Mavis's shoes. Her feet would be cold and uncomfortable all day, but there was no time for her to go home and change. She was not surprised to recognise the car. It belonged to her neighbour, Marie French. It was typical of the woman to give no thought to the effect of her actions on other people. She frequently ruined summer afternoons in the garden by lighting a barbecue or conducting unnecessarily loud conversations. Often, she didn't bring in her wheeled bin until long after it had been emptied. It remained on her driveway where it could easily be knocked over on to Mavis's garden. And there was her cat.

The boy wasn't at the bus stop that morning. The couple were there and the woman nodded toward Mavis.

"Good morning," Mavis was surprised to hear herself speak.

"Worse than yesterday, ain't it?" the woman remarked.

"Quite wet, yes."

"You got far to walk the other end?"

"Half a mile, I suppose."

"Oh, you're gonna get soaked today, love."

"Yes," Mavis agreed. She expected to get very wet indeed.

At work, Mavis hung up her coat and combed her hair before she greeted her colleagues. When she reached her desk, the full tulip mug was sitting on the coaster. Gratefully, she took a sip of her coffee. Tomorrow, the drink would cool untasted; if it was made at all. For the first time, Mavis realised someone must see her arrive and make her drink each morning.

"Thank you," she said.

"Pardon?"

"Whoever made the coffee, thank you."

"No problem, you usually arrive at about the same time as me," Nicola said.

That was true. Mavis had never made the coffee on the mornings when she'd arrived first. She would next time; except, of course, there would be no next time.

Mavis wondered when to give Janice the book. Would the girl be embarrassed if others noticed? Mavis decided to leave it on her locker. Janice arrived a few minutes later, hung up her coat and came in, reading the inscription as she walked.

"What you got there, Janice?" Nicola asked.

"Mavis has lent me a book. Thanks, Mavis." Janice waved the book at her. "Is doubleplusgood like a real word, then?"

"Read the book, Janice."

"You're just like a teacher you are," Janice informed her.

"Oh?" Mavis asked.

"Look it up, Janice then you will remember it." Janice spoke in a voice unlike any teacher Mavis could recall.

"I think that was good advice."

"See what I mean?"

Mavis's coat was dry again by the start of the lunch break.

"You're surely not going out in this? It's still chucking it down out there, and you haven't even got an umbrella," Nicola said.

Mavis had been right to leave it at home.

"Yes, I er, I. I have an appointment."

"Oh, a lunch date?" said Nicola.

"Anyone we know?" Lucy asked.

"Have a nice time. Don't hurry back, we'll cover for you," Janice offered.

Perfect; they thought she intended to meet a man. That would help. They wouldn't raise the alarm in time to save her.

They may perhaps think she'd been jilted when they learnt of her fate.

"Mavis," Lucy called after her as she hurried down the stairs. "Would you like to borrow my brolly?"

Mavis could provide no answer, so pretended not to hear and left the building. Soon her head became wet and a cold trickle crept under her collar and dribbled down her back. Nicola had been correct; an umbrella would, under normal circumstances, have been advisable. She understood Nicola's admonishment for not bringing one, but why had Lucy suggested lending hers? It wasn't Lucy's fault Mavis was ill-equipped for the conditions. Perhaps she worried if Mavis were to catch a cold, she would pass it on to her colleagues.

Mavis felt nervous as she passed under the railway bridge and approached the café. She hesitated outside the tattoo parlour. That establishment, unlike its neighbour, showed no sign of patronage. There were people in the café. Mavis couldn't see them through the condensation and posters covering the windows, but she could hear them. Silly to be nervous, less than an hour before she would slip into the cold water of the Solent. A warm sandwich and plastic chair were surely not more to be feared? She pushed at the door, it resisted. She hesitated. The door opened.

"Sorry, me buggie was in the way," a customer called out. "I've moved it now. Well, come on. Get yourself inside."

"Thank you," Mavis said as she squeezed into the crowded space.

"What'll it be then?" a stout girl encased in a plastic apron enquired.

Mavis stared. She studied the waitresses' tattoos. Roses twined down her arm, a bud unfurled on the back of her hand. The other wrist wore a permanent circle of thorny stems; more roses adorned her partially exposed chest. Mavis wondered what variety they were, the detail in each stage of bud, bloom and blown, so precisely accurate it was surely taken from a horticultural illustration. They were probably done by her neighbour, Mavis guessed. Perhaps he got cheap breakfasts in exchange for cheap roses.

Mavis had never seen so many rings on one person. They were in her ears, her nose, and left eyebrow and on her fingers and thumbs. She wondered if the jeweller who supplied her extensive collection also ate at the café.

"We're famous for our bacon butties. Will I get you one of them?" the woman suggested.

She received a nod by way of answer.

"Eat in or take away?"

Mavis didn't know. She'd intended to eat it at the top of the tower, but it was raining. She knew she would soon be getting wet, but the food would be spoilt.

"There's room just here." The girl whose pushchair had blocked the entrance gestured to the seat opposite her own.

"Sit down then, and I'll fetch it over when it's done. Tea or coffee?"

"Tea. Thank you."

"I'm Karen and the little tyke's Lauren," the girl with the pushchair offered.

Thus introduced, they started a conversation, or to be more accurate, Karen talked and Mavis faced her trying to take in her words and the unfamiliar atmosphere. The girl looked clean and tidy, her hair pulled back into a high ponytail. She wore no make up except mascara. Her unvarnished nails were filed short, with no grime lodged under them. She finished her drink and waved her mug at the waitress, "Any chance of a top up?"

As Karen chattered, she occasionally handed small slices of fruit to her daughter or dabbed the child's chin with a clean white cloth. She explained she was taking evening classes to compensate for the education she'd missed as a result of her pregnancy.

"I was only 15 see, but I'm doing some GCSEs now. It's not easy like, but I want to get a decent job once Lauren's at school."

Mother would have thought this girl a worthless hussy. She would never have spoken to her, but Mavis admired Karen. Clearly, she'd made a mistake, but apparently just the one. Lauren ate fruit and drank milk, not chocolate and Coke.

"There you go," the waitress said.

A large heavy mug of tea was placed in front of each of them.

"Thank you," Mavis said.

"Cheers, Triffid," Karen said.

Mavis looked down at the waitress's sandalled feet; there were rings on two toes and roses climbing her legs. As she returned to the counter, two more roses were visible below her short skirt.

Karen snorted with laughter. "Your face, honestly, it's a picture," she told Mavis. "It's the tattoos, innit?"

"They do seem a little …" Mavis trailed off. It seemed wrong to criticise the woman to her friend after they had both been kind to her. That was not the only reason for avoiding comment; Mavis did not know what she thought of the tattoos.

"Triffid used to wear trousers and polo necks, even when it was redders. She told me it was 'cause of her burn scars. She'd tried next door to see if they could be tattooed over, but they can't do that."

Mavis sipped at the scalding liquid as Karen continued talking.

"Anyway, I said it didn't matter where it was, if she got a wild tat, no one would notice the scars. She got a temporary dragon on her arm and wore a tee-shirt. No one commented on the scars, but a customer called her Dragon Lady."

Karen gave her daughter another slice of apple.

"She told him off, joking like and he called her Angel instead. When she got the first real tat, we started joking about not mentioning the roses. Her real name is Christine, so a bus driver suggested Chrysanthemum. Her boss reckoned the tea'd be cold before she answered, so we dropped that. After she got a few more done the bloke who'd called her Dragon Lady, said they were taking over like Triffids. That one stuck."

Mavis had not noticed any scars on the woman; the strategy had worked.

Karen and Mavis sipped their tea.

"I've never seen you in 'ere before," Karen said.

"No, I thought I would try something different."

Karen didn't look as if she considered eating a bacon sandwich much of an adventure.

Mavis explained, "I just wanted to do something interesting before, well before, it was too late."

She was horrified she'd spoken aloud. She'd never told anyone of her unhappiness, not even Cousin Linda. She'd almost told this stranger everything. Karen seemed to see nothing unusual in the situation. Perhaps other people confided in her?

"You ought to try evening classes then. Not school subjects. There's lots of other stuff, family trees, wine tasting. Hang on; I might've got a leaflet." She produced one, much crumpled and slightly sticky, from her handbag.

"I've gotta go now, but perhaps I'll see you here again? I'm here most Tuesdays at this time, if you fancy a chat."

Mavis's response was cut short by the arrival of her food.

"Well, it was nice to meet you both," she said as Karen fitted the buggy's plastic cover to protect Lauren. The child waved cheerily as she was wheeled away. Mavis waved back and then turned her attention to the sandwich.

She'd heard the term 'doorstop' to describe enormous slices of bread. Two of those, filled with strips of crispy bacon, confronted her. The delicious savoury aroma was as tempting close to, as the tantalising wafts had been on cold mornings. There were no knives and forks on her table; Mavis looked around for some. Other people were holding their sandwiches in their hands, and taking large hungry bites. She had her back to the other customers; no one would notice if she did the same. Carefully, she picked up her lunch. She opened her mouth wide and took a bite. The sandwich was made from proper bread, springy, with a good thick crust. It had both texture and flavour, unlike the insipid, soft stuff Mavis was used to.

Mother had suffered with poor teeth, and could eat nothing else. Mother had been dead for six months. As she chewed, Mavis wondered what other pleasures she'd denied herself, because Mother would not have wanted them. Mother hadn't wanted her to work; Mavis had gained employment. She shook her head; she'd found training and then work, because she'd needed an income. Mother's shares didn't earn much. Taking a job had not been the brave first step of a woman choosing her own destiny, but the only choice open to her. Surely, there were things in her life she'd decided for herself? There was the coffee; she drank coffee at work. No, she still drank tea, from Mother's cups and saucers at home. Karen, she had spoken to Karen, Mother would not have approved of her. True the girl had spoken first, but Mavis had chosen to sit with her. There were very few other empty seats, but she could have sat elsewhere and chosen to ignore any remarks addressed to her. There was the sandwich too; Mother would have been horrified at the idea of buying and consuming such a thing.

Mavis concentrated on her food. The sandwich was delicious, and considering its size, very good value. She thought with regret of the boring lunches she'd prepared for herself; alternating between mild cheddar and bland ham, each laid meagrely between the despised sliced bread. Never again would she eat such food, she vowed. Of course, she remembered, she would not be eating anything more; ever.

Mavis paid for her meal and was about to open the door, when it was pushed open. Karen had come back.

"Got almost to Cambridge Junction when Lauren realised she'd lost Postman Pat." Karen retrieved a knitted toy from under the seat she had occupied. "She makes a real fuss if she hasn't got him."

"I am glad you have found him then," said Mavis.

"Me too. D'you know, I have to take him out of her bed at night, to wash and dry him before she wakes up."

The rain had stopped and small patches of blue were visible between the clouds.

"What are you doing this afternoon? Do you have a job to get back to?" the girl asked.

"Yes."

"Where do you work?"

"McHyvers in Burnaby Road."

"I'll walk that way with you then, it's probably just as quick, that's if you don't mind?"

"No, um, no." Mavis answered; she could no longer walk, as she had intended, in the opposite direction. Karen would realise she wasn't returning to her desk.

"To tell you the truth it's nice to talk to an adult for a change. Lauren's great of course, but well, you know."

Mavis didn't know, but she nodded.

"Most of the people I get to talk to either have children, or they're doctors or people like that and I just talk to them about Lauren."

"Yes."

"So, will you do an evening class do you think? I think you'd enjoy it. You get to meet people, and learning stuff can be fun, if it's the right thing."

Mavis nodded.

"Well, you have a think about it."

"Yes, I shall."

Mavis returned to the office, her plan of suicide again delayed. The computers had again stopped working. Her colleagues sat on desks chatting. By the interest shown in her lunch arrangements, Mavis guessed she'd been one of the subjects under discussion.

"I'd like to think she's meeting a man but, as that's gone, I'm guessing a job interview," Janice said as she came into the office, carrying the tray. She blinked and then looked as if she wished she could hide behind the steaming mugs. "Oh whoops, hello, Mavis. I didn't know you were back."

"That's quite all right. I will fetch myself some coffee."

The door did not close properly and she could hear the voices of her colleagues. She remembered hearing other women speaking from behind a partly closed door. That had been many years ago. She couldn't remember their names or the exact words they used. She could remember the meaning; that it had been Mother's fault that Daddy had gone away, that he was dead. She'd tried hard to forget what she'd heard. Mavis pushed the hushed words from her childhood further back into the past and concentrated on the voices coming from the office.

Lucy said, "Listen to this, 'an unexpected meeting will lead to a change of heart'. That's what her stars say for today. What else could it be, except that she's met a man?"

"It could be a new job, like I said," Janice said. "She could've met someone who offered her a job."

"How are you proposing to find out who won?" Nicola asked.

They'd run a sweepstake on what she'd done at lunch time, Mavis realised. Perhaps their lives were not really much more interesting than hers?

"Maybe someone would like to pop out for biscuits, using the sweepstake fund?" Mavis said as she brought in the drinks. "None of you guessed correctly."

There were a few embarrassed mutterings.

"Plain chocolate digestives please. I think I should be allowed the first choice as I was the only one who knew where I was."

"OK, I'll nip out and get them, but will you tell us?" Janice said. "We just did it for a laugh but now, like I really want to know."

"I went to lunch with my young friend Karen. She was suggesting that I take up an evening class."

"Evening classes at your age? What would be the point?" Sandra sneered.

"Why shouldn't she if she wants to?" Janice asked.

"Yes, Sandra there is no reason why I should not spend my time exactly as I choose. Now get your coat on, Janice."

Janice did as instructed.

"Mavis, I hope you weren't offended by the sweepstake. Honestly we didn't mean any harm," Janice said when she returned.

Mavis smiled. A real smile, it was nice to have people interested in her.

"What class are you thinking of doing?" Nicola asked.

Mavis showed them the leaflet.

"I have not yet decided."

"I thought term started in September. Or is that just schools?" Lucy asked.

"No, says here you can join at the start of any term for some of them," Janice said.

"What's on offer? Computer studies; don't think so! You get enough of that at work," Lucy said.

Everyone crowded around the leaflet to make suggestions, except Sandra who made a show of working, although without the computers, there was nothing to do.

"What did you like at school?" Nicola asked.

"Art," Mavis answered without thinking, and then realised it was true; she'd enjoyed applying colour to a blank paper to fill it with interest.

"Says here, it starts tomorrow. You'd better phone up quick and see if there's like any places left," Janice said.

Only Mavis knew she would be unable to attend the lesson. As she couldn't explain her reluctance, she rang the number.

"I'm so pleased to hear from you," a man told her, after she'd explained the reason for her call. "We were going to have to cancel the class because not enough people had booked. If I sign you up now, it can go ahead."

Mavis looked up, Janice was watching her. She gave the man her bank card details and said she would see him the following evening.

The computers could not be persuaded into working order within the next few hours, the IT department told them. They were sent home.

"Mavis, I'll walk up town with you."

"I don't go that way, Janice."

"But you'll need art stuff won't you? I don't think they'd have it in Gosport. You'd better go to Smiths."

Although the sky was still dark with threatening clouds, the rain had stopped. Janice's chatter about the interesting people who were likely to attend Mavis's class and the fun she'd have, brightened the dull afternoon. Mavis bought a sketch pad and some special drawing pencils. Janice saw a beginner's painting set reduced because of damage to the packaging. Mavis found the girl's enthusiasm enchanting. She couldn't disappoint her by not making the purchase.

At home, Mavis imagined she could feel Mother's presence. The air felt heavy with disapproval. She did feel slightly foolish. She had acquired, and carried home, expensive items she wouldn't use. Perhaps she could use them? The first class would be tomorrow. It would not hurt to delay her plan by another day. It need not even be by a whole day; there was no reason to return home after the class. She could go to the Round Tower and wait for high water. It would be better to jump at night. As other people were drifting into sleep, Mavis would drift in eternal rest.

Chapter 4

'The early bird catches the worm,' was the quote revealed on Wednesday's page of her calendar when Mavis carefully removed, folded and disposed of, the previous day's sheet. She switched on the outside light and looked through the window at her bird table. There had been some early birds there; some late ones too, she imagined. The heap of food she'd left was considerably reduced; the mess, however, was not. Mavis put on her coat, stepped into her gardening clogs and ventured out into the cold damp morning to clear up. Using a spatula, she pushed most of the food from the table into a carrier bag. The spilt food was left for the birds to eat. She took the carrier bag inside, knotted it securely and placed it inside another bag. She folded some newspaper around the package and put it in the fridge. After pouring boiling water over the spatula and leaving it to soak in bleach solution, Mavis washed her hands and prepared her breakfast.

Mavis calculated she would have two hours to fill before the start of her art class, scarcely time to get home, heat and consume a tin of soup and travel to St Vincent College. She would go to the library instead. They served snacks and drinks; she could wait in warmth and comfort. The art materials were not heavy. She could easily carry them.

Mavis planned to arrive at work before Nicola. She would make a cup of coffee for her supervisor and have it waiting. Mavis had made a cup of tea for Mother every morning and taken it in to her. Mother had never thanked her, Mavis hadn't expected it, but she knew Nicola would smile and make a pleasant comment. As she checked her appearance in the hallway mirror, Mavis smiled at the thought of Nicola thanking her. That morning, her appearance displeased her less than usual.

Although she left home at a different time than usual, to catch an earlier bus, her neighbour's cat watched from its customary position on the gate between the two houses. Mavis felt it waited for her to leave, until it could scratch in her borders and torment the birds without Mavis being able to prevent it.

There were people at the bus stop. Mavis didn't recognise them. She'd never noticed them there, or in the library or High Street.

On the bus, she wished she had a book; she usually read during the journey. The previous Saturday she'd returned to the library all those she'd borrowed. She hadn't finished reading Agatha Christie's *4.50 from Paddington*. She'd never know if Cedric Crackenthorpe or his brother-in-law Bryan Eastley were the killer. She would never learn if her guess that the murdered woman was Edmund's widow was correct. Surely she must be; there was no suggestion of another woman whom any of the characters had a motive to kill. Mavis wondered if Lucy Eyelesbarrow would fall in love with one of the men and, if she did, if it would be the right man. Mavis had never fallen in love; for her there had never been a right man.

After hanging up her coat and switching on the office lights, Mavis emptied yesterday's stale water from the kettle. She rinsed it several times, carefully swilling out the pieces of limescale. She half filled the kettle and switched it on. Whilst the water heated, she took her own mug from the cupboard. Nicola's rested upside down on the draining board. It resisted slightly as Mavis lifted it, revealing a dirty ring where both surfaces had touched. Nicola must have simply rinsed and left the mug the previous evening. Mavis looked inside. As she suspected it was stained, the outside perhaps worse. The handle was so grubby as to be slightly tacky and a dark dried trickle obscured a glazed 'S'. Mavis cleaned it thoroughly, dried it and placed it next to her own. The spoons were no cleaner than the mug; she scrubbed one with a green plastic scourer until it was fit for use.

The jar of coffee was newly opened the previous day, and still had the delicious fresh aroma; it also had part of the foil seal attached to the rim. Mavis removed the shreds. Using a sharp knife, she scraped away all traces of glue, leaving a clean smooth edge. She dipped the spoon into the coffee jar, tapped it on the edge to ensure the granules were neatly rounded and poured them into her mug. She repeated the process for Nicola, then cleaned the spoon and added a measure of sugar to her own mug. As she did so, she heard Janice arrive and took the girl's mug from the cupboard and placed it next to the others. Mavis added coffee and put three spoonfuls of sugar in Janice's mug. She wondered how the girl managed to remain slim. Were Mavis to allow herself such an indulgence she would surely become unacceptably stout. Next, she poured a third of an inch of milk into her own and Janice's mugs, then filled all three with water. Before placing them on the tray, she stirred each drink and washed the spoon. She lifted the tray and placed it on the table, wiped down the work surface and took the laden tray into the office.

Nicola arrived. "Morning, Mavis, got here all right then?" she asked as she removed her coat.

"Yes, I got the earlier bus today."

"Probably just as well. Traffic was terrible on the M275, someone had crashed going the other way, so of course everyone was crawling along having a good gawp." Nicola went into her office.

"I'm glad I don't, like, have far to travel," Janice said as she took her mug from the tray. "Cheers, I need this, it's freezing out there."

Mavis smiled at Janice before carrying Nicola's drink to her. She extracted Nicola's coaster from the pile of papers and placed it on a relatively clear area of desk.

"Coffee? Oh thanks, Mavis, you're a life saver."

The other staff arrived within minutes of each other. They discussed the traffic jam and made themselves cups of coffee.

"It's all right for Janice walking in and you coming on the ferry, Mavis, you wouldn't want a journey like that. Didn't move at all we didn't, not for ages," Sandra told her.

"Is this not your usual time to arrive?" Mavis asked.

"What's your point?" Sandra snapped.

"Well, that perhaps ..."

"You don't drive so you don't know what you're talking about."

Mavis walked away. She no longer need listen to people who were rude or unkind to her. There had been other people who'd been unkind to Mavis, she remembered. Mother would never be cruel again. Mother had taunted her, but she was dead now, there was no need to think of her. There were other memories best not recalled. Evelyn, how long ago was it that Evelyn had pinched her arms and pulled her hair? How long ago was that school trip, where Evelyn had asked her over and over why she had no daddy? Over forty years had passed since Evelyn had slipped, screamed, fallen and died.

Janice claimed her attention by holding up the copy of 1984 and asking, "What did you think of it?"

"Read it yourself, Janice, you need to make up your own mind."

"I meant Big Brother."

"I did not watch it."

"Not to worry, it's on again tonight. Except you'll be out, won't you? Never mind I'll remind you tomorrow."

She would not have the chance, Mavis thought, but did not say.

After crossing to Gosport on the ferry, Mavis didn't turn left to the bus station. She walked up through the High Street toward the library. The wind was cold; she walked quickly. For the first time Mavis saw some benefit in the change from a once calm, quiet library to the noisy and rather busy place it had become. It had been renamed a 'Discovery Centre'. The name at least pleased Mavis. She could discover, and forget, so much between the pages of a book.

The library had been one of the few places, other than school; she'd been allowed to go to as a child. It had been her escape. As long as her chores were done, the simple phrase, "Mother, may I go to the library?" had usually allowed freedom until the time for the next meal. She was issued her own ticket and permitted her own choice of reading material. For the pleasure of reading, she owed her mother. She may have provided the need for escapism, but she had also shown the means.

Mavis preferred her local library in Lee-on-the-Solent. The square solid building was pleasant. There were benches and neat evergreen hedges doing their best to be welcoming. The inside however was the attraction. Warm in winter and cool in summer. Always well lit, always quiet. A deliberate, necessary, quiet. Not the quiet of loneliness. There it was not that people did not speak to her, but simply that they did not speak. No one resented her presence. She did not have to justify her visit. People came to libraries, all kinds of people.

The staff were always polite, her contact with them the closest thing to a friendly relationship she experienced. They remembered her, would willingly help if she asked. Would leave her be, to do as she pleased, if not. They needed visitors, without her it would not be a library, just a collection of books. They did not care personally, but at least they cared impersonally.

The books needed her, she knew they were inert, but if they had feelings, they would be glad someone read the titles on their spines. The chosen few would be pleased to be taken up for a more thorough inspection. Disappointed not to be selected or jubilant to be placed in the pile to be stamped, released and read. Mavis shook her head to clear such fanciful thoughts. They did not apply in that bright place. Or maybe they did, a flight of someone's fancy must surely have inspired the oversized pink and orange seats. Who on earth would wish to sit in them? She stifled a laugh as the answer came to her. Art students; they were the people who would use them.

Mavis looked for the *4.50 from Paddington*. There was enough time for her to read to the end and discover if she'd been right in her deductions. Of course, more clues would be provided and the fresh evidence might cause her to revise her earlier opinions. The book was not there. Someone else had borrowed it. Although she would now never know the identity of the murderer and his victim, she knew she'd been right to return it.

She walked to the food counter and looked at the choices on offer. She read the price list first. Many items were things she'd never tried, although the names were vaguely familiar. As cappuccino, latte, and espresso were listed under 'Beverages,' she deduced they were coffee. The food choices were harder to understand. She had no idea what a panini might be, and although she studied the items on the glass shelves, she couldn't differentiate between carrot cake, cookie crumble and brownies. She sighed; she'd been looking forward to trying something new. The only things she could order with confidence were tea, and a choice of cheese or tuna sandwiches. Hardly the food the other members of her class would be eating that evening.

"What can I get you, love?" asked a large lady who approached the counter from a room behind it.

Mavis was startled.

"Not decided yet, that's OK." She smiled and began to wipe down the immaculate surfaces. "Weather's brightening up a bit I think."

Mavis realised the woman had not moved away from her out of rudeness, rather to avoid pressuring her into a quick decision.

"I am sorry, I can't quite decide."

"The muffins are good, if you wanted a cake, but if you just want a drink that's fine."

"Muffins?"

"Yes," the woman gestured to some large and rich looking cakes in paper cases. "Chocolate, cherry or blueberry. Very popular with the students, they are."

"I will try one," Mavis attempted to sound confident.

"Which flavour would you like? The chocolate ones are chocolate of course, with chocolate pieces in as well, they're my favourite. The cherry ones are vanilla with glace cherries in. Then there's the blueberry ones, you ever had blueberries?"

"No."

"They're an American fruit, don't taste of that much to my mind, but they're supposed to be right healthy and they do make the muffin nice and moist."

"I will have a blueberry muffin, please." Mavis's smile was genuine, she was learning of new things, and the chatty woman obviously enjoyed describing her wares.

"A drink with that?"

"Er, yes."

"We've got cold ones, Coke and juice, all that sort of thing, but with this weather, perhaps something hot would be better?"

Mavis nodded.

"Well, there's tea, ordinary, or herbal. Funny stuff that is, but some folks like it."

"No, perhaps not tea."

"Well then, there's coffee."

"Do the coffees all have milk?"

"Some do, we've got cappuccino or latte; nice they are if you like lots of milk. If you don't, we've got espresso, that's really strong and black. Or, as you're going all American, how about hot chocolate with cream and marshmallows?"

"Marshmallows?"

"Uh hm. If you've got a sweet tooth, you've got to try it."

"Well, I suppose…"

"You won't regret it."

Mavis paid for her snack. The friendly woman made the drink and placed the large mug on a tray, next to the small plate that held the muffin. She added a paper napkin and plastic spoon and fork.

"I hope you enjoy it."

"I am sure I shall."

Mavis carried the tray to the smaller of the coloured seats. She placed the tray on the low table and fetched some magazines. Unsure how to sit on the enormous sofas she wished she'd chosen one of the high stools at a proper table. Eating and drinking would have been more dignified there. She would feel foolish moving now. Sliding along to the end, rather than sitting in the middle, helped. The surface sloped less there. She sat upright, alternating between holding the mug and the plate. She was not disappointed by her muffin. The flavour of the fruit was unusual, but not at all unpleasant. The chocolate was too hot and too heaped with whipped cream for her to take more than a few tentative sips. She set it aside, and concentrated on her cake, which was swiftly consumed.

She wondered why she'd been given a spoon. It must be for the chocolate. She lifted a spoonful of whipped cream, it was warm and frothy, strange but good. Mavis ate all of the cream, occasionally capturing a tiny pink marshmallow on her spoon. The ones at the top were slightly chewy; those nearer the hot drink had melted to a silky texture. She sighed, how pleased she was not to be drinking tea and eating a cheese sandwich.

When the cake was gone, and the chocolate cooler and less full, Mavis sat further back into the lurid pink upholstery. Her legs stuck out in front of her, but not she felt, in an immodest manner. She leant into the generous curve of the sofa and took her tube of cream from her bag. She smoothed a tiny dab of it into her chapped hands, rubbing them well to avoid leaving greasy marks on the magazine, and began to read. *Amateur Gardening*; the current copy. Usually, she read that in her local library; it was a few weeks old before it arrived there. Happily, she read of propagation techniques for clematis and sipped her chocolate. What a pity she hadn't read that before. Cousin Linda had some lovely clematis varieties; she would have been pleased to supply cuttings. It would have been nice to have her garden fences draped with those beautiful plants; they would have provided cover for the birds too.

Mavis realised someone was talking to her, the lady who'd served the food.

"Excuse me, I'm just going to start clearing up," she said.

"Oh I didn't realise," Mavis said, beginning to gather together the magazines.

"No, please, you don't have to go, not until seven when we close. It's just that I start clearing up beforehand, I didn't want you to think I was trying to push you out."

"Oh, I see. Thank you, I intend to stay until half past six."

"That's fine, no problem at all."

Mavis checked her watch; ten past six. She had time to read another article.

She read how a vicar and his wife had created not only a beautiful garden, but also a tranquil training environment for people with learning difficulties, out of what had previously been an unofficial rubbish tip. Mavis had just learnt the youngsters grew-on seedlings for the local council when she again had company.

"Sorry to disturb you again, I just wondered if you'd like a croissant?"

"Oh, I ..."

"No charge; the ones that are warm can't be kept until the next day. It's a chocolate one."

"Well, thank you."

The woman used metal tongs to place a croissant onto the plate that had held the muffin.

"There, that'll set you up for facing the cold. You going somewhere nice next?"

"I start an art evening class tonight."

"Oooh. How exciting! I bet you meet lots of interesting people doing something like that." She walked away.

"Thank you," Mavis repeated, to the woman's back.

She ate the crispy pastry with its rich surprises of melted chocolate. She brushed the crumbs from her clothing on to the tray, which she returned to the counter. Mavis visited the lavatory, both for the usual reason and to tidy her hair. As she returned the comb to her bag, she noticed the lipstick; a gift from Linda. Mavis had used it only twice, both times when visiting her cousin. Linda had said the colour suited her, added warmth to her face. "I'm not brave enough to face the day without putting my face on," Linda had told her once. Perhaps an application of make up would boost her own confidence? She applied a tentative slick to her bottom lip and then pressed it onto the top one. She peered at the mirror; the colour was uneven. She applied a bolder stroke and smoothed it out with the tip of her little finger. Better.

As Mavis walked back past the food counter the woman waved, and called out, "Have fun."

Mavis returned her wave, but felt too nervous to smile. Nearing the exit, she saw a large pile of Maeve Binchey books on the fast back section. There was no problem in taking out the book. Her library card was valid for all the libraries in the Portsmouth area, she was informed.

"All except the big one in Guildhall. You need a separate ticket for that one."

Mavis wondered why, but did not ask. She had left the library and walked past the Conservative Club and the museum before she realised she would not read the book. After her class, she would walk to the ferry, cross to Portsmouth, climb the Round Tower and never read again. There was not time to return it; she would have to leave it in the college or the ferry. It would be returned to the library then, faster than if she'd kept it and read it right through.

Chapter 5

Mavis walked briskly to the college; it took her longer than expected. She followed the signs for 'reception' and was soon speaking to the young man who took her details the previous day. He was friendly, yet efficient as he issued a receipt for the fee she'd paid over the telephone and gave her a leaflet before inviting her to take a seat whilst she waited for her tutor.

She almost walked into a man who was patiently waiting in line behind her.

"Mavis? Mavis Forthright?" he asked.

The voice was familiar, the face was not. She looked at the grey eyes, greying moustache and ginger hair that should also have been showing signs of grey. He was smartly dressed, except for the hideous bright yellow shirt that lent his face an unhealthy hue. He smiled. He fidgeted. She remembered.

"Norman?"

"You remember, then?"

"People are waiting," Mavis pointed out the other students queuing to enrol.

"I won't be more than a minute. Then we can talk."

Mavis nodded, but the moment his back was turned, she strode away from him. Norman Merlin, what could he be doing there? She didn't want to know, she didn't want to speak to him, or see him and she most definitely didn't want to think of him. She heard footsteps behind her and lengthened her stride.

"Excuse me," a woman's voice chirped.

Mavis stopped.

"Can I follow you?" the woman, small and neat, asked.

"Why?" Mavis was startled into rudeness.

"Well, I, you see I don't know the way. To the toilets, sorry, I just thought that was where you must be going."

"I am afraid I don't know where they are."

"We'll look together then, shall we? I'm Jenny. I'm doing art too." She offered her hand to Mavis, who shook it firmly.

As they walked through the corridors, Jenny told her how much she was looking forward to the course. Mavis was too; it would be silly to miss it, simply because she had, quite literally, bumped into a man she'd once known. She would go to the lesson. Afterwards she would walk down to the ferry, cross the harbour, climb the tower and all the loneliness, all the suffering, all the memories would be gone. She'd succeeded in not thinking of Norman for twenty years, she could put him from her mind for two more hours. As she waited for Jenny to wash her hands, Mavis resolved to make a real effort to appear friendly and confident. People would remember with sorrow the nice new member of their class who met with an unfortunate accident. More than ever she was determined her death must appear accidental. Norman must not know that, only hours after meeting him again, she had jumped into a cold, dark death.

"Have you taken evening classes before?" she asked Jenny as they returned to reception.

"Oh yes, I did needlework one term, and French, creative writing, local history, oh lots of things."

"Good heavens! You must be busy."

"Oh I haven't kept up with them all," Jenny laughed. "I flit from one thing to another. I like to experience something new, but the best bit is meeting so many new people."

In reception, the waiting students were flocking into groups around their tutors. As each group was complete, they were led off to their classrooms. Norman had gone. Jenny and Mavis stood apart, unsure which group they should join. A young, fair haired man called for the art class to follow him.

Mavis had scant opportunity to study her fellow students as they walked to the class. Some chattered, giving the impression they knew each other. Perhaps they had attended this class during the previous term. It hadn't occurred to Mavis the others would not, like herself, be beginners. Jenny was new to art, but had the advantage of having attended other classes. Mavis had made a mistake; by enrolling for the course, she'd exposed herself to the chance of more unhappiness.

45

"I'm glad we've already met," Jenny interrupted her thoughts. "I always feel a bit nervous walking into a room of people I've never spoken to before. It's silly, really."

"I think it is a perfectly normal reaction."

"Do you? Oh good. I always feel an idiot because I'm shy, then when everyone is nice I feel even more daft for worrying."

Around her, Mavis heard other people asking those closest to them if this was their first time. It appeared the majority were new and anxious to have an acquaintance, however slight, before entering the classroom. Maybe she wasn't so different from them?

The art room appeared much as Mavis remembered from her schooldays. Not the same of course, but still recognisable. There was the smell of poster paints and freshly sharpened pencils. Shreds of sugar paper wafted on the air. The desks and chairs and every surface were coloured and textured with generations of spilt or spattered paint. Around the sides of the room were cupboards, no doubt full of water colours, brushes, glue, scissors, water jars, pastels, perhaps charcoal, certainly pencils, coloured and graphite. Others around her were exclaiming at the memories the room recalled. Mavis smiled, nodded, considered joining in the chatter. She was in the right place; she belonged there, in that room, with that group of people.

The young man began to speak. He gave his name, Tim Bittern, and introduced himself as their tutor. He was the youngest person in the room. Mavis glanced round. No, she was not the oldest. Mr Bittern called a register; there were giggles as he did so.

"Jenny Allis?"

"Oh yes, yes," Jenny whispered. If she hadn't raised her arm, it was doubtful if her tutor would have been aware of her.

"Present," was how Mavis chose to answer her own name.

"Angela Nightingale?"

"Yes, sir, I'm here, sir; but I'd rather be called Flo, if that's OK."

The woman who spoke was large. She had long red hair and wore a brightly patterned floral garment that hung loosely despite her size. The name Flo suited her admirably; her hair, flesh and clothing seemed to flow around her bones. Her continuous chuckling added to the illusion.

"Certainly, if that's what you prefer," Mr Bittern replied. He made a note in his register.

"Cheers. I hope you don't mind about my homework either. I haven't got it. The dog ate it." Flo laughed at her own joke.

Mr Bittern asked them all to introduce themselves, explain why they were there and if they'd any previous experience of drawing or painting. Some had been attending art classes or groups for many years; others like Mavis had done nothing creative since leaving school. Some spoke at length of their motivation and hopes, others gave the barest information.

One woman, called Vera, said the most, in a deep and theatrical voice. She was wasting their time; instead of listening to her, they should have been starting the class. Mavis was distracted by Jenny's constant movements. She tilted her head left and right as people spoke. She kept lifting her legs and hooking her heels over the rungs on her chair before sliding her feet from side to side then allowing them to drop and dangle several inches above the floor. Jenny's fidgeting suggested Mavis was not the only person who thought Vera would talk through the whole lesson.

When at last she finished, a small man spoke. His few words slipped out in a quiet rush; Mavis did not catch his name.

Jenny stroked her hands incessantly. First she ran the fingers of her left hand over the tops of those of the right then reversed the process. Left over right, right over left, left over right. Mavis wanted to take those hands and make Jenny sit on them. She wanted to use her shoes laces to tie her feet onto the chair legs. Instead, she tried to concentrate her attention on each of her classmates as they spoke in turn.

Flo had not painted since her schooldays, "Except for emulsion on walls," she explained.

Some had done a few sketches, just for fun. Only one, Leo, had taken Mr Bittern's classes before.

"I've painted for some time now, but recently felt that the time had come to get back to basics. I thought that the stimulus of a class, the fresh enthusiasm of others might provide the inspiration to lift my work. This will be my second term with our dear Mr Bittern. I hope you all find his teaching as enjoyable and inspirational as I do."

He had a trick of circling his wrists as he spoke, occasionally leading with his index finger and pointing with a flourish at a member of his audience. The movements appeared unrelated to his words, except they stopped when he finished speaking.

"Thank you, Leo," Mr Bittern said. His cheeks were rather pink.

"No more than the truth, I assure you."

Leo looked and sounded, to Mavis, a caricature of an artist. His flamboyant clothes, the deliberate drawl to his voice, the extravagant hand gestures as he spoke all contributed to this, yet he seemed genuine. Perhaps a real painter lay beneath the sham artist?

"It doesn't matter how experienced or otherwise you are," Mr Bittern said. "I will set exercises that will be helpful for everyone, and then as I get to know you all and your work, I will tailor tasks to meet the needs of the individual."

As the students introduced themselves, he strode around the room, setting large sheets of paper before each of them. It felt thick and coarse. Without speaking, he encouraged them to shuffle up, or move into groups of three. Jenny and Mavis were already sharing a table. Vera came to join them. She placed her large hands flat on the table, wide apart before her, as if claiming the space as her own. Mr Bittern placed tubs of paint, brushes and water pots in clusters, within reach of the students and added small palette shaped pieces of board.

"There are many elements to a successful painting. Many of them the viewer will hardly be aware of. Then there is colour, so obvious and immediate. We'll start with colour. Who knows which are the primary colours?"

A few arms were tentatively raised.

"Just call them out."

"Red, yellow and blue," boomed Vera before the others could open their mouths.

"Which shall we start with?" he enquired of Mavis.

"Red."

"Red." He gestured to the tubs of paint.

They began by daubing colour on their palettes, and transferring some to the paper. Jenny formed hers into a small, neat square; Vera created a swirl with a flourish of her brush. Mavis placed her laden brush on to the paper and then dashed it quickly away, leaving a single bold stroke of colour. Next, they added yellow to their palettes and were told to paint some of this on to the paper, a little away from the red. Then they blended in ever increasing amounts of red, to produce gold, peach, tangerine, orange and scarlet until the yellow had become red. Mavis dovetailed her strokes of paint, creating a guttering flame of colour. Jenny's tidy squares were stacked neatly, forming a graduated column. Vera's swirls were too large; they crowded and overlapped each other in lurid confusion.

On another sheet, they used blue again. This time with the addition of white. Mavis's strokes became softer; the liquid paint would still appear fluid once dried on the sheet. She allowed some shades a larger space, and added extra streaks of white occasionally to represent flecks of foam. She added more pure blue, to the lower portion of each wave, to suggest depth. So absorbed was she that she did not notice Mr Bittern pause in his previously continuous circling of the students.

The exercise was repeated with blue and yellow, creating greens, through unripe lemon to deepest bay. Vera reduced her dramatic swirls to meagre tear drops; Jenny created another neat column, parallel to the first. Mavis accentuated the flowing lines of her strokes, adjusted the size and shape so they fitted together more neatly. The effect was of fallen leaves.

On another sheet, they used blue again. This time with the addition of white. Mavis's strokes became softer; the liquid paint would still appear fluid once dried on the sheet. She allowed some shades a larger space, and added extra streaks of white occasionally to represent flecks of foam. She added more pure blue, to the lower portion of each wave, to suggest depth. So absorbed was she that she did not notice Mr Bittern pause in his previously continuous circling of the students.

"Having fun?"

"Oh, I am sorry," Mavis took a long trembling breath and hung her head. She felt as she used to when Mother would see she had decorated the covers of her school exercise books. Lessons were for learning, not for frivolous entertainment.

"Don't be sorry, that's what we're here for, to learn to enjoy our art."

Mavis dragged her head up to look at him. He appeared to mean what he said.

"Tell me what you were doing here."

"The colours reminded me of the sea."

"The sea, yes. Not the contents of Portsmouth Harbour?"

"No, that is a colder colour, rarely blue. No sea is as blue as the one I've painted here. This is a silly make-believe sea."

"Not silly, the pictures in our minds are as valid as the ones we see with our eyes."

"I hoped to paint real things, proper pictures."

"OK, so we'll make this a real sea. Why isn't this colour right?"

"It is too bright."

"So what shall we do about that?"

Mavis pointed to the black paint. Mr Bittern smiled. The class began adding dashes of black to their blue, darkening the sea to a night-time hue. Then they tried touches of yellow, to create a Caribbean turquoise, red to represent a reflected sunset. Another shade of blue was mixed, diluted and washed above the sea to form a sky.

"Oh drat, it looks like it's raining in mine," Vera said. "Tim, can you help me?"

Despite the improper manner in which she'd addressed him, Mr Bittern came to see what was wrong.

"I see what you mean, that's just because the stronger colour of the sea is bleeding into the pale wash of the sky."

"I don't see how I could have prevented that though. If the sky doesn't come right down to the sea, it looks odd."

"You're absolutely right, Vera. Would you mind if I used your picture, and yours Jenny, to explain something?"

They both nodded agreement. Mr Bittern called the class around the table.

"If we'd intended to paint a seascape from the beginning, we would have started with the sky. Painting in the pale background first, allows us to paint on top and avoid harsh lines and gaps."

"That makes sense," Vera said.

"Now, you have your sky. What else could we do to make this more convincing?"

"Paint in some clouds?" the quiet man suggested.

"Yes, clouds, but we don't have to add them."

Mr Bittern demonstrated how colour could be lifted from the paper with a piece of damp sponge, to leave behind a few wispy clouds.

"If I wanted darker clouds, the sponge could be used to add other colours back in as well."

He then showed how a clean brush could be drawn across the page to remove a thin strip of colour, suggesting trails from passing planes. They each tried those techniques then added purple smudges of land on the far horizons. Each of them had created a simple painting.

"You can take these home tonight, if you like."

"I didn't realise we'd be doing actual painting today, so I haven't brought anything to take mine home in," Vera said.

"Neither did I," someone added.

"Don't worry. This is the room I use for my day job and I'm lucky to have plenty of storage space. If people wish to leave other work here that will be OK, if it's raining say, and you don't want to get your masterpieces wet. Of course, that means you'll have to wait until next week to frame them."

The students laughed. Although most were pleased with their efforts, they knew it would be a while before they produced anything worth framing.

They took a short break; some people went to fetch drinks or chocolate from the college's vending machines. Mavis and Jenny helped Mr Bittern to clear away the paints and move the paintings onto the tops of the deep cupboards that edged the room.

After the break, Mr Bittern showed different still life paintings by Jean-Baptiste-Simeon Chardin. They looked at the examples and discussed his subject matter; the mix of metal and glass objects, fruit, flowers and dead animals.

"Seems a funny combination, pretty flowers and dead things," Jenny remarked.

Mavis was surprised at how life-like a dead animal could appear. "You imagine that if you touched them they would still be warm."

"You do indeed," Mr Bittern said. "That's the sign of good still life, you really believe in the things you're looking at. Even if they are not as accurate as a photograph there is a realism that makes you feel you could lift them from the canvas. We'll be looking at different artists and their techniques throughout the term. Now, about your homework."

There were groans.

"It's optional; all I can say is; the more you put into this class, the more you'll get out of it."

"You sound like a teacher," Flo quipped, reminding Mavis of young Janice at work.

"Yes, funny that," Mr Bittern laughed. "I want you to create a still life, a line drawing is fine, but you can paint it if you prefer. It doesn't matter what it turns out like, the main thing is to have a go, make a few mistakes, so that you can learn from them."

"So where do we get hold of dead pheasants then?" the comedienne asked, indicating the last picture they were shown.

"Don't worry, old boy, I'll send out the keeper to bag some," Leo said, before Mr Bittern could reply.

"If you'll just let me finish," Mr Bittern said sternly, over the class's chuckles.

Even Mavis could tell he was only teasing.

"Start with something simple. A piece of fruit, but choose one you don't normally eat, a mango maybe. Anything that you're not familiar with, that way you'll have to look closely at it. Eat it afterwards, fruit's good for you and I want you all back here fit and healthy next week. Class dismissed."

They straggled out of the college calling their goodbyes. Some left through the canteen and went out to the car park. Others walked as she did, under the Bell Arch and out on to the main road. There, they either turned to the right or stepped into waiting cars. Alone, Mavis walked towards the sea. It was dark, but dry and there was no wind. She passed the Railway Arms and felt nervous, without good reason. It was still too early for the occupants to leave. She did not look in and would have been surprised to learn that even a single drinker had noticed her pass.

Street lights reflected in the puddles, the light sparkling and cheerful. She imagined drawing the scene, assessing what to include and what to leave out. Was that an echo of her footsteps, or someone walking behind her? The steps were faster than hers. Should she turn, make it obvious she knew she was not alone? No, better perhaps to walk on. 'Walk purposefully,' she remembered reading somewhere. 'Don't act like a victim.' She walked more quickly. The footsteps behind began to run. Louder, faster, nearer.

"Hello," a male voice called to her.

Do muggers call hello? Probably not. She slowed her pace and allowed him to catch up with her.

"Hi, sorry, didn't mean to startle you." It was the boy from the bus stop. "If you're going to the bus station, I'll walk with you."

Mavis nodded and they walked on, side by side.

"I thought I saw you come out of the college. You doing an evening class?"

"Yes, painting."

"I'm there full time. Doing hotel management."

He was a pleasant boy; Mavis did not mind his company.

"We run a restaurant. Different classes cook and serve different nights. Good food and cheap. You should come, bring a friend; we need more customers. Don't wear your best dress though, one of the girls spilt tomato soup tonight."

"Oh dear."

"Managed to get it on three people. Now that's real skill."

"Do you cook, or serve?"

"Both, we have to learn everything. I work in Luigi's too, at the weekend. I'm a porter at the moment, but as I learn more at college they're going to let me do other things."

Mavis could no longer go across to Portsmouth and climb the Round Tower. She could not walk away from him into the night without him remembering, without him realising, when he read of her death, that he'd spoken to her shortly before. Her plan was again delayed.

He sat next to her on the bus and asked how she'd got on with her lesson. She was surprised at the enthusiastic response she provided.

"Sounds like you're going to really enjoy it. I hope you'll show me one of your masterpieces."

"Yes, yes I shall."

They walked together from the bus stop to her house.

"Perhaps I will see you in the morning?" Mavis asked.

"Not tomorrow, I don't start 'til later. The hours are all over the place. I always do every other Wednesday night though. If you like we could meet in the canteen and come back together."

"Yes, thank you. I would like that."

Chapter 6

Mavis woke in the night. She had been dreaming of walking away from the college, along Spring Garden Lane. She'd heard footsteps. They got faster, louder, closer. Once properly awake, she remembered it had actually happened, but it was the boy, not someone who wanted to hurt her. She remembered too she hadn't wanted to die. Not like that.

The previous night when she attended the class Jenny talked to her and had chosen to sit with her. If Mavis returned to college next week, Jenny would be pleased to see her. They could sit together again and talk. They might even become friends. Mavis did not know if she could keep a friend, but she wanted to try. She wanted to know if Janice at work would read all of *1984*, and what she would think of it. She wanted to feed the birds. Most of all she wanted to paint a picture. She went back to sleep and dreamt of landscapes and portraits.

'Youth is wasted on the young,' her calendar informed her. That was true. When you were young you did not notice happiness, you took it for granted. You did not seize opportunities; you thought there would be time later for adventure, for freedom, so you did as Mother said.

Today's youngsters didn't seem to do as their mothers told them. They always appeared to do whatever they wanted. Perhaps they weren't waiting, they were living. Maybe youth was not wasted on them as it had been on her. They took joy in being alive, in experiencing things. It was easier for them of course; they didn't have a lifetime of unhappy memories to carry around. They didn't have a living to earn either. After putting out half of the food that had been salvaged from the bird table the previous day and stored in the fridge, Mavis washed her hands and prepared to set off for work.

As she unbolted her front door, she picked up a sheet of paper that had been pushed through her letter box. Not the usual flyers advertising things she did not want and frequently did not even understand. This was ruled notepaper and had a message written by hand. It had been folded over, and then stuffed through. Mavis automatically straightened and smoothed it flat. Her name was at the top, spelt wrongly, but there. The ringing phone startled her. It was too early, surely, for anyone to be trying to sell windows or kitchens. She lifted the receiver.

"Hello?"

"Hiya, can I speak to Nikki please?"

"Who?"

"Nikki, is she up?"

"I don't know."

"Oh, could you give her a shout, do you think? I need her to bring something to school."

"I think you must have the wrong number."

"Oh. Oh dear, sorry. I hope I didn't wake you up or anything?"

"No, you did not."

"Oh good, well that's OK then. Have a good one."

Mavis replaced the receiver. People should take more care when dialling telephone numbers. The caller could easily have woken her or disturbed her in some way. What 'one' was she supposed to have that would be good? A good day she supposed the child meant. At least she'd apologised and attempted to be pleasant. Just a mistake then.

She would try to have a good day. To do so, she must get to the bus stop quickly; answering the telephone had delayed her. The note was still in her hand, folded over as she'd talked to the girl. She tucked it into her bag, checked her reflection and left the house.

At the bus stop, Mavis saw the pale girl and attempted to smile at her. There was no answering smile, just a deepening of her scowl before the girl turned her back. Mother had told her people were unkind, that they did not want to be her friends. Maybe that was true.

"Morning, dear, better today isn't it?"

Mavis turned to see the couple had arrived; the woman with the large bag was speaking to her. Her words were not unkind.

"Good morning. Yes it is."

"Going to work are you?"

"Yes."

"Retired we are. Well Bert is. I never worked. Well, I did, housework and the kids … that's plenty of work. You got any kids, have you?"

"No."

"Three we've got. Davie, he's our eldest, he's taken over the business. Plumbing, you know. Pearson's Pipes, ever hear of it?"

"No."

"U-bend it, we'll fix it, that was our motto wasn't it, Bert?"

She turned enquiringly to Bert and gave him a nudge.

"Eh?"

"Our motto, Bert. For the plumbing."

"U-bend it, we fix it."

"That's right. Bert's knees gave out on him, so he had to pack up."

The woman's chatter must be her way of being friendly. Mavis had no wish to divulge personal information, but it might be easy enough to keep a conversation going, without needing to say a great deal herself. Mother had not encouraged idle chatter and gossip. Mavis guessed Bert might not be much of a conversationalist, yet the man had smiled and nodded at her as she arrived. Perhaps there were different ways of making friendships. Maybe it was a skill Mavis could learn.

The bus arrived, and for once Mavis did not select the seat furthest from every other passenger. She chose to sit directly behind the couple. The woman had stopped talking.

"Are you going shopping?" Mavis asked. She had no wish to learn the answer, but felt her companion might enjoy providing the information.

"Shopping, oh no. We do all our shopping at the weekend now. Well most of it anyway. No, we're off to see Lauren."

"Is she your daughter?"

"Granddaughter. We look after her while her mum goes to work. There's just her you see. Dad buggered off, good riddance too. Took drugs he did, nearly got our girl on that too, but then she found she was pregnant, brought her to her senses it did. Got a council flat she has now. She's trying hard."

"It must be difficult."

"Oh she's brave. Had a row we did, when we found out about the drugs n' all. She left home. By the time we found her, she'd already seen through that useless… the baby's father was gone, and little Lauren well on the way. Determined to cope she is. Doesn't live off welfare, got a proper job she has. Didn't want us to have the little 'un she didn't. We insisted, didn't we, Bert?"

The woman turned to her husband, and waited.

"Eh?"

"Lauren, I was talking about Lauren."

Bert grinned, "Lovely girl Lauren is," he said, nodding vigourously.

"Dotes on her, Bert does."

"She sounds lovely."

"Oh yes she is. That's why we're so happy to go and look after her. Don't seem right her mum paying some stranger to do it, when we can. Gets us out the house too."

Following Mavis off the bus and onto the ferry, Bert's wife described the care arrangements of Lauren, and the child's numerous good points for the rest of the journey.

"See you tomorrow then, love," the woman called to Mavis as they left the ferry and went their separate ways.

"Goodbye," Mavis answered. The woman was wrong, she wouldn't see her tomorrow. She would never see her again. Mavis would never again hear her cheery words.

At work, Mavis made a point of smiling at everyone as they arrived and saying, "Good morning."

Her colleagues appeared surprised at her cheerful greeting, but not one of them failed to respond. Janice was full of questions about the evening class. Mavis described her classmates and the teacher. Sandra brought coffee, and Lucy and Nicola perched on Mavis's desk, to drink their coffee and hear the details of Mavis's evening. They asked questions and teased her after she admitted Mr Bittern was 'quite good looking'. Mavis said she felt thirsty and gulped some coffee.

"You're like me," Janice remarked. "I always get really thirsty when I talk a lot."

Mavis had been talking for over ten minutes. No one criticised her; they hadn't called her idle or selfish. They hadn't even appeared bored. They'd treated her as if she was a normal person, with an interesting life.

That lunchtime the other women went out to lunch with the person who'd previously held Mavis's position. She'd left to have her baby, and had arranged to meet up with her old colleagues and show off her daughter. Mavis had been invited, but declined. As she did not know the woman, she would not be wanted. Not until she was alone, did Mavis remember the note she'd received that morning. What had she done with it? She was holding it when the telephone rang. She hoped she hadn't dropped it on the floor and left it there. She looked in her bag. The note, folded neatly into quarters was in the pocket that held her keys. Mavis unfolded it. The writing was untidy and difficult to read. The writer had pressed the pen down so firmly that in places it had pierced the paper.

'Ms Fourthright,

Please clear up all that muck from your bird table. One of my cats has eaten some of it and it made him sick which wrecked my new sofa. Theres a horrible mark and it will probably attract rats. Its not hygienic. If you don't clear it up I'll complain to the council.

Marie French.'

Mavis screwed up the note. She squeezed her hand so tightly around it, her nails dug into her palm. Her neighbour's cat frequently trespassed into her garden. It scratched in her flower beds and left foul smelling mess around newly acquired plants. It stole the fat blocks hung for the birds. It rolled in her seed beds. Worst of all it waited under the table and sprang on the hungry birds. Many were frightened away and several killed. Last spring, it had dragged blue tit chicks from a nest. It was a horrid creature, encased in innocent looking grey and white fur. Marie French should take measures to keep it under control, not allow it to roam

58

free. How dare the woman allow it to invade Mavis's garden. How nasty she was to complain; how spiteful to make threats. Mavis trembled. She'd been fooled, by a few fake smiles that morning, into thinking people were kind. They were not. They were selfish and grasping. They cared for no one but themselves. Mother had been right; if she wanted to avoid being hurt, she should not let people get close to her. She must keep them away; learn to see through their sham friendships and realise it was a trick to get something from her.

The other women were nine minutes late back for work. They'd gone off to have fun, leaving Mavis alone with her cheese sandwich and tea. She should not have expected anything else. She did think it would have been reasonable for them to return to work on time though. They hadn't cared that Mavis worked whilst they were straggling into the building. Mavis would have been the one answering phones, had they rung. She didn't think they'd behaved well and told them so. During the afternoon people hardly spoke to her. Why would they? They did not care; she was not part of the group of friends. Mavis was brought a cup of coffee when drinks were made, but not out of consideration, she knew. They were ensuring she had no grounds for complaint.

"Are you OK, Mavis?" Nicola had asked.

"What do you mean? Are you suggesting that I am not performing my work in a satisfactory manner?"

"No, of course not. I just wondered if something was wrong, you don't seem very happy."

"Is that any concern of yours?"

"Yes, Mavis, it is. You work for me. I have a responsibility and I ..."

"I am perfectly well thank you," Mavis snapped before Nicola could dole out any false concern.

Mavis continued tapping information into her computer. Although she struck the keys quickly and forcefully she made no progress. Her concentration seemed less than adequate for the task. She decided to replenish her stationery instead. Sandra saw her with an armful of envelopes.

"Would you like a hand with those?"

"I can manage. I may not be as young as you, but I am perfectly capable."

"Oooh, sorry I'm sure."

As Mavis left the stationery store, several envelopes slipped from her grasp. Sandra stepped over them and flounced away. By the time Mavis had gathered everything together, Sandra had walked down the corridor and allowed the door to swing closed behind her. As Mavis grasped the handle, her haul slithered to the carpet and the door swung towards her. It banged sharply against her knee. She winced but said nothing. She would not give them the satisfaction of knowing she was hurt.

Mavis was at the photocopier when Janice approached her.

"I've read quite a lot of the book now. It's very interesting."

"Oh?"

"Yes. In the back, it says that he wrote quite a few others, *Animal Farm* was one. Have you read it?"

"Yes, Janice, I have, but I don't have a copy to give to you."

"Oh, I didn't mean that."

"No? What did you mean then?"

"Nothing."

Janice walked quickly away, her head hanging.

Mavis sighed. She'd begun to think Janice might be an interesting person to know, someone she could discuss books and her painting with. She was wrong, as soon as the girl realised she had nothing for her, she lost interest in Mavis.

The rest of the afternoon passed slowly, with none of the usual chatter; at least none where Mavis could hear it. As people left, they said 'good night,' to her and received a curt nod in reply.

Mavis walked to Old Portsmouth and climbed the Round Tower. She tried not to think of the unkind treatment she had received. Soon it would not matter. Nothing would matter.

She was not alone at the top of the tower. In addition to the ever present gulls, a man with a camera stood there; she could not drink her gin and swallow her pills whilst he remained. He might try to stop her. She sat on one of the faded backless wooden benches to wait.

60

Whilst waiting for her own death, Mavis thought of Mother's final hours. Each visit to the bathroom had become an ordeal. It had been possible, with much shame and fuss, to manoeuvre her to the toilet. Mother had often sat there long after relieving herself, before finding enough strength to rise. Worse had been the consequence of Mavis being asleep or shopping or in the garden when Mother had needed such a visit. The removal of soiled bed linen from around the humiliated old woman had never been easy. Sponging off the rubber sheeting, provision of clean linen and cleaning and changing Mother, had always been conducted without speaking. Such incidents were never mentioned.

Mother had asked for pain killers again. She often asked for them. If Mavis had given them to her each time, Mother would surely have died months earlier. Mavis had folded back the plastic packaging to expose a tablet. She shook it into the palm of her hand then extracted another.

"Sit up a little then, Mother. You'll choke again otherwise."

She'd attempted to put an arm around Mother's shoulders to help her rise. She was pushed away. She was always pushed away. Mother stuck out her tongue and Mavis dropped on a tablet. She held the glass to the old woman's mouth. Mother too held the glass as she sipped; careful her thin fingers didn't touch her daughter's hand. She released her grasp and stuck out her tongue again. The pale damp organ provided little contrast to the white tablet. Mother swallowed the second one.

"Another. I want another. Two are not enough."

"Two is the maximum dose. You know that."

"You brought me pain when you started your life. Will you not ease my pain as I end mine?"

"You want another tablet; although you know it is too many?"

"Must you question me always? Yes, Mavis. I want another tablet. When I ask for one, I do not wish to be told how many I have consumed during the last twenty four hours. I do not wish to know how many the packaging suggests I take. I do not wish to know your opinion on this or any matter. Do I make myself clear?"

Mavis had taken another tablet from the pack and dropped it on Mother's extended tongue. She held the glass again to her lips. Mother had swallowed.

A pair of seagulls wheeled overhead, screaming their harsh cries. Mavis didn't look up. She stared out to the Solent, seeing not the photographer who was causing a delay to her plans, but Mother's room as it had been six months before.

Mavis had been woken again in the night by Mother's cries. She'd done what she could to end the suffering. Mavis had known immediately when Mother died. Not only because quiet replaced the rasping breaths. The woman, who'd always been there, was gone. Mavis pulled a chair close and held a cold hand. She waited. There was nothing left to say, nothing to feel. She considered bending close and kissing the head that rested eternally before her. She did not do it. It was too late.

There were six pages of colourful advertisements for funeral directors. She'd called Solent Funeral Services; the simple listing and local address seemed appropriate. The man who answered sounded calm; reassuring. Mavis gave the information he required. He asked if she'd contacted Mother's doctor.

"No." She should have realised the doctor would need to confirm and certify the death. That always happened in the books she read. "I will do so immediately."

The doctor arrived in less time than he'd ever taken when Mother had been alive. He officially confirmed Mother's death.

"Are you all right?" he asked.

"Oh yes, I am quite well."

"That's not quite what I meant. The death …"

"Someone will be here to help me soon."

Mavis sat with Mother until the undertaker arrived; a tiny man, dressed in black and white. He hovered tactfully as though poised to adapt his manner to suit the occasion. He reminded Mavis of a pied wagtail, bobbing around. In answer to his questions, Mavis admitted to a cousin who could be called.

"Perhaps it would be wise to do so?" he'd suggested.

"Of course, Cousin Linda must be told."

"Actually, I meant that she might be of assistance to you."

Mavis hadn't understood. What assistance did she need now she no longer had Mother to take care of?

The body had been taken away.

Mavis rose from the wooden bench and walked to the Tower's edge. She held the safety rail and looked down to where the sea covered the rocks. The photographer removed the large lens from his camera, fitted on a cap and returned it to his bag. He didn't put away the camera, he selected another lens, attached it and returned his attention to the view. Mavis returned to her seat and the memories.

Mavis had boiled the kettle, set out two cups and saucers, warmed the pot and measured tea. Too much tea, only one cup was required. Why, when Mother had been such poor company, did Mavis feel so alone? It was best to get on with things. Linda would be kind; would help.

"Hello," Linda answered.

Mavis had dialled before she had words ready. It was not correct to make a bald statement. Polite talk of the weather before announcing Mother's death seemed equally inappropriate.

"Hello?" Linda said again.

Mavis knew she must speak.

"Linda."

"Yes, this is Linda. Who's that?"

"Mavis Forthright."

"Hello, Mavis. Sorry it's a bad line. How nice to hear from you."

Mavis couldn't think of a suitable reply. For no reason her nose had began to run. She sniffed.

"Mavis are you all right?"

"Yes."

"And your mother? Oh, Mavis, are you ringing about your mother?"

"She's dead. I've just found her dead."

"Oh, Mavis I'm so sorry. Would you like me to come down?"

The undertaker had been right; Mavis needed her cousin.

"Yes, but ..."

"Then I'll come."

Linda had arrived in time to insist Mavis eat an early supper. She'd stayed until after the cremation. Mavis was without direction. Linda had been practical.

"It will be best for you to get a job."

"A job?"

"Yes, don't you think that would be best? You might just manage financially without, but you don't want to sit around here on your own. You want to keep the house I suppose? You could sell, get a flat."

"No. The garden. No, not a flat."

"I know you've never gone to work, but you'd get used to the idea."

"I don't mind the idea. I wanted a job, but Mother ..."

"Yes, things haven't been easy. Now, I wonder what you could do?"

Another seagull cried as it swooped over the top of the Tower. Mavis looked at the bird as it flew free. Mavis had been permanently freed of Mother, but only temporarily from unhappiness.

Time had passed quickly on the government run training course. She'd been one of twelve people learning computer and office skills in order to improve their chances of gaining employment. The other students had greeted her; joked about mistakes and congratulated each other on minor achievements. Mavis hadn't taken part in discussions; she found keeping track difficult when several people contributed. She liked to listen; imagining other conversations, ones in which she would participate when she began working. Mavis had felt optimistic after receiving her certificate. She was pleased when she secured a position at McHyvers; it seemed she would have a future.

She'd learnt her job and become efficient. At first, everyone had been friendly. They'd explained the lunch breaks and arrangements for making tea. Mavis was shown the premises and told the quickest way to the shops. Her colleagues discussed television programmes and films she'd never seen. They'd chatted about themselves and asked her questions; where she went at the weekends, if she had any family. So many questions, to which she had no answers. She'd lived a lifetime with Mother and never got close to her; why had she ever expected to make friends in a few weeks? Why had she thought the future would be different from the past?

The photographer was gone. She could drink her gin, take her pills. When Mavis opened her bag, she saw a folded piece of paper. It could not be the nasty message from her neighbour that had been folded small and thrust into the bottom of her bag. This sheet was folded once. A message was neatly written in Janice's flowing handwriting.

'Dear Mavis,

We are really sorry that we upset you today. It was unkind of us to go to lunch without you. We should have insisted you come. Honestly, when you said you would rather not go, because you don't know Alice, we thought you meant it. We are sorry that we didn't make it clearer to you that we wanted you to join us. Please forgive us.

Best Wishes.'

The note was signed by everyone in the office; everyone except Sandra.

Her suicide must wait. She couldn't allow Janice and the others to believe she'd taken her life because of the lunchtime incident. She climbed back down and walked to the ferry.

"You all right, love?" asked the man who was punching passengers' tickets.

"Oh, yes. Sorry. I am fine."

"Got your ticket?"

Mavis opened her bag. Tears blurred her vision.

"Can you take two from mine, my dear chap?" a man behind her asked.

The ferry worker punched the man's ticket twice and allowed them both to board. The man grasped Mavis's arm and guided her to a seat.

"I'm sorry, I'm afraid I don't recall your name. I'm Leo, from the art class."

Mavis blew her nose and dabbed at her eyes.

"Mavis Forthright."

"Pleased to meet you, Mavis."

He offered his pale hand. It dangled limply in front of Mavis, who shook it firmly in order to remove it from her vision.

"I must pay you for the ferry ticket."

"No, no. Only too pleased to help a damsel in distress," Leo gestured extravagantly. "I do hope the distress was of a minor and temporary nature?"

"Yes, thank you."

"I believe you said that you are newly come to the world of art?"

"Yes."

"I myself have been painting for several years. I enjoy painting immensely, it's so expressive, so freeing."

"Er, yes."

"And our Mr. Bittern! What a talent he is, so inspiring, just divine."

"He does seem quite nice."

"What medium will you use? What is your genre?"

"I beg your pardon?"

"I myself use pastels; I find their infinite subtlety simply exquisite. Oils! You should paint in oils. There is strength in you, and passion. I feel it." He thumped his chest with the flat of his hand. "Yes vivid portraits in oils would be right for you, I'm sure."

"I had not really thought. I did buy a small painting outfit; I think the paints are acrylic."

"Acrylic, oh marvellous! All the drama and excitement of oil, without the tedious wait. Oh yes, superb choice. I look forward to seeing your work progress."

The ferry bumped against the pontoon and Mavis leapt to her feet.

"I must catch my bus. Thank you, for helping me with the ticket."

"Fare thee well, dear lady. Until we meet again, fare thee well."

"Goodbye," Mavis said and made her escape from the incredible man.

Mavis did not head straight for the bus stop; she crossed the road and went into the off licence. She intended to buy some brandy. Brandy was good for shocks and Mavis needed something good for shocks. She hadn't realised there would be so many kinds of brandy, she felt unable to make a choice. Then she saw the distinctive blue bottles of Harvey's Bristol Cream. Cousin Linda always kept a supply of the sherry and on several occasions had persuaded Mavis to sip a small glass of the sweet drink. Half-sized bottles were on sale. Mavis chose a full-sized one.

After her supper of scrambled eggs, she poured a small measure of sherry into a wine glass. She sat on the settee, her legs on a footstool. She took the crocheted throw and covered her legs. Deliberately she blocked all thoughts of her emotional day and concentrated on her Maeve Binchey novel. She savoured tiny sips of her rich, warming drink and read three chapters.

That night, as she waited for sleep, she wondered if she really could paint a vivid and dramatic portrait with her, as yet untouched, acrylic paints.

Chapter 7

The bottles of gin and tablets were still on the kitchen counter. Last night, Mavis hadn't wanted to put them back in her bag. She was not truly ready for them. They were placed in a kitchen cupboard. Not where she would see them each time she prepared food or a drink, but in a far dark corner, out of the way.

The motto on her calendar read, 'Seek and ye shall find.' Mavis could try to seek an improvement in her artistic ability. The course ran for nine more weeks. She'd paid for lessons and paints; it would be a waste not to attend; the tablets would wait.

Bert and his wife were at the bus stop as usual. Bert's wife chatted to her. She felt grateful for the woman's conversation, her words distracted Mavis from the words she must say at work. She had behaved badly; she would have to try to explain. She had to make things right.

"Morning, Mavis, feeling better?" Nicola asked as Mavis walked into the kitchen.

"Better?"

"You weren't happy yesterday afternoon, I wondered …"

"I am fine today, thank you."

"Coffee?"

"Yes please."

Nicola made the drinks. She didn't wash the spoon between dipping it into the coffee jar and using it for the sugar. Mavis didn't comment.

"Good morning, Sandra," Mavis greeted the next arrival.

"Morning, Nicola," Sandra said and walked out again.

Nicola followed her out.

Mavis heard Nicola's voice but couldn't distinguish her words. Sandra's reply was clear.

"No. We didn't do anything wrong. I don't see why we should rush around writing her nice little notes and sucking up to her."

More murmuring from Nicola followed.

"I suppose so, but I still think she should apologise," Sandra said.

Sandra was right; Mavis had sought someone to blame for her unhappiness. The blame lay with Marie French, yet Mavis had punished her colleagues. She wanted to leave, but couldn't; she must explain. She sat at her desk and waited until her colleagues had all arrived and were together in the kitchen.

They stopped talking as she walked in.

"Yesterday, when you …" No, Sandra had said they'd done nothing wrong. They were late, but Janice's note had apologised. She must forgive them if she expected them to do the same for her.

"Sorry. I am sorry I was bad tempered yesterday. I should …"

"Oh, that's all right, Mavis," Janice interrupted.

"Let her finish," Sandra snapped.

"I should not have been rude."

"Go on," Sandra said.

"I am sorry. You did nothing wrong. I behaved badly. I apologise."

For a moment no one spoke

"Get your mug, you must be ready for a refill," Sandra said and switched on the kettle.

"Thank you for the note, Janice," Mavis said later.

"Oh, that's OK. Are you like feeling better now?"

"Yes thank you, Janice."

And she was; things would be all right.

The day continued, much as any other Friday. People spoke to her. Their chatter meant exactly what the words said.

Saturday morning, Mavis cleared the bird table. Because of the note from her neighbour, she was disinclined to do so, but had no alternative. There was too much for the birds to consume. The wet remains would rot. The hungry birds would eat the food, sicken and die. 'If a job's worth doing it's worth doing well', had been the quote for the day. It was worth feeding the birds. She would clear the mess and begin again.

Mavis put on her clogs and stepped into the garden. A ladder was propped against the neighbour's house. A bracket, new and shiny, dangled from the brickwork. The woman must be installing one of those awful dishes. Mavis had seen the advertisements for digital television channels. She couldn't understand why anyone would wish to subject themselves to such horrors, let alone pay for the privilege. Still, that was their business; it didn't matter to Mavis. Once the leaves expanded on her Philadelphus, she wouldn't see the hateful thing. She wondered if Ms French were doing the work herself or if she'd persuaded some man to do the job.

Mavis hadn't noticed a van or a strange car on her driveway, so for once Mavis was spared hearing her gush, "Oh, you're so strong, Steve. Your shoulders must get stiff, why don't you let me give you a rub down," or, "Thank you so much, Dave; come inside and let me thank you properly," nor other, equally simpering and sluttish remarks, to the rest of her hangers-on.

The woman would soon be back up her ladder. She'd look over and see the bird table being cleared and think she'd won. Well, she could think what she liked. Mavis didn't care.

Mavis half filled her washing up bowl with warm water and added a squirt of antibacterial cleanser. As she scrubbed, she wished she'd thought to wear rubber gloves. They would have been impossible to clean properly afterwards, but would have protected her chapped hands. Once all the food had been washed away and all surfaces of the food tray cleaned, Mavis swilled the remaining soapy water over it.

As she carried out the heavy bowl of clean rinsing water, she saw the neighbour's cat in her garden. Mavis could not put up with that. She flung the water toward it, sending it running and clawing its way up the fence towards its own garden. It didn't get wet, and sat on the fence twitching its tail. Mavis advanced; there was still water in the bowl. She wasn't quick enough and the cat escaped. Mavis heard a cry from behind the fence. She didn't give her neighbour the chance to comment, but went inside for more clean water.

After rinsing the table, Mavis boiled the kettle. She poured the contents over the table to scald it, ensuring no germs or bacteria remained. She returned the portion of salvaged food that remained in her fridge to the table, refilled the birdbath and went inside to prepare for the walk to the shops.

The greengrocer didn't stock the mangoes she needed for her artwork. Mavis bought a small green cabbage and two potatoes. As Mavis approached the Co-op, the pale girl, wearing headphones, came out. She looked up; Mavis was sure the girl saw her and surprised the door was let go, just as she got there. Mavis stumbled, brushing against the girl who glared and shuddered as if Mavis were a leper.

The Co-op didn't stock mangoes.

"Try Asda, there'll have them," she was advised.

First, she bought a pint of milk and visited the library. For once, Mavis didn't return a book she'd borrowed. Because of her evening class, she hadn't finished reading it. She'd overheard people asking to have loans extended. The assistant librarian happily did that for Mavis.

"May I borrow more now?"

"As long as you don't have more than eight at a time, that's fine, ducks. If you haven't finished with them you can always phone up to extend them."

Mavis hated to be called 'ducks', but as the assistant librarian had addressed her, and most other readers, in that way for several years now. It was too late to ask her to stop.

She found an Agatha Christie she couldn't remember reading, although she must have done so. There was a new book by PD James too. She could find no other new books by familiar authors. She knew other readers asked for advice, perhaps she could do so?

She approached the assistant librarian and waited until the lady's short fingers had stopped pecking away at the computer keys.

"Ooh yes, ducks. We've got plenty more books on murder n' that. Here, I'll show you."

The librarian stepped out from behind her counter and led Mavis around the shelves. Mavis divided her attention between the books she was shown and the woman's footwear. Her boots were the shape and size of workmen's boots and made of shiny pink leather. As usual, she wore a white blouse, plain grey skirt and matching jacket. She must have damaged her shoes on the way to work and been forced to borrow the boots.

As Mavis handed over the books for stamping, she made an effort to be less abrupt than usual.

"Thank you for your help. I look forward to reading these."

She was rewarded by a beaming smile.

"I hope so, ducks. Don't forget what I said about renewing your loan, if you've not finished 'em or it's raining or summat and you don't fancy popping out, you just give me a call."

"Thank you, I shall remember."

Passing her neighbour's house, as she took the books and her purchases home, Mavis saw the side gate was still open and the garage unlocked.

She put the books, in alphabetical order, on the shelf of her bookcase reserved for library books. The milk went in the fridge. After washing and drying the potatoes, they and the cabbage went onto the vegetable rack. Mavis walked briskly to the bus stop, and hadn't even taken her purse out to look for change when the bus arrived.

There were two kinds of mango on the shelf in ASDA. Small greenish yellow ones with 'buy one get one free' stickers or large fat ones, a voluptuous full bodied red fruit for £1.89. Nearly two pounds, she could get a kilo of apples for that but she was determined to learn how to paint a proper picture. Buying the subject matter for her homework was the first stage in realising that ambition. Unless the start had been reading the college's advertising leaflet, or perhaps meeting Karen in the café.

Mavis decided to undertake each task set by Mr Bittern. She would examine the fruit thoroughly, not just look at it. She would touch, smell, taste it. The tutor had said a painting should teach you something. It should engage all the senses; reach into the viewer's mind. When a person looked at the pictures, they would know what it felt like to pick a fresh mango, to feel they were consuming the fruit. Some of the students had clearly thought that pretentious rubbish, but not Mavis; she'd found it exciting. She didn't wish to draw pretty pictures; she wanted to create meaningful works of art. Mr Bittern would show her how. She stretched out for the ripe, promising fruit and grasped it, and her hopes, firmly.

The red skin was streaked with orange and gold, pitted with purple and had a dull waxy gloss. She caressed its resinous smoothness. She lifted it to her nose and inhaled. The scent was weaker than she'd expected, but the label was correct; fragrant described it accurately. It smelled like walking into a conservatory full of tropical blooms as the owner brewed a pot of Earl Grey tea.

Mavis placed the fruit into her basket, taking care not to bruise it. It would be wasteful to have travelled to the supermarket simply to purchase a single fruit. Mavis walked down every aisle. Tinned soup was on special offer. She chose flavours not stocked by the Co-op; Mulligatawny, carrot and coriander, spicy tomato and leek and stilton. Her other purchases were more mundane: toilet rolls, tea, washing up liquid. As Mavis carried the heavy basket, she noticed the delicious smell of freshly baked bread and was tempted into a further purchase. The exciting soups should be consumed with interesting bread; she chose a large wholemeal loaf containing sunflower seeds. At home, she would cut it into four sections, wrap and freeze three of them, reserving one for her lunch. She wondered if she would enjoy the sunflower seeds as much as the starlings and finches enjoyed the ones she provided for them.

Whilst queuing to pay, Mavis saw display baskets containing packs of four muffins. A sign advised her to buy one pack and get a second free. As she looked at the moist chocolate sponge, an assistant added more packs to the display.

"These ones are my favourite, raspberry and white chocolate," the girl informed her.

"Eight is far too many for me. I could not possibly eat them before they went stale."

"You could always freeze some. Go on treat yourself, really good they are. Chocolate ones are good too though; I'd have one of each, if I was you."

Mavis took the girl's advice and then went in search of drinking chocolate. As the snack in the library had prepared her for her class, it would be sensible to repeat the experience before her homework.

Whilst waiting for the bus, she looked through all she'd bought. There was no reason to feel guilty. She'd earned the money, and the items wouldn't be wasted. She would drink every drop of soup; even if she could not enjoy the actual flavour, she would enjoy the experience of trying something different. Mavis didn't doubt she'd enjoy the cakes and hot chocolate. The other items were household necessities. At home, she took the mango from her bag and set it gently on a small white plate. She placed it on the breakfast table where she'd see it often throughout the day. The other items were unpacked and put in their proper places. Mavis was annoyed to discover the tea was not loose tea, but bags. The vast selection of styles and makes and sizes in the supermarket had alarmed her. She'd snatched up the pack that most closely resembled the type she normally bought. She would have to return it.

Despite the careful way she'd removed her boots before coming inside, the kitchen floor had become horribly dirty that morning. There were several seeds, a piece of dried mud and a mark where spilt soapy water had dried. It had been slovenly of her to go out before cleaning up. Once the floor was clean, Mavis made herself a cup of tea. She drank it slowly as she ate a chocolate muffin for her lunch. She washed up and then gazed at the mango.

Mavis sharpened her pencil and opened her sketch pad at a fresh page. She transferred, as best she could, what she saw onto the inviting white sheet. An outline at first, the rough shape. As her work progressed, she attempted to add depth and shading. She turned the page and drew another outline. Using bolder strokes, she tried, as Mr Bittern suggested, to capture the idea, rather than a faithful reproduction of what she saw. The second attempt was slightly more successful than the first. Mavis drew a third outline, to be filled with colour.

She laid a thick layer of newspaper on the table before opening her new painting kit. She read the instructions for mixing and using the paints.

Congratulations on purchasing this quality set of artist's materials. We are sure they will assist you to realise your full artistic potential. Happy painting!

1: Blending Acrylic Paints.

Because acrylics dry rapidly, you need to work fast if you wish to blend colours. If you're working on paper, dampening the paper will increase your working time.

2: Keeping Acrylic Paints Workable.

Acrylics dry very fast! Squeeze only a little paint out of a tube at a time. Keep the paint moist (you may find a small spray bottle useful for this purpose).

Mavis wondered why, if the spray bottle were required, none were provided in the kit. She had one she used to apply spray to the rose bushes. If its use seemed advisable, she would use that. She continued to read.

3: Blot your Brushes.

Keep a piece of paper towel or cloth next to your water jar and get into the habit of wiping your brushes on it after you rinse them. This prevents water drops running down the brush and on to your painting, making blotches.

Surely, it was a matter of simple common sense to keep your equipment and therefore your work clean? The instructions went on to tell her how use the paints to create both opaque and transparent colour. Mavis read of colour washes and glazes. She was confused by the overabundance of new words, phrases and techniques. Mr Bittern would be able to offer advice, or perhaps the man who'd been kind to her on the ferry. Leo; that was his name. He seemed knowledgeable and eager to help. She might ask him the purpose of masking fluid and to explain the optical mixing of insoluble washes.

She read through to the end of the leaflet.

10: Next Steps

Once you have mastered the basics with this beginner's set, you will require further supplies! We supply a large range of acrylic paints, brushes, papers and equipment. These can be purchased from any quality supplier of artist's supplies, or ordered online from our website, www.slapitonpaints.com

Mavis folded the instructions, but didn't return them to the box. She wouldn't read them again. They'd told her little, except she must work quickly and cleanly; they could go in the recycling bin. Attempting to use the acrylic paint was probably the best way to learn. If she made mistakes, she could ask for guidance in correcting them. Without the benefit of experience, she would not know what to ask.

She opened the tube of brilliant yellow and squeezed a tiny amount onto the plastic palette. She added scarlet, vermilion, cobalt, burnt umber, chrome, olive, raw sienna, yellow ochre and cadmium green. Other than black and white, she used every shade her small kit had to offer. All those colours along with many more were visible in the thick textured skin. She began blending. Quickly, she realised the small water pot provided was impractical. In order to prevent it falling over she was obliged to hold it steady with one hand whilst swirling the brush with the other. She retrieved an empty marmalade pot from the bin of recyclable items. She re-washed it and half filled it with water.

Soon Mavis needed to add paint from the tubes of white and black to her small palette. Silly of her not to have realised she'd need those for shading. As she painted, she occasionally noticed the sound of a gate banging. How irritating! Ms French, must have forgotten to close it.

Mavis worked as quickly as she could. By the time she'd filled the shape with colour, the paint on her palette had begun to dry. She was forced to stop and clean up in order to avoid ruining the brush and palette. The painting, whilst not perfect, was as realistic as she would manage at her first attempt.

It had become dark. She'd spent the entire afternoon at her artwork and was hungry. Whilst trying to decide which soup to have for supper, she heard the gate bang again. Drat that woman, had she no consideration for others? Mavis looked out. There were no lights on in her neighbour's house. Perhaps she'd gone out? Mavis must shut the gate herself, speaking to the woman wasn't something she had any wish to do.

Mavis pulled the gate towards her and latched it. The wood felt tacky; perhaps through grease from the cat who sat there so often. That woman obviously did not trouble to keep the woodwork clean. As Mavis walked back across her neighbour's driveway a car passed. In the light from its headlamps, Mavis noticed the garage door still partially open. Mavis had no intention of trying to close it and risk the woman hearing and accusing her of attempted theft. It was unlikely Ms French would be burgled, but it would show her the error of her sloppy behaviour if she was.

Mavis went back to her kitchen, and washed the dark stain from her hand, before deciding on Mulligatawny soup. She was cold and that would be warming.

"There's no such thing as a free lunch," her calendar warned Mavis as she made tea the following morning. Mavis didn't need to be told, she never expected to get anything for nothing. She decided to have the mango for breakfast. A decadent start to the day, but Mavis felt closer to decadent than she'd ever done previously. She was a painter, for the weekend at least. Artistic people need interesting nourishment. Besides she'd paid for the fruit; it would be silly to waste it.

She took her sharpest knife and cut into the fruit. The skin was thick and unyielding. She soon encountered the large fibrous stone. Deviating around it, she managed to cut the flesh in two. Next time, she would know better and cut to one side. Next time? Was she to become the kind of person who regularly ate mangoes then? Perhaps; surely there were some changes due in her life.

Mavis sliced the remaining flesh from the stone then fetched a spoon to scrape the edible part away from the skin. Her hands were sticky and juice became smeared over the outside of her cutlery drawer and dripped inside. First, she would eat. Then she'd clean up the mess. She'd probably create more smears before she consumed the fruit. To stop each time a drop of juice fell might mean the fruit browned and spoiled before it was all eaten.

With a teaspoon, she dug out a piece of the sweet juicy flesh and tasted it. It was delightful, not at all the challenging acidic flavour she'd expected. It was like a very ripe peach, but smoother, almost creamy. The flavour was different from any other food she'd eaten, yet still comfortingly familiar. Had she encountered it unknown in a jungle, she would have known from the first taste it was edible. Mavis Forthright lost in a jungle, what a thought!

It reminded her of the brightly coloured card she'd bought for Cousin Linda's birthday. The card had been bought weeks ago, written, sealed and stamped ready to be sent. She must post it.

After breakfast, she put the mango skin and stone on the compost heap. How long would that enormous seed take to decompose? She washed up and wiped away the juice spilt on to the work top. She cleaned the handle of the cutlery drawer then checked inside. How annoying, there was a smear of juice on the handle of a spoon and a small droplet by the forks. In her haste to try the fruit, she had made an awful mess. Everything must be cleaned. Mavis emptied the cutlery into the sink, washed and dried the tray that had held them, then cleaned, polished and returned every item. At last the kitchen was tidy and she could leave it to post Linda's card.

As Mavis returned from the post-box, she saw her neighbour's cat scratching in her front border. She hissed at it, much as she'd done many times before. It ran, jumping over the gate that yesterday had been banging. Mavis was surprised to see how discoloured the top of the gate had become. She shuddered as she remembered touching it yesterday. The cat quickly returned. It mewed and walked, tail erect, in front of the garage door; its previously white front paw stained the same rusty brown as the gate.

Mavis walked toward the cat, it seemed distressed. She bent down in a pretence of stroking the animal and peered under the garage door. Her neighbour's car was inside. In front of it, she saw a tool box; the contents in disarray. Mavis remembered seeing the ladder against the wall yesterday and the bracket for the satellite dish. There had been no dish when Mavis refilled the bird bath. It was as if her neighbour had been interrupted during her task. That would explain the unsecured garage, discarded tools and banging gate. The cat mewed again; not the same sound she'd heard yesterday when the cat had leapt her fence, close to where its owner's ladder had been.

Mavis considered ringing the door bell, but what could she say to the woman? The cat did not approach Mavis, but took up its position on the gate. It watched her, but was not quiet and still as it usually was. Mavis walked toward it. The cat disappeared over the gate. Mavis unlatched it and followed it into her neighbour's back garden.

Chapter 8

Marie French had indeed been interrupted whilst fixing up the dish. She would never complete the job. The ladder still rested against the house wall, the dish was thrown clear. Her neighbour's hand still clasped a drill. So much blood had seeped from her body, fouling her clothes and the concrete patio, that it was impossible see the wound. Mavis guessed the bit from the drill had caused the injury. She wondered if it had stopped after puncturing the woman's throat, or if it had continued to whir round until the battery had been discharged.

Mavis recognised death. The woman was paler even than Mother had been, that final morning. Marie French was dead. No cloud of vapour from her nose and open mouth condensed in the cold air. The staring eyes couldn't see. This was not Mother. This time Mavis couldn't wait for office hours before contacting the undertakers. She must call the police and must do so immediately.

Marie French's patio door was open; the light switch in the same position as Mavis's own. Soon she was using an unfamiliar phone to dial a familiar, yet never before used, three digit number.

Mavis didn't know where to wait. Should she stay with the body? She hadn't liked the woman and there was nothing she could do, yet it seemed wrong to leave it, her, alone. She didn't want to stand and look at her. Didn't want to contemplate those small sticky footsteps and think of the cat now washing its paws. Nor did she wish to look at the pool of congealing blood and realise the centre was still vivid and liquid. The woman had died slowly. She was not dead, was a long way from death, when Mavis had slammed shut her garden gate yesterday. Had she heard Mavis's footsteps and thought help was coming? Had she heard the gate crash shut and the footsteps retreating? Did she know who had come and gone? Could her life have been saved then?

The house numbers of Sylvester Crescent were not easy to see from a passing car. Perhaps the police would have trouble identifying the correct address. They wouldn't expect an empty street. She should stand in the woman's driveway and indicate where they were required. Yes, that would be best.

She almost pulled the gate shut behind her, realising just in time that would make entry to the garden difficult. There was a tree; a golden conifer in a pot, Mavis used it to wedge the gate securely open. The tree looked dead. It was difficult to tell with conifers, they died slowly and retained the appearance of life for long after the sap ceased flowing. Mavis felt she recognised death in the pot and elsewhere in the garden. There were dead, or nearly dead, pansies dotted in the front border.

As she waited for the police, Mavis remembered her neighbour planting them. She'd bought a polystyrene tray of pansy plugs and an orange handled trowel. The woman had dumped her purchases on the driveway and begun clearing the weeds. Some had come up with roots attached; most snapped off. The woman stuffed the pieces she'd removed into the wheelie bin. She'd flipped open the top and dropped them in. Towards the end of that stage of her 'gardening' stint, the weeds had no longer dropped into the bin; they'd been mounded on top. She'd shaken the bin, pushed down on the contents, shoving and thrusting in the stems until she could flip the lid shut. Stems of fat hen and a ragwort flower protruded, but she either didn't notice, or didn't care.

Mavis had risen early the morning of the refuse collection. She'd expected the council staff would refuse to empty her neighbour's bin; garden refuse should not be put into bins with household rubbish. It should be composted, either in the garden from which it came, or by the local council. It should be taken to the recycling centre. Mavis knew that; she expected her neighbour knew. Obviously, the council staff did, but still the bin had been emptied in the normal manner. It wasn't fair; the woman had blatantly broken the rules and got away with it.

The sight of the badly planted pansies had further angered Mavis. Plants should be treated with respect. The woman was unused to the task; her trowel cheap and unsuitable. She should have cleared the weeds properly using a sturdy border fork to loosen the soil, to break it down to a reasonably crumbly texture and admit air. The ground should have been irrigated and raked level. She should have dug proper holes, gently firmed the plants into place and cared for them until they were established. None of those things happened. The woman had scraped mean little holes then crammed the dry roots in. Once she'd done that to each vulnerable plant, she'd used a hose to half-heartedly water the bed. Water had been sprayed across the entire area, not administered gently and accurately where required. Some plants received none; others were washed out of place.

Mavis had predicted most would die over the course of the winter. She had been right. The bed was once again covered with weeds, the brown corpses of pansies completely overwhelmed. There were a few plants still, one or two were bravely attempting to flower. Even those had pinched yellow leaves.

What a contrast to her own vibrant garden. Bright leaves in sunny yellow or smartly variegated in white contrasted with the fresh greens. Sunlight lit up the translucent reds of peony stems, sparkled off the pristine hellebores and almost danced amongst the gem-like early bulbs. Mavis's garden was full of life and colour, Marie French's was brown and dead.

"Hello."

Mavis was startled by a woman's voice. She looked up; before her was a policewoman on a bicycle.

"Are you the lady who called about her neighbour?"

Mavis nodded.

"Am I the first to arrive?"

Mavis nodded again and pointed towards the gateway.

"I'd best take a look then," the policewoman said, leaning her bicycle against the garage door. "The area car and an ambulance will be here soon."

Mavis followed the policewoman into the garden. The officer's brisk stride slowed as they neared the body.

"I have not touched her, but I am sure she is dead," Mavis volunteered.

"I'm sure you're right, but I'd better check."

The policewoman knelt, trying to avoid the sticky mess. She held a wrist; the one thrown out as though Marie French were reaching for the satellite dish that had fallen from her grasp. The officer turned to Mavis and nodded.

"I'm sorry to say you're right," she told her, then began speaking into her radio.

Marked and unmarked cars and the ambulance arrived. A crowd began to gather. Mavis could see people leaning out of windows in the houses that backed her neighbour's garden, and her own. The body had lain disregarded, cooling and stiffening for many hours. As tarpaulins were stretched to obscure the view, people developed a curiosity about what lay behind them. A constable went to stand on the driveway in an attempt to discourage the curious, determined to see or hear something shocking.

Mavis sat on a plastic patio chair and watched as death was officially confirmed, photographs taken and an investigation begun. She was not ignored, people were kind to her. They said she need not stay.

"Go home if you like, have a cup of tea. We'll need to take a statement, but you can go home."

Mavis didn't feel able to walk past the gawpers, to ignore their questions and wait alone in her house for the police to arrive and question her. She was surprised at the number of people required to deal with the death. There were various policemen in uniform and other men who although not in uniform, Mavis guessed were also policemen. A doctor attended; however dead a person seemed, there was still a need for that to be officially pronounced. There were photographers, why two she wondered? The subject would wait without complaint for however long was required to take as many pictures as were needed. There were people measuring and recording everything there was to measure.

A couple arrived from the RSPCA to deal with the cat. An ambulance crew arrived and quickly left again. A man who may have been an undertaker spoke in quiet tones to several people and then he too left. Mavis knew from Mother's funeral that the body would attract attention from many more people. Marie French had received several regular visitors and was often collected by all sorts of different cars and taken away for the evening or weekend. Mavis didn't know if she had any family. Most people have relations who, even if not prepared to spare you a thought in life, will insist on 'paying their respects' when it comes to death. That had been the case with Mother. Mavis had expected that, apart from Linda and possibly a few members of her immediate family, the funeral would receive no attention. She was surprised by the number of people who attended. So many women who, although Mavis could not recall them, had been dear friends of Mother's.

Had Mavis's own death come when she'd planned, there would have been few mourners. Now things might be different. Linda would have come of course and probably Nicola to represent McHyvers. Janice might have come on her own account. No perhaps not then, but she would now. Would members of her art class attend? Her death will be delayed until the end of term. There will be people at her funeral. Some of them might be saddened by her death. Mavis shuddered. It was hardly surprising that discovering a body would make her think of death. She was not dying now though; she had more living to do. She no longer wanted to remain within scent and sight of the dead woman and stood up to remind those officially there, she was also present.

The policewoman insisted on walking Mavis back to her house.

"You'll feel better in your own home; this has been a shock for you."

Mavis allowed the constable to take her arm and guide her across the patio; negotiating around blood and working officers. The body had been covered. Mavis could still picture her neighbour's eyes staring at something the living cannot see.

As she reached the gate, Mavis saw people on the pavement, trying to discover what had happened.

"Has there been an accident?"

"Was it a burglary?"

Mavis stopped walking; the policewoman stepped in front of her, shielding Mavis from public view. "It's OK; we won't let them bother you."

She called a colleague, who spoke to the gathered people. He said there'd been an accident and asked for the names and addresses of anyone who knew the owner of the house, or had any information. Some eagerly gave personal details, others melted away. Mavis and her escort walked across the front lawn and into her house.

Once inside, the officer asked if Mavis would like her to call anyone.

"Do I need a solicitor?"

"No. Sorry, I meant a friend or relation."

"Will I have to come to the police station?"

"You'll have to give a statement, but I can do that here if you prefer. There will have to be an investigation. I'm afraid you'll probably have to give evidence at an inquest. It won't be much fun for you, but it should be straightforward."

Mavis nodded, it would not be pleasant, but she was prepared to do whatever was required. "When will that be?"

"Oh, not for a few months, I shouldn't think."

By that time, Mavis herself would be dead and possibly another inquest would be arranged. She didn't mention that.

"Do you feel up to answering a few questions now?"

Mavis swallowed, pulled back her shoulders and answered, "Yes, of course."

"Look, you come and sit down. I think you could do with a nice cup of tea. Shall I make you one?"

"Please."

The younger woman's sympathy touched Mavis. The horror of the scene she'd witnessed began to take effect. She staggered to a chair and her eyes began to stream. The policewoman waited for Mavis to sit, then took the crocheted cover from the settee and wrapped it around her shivering body.

"It's the shock. I'll get that tea."

The policewoman went into the kitchen. Mavis heard her fill the kettle and open cupboards. She soon re-appeared in the lounge. "Would it be all right for me to make myself one too?"

"Oh, yes. Sorry I did not think."

"Thanks." She went back into the kitchen. Mavis didn't want to be alone; she wanted the kindness the officer had shown. Clutching the blanket, she walked to the kitchen.

"Nearly ready now," the policewoman assured her.

Mavis watched as she dropped a teabag into each cup. It was too late to tell her the tea could be found in the red caddy and the pack of bags had been a mistake. The policewoman removed the plastic sleeve and tore the flap from the box; she crushed them together in her hand, before throwing them into the bin.

The kettle boiled and she poured on boiling water.

"Milk and sugar?" the policewoman asked.

"Yes please."

"Me too." She spooned two heaped spoonfuls into each cup, stirred briskly, and fished out the bags. Each was squeezed against the spoon with her thumb, before being thrown away. She took the milk from the fridge and sloshed a generous amount into each cup. The carton of milk was returned to the fridge, with the label facing inward. Mavis said nothing. She would put it right later.

"You sit yourself down. I'll bring them in."

For a minute, they drank their tea without speaking. Gradually Mavis felt calmer and less cold.

"That better?"

Mavis nodded and tried to smile. The WPC produced her notebook and gently questioned Mavis. As she answered the queries, Mavis found herself eager to talk. She was pleased she could give accurate times and a clear explanation.

"I'll get a formal statement typed up for you to sign."

"Will I need to visit the police station in Gosport to do that?"

"No, I can bring it here if you prefer. I am often in your road."

"Yes, I have seen you before, on your bicycle. You must be Constable Martins," Mavis said.

"That's right. Tanya Martins, I'm the local beat officer. There isn't much for me to do on this estate so most people don't know who I am. I try to attend most Neighbourhood Watch meetings and pop into the community centre whenever I can. I don't think I've seen you there?"

"No. I read your name in a leaflet sent by the council."

"So somebody does read those things."

"I like to keep myself informed of local matters," Mavis said.

"Yes, of course."

The silence that followed was broken by a call on Constable Martins' radio.

"Excuse me," she retreated to the kitchen and responded quietly. She returned and approached Mavis.

"Ms French has been taken away now."

The use of her neighbour's name reminded Mavis of the evil note complaining about her bird table.

"Are you sure there's no one I can call for you? Or perhaps you would like to see a doctor?" the policewoman asked.

"No." Mavis made a show of blowing her nose and wiping her eyes as she struggled to regain her composure. She must be calm, as she'd been after Mother died. Death should become easier with practise.

"Do you have to go, now that you have taken my statement?"

"I can stay a little longer if you'd like. Shall I put the kettle back on?"

"Yes please."

As Mavis heard the tap running, she fretted over water splashes on the stainless steel draining board. Knowing Constable Martins would be making a mess, Mavis felt unable to prevent herself witnessing the full extent of the officer's carelessness. She returned to the kitchen.

"I am sorry; I don't have any biscuits," she informed the young woman.

"Not to worry, I eat too many anyway."

That was obviously true, but Mavis managed to keep her agreement silent.

"I love 'em though, biscuits and cakes, they're my weakness."

"I have some muffins; dark chocolate ones, or raspberry and white chocolate."

"Oh, I really shouldn't."

"As you wish."

"They do sound nice though."

Mavis remembered conversations in the office whenever biscuits or cakes were offered. Although several of the women had no need of further calories and remarked on this, it rarely prevented them from eating at least as much as their slimmer colleagues. Maybe the constable had the same problems with self control? Mavis wondered if she did too, as now cake had been mentioned she imagined herself hungry. She glanced at the kitchen clock, it was half past one. Her hunger was justified, and probably that of the police officer too. Chocolate muffins were hardly appropriate as Sunday lunch, but she had nothing more suitable to offer her visitor. She opened the bread bin and withdrew the airtight container.

"Which flavour would you prefer?"

"Oooh I don't know, they both sound good."

Mavis recalled her own difficulties the previous day when confronted with a choice of delicious soups and then the cakes. She placed one of each type on a wooden chopping board and sliced them in half. Two different flavoured halves were placed onto each of two side plates. She swept the crumbs into her hand before transferring them to the blue ceramic jar. The officer looked puzzled.

"I save all my scraps for the birds."

"Oh, good idea."

They carried the food and drinks into the lounge, where the policewoman proceeded to make more food for Mavis's feathered friends. After a few bites, there was a knock on the door. Mavis was startled.

"Shall I see who it is?" Constable Martins offered.

Mavis nodded her agreement. She heard a man's voice, then the officer said, "I'll ask, but I don't think so." She then shut the door.

"Miss Forthright, it's a reporter from *South Today*. He wants to interview you. I'll send him away if you like?"

"Please."

The officer returned to the front door.

"Sorry, she would prefer to be left alone. She's had a nasty shock, I'm sure you understand and will respect her privacy."

Mavis heard the man's voice again before the door closed.

"He's left his card. I've put it on your hall table. He said to call him if you change your mind. It's up to you. Sometimes, it's easier to give one of them an exclusive and get it over with."

"Why would television people want to speak to me?"

"This'll be on the local news tonight I expect. They can't have much on at the moment; they've got a camera crew out there."

"But it's just an accident. You said it was an accident," Mavis said.

"That's just the way these things go. Sometimes minor things make the headlines. Other times bigger things don't because there's something even bigger happening. You must have seen reports of missing tortoise and cats up trees? It's not because it's news; it's just to fill airtime until something actually happens."

"Oh, yes I see."

"There'll be interviewing all her friends and neighbours. They'll say how sad it is and what a lovely woman she was."

"Well, I certainly shall not be doing that," Mavis said.

"You didn't like her?"

"I fail to see how anyone could have done so."

"Oh, a trouble maker was she? Did she upset many people?"

"I imagine so."

"Was there something in particular?"

"Well, she was just rather unpleasant. I am sorry, I know one is supposed to be polite about the dead, but that seems foolish to me."

"Yes, it's probably best to tell the truth."

They didn't speak again whilst they finished their cake and tea.

"I shall have to go soon. Is there anything I can do for you before I go, someone I can call?" the officer said.

"I am perfectly all right now. It was a shock, but I am quite recovered. Thank you for your kindness."

"I don't like to leave you alone. Sometimes you need someone to talk to."

"It is just for this afternoon. I shall be at work tomorrow. I have friends there and there is my cousin Linda, I shall probably call her."

"Good idea. Well, I'll be round with the statement soon. Will Thursday evening be convenient?"

"Perfectly."

"Good, I'll see you then, then. In the meantime, try not to worry too much."

As she spoke, Constable Martins wrote into a small spiral bound notebook and then tore out the sheet.

"Call me if you have anything to add to your statement, or have trouble with the press, or anything. The top one is my mobile, I have that with me most of the time, even when I'm not on duty. The next one is the station, or you can call 101 if that's easier."

Once Constable Martins had left, Mavis began to tidy her kitchen. First, she retrieved the things the officer had dropped into the dustbin. Tea leaves always went on the compost heap; she supposed the bags would rot down eventually. After the cellophane wrapper was separated from the cardboard top of the tea carton, she folded each tidily and put them into the correct bins. The cardboard could be recycled, the cellophane, unfortunately, could not. She checked the milk carton; the constable had placed it correctly after making the second drink. She washed the cups, plates and chopping board, dried them and put them away. The pack of teabags would have to be used, as an opened pack couldn't be returned to the shop. The tea had tasted exactly the same as the loose variety and the bags might be simpler to use. If she could accustom herself to the idea, she might buy bags in future. Mother would have been furious, but Mother's opinion no longer mattered.

Mavis took the teabags outside and put them on the compost heap. People had given up hanging out of the windows opposite. She put the cake crumbs on the table; there was no longer anyone to disapprove of that activity either. There would be no cat to mess in her garden or chase the birds. Mavis wondered how long it would be before she had new neighbours.

She tried to read, but found the fictional world did not hold her attention as well as usual. Her thoughts were focused on the evil note her neighbour had written to her. She wondered why she hadn't spoken of it to the policewoman. Mavis realised she would be asked questions at the inquest. If she mentioned the note, then she may have to produce it. Mavis felt sick to think that others would read those terrible words, would know her shame and anger. She tore the note into tiny pieces and put them into her bin. She would forget the note and its implications. The woman had been unkind to her and now she was dead. That was an end to the matter and she need think of her no more.

She switched on the television. The death of Marie French was mentioned on *South Today* news. It came after the report of the tall weather girl's success in yet another charity run and before details of the little boy waiting for a replacement kidney. Mavis watched the child's worried parents and reflected that, whilst she was trying to forget a death, they were hoping for a fresh one.

Chapter 9

Mavis switched off the television after the news. The report mentioned her. Not by name, but it had stated the body had been found by a neighbour. Mavis had enjoyed that; it made her feel quite important. Pictures of Ms French's house had been shown. People who lived nearby would know who made the discovery. She wondered if Cousin Linda had seen the report. No that was silly, Linda lived too far away to receive the same local news. Mavis knew Linda would have been concerned, would have called if she'd seen it. Mavis had told Constable Martins she had a cousin she could call for support. That support would be welcome; Mavis looked up Linda's number.

She stopped dialling after the area code. Mavis rarely rang her cousin; the last time she could remember doing so was after Mother's death. When Linda had answered Mavis remembered, she'd blurted out, 'She's dead. I've just found her dead.' On that occasion, Linda had known immediately who the dead woman must be.

"Your mother? Oh, Mavis, shall I come down?"

That was what she'd said, "Shall I come down?" as if she lived at the top of the road, rather than hundreds of miles away. She'd helped Mavis to make the funeral arrangements. She sat and talked for hours as Mavis gradually understood the changes taking place in her life. Linda hadn't only helped organise the funeral; she'd arranged the last six months of Mavis's life. They had not been a success. Mavis had done everything Linda told her, but added no plans, nothing at all, to the bare scheme Linda devised for finding a way to survive.

Mavis replaced the telephone receiver and wandered around her house. What a fool she'd been. Mother had squeezed every dream from her. As she'd washed and fed Mother, listened to her cruel remarks and allowed them to erode her personality, she had longed to be free. Once the freedom came, she no longer had the ability to enjoy it.

Standing in front of the bookshelf, Mavis instinctively sought the comfort of her books. Her hand reached out. She selected one, *Unchained Melanie*, by Judy Astley. It looked new. Mavis never bought new books; the few she owned had been gifts, mostly from Linda. Normally, she borrowed from the library, but over the years, she'd collected some of her own. A result of browsing in charity shops. She used to do that quite often, to extend her time spent shopping and therefore away from Mother.

Mavis turned the book over and remembered how she'd acquired it. It had been a free gift with a magazine. Mavis didn't often buy magazines although she leafed through them in the newsagents. She'd known Prima contained recipes and gardening advice. There had been a cake recipe she remembered. She'd baked the cake for Mother's birthday. She'd set out the cake, pretty plates and the good tea set on a tray and then almost not taken them in. Mavis had been sure Mother would rebuke her for her extravagance. Mother hadn't appreciated her gift; after a quick glance at the colourful woollen shawl, Mother had instructed her to place it at the bottom of the wardrobe. Why would she want a cake?

Mavis had been wrong; Mother smiled and made the effort to sit up.

"Well, this is almost a party. Please fetch me my new shawl, Mavis."

Mavis draped her gift around Mother's shoulders.

"I did not imagine I would have an occasion to wear this."

Tears ran down Mavis's face as she remembered that afternoon. Mother had eaten two slices of cake and then asked her to read. She'd been easier to live with for a time after that day. It was not just the cake, but also the reading of stories that made the difference. They'd both remembered how Mother cared for Mavis when she'd been a child. Mother made cakes and read stories then. Their roles became reversed. Mavis tried to forget the years in between when there had been no cakes and no kindness.

Mavis put the book on the table to blow her nose. She picked it up again and put it in her shoulder bag, not back on the bookshelf. She would give it to Janice. The girl must finish *1984* soon and would like something else to read. It would be easy to persuade her Mavis did not want a light-hearted paperback and the girl's mother could hardly complain over a second-hand free gift. Mavis would not regret giving it and the girl would not be embarrassed to receive it.

Why stop at giving her one? Mavis had other books. She did not want to part with them, but would be prepared to lend them. Mavis decided she would lend Janice one book, if the girl returned it in good condition, she would lend her others. It would be interesting to hear the girl's opinions, to see if her likes and dislikes were very different from Mavis's own. It would be fun to guess what would appeal and try to select something suitable from her collection. Janice had tried to be friendly. Mavis had pushed her away. Well, that would change. Mavis would change.

She looked at her painting of the mango. Perhaps she'd already changed. The painting, she knew, was no masterpiece, but if looked at with a generous eye, she felt sure it did resemble the fruit it was intended to depict. She would like to paint other things; to paint them well. Yes, she had changed; she had a dream of a sort, in her desire to paint. If she wished, she could befriend young Janice. The girl was lonely; she recognised the condition from her own unhappy youth. Brief snatches of friendship from Cousin Linda had meant so much. If Mavis tried, she could bring a small measure of happiness into Janice's life; and her own. She would try.

There were other things in Mavis's life too. She had a job that, through hard work and determination, she'd learnt to do. There were friends or at least friendly colleagues who showed an interest in her. She had a dead neighbour; and a cousin who'd helped her before.

Mavis picked up the phone and dialled Linda's number. She told her cousin what had happened.

"Would you like me to come down?"

"Thank you, Linda, it would be nice to see you of course, but your family need you."

"Well you're family too, Mavis. And you're on your own."

"I do live on my own yes, but I will be at work tomorrow and ..."

"You're going to go to work?"

"Well, yes. How can I not? That French woman was no relation and she was certainly not a friend. I had nothing to do with her, and I most definitely don't want anyone thinking I am involved now."

"No, I suppose it's best to carry on as usual. I didn't know she was French. Perhaps that explains any misunderstandings between you?"

"Marie French was her name. There was no misunderstanding; she was a nasty woman. I did not like her and I'm not at all sorry she is dead."

"Mavis! You can't say things like that."

"Why not? Someone should tell the truth."

"Sometimes, telling the truth just causes trouble."

"What a funny idea. I hope you're not suggesting I should rush out to the journalists, who are still loitering, and gush what a wonderful woman she was and how she was a pillar of the community, who will be sadly missed by everyone? There has been quite enough of that already."

"No, I can't imagine you doing that, but perhaps it would be best just not to say much at all?"

"But I will have to say something. The policewoman said that I must give evidence at the inquest and there was a report on the television. It would be difficult to avoid speaking of it at work."

"I haven't explained well. I didn't mean don't talk about it; it's probably not good to bottle things up anyway. I just meant about her being nasty. People don't say things like that about dead people. Before you say that's hypocritical, it isn't just that. Remember when your mum died? Sorry, that's stupid, of course you do. I meant do you remember what people said? Now we both know that for some people she wasn't always easy to get along with. To be honest, if people had tried they could have thought of unkind, yet truthful things to say about her. They didn't though, they said nice things. They didn't do it for her, they did it for you. So you would have happy, not bitter memories. They were trying to comfort you."

"So, what should I say?"

"Stick to the facts and the truth as much as possible. If you can think of a good thing to say, then say it, but if you can't then don't say anything that isn't strictly relevant."

"Just the facts. Yes of course, you are quite right, Linda. Thank you."

"How are you, Mavis, apart from this?"

Mavis described her painting classes. Remembering her resolution to encourage and appreciate friendship, Mavis asked after Linda and her family. She was rewarded with anecdotes of the grandchildren.

"Charlotte's oldest girl, Rebecca, decided to bake a cake for her mother."

"Gracious, isn't she too young? I haven't seen them in a while, but ..."

"Oh yes, she's far too young." Linda chuckled as she explained. "Charlotte hadn't been well, had that nasty flu that's going around. She fell asleep on the sofa while the kids were watching cartoons. A cookery programme came on next, we guess it was boring for the girls but it made Becky think of making Charlotte a cake to cheer her up."

"It sounds like a nice idea."

"Yes, the idea was all right. Charlotte hadn't even realised Becky could open the kitchen door, but she managed. She gave her sister a wooden spoon and sat her on the carpet tiles, then looked for ingredients. She emptied a bag of flour, some sugar and a tin of cocoa on to the kitchen floor."

"No! Oh, Linda, the mess."

"You think that's bad? I haven't even told you about the eggs."

Although horrified, Mavis chuckled at the picture in her head. Linda laughed so hard she had difficulty explaining Charlotte's reaction, when she awoke to find Rebecca spooning the mixture into a cake tin and Lorraine spooning it over herself.

"Of course, Charlotte couldn't be angry, the girls hadn't intended to be naughty. I'm afraid she didn't get much sympathy from me either. After I'd had a good laugh, I just told her it was a payback for all the mess she'd made as a kid. Then of course

Becky wanted to know about her mummy when she was a little girl."

"Charlotte was not untidy, was she?"

"Wasn't she? She was obviously on her best behaviour the times you saw her then. Did I tell you about the time she heard me say the wallpaper was dull, so she brightened it up? Becky loved that one."

Giving Linda a chance to discuss her family had been a good thing to do. Mavis ended the call feeling happier than for some time. She hadn't laughed with anyone since before Mother had become ill. Although it had been a long call, it was worth however much it would cost. She laughed again, as she recalled her contract entitled her to free weekend calls, the conversation had cost nothing. She wondered why she never called Linda then corrected herself; she had not previously called her, but she would do so in future. Possibly, she would call to wish her a happy birthday on Tuesday. That call wouldn't be free, but no matter, it wouldn't be long, as Linda was unlikely to be alone.

She felt guilty she'd made little effort to stay in touch with Linda. After the funeral, Linda had rung regularly to find out how she was doing in her training course and attempts at finding work. Mavis had rung once, she remembered, when she'd been accepted for her present job. Linda had been delighted and they'd talked for some time, making imaginary plans for Mavis's future. Mavis never asked after Linda's life, the few details she knew had been volunteered by Linda herself. Mavis sighed, no wonder she had no friends; she never made any effort to be one herself. She'd done slightly better at work, simply because she was forced to take part in conversations and return greetings. It was not possible to work there without at least a pretence of good manners. Mavis had rarely gone beyond that. She didn't know how to change things, but change them she would.

Mavis took her notebook from her shoulder bag and began listing book titles and author names to show Janice. If the girl had heard of any of them, she was likely to be especially interested in reading them. As Mavis wrote the familiar names, she couldn't help touching the books. With some, she merely brushed a finger down the spine, with others she took the volume from the shelf and leafed through. She looked at the inscriptions too and noticed how many were written by Mother. As a child, she was given a great many adventure stories and picture books. Those that were birthday gifts or were presented at Christmas were inscribed, but there were many others. She could not mark the year Daddy had died by a reduction in the number of books acquired. Mother had bought most of them. Even as Mavis got older, and Mother's concern for her child's development had turned to quiet dislike and thwarting of all ambition, there had still been books.

So many books and all of them greatly enjoyed. Mother had not selected the first bright cover on display, but had carefully chosen the books she had given her daughter. Mavis wept for the difficult woman who had, in an awkward, selfish way, loved her.

Chapter 10

'If life deals you lemons, make lemonade,' her calendar instructed on Monday morning. Mavis did not make lemonade. Instead, she made herself a cup of tea and ate her cereal. She'd not slept well and felt cold. She was tempted to go back to bed with a freshly filled hot water bottle. Had she not had a job to go to, that's exactly what she would have done.

There was still some sliced white bread left. It was slightly stale because she'd passed over it, in favour of the crusty loaf, at the weekend. She spread on butter and positioned thin slices of cheese to cover one slice before placing the second on top. Once the cut and wrapped sandwich was put in her lunch box, she wrapped that in a plastic bag and put it on the hall table.

A sound startled her. It was probably just the wind; not a gate banging. Mavis shivered. It was perfectly normal to feel disturbed by what happened yesterday. Once back at work she could forget the incident. If she could get warm, she'd feel better. She changed her cotton blouse for a polo neck sweater and added a cardigan. She pulled on woollen socks and wore her suede boots in place of her usual grey court shoes. Although she'd wanted to travel in them before, she couldn't wear boots at work. Janice and Sandra often arrived at work wearing trainers and changed into smarter shoes kept at work for the purpose. Mavis could do the same. After placing each shoe into a separate plastic bag and wrapping them in a third bag, she emptied her shoulder bag, put in the shoes and replaced the most essential items.

There wasn't room for everything, but she doubted she'd need the pocket dictionary, the antiseptic wipes, the Dettol or her binoculars. Mavis noticed the time, if she put away everything that wouldn't fit back in her bag, she would miss the bus. She had to leave them, jumbled on the table.

She wrapped a pale blue scarf around her neck, buttoned her coat and selected gloves to match her boots. Mavis locked the door behind her and walked towards the bus stop.

Bert and his wife were waiting.

Bert's wife asked her, "Did you hear about that poor woman crushed to death by a meteor?"

"No. How could that happen?"

"The telly didn't really say. I didn't pay much attention, until I realised it was in Sylvester Crescent. That must be near you?"

"I live in Sylvester Crescent, but I'm sure that no meteor has landed there," Mavis said.

"Well maybe I got it wrong then. I often get things wrong don't I, Bert?"

She nudged Bert.

"Eh?" he asked.

"I get things wrong don't I, Bert?"

"No dear."

"Oooh, I do, you know I do."

"Yes, that's right," Bert agreed.

Bert's wife turned back to Mavis. "Like I said, it must have been somewhere else, maybe it was Southampton? There could be a Sylvester Crescent in Southampton, couldn't there?"

"Yes, I suppose so."

"Southampton it was then, mark my words. TV cameras were there." She laughed. "Well, course they were. How else could it have been on the telly? Anyway, they was interviewing all the neighbours and they said how nice she was and everything. Like they always do. Used to say 'pleasant girl with no men friends' didn't they? Always made you laugh that didn't it, Bert?"

She lifted her elbow in preparation for another nudge, but he'd noticed and said, "Yes, dear," before she made contact.

"Used to say, if they was as pleasant as they was made out, then there'd've been plenty of men friends all right!"

The bus arrived and they got on, behind the flock of schoolchildren. The boy ran towards the bus stop, as Mavis, the last to board paid her fare.

"Driver, please wait just a moment."

"Didn't you want a return?"

"No, I mean yes, I did. That is not why I asked you to wait."

"Well, what is it then?"

The boy reached the bus. He jumped on and flashed his pass at the driver.

"You was lucky there, lad. If it wasn't for this lady youd've missed me."

The boy thanked Mavis. She sat behind Bert and his wife, the boy sat opposite her.

"I wonder if they showed it in France?" Bert's wife asked.

"I beg your pardon?"

"About that woman being killed, they said she was French, so I suppose they would."

"Her name was French." Mavis explained.

"Well, yes, it would be. I can't remember what it was though."

"Marie French, she was English. She was putting up a satellite dish when she fell."

"You did see it then?"

Mavis explained she'd found the body. Bert's wife asked questions, but was sympathetic. The boy and other passengers joined in the conversation. Mavis was the centre of attention. Everyone was kind; she enjoyed the fuss.

At work, Mavis went straight into Nicola's office and explained what had happened and that she might need time off work, for the inquest.

"Oh, Mavis what an awful shock that must have been for you. If you don't feel up to work today, I'd quite understand. Just say if you'd like to go home."

"Thank you, but I would prefer to be here. There were reporters at the house. They will probably come back and there are policemen there still. I think some stayed all night. When I walked past this morning, I could still see the blood on…"

"Right, yes. OK."

Nicola buzzed through to the main office and asked for Mavis to be brought a cup of tea.

"Finding a body must have been horrific. I hope nothing like that ever happens to me."

"It's not the first time; Mother, I found my mother ..." Mavis began to cry.

Sandra brought in the tea. She stood by Nicola's desk staring at Mavis.

"Thank you, Sandra," Nicola said, gesturing for her to leave.

Mavis accepted the drink, the mug shook in her trembling hands and tea spilt onto Nicola's desk. As she tried to put down the mug, apologise and reach across the desk for the box of tissues, more spilt. She tried to mop up the spillage with the tissue. Because her eyes still ran with tears, she was clumsy, making the mess worse.

"Don't worry about it, Mavis. A bit of tea won't damage the desk."

Nicola walked around to Mavis and gently pushed her back into the chair. She picked up the mug, wiped the base dry with a tissue and returned it to Mavis. She lifted her other hand, encouraging her to hold it securely.

"Drink the tea, Mavis."

Mavis drank. Her shivering stopped; she drew in two long shuddering breaths then drank more tea.

"Sorry, I ..."

"It's all right. Do you feel better now?"

"Much, thank you."

"The others might have heard what happened yesterday, they'll certainly know you're upset. Do you think it might be best if I explain?"

"Yes. Yes, please do that."

Nicola placed the tissue box near Mavis and went out. Mavis finished her tea and took the mug into the kitchen. As she passed through the main office, all conversation stopped. When she returned, after having washed her mug, visited the toilet and splashed cold water on her face, her colleagues were discussing the weather.

Mavis sat at her desk and switched on her computer. Everyone worked quietly for an hour, until Lucy offered to make more tea.

Mavis said it was her turn, and stood up.

"No, you sit down, you've... um."

"I'm quite capable of making tea," Mavis declared and gathered up the mugs. She made the drinks and carried the tray back in.

"Sorry, Mavis, I er ..." Lucy said.

"I'm fine now. It was just a shock."

"It must have been awful for you. I think you were brave to come in to work today," Lucy said.

"No, I'm not brave. It would have been worse to stay at home, alone."

"Did you get questioned by the police?" Janice asked.

"Shh, Janice," Lucy said, flapping her hands at the younger girl. "Mavis doesn't want to talk about it."

"It's all right," Mavis assured them. "It's natural to be curious. The local policewoman did ask me some questions, yes."

"Oooh, were you kept in a cell, like they do with suspects on the telly?"

"No, Janice. I was questioned at home; Constable Martins was sympathetic. I don't believe I'm a suspect." She attempted a smile to show she hadn't been offended by the question. If she seemed upset, they might stop the conversation. "I will have to sign a statement and I will be going to court for the inquest."

"Cool. You'll be, like, an important witness, won't you?"

"Yes, Janice. I suppose I shall."

Soon everyone began asking questions. Mavis took centre stage again. Previously she'd held a poor opinion of those who sensationalised anything that happened to them and then sold their stories to the newspapers. She began to understand their motivation; the novelty of the attention was exciting.

At lunchtime, it was decided Mavis should not be on her own. She should do something different, to take her mind off things.

"I've been invited to a posh wedding," Janice said. "I've seen a dress I could wear. Would you come and look at it with me, Mavis?"

"I don't know anything about fashion."

"That's OK; the people getting married are quite old. Sorry, I don't mean to be rude. The bride isn't really old, just old to be getting married. She's about your age. She's my godmother and I want to wear something she'll approve of."

Mavis felt flattered anyone would seek her advice and pleased Janice recognised she would know what was appropriate.

Sandra went too. She thought they should go to Gunwharf and look at designer stuff.

"I've already seen something I like, in town," Janice said.

They went to Commercial Road. Sandra turned toward Debenhams.

"Not in there. It's in New Look," Janice told her.

"If you insist on going somewhere tacky, you can do it on your own," Sandra said before striding away.

Mavis had never been in New Look. After hearing the thumping music and looking at the crowded racks of bright clothing and being jostled by the young customers, she agreed with Sandra's opinion. She kept quiet. Janice showed her the dress. The full length floral garment was perfectly suitable for an early summer wedding.

Whilst Janice tried it on, Mavis looked at the racks of clothing. She saw a long cream skirt with a pattern of huge pink poppies. A vest top in the same glowing pink was available as well as a matching jacket. The whole outfit cost the same as the last item of clothing she had bought. That had been a sensible beige cardigan for wear in the office. For a moment, Mavis considered trying on the outfit; she'd like to think she could ever wear something so impractical.

"What do you think?" Janice asked.

Mavis turned to see Janice's neat figure decorated by the softly flowing material of the dress. With her hands on her hips, Janice spun round. The skirt billowed out. The dress suited her.

"Very nice, Janice."

"Are you going to, like, try this?" Janice asked, indicating the skirt, Mavis had been inspecting.

"No." Mavis blushed. Had the girl understood her foolish thought?

"I reckon with your lovely green eyes, it'd look fab on you. It'd bring out the highlights in your hair too and you've certainly got the figure for it."

Mavis shook her head. Why would Janice say such things? She didn't appear to be making fun of her. Perhaps she felt ridiculous flattery was suitable antidote to the shock of death? It seemed likely she was trying to be kind.

"I have no need of a new suit, Janice. Perhaps you had better get dressed?"

Janice returned to the changing rooms. Mavis held the pink top against herself. The colour didn't make her look any worse than usual. When she next needed new clothes, she might try a brighter shade.

Mavis stopped Janice buying the dress she'd tried on, as there was a pulled thread. Mavis checked all the seams and hems to select the best garment.

"Thanks, Mavis, I would never of thought of that. You're like a proper Miss Marple, looking into everything."

"Miss Marple?"

"Ooops, sorry I shouldn't have said that."

"Why did you?" Mavis asked.

"I didn't mean to be rude, or nothing, like. I expect it was because of you finding a body made me think of it. Sorry."

"I think it is rather a compliment. Miss Marple, although fictitious, is remarkably shrewd."

"Actually, you're more like that Poirot. Always straightening stuff like, and being tidy. I've always thought it would be fun to be a detective and work out who done the crimes."

"Really? I have occasionally thought I would be good at detection, in an amateur way. I am very observant."

"Yes, you are and I'm good at imagining all kinds of things. We'd make a good team. I don't suppose your neighbour was murdered though?"

"The police seem sure that it was an accident."

"I suppose that's more likely. Still if you hear about anything mysterious will you let me know?"

"Yes, if I do."

Janice bought a salad box for lunch. Mavis would have liked one too; she had little appetite for the cheese sandwich she'd prepared. On the way back to the office, Janice confided, "Mum won't buy salads. Says they're a waste of money."

"They are rather expensive to buy ready-made; they're more economical if you buy the ingredients separately."

"I don't think it's just that, she only buys stuff that can be put straight in the oven, she wouldn't think fiddling about chopping and stuff was worthwhile."

"It is frustrating to have to live according to the wishes and needs of another person."

"You don't have to; you can eat whatever you like."

Mavis thought of her bland sandwich and the crisp leaves and juicy prawns Janice would soon consume.

"Janice, my mother used to dictate what food we had in the house. There was nothing I could say about the matter, as it was her money that provided for everything. I would have liked to work, to be less dependent on her, but it just wasn't possible."

"You had to nurse her and everything didn't you?"

"Only towards the end. She always wanted me to be there with her. She felt it was right as she had no one else."

"At least I'm not stuck with my mum all day. I think that'd drive me mad."

"Well as you're not and you earn a wage, perhaps you should contribute towards the household expenses? Then you could have a say in what was purchased," Mavis said.

"I do. Mum gets nearly all my money. She's got the rent to pay and my little brother to keep. He's still at college."

"Does she have an income?"

"She gets some benefits like, but most of that goes on fags, the Lotto and Sky TV," Janice said.

"So you pay all the bills, yet have no say in what is bought or what happens in your home?"

105

"That's about the size of it. I've thought of moving out and getting me own flat. It'd cost even more though and I'd be lonely. Mum gets on my nerves, me brother too, but I suppose I love them really. Dunno, like sometimes it seems you just can't win."

The boy travelled home on the same bus as Mavis. They talked all the way. He was kind; sympathetic about her discovery. She told him she'd not liked her neighbour much.

The boy seemed pleased. "It's just the shock then, you'll soon get over that. Sometimes, things are a shock, but once you get over that, then things are OK. Sometimes, it turns out for the best."

Once he'd walked away from her, she wished she'd asked the boy his name.

There were bunches of flowers outside Ms French's house. Mavis wondered why a sudden death always prompted people to leave litter at the scene. They would be left there until they began to rot, the notes would blow into people's gardens and eventually the council would be forced to remove them. People were inconsiderate; they ignored the living and presented the dead with gifts.

Mavis found a cellophane wrapped bunch on her own doorstep. If someone had chosen to honour her death, they were early; however it was more likely they'd simply made a mistake with the address. To those who took no notice of gardens, and there were such people, the two houses were superficially alike. Mavis picked up the flowers. They were yellow chrysanthemums. A small card bore the message,

'Mavis,

I saw the report on the news yesterday. It must have been a terrible shock for you. Give me a call, we need to talk. 02392 981723

Norman.'

There had been no mistake over the address or her state of health then. The flowers were a gift for her. Mavis had no wish to discuss her neighbour's death, or any other matter, with Norman. She took the flowers inside.

On the dining room table were the items removed from her bag that morning. She began to pick up the discarded items, putting them down again to remove her coat and boots. Hanging her coat in the garage reminded her to fetch a vase for the flowers. She filled one and placed it next to the discarded items. Mavis began to feel queasy. They had lain there all day, exposed to dust and germs. What if anyone had come in with her? That wasn't impossible; Constable Martins might have had another question.

She'd had little choice, Mavis tried to reassure herself. There simply hadn't been time for her to put everything away, nor to take her shoes out of the bag and repack it. If she hadn't left the items, she might have missed the bus. Then her whole routine would have been upset; the day would have been wrong. It hadn't been a bad day; she'd done the right thing. It would never happen again. Her work shoes were safely stored in the cloakroom at work. She would wear comfortable footwear for the journey from now on. Not only would her feet not ache at the end of the day, but her shoes would stay in good condition for longer. Every morning, throughout the winter, she had suffered from cold feet. Why had she not thought of this plan earlier? She hadn't given a thought to physical comfort since Mother died. Although she'd done what she could for her, she'd not thought to extend the same consideration to herself.

Mavis began cleaning each item with an antiseptic wipe. She looked down at the involuntary movements of her hands and laughed at herself. Of course, she'd needed to clean the other things, but wiping the outside of each cleansing wipe sachet was excessive.

Once order had been restored, she saw to the flowers. She'd not been given flowers for a long time. Cousin Linda brought some, when Mavis had been in hospital to have her wisdom teeth out. The time before had been over twenty years ago. They too had been a gift from Norman. These flowers could not mean what those others had meant.

She removed the stiff outer wrapping and discovered a sachet of flower food. After snipping off the corner, she added half the contents to the water and sealed the remainder with tape.

As she removed the inner wrapping and separated the flowers, a pleasant scent filled the room. In addition to the yellow chrysanthemums, there were sprays of gold carnations and white

107

freesias. With her secateurs, she snipped the ends of the stems, then stripped away the leaves that would be below the water line. Each stem was the same length; Mavis cut two inches from some, to make a more pleasing display. She folded the cellophane and put it into the bin. The pieces of leaf and stem were put into the plastic box she kept for compostable items. She wiped the table. Mavis felt tired. She didn't immediately fetch her coat and take the box out, to empty it. The task could wait until she had eaten; she'd need to go out again then, to dispose of her used teabag.

Mavis removed a slice of bread from the freezer and placed it in the toaster. Once, after forgetting to take the loaf from the freezer the evening before, Mavis had found Mother unusually hungry and asking for toast. Lacking the confidence to explain her error, she'd toasted a still frozen slice. Mother hadn't noticed a difference. That mistake had taught her something; she could learn from this morning's mistake too. She would in future prepare everything she could, ready for the morning. She could, of course, not put in her lunch, but she could pack the items that were to go below it and then arrange the other items in order, ready to be added once she'd prepared her sandwich.

Mavis thought through each action she took in the mornings. She could put the bird food out before she went to bed. She would not put out the breakfast crockery, the time saved by not having to remove it from the cupboard would not compensate for having to rinse the items, in order to remove the night's accumulation of dust.

Her mind was so full of her morning routine, she lifted the day's sheet on the calendar and folded it back on itself. As she ran her thumb nail along the perforations, she realised her error and stopped before she tore at the paper. She'd seen the quotation; 'Attack is the best form of defence.' Mavis had begun to attack her problems. Loneliness and boredom had been enemies of her happiness. Painting provided a way of lessening those troubles. Enrolling in the classes had been a good suggestion. Perhaps she should thank Karen. She would enjoy talking to her and having another of those substantial bacon sandwiches. Her life had begun to improve after speaking to Karen. Mavis had intended to die, but instead she'd told the girl she would take classes and improve her life. She'd not believed it then, but it had been true. She would go to the café and see Karen. The girl had invited her to do so, if she wished to talk. Mavis would tell her she was beginning to make friends and that she would become good at painting. Perhaps those wishes would also become true.

That evening everything except her keys were packed; there was no need to leave space for her lunch as she would be eating at the café in, she hoped, the company of Karen and her daughter.

Although her shoulder bag was ordered, her mind was not. Her dreams were of Mother and Ms French and Sandra taunting her. She awoke distressed. The words spoken in the night quickly faded; the meaning and her reaction were still vivid. She reassured herself that Mother and her dead neighbour could never displease her again. She wouldn't let Sandra's remarks hurt her either; not that they were directed at her. Janice must be advised to stand up to her. Her tormentors were silenced briefly, allowing another hour of sleep.

Chapter 11

In the morning, Mavis revealed the quotation she'd read the evening before and tidily disposed of the tiny sheet which had covered it. Then she gently raised several sheets together and learnt, 'Nothing is a waste of time if you use the experience wisely'. She must have wasted much of her life as very little of it had been spent gaining experiences she could put to use. She had learnt how to keep to herself, how to rely on nothing outside her own home. She'd learnt those lessons well, but they were no good. They'd not kept her safe; they'd kept her lonely and unhappy.

Mavis was ready to leave long before her normal time. She didn't wish to remain in the house, she might think of a task that needed doing and would then either chance being late for the bus, or have to leave before it was completed. She could not risk either situation.

Mavis walked to the Co-op, it would be warm in there, much better than standing at the bus stop. As she strode toward the shop, sharp angry gusts of wind jabbed at her legs and face. When she stepped in through the door, a soft swathe of warmth, from the heating system, draped itself around her. Mavis slowed her normal walking speed, to wander around the shop taking careful note of everything they sold. Amongst the brightly coloured plastic rubbish, were items that attracted her attention. There was a small book of outline shapes for a child to colour in. Mavis had enjoyed those when she was young. She must have been Lauren's age then; perhaps Karen would accept a small gift for her daughter?

The books and many other items were piled into wire baskets. '75p each or 2 4 a £1' a handwritten sign announced. Mavis chose one with outlines of animals and another depicting various fruits and vegetables.

When the young Mavis had coloured in similar drawings, she usually used wax crayons. Occasionally, she'd been permitted to put on an old shirt of Daddy's whilst Mother laid newspaper on the dining room table and on the floor. Mavis was then allowed to use her watercolour set. She wondered if Karen had coloured crayons for Lauren. It was likely she would, but how sad for the child if she were given a gift she could not make use of. She looked around for crayons, she found only coloured chalk and felt tip pens. The chalk would produce a disappointing result. The pens were rather expensive; they were also liable to stain should Lauren use them anywhere other than on the drawing books.

"Can I help?"

Mavis was startled by the question.

"Two for a pound they are," the blonde girl said, indicating the books Mavis held.

"Do you supply wax crayons?"

"Yeah, they're the same price. They'll be here somewhere; everything's got all mixed up." As she chattered the assistant rummaged in the baskets, pulling out items wrongly placed or damaged. She picked up a tin box of watercolours.

"I think I will take that, thank you."

"That's more expensive, I think."

"What is its price?"

"About two quid, I'll have to check."

"Very well. Does it have brushes?"

"Dunno, don't think so." The girl studied the tin. "Don't say. It would if there was, wouldn't it?"

"I imagine so."

"Tell you what; I think we have some brushes out the back." The girl handed Mavis the box and walked away.

Conscious of the time, Mavis waited by the till.

"I'll take them for you, love," the assistant behind the counter said. Mavis stared at the girl, for a moment she thought the girl who'd walked out the back of the shop had somehow raced around and in the front door. The girls were so alike they must be sisters.

The second assistant was unable to scan the paint box.

"Sorry, I'll have to get someone."

"Your colleague is just looking for something for me."

"Oh."

The first assistant then returned.

"Here you go," she handed Mavis three packs of brushes to examine. Mavis selected the pack with pink stems.

"Same price as the books," she informed her look-alike before walking away.

The second assistant scanned the brushes and tried again with the paints.

"That'll be two pounds then, please."

Mavis handed over a five pound note. Worried she would be late, she dropped the change unchecked into her purse. The assistant put the receipt and Mavis's purchases into a carrier bag. Mavis left the shop, pushing the painting things into her shoulder bag as she went.

She walked, briskly, back to the bus stop. When she arrived, she was alone. A check of her watch assured her, rather than having missed the bus, she was earlier than usual. Schoolchildren began to arrive. The girls had either yielded to the cold or there'd been a radical change in fashions recently. All of them were wearing brightly coloured woollen scarves with matching gloves. The boys, as usual, were ill-prepared for winter weather.

As Mavis opened her purse, to extract the bus fare, she found only one five pence piece. That was not right; after her shopping there should now be a second. Once on the bus, Mavis tried to work out what she had paid for Lauren's gift. The books were one pound for the two, the paints two pounds and the single pack of brushes would have been seventy five pence. She should have received one pound and twenty five pence in change. The girl had short changed her by five pence. It was too late now to go back and say she thought there'd been a mistake. It probably had simply been a mistake, but still it was annoying.

She took out the carrier bag and looked for the receipt. Four items were shown at seventy five pence each; that totalled three pounds. Two multi purchase discounts, of 50 pence, were given. The total cost had been two pounds. Mavis checked her purse again a realised the three coins change she'd been handed where all pounds. The mistake, if there was one, had been Mavis's. When she'd thought the girl was confirming the price of the paints, she'd actually been quoting the total due.

112

Mavis was the first to arrive in the office. She made herself and Nicola a cup of coffee. Nicola arrived as Mavis put the milk back in the fridge.

"Oh thanks, Mavis, just what I need," Nicola said as she picked up the freshly made drink.

Soon the others arrived, calling greetings as they came in and prepared themselves to begin work. Mavis had found it strange at first, for young girls to call her Mavis. It seemed strange too to call her immediate supervisor, Nicola, by her Christian name, but everyone did it. They even called the managing director Allen. She had to do the same to fit in. It had seemed disrespectful, but once she'd become used to it, she realised it made things more friendly.

Sandra arrived wearing a new jacket. It looked like tweed, but was not old-fashioned. The colours were lovely, soft lavenders and pinks, woven into a background of warm beige and rich cream. It looked like the delicate plumage of a bird, pausing to feed or bathe, in flattering evening light. A common bird could reveal a complex pattern of delicately coloured feathers, when carefully studied. Mavis would love to wear something so beautiful. Although it would fit her trim figure better than Sandra's stout frame, the jacket would not look good on Mavis. No light was so flattering; no study from those around her so generous she would feel comfortable in something so individual. She stuck to plain classic clothes.

Nicola escaped to her office, but Sandra ensured the rest of them all took a careful look at her coat as she bragged it'd been a bargain. She informed them she'd gone to Gunwharf after work and bought it on impulse.

"I couldn't resist when I saw it had been reduced by £200."

"Two hundred quid for a jacket?" Lucy queried.

Sandra ignored her. "Did you get that dress for your wedding?" She asked Janice.

"Yes, thank you, I did."

"You should have listened to me and got something designer, not that tacky high street stuff."

"Sandra, I know it's not designer, but the dress I bought isn't tacky. I don't have much money for clothes."

"Silly girl, there's a sale on. You could have got something really stylish for very little."

"I expect your idea of 'very little' is different to mine."

"Well, if you want to continue looking cheap, Janice, that's up to you."

Lucy gasped and left the room.

"So what did you get up to last night, Mavis?" Sandra asked. "Did you find any dead bodies?"

She received no answer.

"No? What a shame. I suppose your life will get back to its sad routine, won't it?"

Sandra turned and walked towards her desk as she spoke.

"Why is she so horrible?" Janice asked. "I can't believe she, like, just said all that."

"It was certainly unacceptable," Mavis agreed. "Perhaps we should say something to Nicola?"

"No, it's not worth it. It'd just create a bad atmosphere. I can't be bothered with all that here as well."

"What's wrong, Janice?" Mavis asked. The girl appeared more distressed at seeking a solution than she had at the insults passed by Sandra.

"Well, I thought about what you said yesterday, like. About Mum? I decided that as I'm paying for all the food in the house I should be able to eat the things I like sometimes. I had a real row with Mum over it because she said I was just being selfish. I told her I wasn't. D'you know what she said?"

"No," Mavis answered the question, even though she suspected no response was required.

"She said I was too controlling. Can you imagine that?"

That time, Mavis knew she need not speak.

"I told her she could still eat what she liked and do what she wanted. It's just that I want the same. She, like, shut up for a minute then, so I got a lot of other stuff off my chest. I pointed out as I was paying all the bills, I was entitled to some say over things. I told her just because I paid the TV licence didn't mean I wanted to watch it all the time. Sometimes, I'd like to read a book in my room."

"You mean you cannot do so?" Mavis queried. However bad things had at times been with Mother, she'd always been allowed the comfort of escaping into fiction, once she'd done her chores.

"Mum says it's not fair. She's only got me and I'm at work all day. Dunno how my brother felt about that, poor kid. Anyway, she says it's only fair I spend the evenings with her, like. I wouldn't mind, but she doesn't want to talk, we just watch TV. I might as well not be there. I told her that an' all. Said I'd be better off on my own."

"I think you might be right."

"But I don't really want to be alone, Mavis. No offence like, but you don't seem all that happy. You can do what you want, but you never go anywhere. You can eat what you like, but you still always bring a cheese sandwich for lunch."

Why must the girl say she intended no offence? Did she think that excused her rudeness?

"Are you suggesting that you don't approve of my life and eating habits?"

"Yes. No. Oh, I give up." Janice walked away.

The office stayed unusually quiet for the remainder of that morning as everyone concentrated on their work, saying no more than required to complete their tasks.

By lunchtime, Mavis was glad to escape to the café. Karen was there and waved when she saw Mavis. After placing her order, Mavis sat next to her new friend.

"Oh, I'm ever so pleased to see you," Karen said as soon as Mavis was settled.

"You are?"

"Yes, when we met you seemed real unhappy. Of course, I don't know you, so it was difficult to tell, but I've had awful depression. Before like, not now. Anyway I thought you seemed real down. Not just bored like you said, but like summat was really getting to you. That's why I suggested doing the evening class. Maybe it weren't the best idea, but it was all I could think of. I turned my life around. I thought you could too, if you wanted."

"Well, you were right. It was a good idea. I enrolled for art classes and started last week."

"Yeah? Cool."

Mavis produced the books and paints.

"I brought these for Lauren, as a way of saying thank you."

"That's very kind of you. Cheers."

Karen showed the gifts to Lauren and encouraged the girl to say 'thank you.' Lauren made no sound, Mavis didn't know if she was still too young to speak or simply shy. The child turned the pages of the book, stroked her mother's cheek with one of the brushes and began trying to prise open the tin of paints.

"So things are all right for you?" Karen asked.

"Well, yes. Yet it seems strange to say so."

"Strange, why's that?"

"I found a body."

"A body? That can't happen often."

"I hope not."

"It can't be coincidence; you must know me parents, they get the bus with a lady who found her neighbour dead. That woman what was on the news?"

"Oh, yes. Yes, I know your parents. They talk to me in the mornings."

"Mum does, I expect you mean? Dad don't usually get a word in, unless she prods him one. Then he's just got time for, 'Yes, dear' and she's off again. I don't suppose you get to do much more than agree with every word either?"

Mavis could think of no suitable reply. To agree would have implied criticism of Karen's parents, not to do so would mean disagreeing with her friend.

"Don't look so worried, I'd like to think we're friends, so it's not like you've got to watch what you say."

"I shouldn't like to say anything to upset you," Mavis explained.

"Well you haven't. I love 'em dearly, but I can see the comical side of their double act."

As they ate their lunch, Karen told her of several occasions when Bert's lack of attention to his wife's conversation had amused their daughter. When Mavis parted company with Karen and Lauren, the child waved energetically and said, "Guy guy."

The tense atmosphere in the office was even more noticeable on her return. Janice wasn't the only one who wished to avoid bad feeling; Mavis wanted the office to regain its usual agreeable ambience. She searched her mind for a safe topic of conversation.

"How much of *1984* have you read, Janice?"

"Eh?"

Mavis understood the girl's surprise. It was rare for Mavis to be the one who began a discussion.

"This morning's conversations were not particularly pleasant. I didn't wish to continue them, however I do not wish to avoid talking to you."

"Aww thanks, Mavis, you're right we shouldn't fall out. One person in the office being bitchy like is bad enough. What did you say?"

Mavis repeated her question.

"That your idea of cheering me up?" Janice laughed.

"Are you not enjoying the book?"

"I'm nearly at the end. I've got to where they meet in the park. Big Brother has got to them and they think they were wrong when they cared about each other and tried to do their own thing. In a way that's scarier than the bit where he's got that thing on his face with the rats and he tells them to do it to Julia."

"You're right. That is not very cheerful."

"Actually, the whole book's not very cheerful. Interesting though; it makes you think about things like, and it takes your mind off your own problems."

"You are right. That reminds me, I have another book for you." Mavis delved into her bag and produced, *Unchained Melanie*. "You may borrow this one, if you wish. I cannot remember it very well, but I'm sure it is more light-hearted."

"Good. Thanks, Mavis. I'm sure I'll enjoy it. Not that I'm not pleased you lent me the other book."

"I gave it to you, Janice."

"I read the message. A friend gave it to you. I'll give it back. I haven't quite finished it yet, I sort of feel like I need to concentrate on it, not just read it. I will finish it though, and then I'll give it back."

"Well, in that case, I will lend you others."

"Thanks, Mavis."

Janice leafed through the book for a moment.

"Mavis, do you think anyone would, like, let the rats bite them, to save someone else?"

"You have to remember, it was not just rats to him. He was extremely frightened of them. For him, it was the worst thing in the world."

"Yes, I suppose so. I'm not sure he really loved Julia anyway; he doesn't always act like he does."

"People can care yet act as though they don't."

"Oh, you said that like you know what you're talking about?"

"There was someone, but it was a long time ago."

"There's no one now? You went out at lunchtime; Tuesdays is when you see your mystery man isn't it?"

"No, Janice."

That was true. Last week, she'd bumped into Norman, but that had been on Wednesday. He was probably joining a class too; it was possible she would see him again. If she wanted to, she could go early and wait for him, thank him for the flowers. He had wanted to talk. She didn't know if she wanted to speak to him.

Mavis did want to speak to Cousin Linda. Mavis rang her that evening to wish her a happy birthday.

"Are you having a nice day?"

"Very nice, thanks. Phil is taking me to dinner later. Well, any minute really. I've had some lovely presents. The kids clubbed together and bought me some rather nice planters. I'll use the voucher you kindly sent me, to buy some plants. I haven't decided what yet. Sometimes, it's fun to just wander round until something catches your eye, isn't it?"

Mavis agreed with her cousin, although she had never bought anything for herself on a whim.

'Rome wasn't built in a day,' her calendar advised. She supposed that to mean things happened gradually. Sometimes, they did; but not always. Changes in her life had occurred rapidly, since Mother's death. The days collected on each other like falling snow flakes. Her eyes distinguished very few individuals as they fell from the dark clouds, yet when she lowered her gaze, the entire world had changed to a softer more beautiful place. The flakes were cold, but the covering they formed insulated the earth, protecting it from cold winds.

There was no snow that day, just an icy wind with occasional squally showers. Mavis hurried to the bus stop, it offered little shelter and no comfort.

Bert and his wife soon arrived. They walked closer together than usual, reminding Mavis of the pigeons on her garden fence. In cold weather, they fluffed up their plumage when they had landed. They then sidestepped until they were resting against each other, giving and receiving body heat. Bert's wife put her bag by her feet and settled close to her husband. They were not close enough for Mavis to benefit from the generated heat, but sharing the draughty space with people she knew seemed to warm her.

Mavis again spent the time between work and her class, in the library. She left at the same time as the previous week. As she did not have to register, she would be able to get to her classroom early and avoid bumping into Norman.

She was walking in through the automatic door when she heard her name called from the car park. The voice was Norman's. If she kept going and pretended she hadn't heard him, she could climb the stairs before he reached the entrance. He would not know where she'd gone or be able to follow.

Chapter 12

Whilst Mavis was deciding how to deal with Norman, she heard her name called again, this time by Jenny. She and Norman both walked towards Mavis, leaving her no option but to wait for them. She would have to thank Norman for the flowers and introduce the two of them. She briefly did so, but did not wait for a reply.

"Come along, Jenny, we don't wish to be late," Mavis said, turning towards the door.

Jenny didn't seem to notice Mavis was anxious to go inside.

"It's so nice to meet another friend of Mavis's, Norman," she twittered. "We are really enjoying our class, I hope yours is interesting. What class are you taking?"

"Rather a coincidence, actually. Mavis here, is studying art and here I am studying art history and appreciation. Amazing how much we still have in common, even after all these years."

"We really must go," Mavis said. She strode away, trusting Jenny would follow.

"Sorry, Mavis, I didn't mean to interrupt. I didn't know you …" Jenny said as they climbed the stairs.

"There is nothing to interrupt and nothing to know."

"Oh, but he gave you flowers, you …"

"My neighbour died suddenly, they were to cheer me up."

"Oh, what a shame. Had she been ill?"

"No, she fell whilst attempting to install a satellite dish."

"That lady on the news? That was awful. It must have been terrible for whoever …Oh. Was it you who …?"

Mavis didn't wish to think of dead bodies and answer endless questions, instead of concentrating on the lesson.

"It was a shock, nothing more. I would prefer not to discuss the matter."

Once in the classroom they, and everyone else, sat in the seats they'd occupied the previous week. They discussed their work with each other as they came in.

"Hope you've all done your homework, or it'll be detention all round," said Flo, the woman who'd made the jokes the previous week. The enormous swathe of material covering her was patterned in zigzags of green, yellow, orange and white. That was overlaid with spirals of turquoise and black. Mavis was pleased Flo didn't sit directly in front of her. To have focused for any length on the complicated design would have made her feel dizzy.

"Yes, I've done mine, Flo," Jenny said. She opened her sketch pad to show a neat pencil sketch of a pomegranate. "When I was a little girl, an uncle used to bring me pomegranates sometimes. I haven't eaten one in years, so that's what I chose. I'm not sure I've done it right."

"Well, I can see what it's supposed to be. That's a good start," Flo said.

"How about you, Flo? How did you get on?" Jenny asked.

"I had a go; no one can say I didn't try. Bit of a mess it is to be honest. I squeezed out far too much paint and then it seemed a waste not too use it. It's still a bit squidgy in the thickest bits."

"Did you use oils?" Vera asked.

When Flo nodded, she continued.

"You have to be build it up in layers. Otherwise it gets all mixed together as you work."

"Oh bugger, now you tell me." Flo laughed. "That's exactly what happened; still I'll know better next time. Anyway, I've eaten the blessed thing now, so no one can say it didn't really look how I painted it. I should have brought in the trifle I made with the mango afterwards. Now, that really was a work of art!"

"How did you get on, Mavis?" Jenny asked.

"I am reasonably pleased with the result, although it was quite a challenge to mix up all the colours accurately," Mavis said.

"All the colours? Why, what did you paint?" Vera asked.

"A mango," Mavis answered.

"Me too. I thought that was the idea?" Flo said.

"The idea was to express ourselves artistically using a mango or other fruit as inspiration. I've been a little abstract in my own interpretation," Vera told them.

Jenny pulled a face from behind her sketch pad. Mavis felt a sudden need to look in her shoulder bag and Flo laughed energetically.

Mr Bittern arrived, took the register and began the class. Their work was spread out and admired by the other students. Mavis, Vera, Flo, Leo and one other person had attempted to use colours. The rest were pencil drawings. Mr Bittern said he would ask a different person to give their thoughts on each one.

"We must learn to look critically at our work. By that, I don't mean just that we see if there's something wrong, but that we see what is good and what can be improved. Leo, perhaps you would like to start?"

Mr Bittern indicated Mavis's picture.

"Well, I can clearly see that it is a mango, which of course is an excellent starting point. The outline demonstrates the typical shape of the fruit. A creditable attempt at shading has been made, perhaps just a touch more emphasis would improve that elusive three dimensional image. This work shows a splendid use of colour, the variety of tones is, I'm sure, very accurate. One truly feels that the painter has looked closely at this fruit. Once cut, I'm sure that it was beautifully ripe."

"I agree," Mr Bittern added. "This work shows great use of colour, really good. Whose is it?"

Mavis raised a hand to shoulder height and blushed.

"Well done, Mavis. For a first attempt this is excellent."

"Thank you, Mr Bittern."

"You're welcome, but please call me Tim."

Each work was discussed in turn. Mavis enjoyed that; pleased to note that Mr Bittern's opinions, although far more generous, were broadly similar to her own. She felt if she was able to spot errors in other people's work, she might be able to do so in her own and therefore correct them.

It was interesting to see how different the paintings were considering all were based upon a similar subject. Most people had painted a mango; there was also Jenny's pomegranate and something that looked like a slightly deformed orange. To her embarrassment, Mr Bittern chose her to give an opinion on that drawing, telling her the subject was an ugli fruit. She looked at the coloured pencil sketch.

"It is difficult for me to say how accurate this is, because I do not recall ever seeing an ugli fruit."

"Well, never mind. Just say what you think," Mr Bittern encouraged.

"Well, um, the shading is, I think, quite good." She didn't think it particularly good, but guessed the person had tried to get that right. "I am sorry, but to me, it looks like a rather insipid and unevenly shaped orange."

"Thank you, Mavis," whispered the small man who had been so quiet last week. He glanced at her and gave a brief smile.

Mavis was pleased the man had taken no offence at her honesty, yet surprised he seemed happy at her criticism. She was sorry the man, who was obviously shy, had been chosen to receive her remarks. Jenny should have commented; she would have said something nice.

"For those of you unfamiliar with the fruit, an ugli does indeed look like an insipid, misshapen orange. I believe that is how they came by their unfortunate name," Mr Bittern explained.

Mavis let out her breath. Telling the truth had been the right thing to do. The quiet man glanced at her again. Mavis smiled, he smiled back.

Vera's painting was especially different. She had not only painted a mango, but also one that had been peeled, and the peel, and dried mango, and a pot of mango yoghurt, and mango chutney in a jar, and on a spoon.

"Geoff, what do you think of this one?" Mr Bittern asked the quiet man to give his opinion.

"There is obviously a great deal of work involved in this one. I think the artist should be commended for his, or her, effort." He spoke quickly.

"Yes, it is a very full scene." Mr Bittern said. "Anything else?"

"Um, well it does seem that things are a little out of scale. Mind you, I cannot pretend that I would do better." His voice grew quieter and his speech faster as he gave his opinion.

Mavis considered the painting to be a mess. Most of the others must share her view, although no one said so. Mr Bittern tactfully explained to Vera she'd rather overdone things.

"I too admire the effort and enthusiasm shown here. You have attempted a large amount of work. To get all the items to not only look good individually, but also correct in relation to each other, is not easy. Perhaps next time you might consider something simpler?"

Later, Vera moaned to Mavis and Jenny that he was suppressing her artistic talents rather than encouraging them. Jenny tried to soothe her. Mavis remembered how she had been suppressed by Mother and tried to sympathise. She was unused to saying such things and it came out wrong.

Vera sounded upset. "I've tried to be creative; perhaps the idea of looking beyond the obvious scares some people. Well, not me. I wouldn't be content to paint something dull and unimaginative."

Mavis said loudly, "I have painted a mango that looks like a mango. Forgive me if you don't like reality."

An embarrassed silence followed.

After a moment, Jenny said, "I think it's called realism? Where you just paint exactly what you see. I don't mean 'just;' yours is very lifelike Mavis, but Vera's is more, er, um ..."

"The reality is that some people feel threatened by what they don't understand. They are narrow minded and ..."

"Ladies?" Mr Bittern interrupted. "You can each learn much, not only from each other, but also from other works of art. For that reason, I'm trying to organise a trip to look at art galleries with the art history and appreciation class."

"Oh that's good, I have a friend on that course," Vera said.

"So does Mavis," Jenny said.

Mavis wondered why other women seemed intent on volunteering personal information. She had no wish to know anything about their lives.

The class continued with a lesson on shading to create a more realistic 3D effect. Mr Bittern set another task for homework. They were to attempt a still life using several different objects together. They could paint whatever they wished, even pheasants, but were urged to pick items of different shapes and surface textures.

Mavis decided she would talk to Norman if she saw him on the way out. Why not? Jenny and the others would think she was the sort of person to have friends. It surprised her to note she cared what they thought of her. She didn't care about Norman's opinion, he was nothing to her. Almost nothing, he had left her the flowers; that had been a kind gesture. He must have assumed the death had upset her and come to visit. Of course, he did not know she had a job now. It was good to know he still thought well enough of her to wish to comfort her.

Once everything had been packed up, Mavis left. Some stopped to chat; Mavis did not. Outside the college, Norman was waiting. He smiled and came towards her.

"Oh, Norman, you've waited to give me a lift," Vera said as she pushed past Mavis and Jenny. "How kind, especially as you didn't think you'd have time."

She took his arm and dragged him away. For a moment, Mavis regretted she had previously thanked Norman for the chrysanthemums; it would have been interesting to watch Vera's reaction, had she mentioned them in her presence.

The boy was waiting under the Bell Arch.

"I didn't expect to meet you until next week," Mavis said.

"Normally, it's every other Wednesday evening, but I was in Gosport anyway, so I thought I'd come and meet you. I don't like the idea of anything bad happening to you."

On the way to the bus station, Mavis complained about Vera and Norman. Suddenly she understood how bitter she sounded. She shouldn't be talking to the boy like that especially as she hardly knew him.

"I don't really know what to call you," she said.

"No; difficult isn't it? Let's make it simple, call me Jake, most people do."

"Jake? But that is not your real name?"

"No, it's not, but I'm never called by my true name. My adoptive parents called me Jacob, but Jake is what I'm used to now."

"Your adoptive parents?" Mavis asked.

"Let's not talk about that. Now, what should I call you?"

"I don't know."

"Well, what do your friends call you?"

"Mavis, my friends call me Mavis."

It was true she had always been called Mavis and now, at last, there were friends to use the name.

"And me?"

"Yes, please call me Mavis."

"I hope that means you think we can be friends?"

"I would like that."

"Yeah, me too."

Despite the darkness, Mavis smiled, she couldn't clearly see his expression, but knew he too was smiling.

"Well, Mavis, we both live on the same road and we go to the same college. D'you think we've got anything else in common?"

"I suppose it's possible."

"What things do you like then?" the boy asked.

"I like to read."

"Me too," the boy said as they reached the brightly lit station. "Fantasy novels mostly, adventurous worlds populated by dragons and trolls, where beautiful princesses battle the forces of evil and sorcerers from other worlds impart wisdom."

"I prefer something a little more realistic," Mavis told him.

"Which authors do you read then? Anyone I might have heard of?"

"Perhaps. Agatha Christie? P.D. James? Margaret Yorke?"

"I've heard of Agatha Christie, My gran, I mean my adoptive Dad's mother, she likes reading that kind of thing. Are they all detective stories?"

"Yes, mostly."

"I'm not sure they're more realistic than the stuff I read. Real murders aren't like they are in books. I bet you were shaken up when you found your neighbour. No one seems to get upset in those things, well judging from when I've seen them on TV."

"At least the characters are people."

"Maybe, but they don't act like real people. The dragons in my books behave exactly like a real dragon would."

He winked as he said this. For the rest of the journey they discussed their likes and dislikes. Neither enjoyed marzipan, neither were keen on sports. Although they disagreed on many things, they did so in a friendly fashion, each listening to the other's point of view and then attempting to alter it.

The next morning, 'If you can't beat them, join them,' was on her calendar. Mavis had no desire to beat anyone; she was not in the least competitive, unlike the loud and flamboyant Vera. The woman was quite impossible, every time anyone expressed an opinion she would swoop into the conversation, squawking out her own ideas.

Neither Bert and his wife, nor the boy, were on the bus. Mavis read, strangely Margaret Yorke made poor company that morning. Despite the chattering children, the bus seemed too quiet.

Janice did not arrive for work. Nicola received a call to say the girl had been sick during the night. Sandra was spiteful, first saying Janice wouldn't be missed because she did nothing all day, next moaning she had to do extra work to cover for her.

A visitor from head office arrived and was offered the special biscuits they kept in reserve. Mavis decided she should buy herself a packet in case she had visitors. At lunchtime, she went to Tescos and bought some that were on a special offer. She had never done so before, because no one ever visited, but Jenny had suggested they meet up for a chat and there was the boy. No that

127

was silly, she could not invite the boy in, but there might be other people she could invite, if she wished to make friends.

Mavis went home via the Lee-on-the-Solent library. The assistant librarian was preparing to call her 'ducks' when Mavis talked over her and said, "Please call me Mavis."

The woman seemed pleased and it worked. Once Mavis had chosen her books, the assistant librarian called her by name. Why had she never thought of that before? Because Mother had always told her to avoid over familiarity, that was why. Mother had not wanted her to have friends. Well she had them now, almost, and they called her Mavis.

Constable Martins was on Mavis's driveway when she arrived home. The combination of her black and white uniform and the fluorescent strips illuminated by passing cars made Mavis think of a magpie that had collected some silver, although she supposed in the policewoman's case it would have been retrieved and returned to the rightful owner.

"Hello, Mrs Forthright. I saw the 34 go by and wondered if you'd be on it. If you can spare a few minutes, I've got some information about the inquest."

The young woman was doing her job, but it was still pleasant to have someone wanting to see her. Mavis invited her in and offered tea.

As Mavis put away her coat the policewoman said, "Shall I put the kettle on and get the tea ready? I think I can remember where everything is."

"No," Mavis answered quickly. "No, I will do it. Please sit down."

That meant she had to leave things in her bag to be put away later, but that was better than the thought of the untidy constable disarranging her kitchen. She did take out the biscuits; she had been right to buy them.

Mavis arranged the tea and a plate of biscuits on a tray and carried it in.

"Thank you very much, Mrs Forthright," the policewoman said.

"Please, call me Mavis."

"The inquest will be opened next week." Mavis was told, after pleasantries had been exchanged, tea sipped and biscuits crunched, though thankfully not dunked.

"Will I be required to attend?"

"Not yet. It will just be opened and adjourned, that only takes a few minutes. It's just to set things in motion."

"I have read about adjournments in books. It seems so strange to be involved in a real court case."

"I'm afraid even the full inquest will be pretty tame compared to anything you're likely to have read." As the constable spoke, she reached out for the last biscuit, withdrawing her hand just before she touched it.

"It will be interesting to see how reality compares with fiction."

"Well, I suppose so, if you're interested in crime and stuff. I wouldn't bother with the opening though. Really, all they do is confirm the deceased's name and the date death occurred, that sort of thing. You're allowed to attend if you like, anyone is, but it wouldn't be worth taking time off from work for. Well I don't think so anyway."

Mavis had yet to take any of her holiday entitlement. She wondered if she could do so at such short notice. No, the officer was right. It would be better if she didn't attend. To do so would appear unusual. She offered the biscuit plate.

"Thanks," the policewoman said. "Working shifts always seems to make me hungry."

"Would you like more tea?"

"I wouldn't mind, that's if it's no trouble?"

"Not at all," she said as she gathered the cups.

Mavis returned with more tea in clean cups and another plate of biscuits. "What will happen about the funeral?"

"The family should be able to arrange it soon; the coroner will probably release the body. That's only delayed in the case of murder or if tests have to be done or anything like that."

"An autopsy, do you mean?"

"No, that's been done already."

"When will the full inquest be held?"

"The coroner will set the date when he adjourns next week. It depends how long it'll take to gather evidence. I shouldn't think it will be long in this case, maybe a couple of months. The coroner's officer will write to you with all the details as soon as a date is set."

"Will you be there?"

"I was the attending officer, so I'll be asked to give evidence. I'll see you there."

Mavis wasn't sure that last remark was true, but still nodded her agreement.

As Mavis watched the girl leave, she again thought of a magpie; the stiff walk down the path, the black uniform disappearing into the night and the buttons gleaming under the street light were probably responsible. The girl had her silver, though she'd earned, not stolen, her symbols of authority, Mavis reflected, as Constable Martins mounted her bicycle and flew into the darkness.

Chapter 13

After weeks of dark skies and drizzle, Mavis opened her bedroom curtains to a beautifully sunny morning. The few fluffy white clouds threatened neither rain nor snow. Their role was to emphasise the clear blue. The sun reflected along their wispy outlines, sparkling like polished crystal.

She was disconcerted to read on her calendar, 'Every cloud has a silver lining'. What a coincidence. The compiler had selected a quote that aptly and surprisingly fitted the day's weather conditions. It fitted less well with her emotions at work. Janice was still away. Mavis missed her and could see no bright side to her friend's absence. The prospect of a lonely weekend was all the more dismal after a lonely few days in the office.

Over the weekend, the sky darkened again. The clouds were no longer edged in silver, but cold, dull lead, weighing down her spirits. Her calendar provided the opinions; 'One lost, ten found' and, 'You can't have it all'. She wondered if that meant she couldn't have what she'd found; in which case, it would surely be poor consolation for whatever she'd lost. Her boredom possibly made her pay too much attention to the quotes, causing them to take on a significance they didn't warrant. Perhaps she should follow Lucy's example and begin reading her horoscope. By choosing the right newspapers, she could be sure of good fortune every day for the rest of her life.

The wind blew, cold and unrelenting, making gardening an unwelcome way of filling her time. The light was not bright enough for her to paint without artificial aid, yet not quite bad enough for her to feel the use of electricity was justified. There was nothing she felt inclined to paint.

Monday's quote was of no use at all. 'When in doubt, consult your inner child,' she was advised. Mavis didn't have an inner child and doubted she would consult one if it were present. A child would not reason out a situation, but would do whatever seemed the most fun.

Janice returned to work. Mavis was pleased to be able to speak to her. Despite seeming almost childlike on occasions, Janice was pleasant company.

"Are you sure you're OK, Janice? You look a bit peaky," Lucy said.

"Yeah, I'm OK. I was still throwing up like, on Thursday and Friday. I hardly ate anything over the weekend in case it started up again. I just stayed in bed."

"I'm pleased you are back," Mavis told her.

"I'm glad to be back, to be honest. I was pretty bored. That reminds me, here's your book back, I finished it on Saturday." Janice gave her *1984*.

"What a shame I had not lent you more."

"You did; that Melanie one. I've nearly finished that an' all."

"Are you enjoying it? It's so long since I read it that I cannot remember the subject."

"Yeah, it's good. It's all about this woman who had a rotten mother, a bloke who didn't stay around and suddenly she's got the house to herself like and can do what she likes. She starts eating and drinking whatever she likes and generally trying to have a good time."

"Perhaps I will read it again when you have finished."

'You can't make an omelette without breaking eggs,' Mavis learnt on the morning before her next art class.

Mr Bittern showed them some of his own paintings; landscapes. He produced photographs of the scenes they were based on and explained how he'd left out an electricity pylon, or added a tree where doing so improved the finished image.

The students would not have to break any eggs to do their homework they were told, but they could if they wished.

"I want you to draw or paint an egg. You can do it however you like; on its own, as a part of your picture, whatever you like," Mr Bittern said.

Mavis felt uncomfortable with such an imprecise task. How would she know if she was doing the right thing? Vera said she'd learnt her lesson from the mess she'd made of the mango collection she'd attempted.

"I'll go for something a bit simpler this time, so don't be worried you're going to see boiled and poached and scrambled eggs all over the place."

On the journey home, Mavis tried to think of ways to make an egg more interesting. All she could think of were recipe suggestions. The moment Mavis had removed her coat and boots, her phone rang. It was Cousin Linda.

"Are you all right, Mavis?"

"Yes, perfectly. I've just come in from my art class."

"Oh, of course; how silly of me. I rang earlier, when I thought you'd be in from work and there was no answer. I tried again a bit later and when there was no reply I began to get concerned."

"There was no need; I am unlikely to come to any harm," Mavis said.

"No, of course not. It was just my neighbour's accident that put it into my head."

"Accident?"

"Oh, nothing really. She's quite old and was putting her bin out and fell just as I came home from shopping. I heard her cry out. If I hadn't been there just at that moment she might have lain there for a long time before anyone noticed."

"Oh dear, was she badly hurt?"

"No, just shaken, but the ground was slippery. She might not have got up on her own and it's so very cold. Still, she's fine now."

Mavis was glad of the textured surface to her own paths. She was unlikely to fall. It was kind of Linda to be concerned.

"I will be careful, Linda. I hope you will, too."

"I'll be fine. Phil's put some grit down; he's good at that sort of thing. How was the class?"

"Very interesting."

"What do you do? Is it like I remember from school, not that I do remember really."

"We are given exercises and set homework, so it is a little like school. It's very informal, though. People do different things. Mr Bittern does not consider that there is a wrong approach to art and he encourages us to interpret things in our own way."

"That sounds very arty," Linda chuckled.

"I find it a little disconcerting, but it's interesting. I'm not sure if I have any real ability, but Mr Bittern does not seem to worry about that either. He wishes us to express ourselves." Mavis made a noise similar to a giggle. "Expression is very arty too."

"It all sounds rather fun. Are the other people nice?"

"Yes, Mr Bittern is very agreeable and so is Jenny. I sit with her and another woman called Vera. I didn't like her at first, but she was pleasant today. Perhaps we just need to become accustomed to one another."

"I think this class was a wonderful idea, Mavis."

"Yes. I'm pleased that I enrolled."

The next morning, Mavis was reminded, 'Charity begins at home'. Plastic sacks requesting donations of clothes and bric-a-brac were often pushed through her letter box. Perhaps next time she received one, she would look through Mother's things and give some away. There was no such request that morning. She would wait until one arrived and consider the matter then.

As Lucy arrived at work, she asked if anyone knew what had happened in Gosport last night.

"Perhaps you could be just a touch more specific, Lucy?" Sandra suggested.

"Eh? Oh, well it was my sister. She rang me and said she'd not been allowed down her road for a while. Police were all over the place. One of her neighbours said a girl had been murdered in the street. Did anyone hear anything about it?"

"No, I didn't. Was it anywhere near me?" Sandra asked.

"No, other end. My sister lives just up past The Castle pub."

"Is that near where you go to your evening classes, Mavis?" Janice asked.

"Quite close, but I don't go that way to college."

By lunchtime, the weather was much brighter than it had been for days.

"Would anyone care to come for a walk?" Mavis asked.

"You must be joking, it's chuffing freezing," Janice answered.

"It's too cold for me too," Lucy said.

"Well, I shall go. I've been inside far too much recently. I think some fresh air would do me good."

Mavis crossed the road and walked through Ravelins Park. There was little to see, even if she'd felt warm enough to linger. The park with its benches and wild flower meadow had been more inviting in the autumn. Mavis remembered she'd taken her lunch and a book and sat there, amongst the long dry grass and last few flowers, during her first few days at McHyvers. She'd planned to explore all of Portsmouth. First, she'd thought she'd accustom herself to having a set time to return to the office then she'd planned to visit the museum, walk through Victoria Park to see the bedding displays and aviaries. She'd expected to walk briskly to the historic dockyard and wander around surveying HMS Victory and Warrior. She'd done none of those things.

One day, she had walked to Old Portsmouth. There, she'd climbed the Round Tower in the hope of seeing out to the Isle of Wight. The day had been overcast. Behind the fortifications, she had been sheltered; once she reached the top, cold wind buffeted her. The Tower had been deserted; the weather seemed determined to maintain that situation. That had been the very last day of summer. Since then, until she had planned her suicide, her lunchtimes had been spent in the office with only an occasional walk to the shops for variety.

Mavis exited the park and circled back towards the office. Although cold, she didn't take the quickest route down Museum Road. She would walk that way soon and visit the museum. She could do that even in bad weather. In a way, by taking the alternative route she was exploring. She was almost sure the road

135

would lead her to the big bookstore on the corner. From there it would be a short walk back to work. If she were wrong, it wouldn't matter; she had time enough for a few wrong turnings.

"Mavis, can I give you a lift?" a familiar voice called.

Norman sat in his car, across the road.

"You are going the wrong way."

"I could turn round."

"There is no need."

"Please, I'd like to talk to you. It's been a long time."

A few heavy spots of rain spattered on the road. Mavis crossed and slid into a comfortable leather seat.

"Where to?" he asked.

"Burnaby Road."

Mavis admired Norman's car.

"It's a Jaguar, Mavis. Better than that old Austin Allegro I used to have."

Mavis had liked his old car; it had represented freedom to her. She was driven about in it, to spend several happy hours away from Mother. She'd even tried driving it a few times.

"What's the great attraction in Burnaby Road then?"

"That is where I work."

"Work? Ah, that's why you weren't in the other day. Somehow it never occurred to me that you'd have a job."

"I have worked at McHyvers since September."

"And what does your mother think of that?"

"Mother is dead."

"Oh, I'm sorry, Mavis."

"Are you?"

Norman didn't answer.

"I saw the report of your neighbour's death ..."

"Death is not something I care to discuss."

"Sorry, no, of course not. I didn't mean ... So there's just you in the house now?" he asked.

"Yes, I still live in the same place."

Norman knew that. He'd left her the flowers.

"I did think of selling it, but I would have missed the garden. Besides I'm used to it."

"And you keep busy, your art class and things?"

"Yes. I believe you are friends with someone in my class?"

"You must mean Vera Parrotte? I do know her, but we're not exactly friends. We both went to an art appreciation lecture-come-workshop in the library. Obviously, I spoke to her and we had lunch together. I discovered she lives near me. Now the woman thinks we're an item and I'm having trouble shaking her off."

Norman negotiated the roundabout and turned on to Cambridge Road, then left into Burnaby.

"Say when."

"Just here, thank you."

Norman stopped the car.

"Mavis, it's been nice to see you. We must have a proper talk at some point in time. Maybe over dinner, or ..."

"Oh look, there's Janice. I had better not get in after her."

"Is she the boss? Will she tell you off? I can tell her it's all my fault," Norman offered.

"There is no need for that, she is not my supervisor and I would rather you did not speak to her," Mavis said as she got out of the car.

As she ate her toast the following morning, Mavis read, 'The longest journey starts with a single step'. That was true, even people who drove to their destination first had to step outside their own homes. She guessed that wasn't the reason the remark had been included in her calendar. The journey was probably symbolic of life. Mavis hadn't been on any long exciting journeys. She had, however, taken a few short trips.

Bert's wife spoke of the dead girl as they waited for the bus.

"It's all so sad, the pressure of exams and things. Local girl you know, went to school with our Karen. You know Karen

137

don't you? Lovely girl, of course, she didn't have the pressure of exams. She had the pressure of Lauren, not that she's any trouble, but you know what I mean."

Mavis didn't, but as she'd done with Lauren's mother, she nodded as though she could understand the relationship between a loving mother and happy child.

"Done some lovely pictures Lauren has with those paints you gave her. Very artistic child, she is."

"I'm pleased that she is enjoying them."

"Oh, she is. Loves that little paint box, she does. We've given her crayons before, haven't we, Bert?"

She jabbed her elbow out. It didn't connect with Bert. He'd left the seat and was standing in the corner usually occupied by the pale girl.

"Well, we have. We've given her crayons," his wife asserted.

"I'm sure she enjoys them."

"Yes, she did anyway. Now, it's painting. Proper taken with that, she is."

Mavis felt uncomfortable.

"Paints everything she can."

"Oh dear, does she make a mess? I ..."

"Bless me, what'd that matter? A bit of mess don't hurt none. Didn't mean there was anything wrong with you getting them paints. I meant she does pictures of anything. Fills things in, in those little books, then has a go doing it herself. She's not really very good at that bit, but then she's young yet."

"Yes, of course. She must be very clever to try."

"She is. Very clever is our little Lauren. Proud as anything we are of her."

"She is a lovely child."

"She is and you was nice to think of them paints and encourage her like that. It's nice our family's got you as a friend."

Mavis felt a stinging in her eyes, she swallowed and looked away. She was pleased the bus arrived at that moment as continuing the conversation might have made her cry. It would be silly to cry when she wasn't unhappy.

Within minutes of switching on the computers, it became obvious there was a problem. They were slow to start up. Once they'd all successfully logged on, the staff were unable to access the company's database. The technical department were called. Each of the women were talked, in turn, through the steps of a process it was hoped would restore the system. Mavis felt alarmed as she watched both Lucy and then Janice, hold the telephone in one hand and press keys with the other. The screens were black and page after page of white symbols flashed by. When her turn came, she hoped someone more experienced with computers would offer to work on her machine. Instead, Janice simply transferred the call to her.

"Your go, Mavis. Don't panic; Steve'll talk you through it."

Janice was correct; there was no cause for concern. The young man gave clear instructions and didn't assume knowledge she didn't possess.

An hour later, error messages began to appear. On each occasion, they rebooted their machines. Work progressed slowly and was frustrating as the time spent logging back in roughly equalled the time spent entering data.

"Oh shitting hell," Sandra exclaimed. The others turned to her.

"Sorry, but if you go and look up what you entered half an hour ago you'll be swearing too."

When they discovered none of the data they'd entered was still on the system the others didn't swear, but they did tell Nicola.

"OK, switch off everyone. It's pointless doing anything else until this has been sorted out. I'll get someone to come out," Nicola said.

"I'll put the kettle on," Lucy said and began gathering the mugs.

They had emptied them again by the time the technician arrived. After two minutes, he said, "It's gonna be a couple of hours at least, I'm afraid."

"Tell you what," Nicola said. "There's not much we can do here. Let's go early for a long lunch and let Steve work in peace."

After discussion, they decided to go together, to the Duke of Buckingham, for lunch. Mavis didn't want to go. Mother hadn't approved of public houses so Mavis had never been in one. Then she remembered the last time the other women went out for a meal. She'd been invited then and hadn't gone. That didn't appear to be preventing them from assuming she would come. They put on their coats and Lucy handed Mavis hers. She said, "Come on, Mavis, it's not far, but you'll need your coat."

Mavis hesitated.

"Come with us, Mavis, please," Janice said.

Mavis's previous refusal to join the others for lunch had been a mistake; one she must not repeat. She nodded and tried to smile.

Chapter 14

The pub wasn't as alarming as Mavis had feared. The other customers were couples or small groups of people who looked as if they were also taking a break from work. There didn't seem to be any of the drunken unemployed layabouts whom she'd supposed would be the customers of such an establishment. There was a bar of course, and people were drinking, but the focus appeared to be on the food. People were talking, not brawling or otherwise behaving inappropriately.

They studied the menus, and discussed drinks. Lucy decided on Coke as she would be driving home later. Janice too ordered Coke.

"I'd better make it a diet one as I'm bound to want afters."

"That's so nearly sensible, Janice," Sandra said.

"What do you mean?"

Sandra shrugged in lieu of an answer.

"I'm going to have dessert, too," Shelia said. "Janice, don't worry about it. We've got plenty of time."

Sandra started to speak, "Actually..." She was talked over by Nicola asking what Mavis would like.

"I'm not sure."

Lucy said, "There's quite a good choice, isn't there? I think I'm going to have a proper meal. The kids are at their dad's this evening, so I needn't cook tonight."

Mavis decided buying a meal would be less of an extravagance if it replaced her usual supper. She could eat the sandwiches, intended for lunch, as her evening meal. Unsure what all the items were, she settled for steak and kidney pie. She was persuaded to share a bottle of wine with Nicola and Sandra.

The pie arrived, served in a china dish with a huge puff of pastry on top. There was a separate dish of vegetables to be shared amongst those who were having cooked meals. The pie was delicious and as the others weren't keen on the vegetables, she ate most of those too.

Janice ordered hot chocolate fudge cake for dessert. Nicola chose fresh fruit salad.

"Would you like cream?" the waitress asked.

Nicola said, "No."

"Oh, yes, please," Janice said.

Sandra pursed her lips and made a disapproving hiss. Janice's smile disappeared.

Nicola said, "Sorry, can I change my mind, please?"

"Yes, of course," the waitress said. "What would you like?"

"A piece of caramel cheesecake; with cream. I don't go out to lunch often, so I think it won't hurt to treat myself just this once."

Lucy sighed. "Oh you've done it now. I fancied that cheesecake. I'm not sure I can sit and watch you eat it without having some."

"Two cheesecakes, then?" the waitress asked.

"How about you, Mavis; can we lead you astray?" Nicola asked.

Mavis liked the idea of being led astray in such a relatively harmless way. She had also been watching Janice. The girl had been like a child promised a treat when she'd ordered. The child's treat had been spoilt by the unkind behaviour of an older woman. Mavis knew how the child inside Janice felt. She remembered Cousin Linda sharing her sweets with Mavis after Mavis's had been taken away. Mother had never asked people not to give her sweets. Instead, she'd waited until Mavis had accepted them, opened the pack and made her selection, before deciding it was too close to a meal time, or that her teeth would suffer. She understood Nicola and Lucy's change of order. If she'd been hungry, she would have increased the cheesecake order to three; it sounded good. How could she show support, without ordering food she might be forced to waste?

"I would like dessert, but I have eaten enough," she said.

Sandra smirked. Mavis saw she'd got it wrong.

142

Lucy said, "Oh go on, have some cheesecake."

"Yeah, go on, Mavis. You have duff, too," Janice said.

Mavis hesitated.

"We could share a piece couldn't we?" Lucy coaxed.

"Yeah," the waitress agreed. "I don't see why not." She left to fetch their order.

After a few moments, Sandra stood up, "I might as well have one, too. I don't much fancy sitting and watching you lot stuff your faces. A bit of self control isn't always a bad thing you know, but it seems that demonstrating it in present company makes me the bad guy." She stomped off to find the waitress.

Janice said, "Oh dear." She didn't sound sorry.

"I wonder what's wrong with her?" Nicola asked.

The desserts all arrived together. Sandra had coffee as well as cheesecake brought to her.

The bill totalled £59.75. Sandra said, "Twelve quid each then," and put that amount on the plate. The others began to look in their bags. Mavis mentally added up what she'd eaten, satisfied twelve pounds was reasonably accurate. She did not think they'd all spent the same though. As well as taking her purse from her bag, she took out a notebook and pencil. She picked up the bill and collected a menu from another table. She compared the two and worked out what they each owed. Mavis had drunk only one glass from the bottle of wine, whilst the other two shared the rest, however she'd agreed to share it. She divided the cost equally into three and added that amount to the cost of the meals. She turned over the menu, searching for the price of Sandra's coffee.

Sandra snapped, "For goodness sake, how petty can you get?"

Nicola leant over to point out prices to Mavis. Mavis could see her supervisor did so in order to disguise her amusement. When Mavis had finished writing, she showed her sums to Nicola.

Nicola said, "Twelve pounds is about right for Lucy, Mavis and myself. Janice, yours is nine and Sandra's fifteen."

Sandra threw the extra coins onto the table and left without speaking. The others paid and walked back to the office, laughing and chatting. When they arrived, Sandra made a big show of working. With shock, Mavis was reminded of her similar behaviour on the day the others went to lunch without her. She guessed Sandra was probably as upset as she'd been. She also guessed Sandra's unhappiness was as self inflicted as her own.

"Mavis?" Janice said as they passed in the corridor.

"Yes, Janice?"

"Thanks for like sticking up for me an helping me an' stuff. Not just today, but you know, the books and Mum and everything. It's like, really good of you."

Mavis could not have replied without releasing a sob. She didn't wish to embarrass Janice by a silly show of emotion. She smiled and nodded, hoping the younger woman would guess at her meaning.

"We're like mates now, aren't we?"

Again, Mavis smiled and nodded. Janice grinned back, looked for a moment as though she had more to say, then continued towards the stationery room.

"Janice?"

"Yes, Mavis?" Janice turned back.

"Now that we are friends, perhaps you would do something for me?"

"Yeah, like sure."

"Try to stop saying the word 'like' in every sentence." Mavis didn't wait to see Janice's reaction.

'You can't get blood out of a stone,' Mavis learnt on Saturday morning. The information was of no value, as she had no intention of trying to do so. Instead, she would tidy her garden and begin her art homework. An egg, or more than one, Mr Bittern had said. He'd spoken of interpretation. Mavis was unsure what he meant by that. She'd tried to ask for clearer instructions, but he'd supplied none. She could simply paint a picture of an egg, but knew that wasn't what he intended her to do.

As she took the milk from the fridge, for her morning tea, she looked at the eggs in their rack. There were two. Two were no good, she needed an odd number. Plants and flowers looked wrong in even numbers. The same would hold true of the eggs in her painting. Two was the correct amount for scrambled eggs on toast.

A cooked breakfast would be a good idea before she tackled the garden. She could see there was work to be done; could see, too, the frost on the ground. Mavis broke the eggs into a jug and beat them vigourously. She would buy more from the Co-op and use as many in her picture as she felt looked good. Her artistic endeavours would not be restricted by the meagre contents of her fridge.

Fortified by her breakfast, Mavis set out to restore order to her winter-ravaged garden. Sodden leaves had accumulated in odd corners and threatened to rot the new shoots that would soon emerge. She gathered them up and put them on the compost heap. The young growths would benefit from more light and air. Some climbers were no longer attached to their supports; Mavis carefully tied them back into place. She cut down the sere stems of verbena bonariensis, teazle and cornflowers. These had been left to provide winter food for the birds. The seeds had long since been consumed or wind scattered. Her compost heap received the desiccated remains.

Not everything in the garden was dead. The bold snouts of daffodils were sniffing their way into daylight. Mavis smiled at them. The tips were thick and strong; there would be a good display in spring. The viburnum was thickly encrusted with shiny buds just flushed with pink. In the first warm spell, they would begin to open and release their sweet scent. Snowdrops were open. Mavis wasn't positive she could accurately name each of the different varieties she possessed. She was sure of the Flore Plena and *nivalis*; everyone could recognise those. The doubles would not open for another week or so, but flashes of purest white showed through the green. The tall one, bought from the church sale, stood proud, the slender stems hardly bent under the weight of the substantial flowers. The glaucous leaves surrounding the flowers were beautiful too.

Mavis bent to remove a weed seedling from the base. As she lifted the offending greenery, she exposed the furled bud of an aconite. It always pleased her to see they'd survived the winter. With her, they didn't merely survive; they flourished and increased. She wondered how many there would be this year, how much more new territory they would have claimed. She looked again; once she had spotted the first one, she often noticed others. There were more, many more. Most were barely breaking through the surface.

Once she stood up again, they would no longer be visible. That did not matter; she knew they were there. Other plants were there too, she could not yet see them, but sensed their presence in her rich soil. They were waiting their chance to burst through. The tiny threads of crocus leaves formed delicate drifts across her borders. The strangely twisted tips of tulips nestled in thick clumps. Anemones peeped out from under the skirts of shrubs and amongst the luscious greenery of over-wintered escholzias.

Mavis straightened up and looked across the bed she'd worked on. With the debris gone the clear colours glowed in the bright winter sun. Spring would soon be here. The birds would begin to nest and lay eggs. Eggs; of course, they were a sign of spring, of new beginnings and optimism. That's what she'd paint. She snipped pieces of greenery, gathered the better specimens of dry leaves and seed heads from the compost heap and picked up a large flat stone. She put those items by the back door before returning for a few precious flowers.

Once Mavis had put the plant material in water and cleaned herself up, she walked to the shop for more eggs. A newspaper headline caught her eye as she collected a shopping basket. 'Local girl dead', it declared. Mavis read the short report. A girl had been struck by a car shortly after seven in the evening, last Wednesday. That must have been the girl Lucy mentioned. Mavis was glad she would have the company of the boy next week, for the journey home from college.

Walking back through town, Mavis looked in the window of the estate agents' who were selling Marie French's house. The house was the same size as hers, the same layout, and the same location. It was advertised for sale at £285,000.

'One thing you can't recycle is wasted time' Mavis read, as she buttered her toast the following morning. Over the course of the day, she wasted no time; she used it to paint several sketches and a painting of a spring scene. The painting perhaps verged on the abstract, but she was pleased with her efforts. First, she'd applied a wash of earth coloured tones as a base. Once it had dried, she added the dry plant material. These were painted as a glaze on her soil. She diluted the colour more than she intended. The result was a ghostly shadow of dead plants. With the greenery, she over compensated. The green was more vibrant than it would appear in life, the flowers gaudy in comparison to the drab background. With the eggs, she deliberately reduced their scale and exaggerated the speckling. She hadn't intended to do so, but created an accurate depiction of three cuckoo eggs.

The sketches were far more realistic than the painting. Mavis liked her painting; she liked the fresh greenery eclipsing the browns of winter. She smiled at the tiny flowers flaunting their beautiful petals. She was not sure what would emerge from the eggs, but she felt sure something would. The chicks would grow, find their wings and leave the nest. That didn't matter, the garden, with its assurance of beauty and warm days to come, would remain.

That night, Mavis lay in bed reflecting on her productive weekend. She smiled; slept untroubled by dreams and woke eager to look out at her garden. She smiled again. Her session of tidying had removed much of winter. The sun shone through the still bare branches, highlighting the promise of spring.

'What goes around comes around,' the calendar declared. A stomach bug appeared to be going around. Janice was again absent from work, having been sick during the weekend.

After work, Mavis looked at the stems of berberris, arum and ivy she'd gathered for her artwork. The vase of leaves, on the kitchen windowsill, looked good. She'd decided that when the daffodils bloomed she would pick some, perhaps those brought down by the wind or the weight of their extravagant flowers. She'd pick more leaves too and make another arrangement. The ringing bell interrupted those thoughts. The sight of Norman clutching just opening daffodil buds confused her. It was as though her mind had summonsed them.

Norman offered her the flowers. After a moment, she took them.

"Thank you."

He smiled. "May I?" he said and gestured into the house.

"Oh, er yes. Please come in."

He followed her to the kitchen where she unwrapped the flowers. She added them to the greenery.

"They look good like that. It's almost as though you'd been expecting me."

In a way, she had. He'd come to the house and tried to speak to her at college and in Portsmouth. She'd known she would have to speak to him again.

"Would you like a cup of tea?"

"Please." He followed her to the kitchen.

"So, what have you been doing with yourself?" he asked as she filled the kettle.

Mavis told him how she'd learnt to use a computer and found a job. She mentioned her friends at work and her art class and visits from Cousin Linda. She didn't say these were recent developments.

Norman said her friends sounded fun, her work interesting, that he remembered Linda and would like to see the paintings. She showed him her efforts.

"You've made good progress, Mavis, well done. These show real promise, especially this one." He indicated the spring picture. "Is this the latest one?"

Mavis nodded.

"I thought so. It's good; it looks somewhat hopeful, symbolic of a fresh start. Sorry, I sound as though I'm doing my homework now. I don't mean to seem pretentious."

"That is what I thought," Mavis said.

Norman's expression changed. Mavis laughed.

"Oh Norman, not that you were pretentious. I meant, that was what I intended for the painting, that it would show the optimism of spring."

They smiled at each other. Maybe she'd misjudged him; he seemed far more interesting than she remembered.

"Would you like to come out to dinner on Saturday?" he asked.

"No."

He stopped smiling.

"I meant that I cannot."

"Oh, are you going somewhere else?"

"No. Cousin Linda may come to visit. It is, I mean …"

"Sunday then?"

"If Linda comes then she may stay for the weekend," Mavis said.

"Well, give me a call then, if she doesn't come, and we'll arrange something."

He gave her a business card. As well as his name and the title, 'Executive Consultant' there were two telephone numbers.

"Please ring me anytime, Mavis. Not just to arrange when we will go for a meal, but if you have any problems or worries."

"Worries? What would I worry about?"

"You might want someone to talk to if you're nervous or anything," Norman said.

"What do you mean, Norman? Is there something I should be nervous of?"

"No, no. I was just thinking of the deaths. They could be unsettling."

"Deaths?"

"Marie of course, and that young girl, the one killed down by the college, didn't she live near here?"

"I have no idea." Why should the deaths of her annoying neighbour and an unknown girl worry her? One had been an inconvenience when alive, but that ended with her death.

"I don't know, but that has nothing to do with me," said Mavis.

"No, of course not. Well, goodbye, Mavis. I look forward to hearing from you soon."

When he'd gone, Mavis felt silly for having lied to him. Perhaps she could ring Linda and invite her? She did so. Linda was pleased to be invited, but unable to come as she had promised to look after her granddaughters.

"I'm sorry, Mavis, are you all right? Shall I try to come next week?"

"I am quite all right, please come if you would like to, but there is no problem. Actually, I suppose I must confess; I invited you as my alibi."

"Alibi?" Linda asked. "Why? What have you done?"

"Maybe alibi is the wrong word; I used the possibility of your visit in order to avoid accepting a meal out with Norman."

"Norman? Who's Norman?"

"He was a man I knew several years ago. I think he was considering proposing until Mother frightened him away."

"And he's been carrying a torch for you ever since? Well, Mavis my girl, I'm not coming this weekend so your alibi has vanished. Do you have Norman's telephone number?"

"Yes," Mavis said.

"Then you had better ring him up and accept."

"But I am not sure I want to get involved with him."

"You don't have to be involved to eat dinner. Accept his offer, unless you have something better to do with your evening?"

Mavis did not.

A brighter sky the next morning suggested an unseasonable improvement in the cold weather. Mavis knew, 'All that glisters is not gold.' Things were often not what they seemed. Sometimes, that mattered; and sometimes, it didn't.

Janice was back at work.

"Poor you, you've had a rough time of it lately. Do you think you're allergic to anything?" Lucy asked her.

Sandra made a strange coughing noise that sounded like 'hard work'. The others ignored her.

"Not so far as I know, I don't think I ate anything odd," Janice said.

At lunchtime, Mavis asked if Janice would like to come out for fresh air.

"No thanks, Mavis. I think I'll stay in, I still feel a bit weak, that's why I was off yesterday, I just didn't feel up to walking in."

"I'm sorry you've been ill, Janice. Perhaps you should not have returned to work so quickly?"

"I'm all right really. I was sick again on Friday night. It wasn't too bad though, once I'd stopped throwing up. Mum insisted

I stay in bed for the weekend. I was nice and warm and I just sat there drinking tea and reading."

"You had a good book I hope?"

"You're not going to believe this, but my mum bought me them."

"Your mother?"

"Yep, she saw some books in a basket outside a charity shop priced at five pence each and so bought some."

"That was thoughtful of her."

"Yes, I think she's accepted that we're not the same. She said she picked out the ones she thought I'd like best. She did well; they are all detective type stories. I'll lend them to you if you like, Mavis."

Lucy bought a copy of The News in her lunch break. It named the dead girl as Emily McBride and showed her photograph. It was the pale girl. Another who'd been an annoyance in life and who'd trouble Mavis no more. The article talked of a tragedy, but did not give any reason for the death. The words 'accident', 'suicide' and 'murder' were all avoided. Mavis could not decide if the details were vague because they were not known, or if they were being withheld for a reason.

Chapter 15

'Don't worry, be happy!' the calendar suggested. What a silly idea. A person cannot choose to be happy or not to worry. Mavis worried, but only in a sensible way. She worried things wouldn't be clean, but only if she was unable to remedy the situation. Otherwise, she simply cleaned them. Perhaps then, cleanliness should make her happy, yet it didn't seem to. A clean environment seemed empty; devoid of a reason for her to be there.

As was now her habit on Wednesdays, Mavis went to the Gosport Discovery Centre after work. There she had a snack, a cheese-filled toasted panini. The day had been cold and sleety rain had thrown itself against her as she hurried up the High Street to the inviting warmth of her familiar refuge. She felt warm food was required to counteract the cold weather. The woman who served her agreed.

"I'm not surprised you fancy something hot today. Bitter out there, ain't it?"

"Yes, very cold."

"What would you like to drink then? I can do you a nice mug of soup if you fancy that?"

Soup was properly another meal, not an accompanying drink, Mavis felt, but the idea of sipping piping hot soup appealed. It would be strange to consume it from a mug. Strange for her that was, she knew it was a common practice for other people. The women at work often made themselves mugs of instant soup. She correctly guessed that was what she'd be presented with if she agreed to the suggestion.

"Do you have tomato? I think that would go best with the cheese."

She paid for her order and selected a gardening magazine from the shelf. The sofas were all occupied, but that didn't bother her. She intended to drink her soup sitting on a proper chair at one of the tables. Once she'd decided which was cleanest, she sat and opened the magazine.

The soup and sandwich were very comforting. Mavis was surprised at the rich texture and full flavour of her soup. She had expected it to be watery, but it tasted every bit as good as the canned varieties she drank at home. Next time she went shopping, she would look out for some. She could keep a pack at work. They would be a welcome addition to her usual lunch, especially when the weather was unpleasant.

Once she'd eaten, Mavis visited the toilet. She was distressed to see there was not enough paper left. Normally she pulled several sheets and folded them, so there was no need to touch herself with paper previously handled by someone else. There was insufficient for that precaution. She separated the sheets into single ply and turned them so the outside went to the centre, before she used them.

As she strode through the onslaught of sleet on her way to college, Mavis tried to feel the soup warming her from the inside out. Either the thought, or her hurried pace in fur lined boots had the desired effect; she felt no regret at removing her heavy coat and woollen scarf on arrival.

Mavis was delighted Mr Bittern and Leo seemed to understand the idea behind her spring painting. Leo applauded the insubstantial nature of the background and the extra vibrancy of the living plant material.

"Such a clever idea, to show the temporary, transient nature of winter, and the life force behind the emergence of new life. It's a powerful image."

Mavis smiled at his praise. Although the effect was the result of her unfamiliarity with the acrylic paints, she had chosen to leave it as it was; not tone down the brighter colours, nor strengthen the browns and greys of the decaying remains.

"You have interpreted your idea very well, Mavis. Well done," Mr Bittern said.

"The leaves are not very good," Mavis admitted.

"There is certainly room for improvement, but you should be proud of what you've achieved, your progress is quite marked. This is a good piece of work."

Mavis had an urge to hug him, then rush to the windows, throw them open and shout 'I can paint, I can paint,' to the moon or passers by. "Thank you," she said.

She knew the painting that she was asked to comment on was Jenny's. It showed kitchen utensils and two eggs. The utensils seemed slightly distorted and were two dimensional, they were easily recognisable though. The background colour had been applied after the objects, judging by the way it didn't always meet the next colour. The direction of the brush strokes further indicated the paint had been put on around, rather than under, the subjects.

"The eggs in this still life are good, the colour is just right. The background colour is very pretty; I like that shade of blue."

"Thanks, Mavis," Jenny said. "Oh sorry, I didn't mean to say that, I wasn't supposed to say anything yet, was I?"

"That's all right, Jenny. Mavis, anything else?" Mr Bittern said.

"It is very different from mine. I think that's good, that we have done different things?"

"Yes, it is," said Mr Bittern. "The shading on the eggs is good, Jenny. You were obviously paying attention last week."

Jenny grinned. "It wasn't to start with, I made the shadowy bit too dark, but I kept adding white until it suddenly seemed OK."

"That's the key to getting a painting to come right, keep making changes until you are satisfied and then stop."

"My dear chap, you make it sound so simple. Knowing when to stop, that itself is an art," commented Leo.

Mavis smiled. She'd been right not to alter her painting although it hadn't looked exactly as she'd originally intended.

Someone had painted a pavlova oozing with cream and chocolate sauce. It was topped with strawberries, slices of kiwi fruit and halves of black grapes. Sharp looking pieces of something toffee coloured were piled on top.

Vera was asked to comment.

"I wish I had a cake slice and a fork; I quite fancy a slice of that."

Flo, who's painting it was, said she'd thought the same when looking through a cookbook.

"I'll confess that I only managed a quick sketch before it was eaten. I finished the painting off from memory. I couldn't even go by the recipe book, because the sauce, whipped cream and caramelised sugar were my own idea."

"Ah, is that what they are?" asked Vera.

"I didn't get them quite right. In the picture I mean, they were fabulous on the pavlova."

That evening's lesson concentrated on landscapes. They were shown how to look at a scene and choose what to include.

"You might like to paint an entire view as realistically as possible; you might prefer to simplify what you see to represent the scene before you. Perhaps you will prefer to concentrate on a small detail that captures the spirit of the place. Sometimes deciding what to paint or draw is as important, perhaps more so, than the quality of your technical execution."

"What was that last bit?" Jenny whispered.

"He means we can paint it however we like," Vera explained.

"Is that our homework?" Flo asked.

"Yes. You're to paint a view; I'd like you to look either to the sea, or some other local feature, for your inspiration."

As Mavis wrote the assignment into her diary, she saw how sore and dry her hands were. She'd better be careful; it would be easy to get an infection in broken skin. She must be very thorough in keeping them clean. Maybe she should try a stronger antiseptic wash. Her mind was distracted and she nearly missed what Mr Bittern said. Or Tim, perhaps she should do as he asked and call him Tim.

He told them the proposed date for next term's trip to London was Saturday the eighteenth of April. Tim hoped they would be able to hire a coach as it would be cheaper than going by train.

"I don't know if that will be possible, but I'm making enquiries and I'll keep you informed."

Jenny hoped they would travel by coach.

"I'm not keen on the underground. Anyway it would be nicer, more of a group event, to go by coach."

"I agree," Vera said. "I hope the art history and appreciation group will be invited to join us. I'll go regardless, though. I hope you'll both come?"

Jenny said, "I will if we go by coach. Otherwise, I'm not sure."

"Don't you go worrying about the underground, there's nothing to fear there."

Mavis said, "I shall definitely come. I am looking forward to it, although using the underground system will be rather unnerving for me as well."

"Well, not for me. I'm quite used to it. You both stick close to me and you'll do fine," Vera said.

Mavis smiled; Vera enjoyed reassuring them she was a seasoned traveller and promising assistance. Her familiarity with the train system would undoubtedly prove valuable, should that be the method of transport adopted.

When Mavis next spoke to Cousin Linda, she told her how much she'd changed. Even if she'd wanted to go on a trip to London before and had found the confidence, she would have wanted to go alone. Now, she thought it would be an advantage to hear what the others thought of pictures and compare their opinions with her own. Vera would be good to discuss things with; she wouldn't be afraid to say what she thought and wouldn't mind if Mavis had a different opinion. Jenny was a nice person, but not much good as a friend to Mavis; she'd just agree with everything.

Mavis considered telling Linda of the day she'd stood on the Round Tower and planned her death. She wanted to tell someone, to let the thought out of her head. It wasn't fair to burden Linda though. She'd helped her after Mother died and helped her plan a future. She couldn't tell Linda of her failure, her shame. Mavis spoke only of positive things. She was surprised how much there was to tell.

'You can't tell a book by its cover,' Mavis read whilst making breakfast. Of course not, you had to read it and judge for yourself. Not many people realised that. They bought books because of a celebrity author, not for the quality of the writing. Mavis would never buy a book written by a model, footballer or pop star.

She took the last teabag from the pack. Her next cup must be made with loose tea from the caddy. When that had been used, she would buy more of the bags Mother had disliked. She didn't have to do what Mother did. Bags were far cleaner; they could go on the compost heap. It was difficult to do that with leaves. They made a mess and it took a long time to remove every last one from the sink.

In addition to teabags, she bought quiche; just a portion. Previously, she wouldn't have bought ready-made food, but was encouraged by her experience with the muffins, lovely seeded bread, and the interesting soups. She bought more of the bread and a pack of instant soup to make in a mug. Quiche wasn't a meal on its own. What would go with it? When she'd made it for Mother and herself, she'd accompanied it with salad. There was none in the garden yet, except a few burnett leaves and the chives, so she bought a bag of mixed salad leaves.

At home, she found a letter informing her she was summonsed to attend and give evidence at the inquest into the death of Marie Fiona French. It was scheduled to be held at 10.00 on the fourteenth of April in the Magistrates' Court, Portsmouth. A leaflet, explaining what was required of her, was enclosed. She read it carefully; learning nothing Constable Martins hadn't already told her. Mavis entered the date in her diary.

The quiche and salad leaves were disappointing. They were tasteless; both had a soft, flabby texture. They were not as good as she could make or grow herself. Some new experiences were not a good thing. Sometimes, it was better to rely on yourself than to put faith in the efforts of others; Mother had taught her that.

She rang Norman and told him Linda wasn't coming after all and that she would be pleased to go to dinner with him on Saturday.

"I won't pretend to be sorry that your cousin won't be coming; that would be hypocritical of me. Will seven-thirty be convenient?"

"Perfectly."

"I shall look forward to it. Goodbye, Mavis."

Mavis dreamt of a man eagerly waiting for her. The man was not Norman, but Tim Bittern. He was waiting to see her next painting as he knew it would be good.

The frost that held a tight grip on her garden the next morning would provide a good subject for a painting. Mavis wondered if she could accurately portray its cold rigidity. A pretty scene with hoar frosted seed heads and fluffed up robins held little appeal. If she painted winter, she wanted to capture the cold; to leave no doubt the dark corners would still be icy, long after the sun had passed overhead.

'Some people pretend to despise what they cannot have,' she read as she poured boiling water over a teabag. There was nothing Mavis pretended to despise.

An hour later, Mavis was at work, again pouring boiling water onto tea. As she added milk and sugar, Janice chatted about her new boyfriend. Her mum didn't like him, Janice said.

"Pretends it's because she don't approve of his job and because of the earrings, but really she's just jealous, because she's single. Anyway she thinks I'll go and live with him and then she'll have to pay all the bills herself and have no one to help with housework."

Mavis didn't like sound of him either; mothers were usually right about such matters. Mother had probably been right with regard to Norman. If he'd truly cared would he have been scared off so easily? She must not interfere with Janice and her boyfriend, especially as she did not know him. She limited herself to warning the girl not to rush into anything.

'Don't look a gift horse in the mouth,' Mavis was instructed on the morning of her date with Norman. Linda had urged her to enjoy the evening and not worry about the possibility of a future relationship. Mavis would try to do as advised. She didn't know what to wear. For a moment, she considered phoning Linda for advice. There was no need, she realised. Mavis would wear the suit she'd worn for her job interview. She liked the outfit and didn't imagine she'd have many other suitable opportunities to wear it. It had been purchased for Charlotte's wedding. Mother had refused to attend and Mavis had travelled alone on the train. Mavis thought the quality cloth and strong colour would give her confidence. It had worked at the wedding and the interview; it would work again.

Norman arrived promptly at seven thirty and drove her to The Alverstoke.

A waiter took their coats and showed them to a table. A younger member of staff pulled out a chair to allow Mavis to sit and then presented them with menus. Mavis read through the exciting sounding choices. Pan fried duck with oriental vegetables in a plum sauce glaze sounded good, but then so did the tender medallions of lamb served on a bed of wild rice and finished with rosemary. There were fish dishes too; she'd never eaten turbot, or mullet.

"There are so many things to choose from, I cannot decide," Mavis said .

"That's all right," Norman said.

The older waiter approached.

"Two soup of the day, one fillet steak medium rare and one chicken breast with new potatoes please."

"Certainly sir, anything to drink?"

"A sparkling water and, would you like wine, Mavis?"

"Yes please."

"A glass of Piesporter, thank you."

"Very good, sir."

Norman smiled. "You can't really go wrong with chicken can you?"

He was right, that's why she cooked it so often for herself.

Norman complimented her on her outfit and said how pleased he was that she had, after all, been able to come out for a meal. He briefly spoke of the past. His version of events at odds with her memory. He gave the impression she'd dumped him because he wasn't good enough. Mavis remembered how he'd abruptly left her house after Mother had returned early one evening and caught them embracing on the sofa. Mother had been angry. Norman had not returned.

Mother had said, "Men are only after one thing and that Norman is no good for you." Mavis had been thirty-two at the time; no man prior to that evening had got the one thing they were after. Norman hadn't attempted to that evening, but perhaps one day he might have. Mavis had felt then, if she waited for a man who was good enough, she'd never get one at all. It hadn't mattered anyway, Norman never came back and Mother had never left the house again. Mother was probably right; but Mavis would have liked to have made the decision for herself.

The soup arrived. Mavis realised Norman had been talking and she'd not listened. A glass of wine sat to her right. She must forget the past and enjoy the present. Large shallow soup plates held soup of a rich golden colour. They were decorated with a swirl of what Mavis guessed was cream and a few leaves that resembled parsley. She sniffed at the fragrant aroma, but couldn't guess at the flavour.

"What flavour is this?" Norman asked.

"Curried pumpkin, sir."

"Curry?" Norman didn't sound pleased.

"Yes, sir. The pumpkin is roasted and then pureed into a mild creamy soup and garnished with coriander and yoghurt."

"It sounds and smells delicious," Mavis said as she picked up her spoon.

The waiter gave her a small bow and left. Mavis tasted her soup. As promised, the flavour was mild and creamy.

"I'm sorry, Mavis. I expected it to be vegetable."

"Pumpkin is a vegetable, Norman." She took another spoonful of soup. It was very rich. Perhaps it was a good thing her main course would be a simple one.

"Is it all right?" Norman asked.

"Very nice."

He tasted his.

"It isn't as bad as it sounds. Curried soup always sounds a bit odd."

"I would not have thought of trying it myself, thank you for ordering it."

Norman smiled and lifted his glass. "To new things."

Mavis clinked her glass against his and sipped the wine. It tasted sweet, much more to her taste than the wine she'd drunk during the meal shared with her work colleagues.

"The wine is very nice, Norman. What name did you give it?"

"Piesporter. It's German; I thought you would like it."

"I do, very much. I know little about wines, when I've been out before I've not known what to order."

"You can't go wrong with a nice German wine, Mavis. The wine list always states the country it was made in, so just look for German and you'll be fine with whatever you pick."

"Are different types of wine made there?"

As they continued eating, Norman told her of a vineyard he'd visited in Germany and after learning Mavis had never been abroad, he described some of his many foreign travels. Mavis listened; fascinated by the interesting sounding places, tales of his journeys and the things he'd seen and done. He was as knowledgeable as the presenters on the travel programmes and far more entertaining. He told her of the exotic plant life and birds; not the children's entertainment and shopping opportunities. He was eager to explain anything she didn't understand. Mavis hardly noticed eating her chicken as she listened to his story of a beach barbecued Christmas lunch in Australia.

After they'd eaten dessert and whilst they waited for their coffee, Mavis visited the toilets. To her relief they were clean and tidy, with automatic hand driers. As she applied cream to her clean hands, she saw her watch indicated it was quarter past ten. How annoying, it must have stopped that morning; she would need to buy a new battery and have it fitted.

The coffee was brought to them in tiny cups, with a small jug of cream and a dish of huge brown sugar crystals. They sparkled in the candlelight. Mavis couldn't resist spooning several into her coffee.

"They drink coffee that way in Turkey," Norman told her.

"In small cups?"

"Well, yes, but I meant black and incredibly sweet."

"Oh, have I …"

"Mavis, you drink your coffee however you like."

She added cream, stirred carefully and lifted the delicate cup to her mouth. Their cups were refilled several times as Norman shared his experiences of haggling in Turkish bazaars. He drove her home and walked with her to her front door. When he bent towards her, it seemed natural to offer him her cheek to kiss.

Once inside, she thought for a moment her kitchen clock had stopped working on the same day as her watch. That didn't seem likely. She looked again at her watch; it hadn't stopped and neither had the clock. The time really was twenty five past eleven; she'd spent almost four hours enjoying a meal and Norman's company.

Chapter 16

'Treat others as you hope they'll treat you,' the calendar advised on Wednesday. Mavis stared at the newly revealed sheet of paper. Her hand tightened around the piece she'd removed, crushing it. She'd heard the phrase before, but never considered it. She treated people as they treated her; usually with indifference. If she were to behave differently, perhaps others would do likewise? She wanted friends, but didn't know how to encourage them. Perhaps she was not the only person to feel that way? She'd told Linda that Jenny was a nice person and Vera would be a suitable friend. If she tried, Mavis could encourage friendships. She only saw the two women for one evening a week; how badly wrong could her advances go?

Mavis had made a mistake in screwing up the paper in her hands. She smoothed it and folded it as best she could. She dropped it in the bin and tried to forget it.

Bert and his wife were at the bus stop. They shuffled along to allow her to sit. She'd noticed before that no matter how many people were standing around the shelter, the woman didn't move her bag and the man didn't slide along the bench, until Mavis arrived. Mavis greeted them and asked after Lauren. As the child's grandmother talked, Mavis remembered they'd called her a friend. She'd done little to deserve the tribute; done nothing but accept, when Karen had offered her a seat in the café and allow Bert's wife to chat about Lauren.

At work that day, Mavis talked to Janice of books, she looked at the holiday brochure Lucy showed her, agreeing Italy sounded romantic, and she told Sandra her new hairstyle suited her. Her colleagues asked about her art class and wanted to see her pictures. She showed them some sketches and they admired her skill.

"What about people?" Sandra asked.

"People?"

"Yes, portraits, do you do those too?"

"We will, but not until later in the term. It's not something that I've ever tried."

"Oh go on, Mavis, do me," Janice said.

"I don't know how."

"Oh go on, I've never had my portrait done."

"Well, I ..."

"Oh, purr-leese," Janice said. She grinned widely and waggled her head at Mavis.

Sandra picked up Mavis's bag of art materials and handed it to her.

Lucy wheeled Janice and her chair away from the desk. "Do you want to do her nude, Mavis?" she asked.

Mavis pretended to think for a moment.

"No," Janice squealed.

"Perhaps not," Mavis agreed.

She turned to a clean sheet in her notebook, selected a pencil and held it poised above the paper. She had no idea how to begin. Lucy and Sandra moved round behind her.

"Hmmm, interesting subject, Maestro," Sandra said. "It puts me in mind of a Picasso, or a Dali."

"Picasso, that's a car, innit?" Janice asked.

"Picasso was a very famous artist, with a distinctive style," Mavis said.

"Isn't he the one who ...?" Lucy mimed severing an ear.

"No, that was Van Gogh," Sandra said.

"What're you lot going on about?" Janice asked.

Sandra approached Janice and turned her chair. "Now, we need a pose; sit up straight, Janice. What do you reckon?" she asked Lucy and Mavis.

"Try to look enigmatic, Janice," Mavis said.

"Eh?" Janice scratched the back of her head.

"Yeah, stay exactly like that," Lucy said.

Sandra returned to Mavis's side. She held up a thumb and squinted past it at Janice. Lucy giggled, lifted both hands, formed her fingers into a square and peered through. Mavis drew an oval on the page; it was not at all like the shape of Janice's face.

The three women looked at it.

"So, which one is Picasso then?" Lucy asked.

Mavis drew a triangle on the side of the oval.

"That's her nose isn't it?" Lucy asked. "I'm with you now."

"Sounds like I've got three art experts working on my picture," Janice said.

Mavis added two circles to her sketch, they were in approximately the right position for eyes and nearly equal in size.

"Don't forget her lashes," Lucy suggested.

Mavis continued to add to her sketch, following the advice she was offered. Janice asked many questions. The only reply was, "Sit up straight, Janice." That instruction was repeated frequently.

Lucy and Sandra laughed so hard Mavis was unable to avoid following their example. That didn't improve the accuracy of her drawing.

"What on earth is going on out here?" Nicola asked as she strode across the room from her office.

"Mavis was just showing us what she's learnt at college," Janice explained.

Nicola glanced at the sketch pad. She chuckled. "Well, I hope the course isn't being subsidised by my taxes," she said.

"Here, let me see," Janice shouted and ran around to look.

She stared at the drawing. The others stopped laughing and watched Janice. The girl reached out her hand and took the sketch book. Mavis wanted to take the drawing from her and rip it into pieces. Janice had shown an interest in her artwork and Mavis had made a joke at the girl's expense. She wanted to run, but the other women surrounded her chair. She couldn't leave without pushing them away.

"I don't think you've got my hair quite right," Janice said in a slow, calm voice.

"Janice Quicke, you obviously don't appreciate true artistic genius," Sandra said. She indicated the top of the face. "Those are your eye lashes."

Janice pressed a hand to her mouth. Her face became red and her body shook. She began to giggle. The laughter that followed left Sandra holding the back of Mavis's chair for support and everyone's eyes streaming.

"If I make you lot a cup of tea, is there any chance of getting some work out of you?" Nicola eventually asked as she collected their mugs.

Later, Mavis approached her model. "Janice, I am sorry that I played a joke on you."

"That's all right, Mavis. I have to admit, you got me good and proper. I wasn't expecting nothing like that."

"I'm very pleased that I did not upset you."

"'Course you didn't. Actually, I wanted to ask if I could take a copy of it. See, it really is the first time anyone's done my portrait and well, I sort of like it."

"You can have it, if you would like."

"No, it'd spoil your book if you ripped it out. You keep it, I'll take a photocopy."

At class, Mavis and Jenny were the first to arrive. They'd both produced seascapes. Both were views looking out toward the Isle of Wight. Jenny's included people and a dog in front of Southsea pier. It had a precise quality to it, making Mavis think of a simplified photograph. She imagined Jenny must have seen the people in exactly the positions she'd drawn them. It seemed likely the dimensions of the pier and relative placement of the individual elements were calculated with the aid of a ruler. Although Mavis was unable to define why, the picture didn't look real. The tide neither advanced nor receded, the dog wasn't playing. The people were not talking or feeling the sea breeze. Everything in the picture was just there.

Mavis's own painting showed an oblique view of the beach down past Lee-on-the-Solent and on toward Hill Head. There was enough colour to suggest the beach huts in the distance. The rest was done in a monochrome of greeny grey. It was bleak; but not dead. The waves were crashing on the rocks, pulling at the pebbles in their fight to reach land. The wind was insistent, damp and cold. No litter remained. It had blown away and no one would venture out in such conditions to discard more.

"Oooh, it makes me cold to look at it. The weather there looks worse than it is now."

"Thank you, I was trying to show a winter scene."

"You've done that all right. Is that the beach by Lee?"

"Yes, it is, and yours is Southsea."

"Yes. I'm so pleased you can tell."

"It is very accurate."

"Thank you, Mavis."

Other people arrived as they talked; soon Vera bore down on them.

"I'd not have the patience to be as neat and precise as you Jenny, nor as disciplined in my use of colour as you Mavis. What do you think of my latest effort?"

She opened her portfolio case to reveal an extremely colourful painting. It depicted a seascape, but surely, one based on vivid imagination rather than a real place.

"It's somewhere I went on holiday, well a sort of combination of a couple of places really as I couldn't decide which to go for."

Jenny said, "It's different, very nice, very brave."

Mavis didn't think it was successful. She said so but, remembering being criticised for your efforts hurts, she tried to be tactful.

"Actually you're right," Vera agreed. "It is a bit of a mess, I tried to do too much. I do think the flowers look good though? Maybe not quite to scale, but they're the best part of the painting I think?"

"Yes, they are. Perhaps you should concentrate on painting flowers as you do them so well."

"Good suggestion. Thanks Mavis, I'll get and look at some in the summer. I think I'd rather do them from real life than photos and such."

"I have some in my garden, perhaps ..."

Tim began the lesson; Mavis finished neither her sentence nor the thought behind it. After taking the register and asking them to lay out their pictures, Tim told them, "The college has had trouble with trips before and therefore has not agreed to the art classes visiting London."

People began to mutter; he held up his hand to silence them.

"The college won't support us, but I will still be going to London and will visit the galleries that day. If anyone else would care to join me then that's up to them, but the college will take no responsibility."

"We'll be going too," Vera declared. Jenny, Mavis and several others agreed.

Tim showed them how to use perspective and shadows in their artwork to create depth and a sense of scale. He demonstrated how lighter, softer colours and less precision in the shapes could suggest distance. The class practised the new techniques.

"For homework you are to have another go at a landscape. I would like you to choose a place you are familiar with, but more important than that, is that you choose a place that's important to you in some way. It could be somewhere with happy memories, or even somewhere you dislike, but not a place you don't care about. I would like you to think about your emotions as you paint."

As she walked through the college lobby after class, Mavis was pleased to see the boy waiting for her. No one would wish to harm her, yet still she didn't wish to walk close to where the girl had died exactly a week before.

As she waited for sleep, she wondered where to paint for her homework. She thought of the Round Tower; it fitted the requirements. The place was important to her. If she were to go out on Victoria Pier, she could paint the Tower with land, not sea, as the backdrop. Mavis didn't want to think of the emotions the Tower represented. She would paint somewhere else.

'He who aims at perfection in everything achieves it in nothing,' Mavis read on Thursday. Another silly thing to have included, if the intent of the calendar was to inspire. Achieving perfection was difficult, but surely, that should be one's aim? Mavis might never be able to produce a perfect painting or a completely clean house, but that was no reason for not trying. Dust would fall whilst she was at work, but that was a poor excuse for not cleaning and polishing before she left home.

On Friday morning she was informed, 'Familiarity breeds contempt'. Mother had told her that often enough. Mother had sometimes been wrong. Janice had begun to treat Mavis in a familiar manner; she didn't think the girl had formed a lower opinion of her as a result.

Saturday's quotation was easier to agree with; 'One swallow doesn't make a summer'. There would be no swallows for several months. Other birds populated her garden. Mavis watched them from her bedroom window. They reminded her of people she knew. The cooing wood pigeons were Bert and his wife. One sat still on the top of her fence, the other kept fidgeting, knocking into the first. The jerky head movements suggested a lively one-sided conversation. It was easy to decide which bird represented which partner.

She noticed a wren, venturing toward the food supply then darting for cover. Mavis thought of Jenny; was that just because of the term Jenny Wren? No, she didn't think so.

Blackbirds with young searched for food, they were Karen and her daughter Lauren.

Starlings; Mavis thought of school children at bus stop that way, but they could be any group of people. At first, they seemed all the same, but in reality, there were many different personalities. The ones that kept look-out for danger and flew off alerting others, they could be Nicola at work, leading and directing the others. Or perhaps they represented Timothy Bittern; advising but with no power to make others do as he suggested except by example. With starlings, there were often one or two who didn't fly away when advised. They were like Sandra at work. Everyone occasionally complained, but Sandra was more spiteful than the others. She didn't pay attention when Nicola tried to change the subject. It was as if she didn't realise she was behaving inappropriately. Mavis never used to think how her words affected others; it was likely she too had upset many people without knowing it.

Once the main flock of starlings had flown away, taking Lucy and Janice from the office with them, then an occasional singleton arrived. It looked like the others, yet was slightly different; like the boy. He joined in with the other schoolboys, but he also went out of his way to come and meet her from college and seemed to be interested in her. Most youngsters would not be; he was different. More than different, perhaps special; almost a guardian angel? Because of him, she hadn't jumped after that first art class, his presence stopped her. His kind ways and interest in her painting helped her own enthusiasm. He'd been partly responsible for her change of heart. She had changed; she was no longer putting off suicide until the end of term, but beginning to think she didn't really want to do it, even then. There were things she wanted to do first; and she wanted to have fun.

One of the things Mavis wished to attempt was to make friends with Vera. She looked around the garden, trying to find a bird to represent Vera. Of course, there were none; it was unlikely that tropical birdlife would visit her bird table. Vera wasn't what Mavis was used to, but maybe that was a good thing?

There were other things she wished to do. Norman had suggested going to the theatre. She would like that. Norman might not be an ideal life partner, not that she wanted one, but he was very charming and generous. She would like to go to some of the places he'd suggested. As she considered spending time with Norman, the birds flew away. It became very quiet. Mavis looked in the sky to see if a bird of prey circled overhead.

Chapter 17

'55% of all statistics are made up', were the next words of wisdom from her calendar. Mavis thought that quite likely, especially the things reported on the news.

At work, Lucy and Janice were dreaming of what they'd do when they won the lottery.

Sandra said, "You two are living in a fantasy world. You won't win; life's not like that. Your problems won't just get magically solved."

"I haven't got problems really and I know I'm not likely to win, but it's nice to dream," Lucy said.

Janice said, "Yeah, lighten up, Sandra. I know we'll probably always have to work for a living, but there's a chance of winning. Always look on the dark side you do."

"I'm not looking on the dark side," Sandra said. "Just being realistic. The chances of winning are extremely small. You're far more likely to get hit by a bus."

"I heard that there's a fourteen million to one chance of winning," Nicola said.

"Come on, it must be better than that or no one would play it," Janice said.

"Nicola's right, those are the odds," Sandra said. " People play it because, like you, they delude themselves that there's a chance. Like I said, life doesn't work like that."

"I've heard that fourteen million to one thing too," Lucy said. "That's for the jackpot though isn't it?"

"You could be right," Nicola agreed.

"What's your point?" Sandra asked.

"The chances of getting a few hundred are much better. I could do with a couple of hundred quid. That'd pay for a few days at Butlins with the kids," Lucy said.

"Oh yes," Nicola sighed. "A couple of days with no cooking and cleaning and someone else to occupy the little darlings; bliss."

"Don't know why you have kids if you're not prepared to look after them," Sandra snapped.

The other women stared. Normally Nicola would try to change the subject to keep the peace, but it was difficult as she was the one being snapped at. Someone else must say something.

"I read this morning that 55% of statistics are made up," Mavis said.

Lucy quickly agreed, "You can't trust what some of these experts say."

Mavis told them she'd stopped watching the television news, because it was alarmist.

"You're right, Mavis," Nicola agreed. "If you were to believe everything that's reported you'd never leave your house. I'm sure that facts are distorted just to increase viewing figures."

"One minute they say red wine is good for you, the next that binge drinking is a killer," Janice said.

Discussion on the rubbish spoken by experts continued. Sandra did not contribute.

After lunch, Janice limped back into the office. Her coat was muddy and her face pale.

"Are you all right?" Lucy asked her.

"Yes, I'll just get myself a cup of tea," she mumbled.

Janice didn't look all right and she hadn't offered to make the others a cup of tea. She didn't even sound all right. Mavis went out to the kitchen. Janice still wore her coat and she was shivering.

"Has something happened, Janice?"

"There was a car, Mavis. It didn't stop, well it did, but afterwards and now I'm so cold."

Her trembling became worse as she spoke. She looked frightened; Mavis thought the girl might cry.

"Come and sit down, I'll get Nicola."

Mavis coaxed the girl back to the office and into a chair. She walked across to Nicola's office and opened the door.

"Janice has had an accident."

Nicola rushed into the main office. She spoke gently to Janice and asked what had happened. Janice explained a car had hit her. She hadn't been caught under the wheels, but thrown clear. She was bruised, she thought, from impact with the car as well as falling hard on to the pavement. As Janice answered the questions her shaking grew worse, her face became pale and sweaty. She began to claim someone had it in for her; that it was a deliberate attack on her.

Sandra said, "You should have looked where you were going."

Janice replied, "I did, I didn't even want to cross the road. I was walking along and ended up off the kerb. I'm sure someone pushed me."

"Nonsense, why would they?"

Janice shook her head. She'd stopped shaking.

"What you need is a nice cup of tea," Sandra continued more gently.

"I'll get it," Lucy offered.

"Did you see what type of car it was?" Nicola asked.

"Yes, the driver stopped."

"Well he wouldn't have done that if he'd meant to harm you, would he?" Sandra said.

"I suppose not," Janice said.

After they'd drunk their tea, Nicola told Janice to go into the ladies toilet and see if she'd been badly hurt. Janice did as suggested and reported she was fine.

"I'll have some cracking bruises though. I'd better not let my boyfriend get too romantic for a while. Purple thighs might be a bit of a turn off."

For her evening meal, Mavis decided on soup. She drank it quickly, anxious to begin drawing. On the way home, she'd had the happy idea of painting her garden; not the whole thing, but little glimpses. The moment she'd got in from work, she'd taken out her book and sketched the angles of the side of the house, path and adjacent fence. The hard materials should act as an interesting contrast to the froth of new growth in the narrow border. She'd picked a few leaves and stems of the key plants; they were standing in water waiting for her to begin. Her customary after supper cup of tea would be drunk in the dining room as she studied the sketches and plants. As she filled the kettle, someone knocked on her door.

"It's only me," a voice called as she approached the door. It was Norman.

"Hello, Mavis. I hope I'm not interrupting anything?"

"I was just making a cup of tea."

"Oh, good timing then."

He clearly expected to be invited in. He'd taken her for a lovely meal; it would seem ungrateful to refuse him a cup of tea.

"Come in, Norman."

As she made the tea and listened to his chatter of the weather and the traffic congestion, she wondered what he wanted. It would take several minutes for him to finish his drink; she supposed he would come to the point eventually.

"Shall we sit down?"

She carried the tea, on a tray, into the lounge. She placed Norman's cup onto a table by the settee. Mavis sat in an arm chair.

Norman looked around him. "It's a lovely house, Mavis. You've kept it up well."

"Thank you, Norman."

"It's nice to see you again."

She gave a small smile and sipped her tea.

"We had a nice evening out the other day."

"Yes we did. Thank you for taking me, Norman." She drank more tea, hoping to encourage him to drink his.

"I thought we could go somewhere tonight, if you're not busy?"

"No. I am, sorry."

"No?"

"No. I shall be painting."

"Ah, painting." At last, he picked up his tea and began to drink.

"Yes, once I have drunk my tea I shall begin painting."

"Are you going on the college trip to London? Well, I suppose we shouldn't call it a college trip the way things stand at this point in time, but you know what I mean."

"Yes, I shall be going."

"Then I'll treat you to lunch; make it a proper day out."

"Vera is going too, I believe."

Norman said, "No problem, the more the merrier."

Mavis felt relieved; she didn't want to have to choose between two possible friends.

"I am going to do my painting now, Norman," she said as she took his almost empty cup from him.

"Where do you do it?"

"In the dining room; alone."

"Thanks for the tea, Mavis. Sorry I can't stay, but I've got things to do. See you soon."

"Goodbye, Norman."

"Give me a call. We'll go out another time."

"Goodbye, Norman."

The following morning, Mavis was advised to, 'Count your age by friends, not years'. What was that supposed to mean? School children had many friends; old people had few. It didn't make sense.

With six days to go before the inquest into the death of Marie French, Mavis began to get nervous. Would the family know who she was? Would they think she should not be involved? What would she be expected to do? She'd read the information provided by the court and Constable Martins had told her there was no need for concern. Perhaps that was true.

She'd said, "You'll just be asked to confirm what you said in your statement. You might be asked a few more questions, just to make sure the coroner gets a clear picture. It won't take long, I shouldn't think."

Mavis hadn't been concerned then, but as the day approached, she worried. How long would it take her to get there? If she arrived too early, would she be taken to the wrong enquiry?

Was she sure she knew where to go? She was worrying for nothing. She could walk down at lunchtime and time the journey. That was a good idea; if she were familiar with the location, she would feel more comfortable.

Mavis entered Guildhall Square and climbed the steps to her right until she reached the library entrance. A blue painted metal signpost indicating the court pointed to a small, brick paved bridge. The bridge looked more inviting than the formidable exterior to the library. She walked past buildings that were either flats or offices. A sign, bearing Portsmouth University's logo declared them to be 'Guildhall Halls'. They must be halls of residence. She saw a building named 'Crown House', could that be the court? She saw another blue signpost and walked a few yards further. To her right another building was clearly marked 'Courts of Justice'. Mavis climbed the steps and hesitated. She looked for an instruction to guide her. A sign invited her to, 'ring for assistance'. It had the symbol for a wheelchair on it. Mavis wondered how those who couldn't walk negotiated the steps to request assistance.

Two women climbed the steps; Mavis stood aside to allow them to enter. They handed their bags to a man inside the door. He placed the bags on a conveyor belt and waved the women through an archway. Mavis had seen similar archways on the television news. She was watching a security check. Mavis decided she need not go in.

In the afternoon, Mavis, on her way to the stationery store, overheard a discussion between Sandra and Nicola. Sandra asked if it were true Mavis had been given a day off for the inquest. Mavis stopped walking; she had a right to know anything said about her.

"Yes, Sandra, she will have to be absent from work for however long the inquest takes. Why? Is that going to cause a problem for you?"

"Me? I don't know why you're interested in me all of a sudden. Mavis gets to swan off to court and Janice is off sick half the time, why worry about me? I'm just the one who's left struggling at work covering for them. I don't always feel well, but I still come in don't I?"

"Yes you do. I appreciate that when anyone is away the others may have to work a little harder."

Sandra snapped, "Are you trying to say I can't cope?"

"No, Sandra. I'm not. I'm trying to say that I don't expect you to overwork or to come in if you feel unwell. I wouldn't expect any of my staff to work if they were sick."

"Mavis isn't sick though is she?"

"No, she isn't. She's been summonsed to give evidence in court. She doesn't have any choice in the matter and it's hardly going to be much fun for her."

Sandra said, "She shouldn't have been so nosey, poking into other people's business."

Mavis went to fetch envelopes. On her return to the main office, Lucy and Janice were discussing what they would do during the Easter break.

"Me and my boyfriend are taking my little brother to Marwell Zoo," Janice said.

"I want to take my kids somewhere like that; the oldest one went there recently on a school trip though. What about the sea life centre, would it keep my little darlings occupied for a day?"

"I don't know, I think maybe it's better for older kids," Janice said.

"Hmm, you're probably right. I'd rather take them somewhere they can run around and make a noise without annoying people," Lucy agreed.

Mavis thought of the Round Tower. Children could climb the steps and run along the sea wall making as much noise as they liked. Mavis had done so as a child; Daddy had taken her. She was almost sure that had actually happened. Children ran there still, she'd seen a girl run round and round the top; but the tower wouldn't occupy them for a whole day.

"The Millennium walk," she suggested.

"The what?" Lucy asked.

"The Millennium walk. A route from Gosport, around the dockyard, down to old Portsmouth, all marked out in tiles linked together," Mavis explained.

177

"Oh yeah, I know what you mean now," Lucy said.

"That'd be good, Lucy," Janice said. "You could go over to Gosport and back on the ferry, then take them round the dockyard; it's free to get in if you're just walking round, not going on the ships. Then, after you'd been down along the sea front for a bit, you could take them to Gunwharf for something to eat. That'd keep you busy for ages."

"It would wear them out too. Thanks, Mavis that's a brilliant suggestion." Lucy said.

"What's brilliant?" Sandra asked as she came into the office.

"We were just discussing what we're doing for Easter," Janice said. "Are you going away or doing anything interesting?"

"No." Her tone didn't encourage further queries.

"Oh, OK. What about you, Mavis?"

"I'm looking forward to spending time in my garden and being able to work on my painting."

Compared with Sandra's answer, Mavis had sounded as though she had an interesting life, but she knew she needed more than those solitary activities. Norman was good company in a way, but she didn't want to spend every evening with him. Her loneliness might encourage her to accept more of his invitations than was advisable. She would invite Vera to visit. Perhaps not for a meal, Mavis could not host a dinner party or anything of that nature. If Vera were invited to look at the flowers in her garden and to stay for a light supper, that might be all right. Vera was not the sort of person to worry over the etiquette of a situation anyway. If she wanted to come, she would; otherwise she would simply decline.

The next morning, 'Procrastination is the thief of time,' was on her calendar. That was true. Mavis had wasted years by not getting around to having friends and a life. She'd had friends at school, but she and Mother had moved when Daddy died. Was that right? Surely Daddy had been at this house too? She wouldn't think about that. Trying to understand when and why Daddy had gone from her life, could bring her no pleasure. Few thoughts of the past were pleasant. At her new school, the other girls had friends;

Mavis had been befriended only by the unpopular girls. She hadn't kept up those unsatisfactory friendships after school.

Because she'd not gone to work, she hadn't made new friends. On a few occasions, boys had asked her out. She'd nothing in common with them and hadn't known how to act. There was only Mother to ask for advice and she'd thought all boys were out to hurt and ruin Mavis. She was too shy to ask Linda. No relationship had lasted long. Then there had been Norman. That had ended in disaster. She hadn't wanted another boyfriend after that.

Mavis determined she would not waste more time. There were people who said they were her friends; Janice and Bert's family. Linda was a relation, but she acted like a friend. Mavis could learn to have friends. She'd carry out her plan of inviting Vera round when classes resumed after Easter.

The day before the inquest, her calendar suggested, 'Smile. It makes people wonder'. She wasn't sure she wanted people to wonder about her. Maybe tomorrow she would be told, 'Scowl and you'll be left in peace'. She would smile if that proved to be the case.

Chapter 18

Although Nicola had said she needn't come in to work, Mavis woke at her normal time on the day of the inquest. She preferred to stick to her usual routine as much as possible.

She removed yesterday's page from her calendar and read the new quote. 'Life can only be understood backwards; but it must be lived forwards'. Mavis was soon to learn the details of a death, not a life. She had no interest in understanding the life of Marie French.

Mavis was pleased Bert and his wife weren't at the bus stop. She didn't feel like chatting. She would have to answer the coroner's questions. That would be enough talking about an event she'd rather forget. The couple might not know it was the day of the inquest and have wished to talk of other matters. That would have been no better.

At work, she made coffee for the other women and herself. They talked only of the weather. Nicola asked her to step into her office for a moment.

"Mavis, I don't know how long the inquest will take, but please don't feel you have to come back to work straight afterwards. You might want some time to yourself. If that's the case, just give me a call to let me know, and perhaps you could let me know tomorrow if they say how long you'll be needed for?"

"I don't expect it to take long, perhaps just a few hours."

"Really? I imagined it would go on for days, weeks maybe. Court cases seem to take ages," Nicola said.

"The policewoman who spoke to me said that inquests are different. It's simply a matter of people giving statements so that a verdict may be reached."

"Oh, well good. Still even so, if you do feel that you need time …"

"Thank you."

"Mavis, I don't mean I don't want you to come in, you do know that? If you'd feel better at work then that's fine, you do what's best for you."

Mavis smiled. "Thank you, Nicola. I expect I shall return this afternoon or possibly tomorrow morning. If for some reason I shall not be at work as usual tomorrow, then I shall telephone you."

"That's fine. I hope it goes all right."

Mavis walked down to the court. Before she climbed the steps, she took out her letter. Once inside the glass doors, she showed it to the security guard.

"I am here to attend the inquest into the death of Marie French."

"Inquest? Hang on." The man turned away from her and called to the women behind a desk situated beyond the security equipment.

"Have we got a coroner here today?"

"No, nothing this week," he was informed.

He turned back to Mavis. "You must want the Magistrates' Court. Know where that is?"

The man was right; her letter stated the Magistrates' Court. Mavis hadn't realised that was different from a court of law.

"No."

"Down the steps, over to your right a bit, to the building opposite. Down the side of there and you go in on your left."

"Thank you."

Mavis followed his directions and reached a short queue of people. Mavis joined the queue. Most of the people waiting were, she was sure, guilty of whatever they were accused of. Most were silent and smoking. Those who weren't silent were swearing loudly and gesturing with their cigarettes. When she reached the front of the queue, Mavis handed over her bag. A uniformed man glanced inside it before placing it on a conveyor belt. As her bag was x-rayed, Mavis was ushered through an archway. Once inside, she reported at the desk, in accordance with the sign directing all visitors to do so.

"Straight through the hall to the end. Court number eight on the right," said a woman who looked at her letter, but not at Mavis.

Court eight had a sign above the door confirming it to be the coroner's court. She tried the door, it opened. Mavis took a few steps into the small wood panelled room; it was empty. She went out and sat on one of the metal chairs fixed to the floor around the perimeter of the hall. They were red and uncomfortable. People sat or stood in groups, speaking quietly. Most wore jeans with sports tops and trainers or very short denim skirts and tight sleeveless tops. One woman wore orange rubber flip flops. She had tattoos; they were different to those of the woman in the café. In place of artistic, colourful roses were crude outlines of daggers and sets of initials in washed-out blue. It looked as though she'd done them herself. Perhaps she had, Mavis thought as she looked at the woman's stained fingers.

Many people had yellow forms and were completing them as they waited. No one looked happy to be there. A few men wore suits; they stood and questioned those who sat. Were they solicitors? A woman, gowned in black, strode down through the hall. She smiled at a suited man and entered the court opposite Mavis. A judge? Mavis didn't recognise the woman's clothing as anything she'd seen in a television drama.

Mavis read a sign on the courtroom door, informing her mobile phones must be switched off before entering court. Did people need to be told that? She looked around her; yes, perhaps they did. There was a coin operated drinks machine, toilets; no windows. People must be looking at her, wondering who she was and why she was there, alone. She went into court eight and chose a seat at the back.

There was a raised area against the opposite wall. A microphone sat on the wooden desk. She guessed that was where the coroner would sit. There was a table in the centre: surrounded on three sides by blue upholstered chairs. On the table sat another microphone. There was no sign of speakers. It was quiet in the courtroom; peaceful. There was no need to be afraid. There was nothing to fear until she had to speak.

The door opposite the one Mavis had used opened and a smartly dressed man entered. He placed a briefcase on to the table and brought out some papers. Mavis looked in her bag for the letter the court had sent her. She approached the man. He looked up and smiled.

"Hello, I'm David, the coroner's assistant."

"I am Mavis Forthright. I am here for the inquest." Mavis held out her letter.

"Yes, you're a witness aren't you?"

"Yes. I am early. I came in here because it is quieter and I …"

"That's fine. I will be bringing in everyone together and briefing them, but you may wait here if you prefer."

"Thank you."

Mavis sat and waited.

Tanya Martins came into the court and introduced herself to the coroner's assistant. She wasn't wearing her uniform.

"Have you given evidence at an inquest before?" David asked.

"No, no I haven't," the policewoman said.

"It will be quite informal. The coroner will ask questions and it's possible that the family may wish to do so, but this is not a trial. You won't be cross examined."

"Will I be able to use my report to refresh my memory?"

"Yes, in fact the coroner will probably ask you to read directly from it."

"Thank you."

Tanya Martins turned away from him and saw Mavis.

She said 'Hello', and took a seat near the front.

A young man and a woman entered. They nodded at David and took seats in the area Mavis assumed was the witness box. They seemed at ease; presumably, they were court staff.

David went out. He soon returned with an elderly couple whom he sat at the table. Other people followed them in and took seats on the other side of the room to Mavis. Because the entrance jutted into the room, Mavis couldn't see everyone; those she could see were dressed casually. David stood in the centre of the room and waited until everyone was settled.

"Hello, my name is David and I'm the coroner's assistant. We are here today to enquire into the death of Marie French." He paused. "The microphones are there to record what is said, they are not for amplification, so please speak clearly so that everyone can hear. If there is a fire or other emergency we will leave calmly through the doorway behind me." He indicated. "Are there any questions before I tell the coroner we are ready to begin?"

There were none. He left through the door he'd brought to their attention. No one spoke in his absence.

The door opened, David walked back in and said, "Court rise."

Everyone stood. A man, dressed in a dark suit, entered.

"Please sit," he said.

They did.

The coroner addressed most of his remarks to the elderly couple. After confirming their identity as Ms French's parents, he said, "I am sorry to have had to ask you to come here today. The purpose of this enquiry is to allow me to reach a decision on how Marie died. First I must ask you to confirm a few details about Marie, so that I can register the death."

He went on to tell them medical evidence would be provided from Marie's doctor and from the post mortem examination. Further information would be provided by the neighbour who discovered Marie and by the police officer who attended. Mavis was the neighbour he'd referred to. She'd have to explain to the parents that she'd found the woman lying in a pool of her own congealing blood. The coroner would ask why she'd gone into the garden and why she'd done so too late to save her. The thought of the stains the cat had licked from his paws might not be an image the parents would welcome. It was also likely they wouldn't wish to know of her daughter's unkind treatment of Mavis.

The father, still seated at the table, held a book and read the oath. In answer to the coroner's questions, he confirmed Marie's name and date of birth. The questions were asked gently, just as Constable Martins had questioned Mavis after the discovery of the body.

"Miss Forthright?" the coroner's assistant stood at her side, inviting her to stand. She followed him and was taken to the witness box. She was handed a book and a piece of laminated card. Her voice hardly faltered as she read the oath.

"You may sit if you prefer," the coroner said.

Mavis sat.

"Marie was your neighbour for almost four years, is that correct?"

"Yes."

"And did you know her well?"

"No."

Everyone looked at her. They expected her to say more.

"She, Marie, was at work in the day and often out in the evenings. Mother and I lived quietly we did not see her socially."

"I see, so you were not close friends. You would not have known of any problems she may have had?"

What problems would she have had? Mavis had been the one with a sick mother, a nasty neighbour and a lonely life.

"No, she appeared to be happy."

"You went into Marie's garden on Sunday eighteenth of January this year; is that correct?"

"Yes," Mavis said.

"Can you tell me why?"

"The cat, the garage door …" Mavis didn't know what she was expected to say.

"You say in your statement that you saw, on your return from posting a letter, that Marie's garage door was slightly open. As you had thought she was away, you were concerned and went to look."

"Yes, that is correct."

"You thought she was away because her gate was banging the night before. You went round to close it and there were no lights on in her house?"

"Yes."

After that, it was easy; the coroner read from her statement and she agreed it was correct. He then asked her if there was anything else she remembered or would like to add. There was nothing. Marie's parents were asked if they had any questions. They had none.

Details of Marie French's medical condition were read out. She'd been a reasonably healthy woman with no children.

She'd visited her doctor two months before her death and appeared to be suffering mild depression. He gave her advice and suggested she return if her condition didn't improve. He hadn't seen her again.

Details of the post mortem report were also read aloud by the coroner. Those revealed no serious medical condition. Her liver had indicated mild alcohol abuse. There was sufficient alcohol in her blood to have just put her over the legal limit for driving. She'd been wearing high heeled shoes. She'd received a significant injury to her head, consistent with falling from the step ladder. The injury alone would not have caused death, but would have been likely to render her unconscious. There was a puncture wound in her neck consistent with having fallen on to the bit of the drill that was in her hand. The drill was of the type that stopped working once the trigger was released and in good working order. Ms French had died in the early hours of Sunday morning as a result of massive blood loss.

Again, the parents were asked if they had any questions.

"Did she suffer? Did my girl suffer?" the mother asked.

"It seems most likely she was knocked unconscious by the fall and that she did not regain consciousness. I don't believe she would have felt any pain or been aware of what had happened to her."

Constable Martins was asked to step into the witness box and take the oath. The policewoman preferred to stand rather than sit, but otherwise there was no difference from when Mavis gave evidence. The coroner simply confirmed key points from her report. Mavis smiled when she heard that the neighbour who'd discovered the body had acted properly by promptly calling the police and had provided a clear statement. Mavis had acted properly; it was good this was recognised.

Marie's parents were asked if they'd been in regular contact with their daughter.

"We spoke often on the telephone, at least once a week," the father said.

"When did you last see her?"

"She came to us for Christmas and stayed for a couple of days."

"And did she seem her usual self then?"

"Yes," the father said.

"Yes," agreed the mother. "We did notice she seemed to be drinking more than usual though, didn't we?"

Her husband nodded in agreement.

"Was it unusual for her to drink alcohol?"

"No, but she didn't always have so much."

"I see. And when you last spoke to Marie on the telephone, did she seem much as usual?"

"She seemed quite happy," the father said. "She said she was sticking to her New Year's resolutions. She'd told us she wasn't going to sit around waiting for a man to make her happy, something like that. She'd said she was going to try for promotion at work and she'd get on and do things herself. She wouldn't wait for the satellite man either. She'd bought that dish and reckoned she was quite capable of putting it up herself."

"Do you know why she did not have the dish fitted by the company who supplied it?"

The father answered. "They came to do it, but the man's drill wouldn't work. Said he couldn't use hers because of health and safety."

"Why didn't she wait?" the mother cried. Her husband comforted her.

The coroner waited a few moments.

"Thank you. I know this is distressing for you, but I must ask these questions."

"We understand," the father said.

"When she spoke of a man, did you gain the impression that she was referring to a particular person?"

"Yes. Norman Merlin; her ex-husband," the mother said.

Mavis must have heard the name wrong.

The mother continued, "There'd been some talk of them getting back together. She didn't say much to us as she knew we weren't happy about it. He'd treated her badly when they was married, he'd messed her about with payments and things after they was divorced. We never liked him much, couldn't see why she'd want anything more to do with him."

Norman stepped into the witness box and read the oath. Mavis hadn't misheard. He confirmed he'd been married to Marie and had spoken to her a few days before her death. Norman denied any trouble between them since the divorce. He said he'd paid the sums agreed; they hadn't involved solicitors in the divorce proceedings and financial arrangements had been agreed informally. He'd kept to that agreement; but there was some confusion over shares bought, by him, in her name.

"We met to discuss this on a couple of occasions. The matter hadn't been resolved, but we were discussing the best way to sort things out."

"You did not argue?"

"Certainly not. We were on very good terms."

"Were you considering resuming your relationship?"

"I wasn't and I don't really think she was."

"I see. When did you last speak to her?"

"On the nineteenth. We went for a drink."

"And how did she seem?"

"Fine. She didn't stay long as she suddenly remembered an appointment and had to rush off."

"Did you visit her at home?"

"No, never."

That was probably true; Mavis had never seen him there.

"It is my belief that the death of Marie French was an accidental one," the coroner said.

"Must have been," said the father.

"It seems likely that the alcohol she consumed would have made it more likely she would fall from the ladder whilst performing a task that was unfamiliar to her. The newly acquired satellite and television equipment and the absence of any note make it seem unlikely that she intended to harm herself."

"She wouldn't have done that. Never," the father said.

"It is my duty to determine the reason for Marie's death. It is good that it accords with your own view. There is no evidence that another person was involved. Whilst it is possible that her life could have been saved had she been discovered the previous day, I do not believe that anyone can be blamed for this not happening. I shall register this death as an accident."

That was it; it was all over.

Norman followed Mavis out of court and persuaded her to come for a drink with him, 'to settle their nerves'. She felt more unsettled at learning Norman had been married to her neighbour than by the inquest.

"Norman, why did you not tell me you were married to her?"

"We divorced four years ago. I thought it would be distressing for you to talk about her as you'd found her. It was a shock to know it happened just after I'd seen her of course. I would have liked to have talked, made sure she hadn't suffered, but it seemed wrong to burden you with my concerns as well as your own."

How thoughtful he was. Mother had always told her of every worry, every pain; Norman wished to shield her from unpleasantness. She couldn't tell him she'd been unconcerned by the death. He'd been right to say nothing.

"Come on, Mavis. Let's have that drink and talk about something more pleasant."

As they reached Yates's bar, Janice and Sandra passed them on the opposite side of the road. Janice called out to Mavis. Mavis acknowledged them, feeling embarrassed to be seen going into a pub instead of returning to work. She was even more embarrassed to be seen with Norman, whom she'd learnt was divorced, after warning Janice to be careful with men.

"Friends of yours?" Norman asked.

Concerned Norman might expect to be introduced she replied, "Just some people from work."

"I must meet your friends at some point in time."

Mavis didn't reply.

Norman asked her what she would like to drink. Mavis didn't reply; she had to wash her hands before she could think about anything else. She felt unclean after spending time in the court room. When she returned from the toilets, he carried a pint of beer and a white wine, to a window table. She followed.

Mavis told him her boss, Nicola, had been very kind.

"She allowed me the time off work and said that I wasn't to rush back if I didn't feel up to it."

"Good. We can have lunch together then."

Norman explained he made his own appointments and didn't have to worry people might not like him to be absent.

Mavis mentioned Sandra seemed to be jealous Mavis had been permitted time off. "She made it sound as though I shall be finding bodies and giving evidence on a regular basis, which is ridiculous."

"Tap a plank," Norman advised. "You never know what will happen."

"Tap a plank?"

"Oh, that's what my daughter says; it means touch wood."

Mavis said, "I did not know Marie French had a daughter, it was not mentioned at the inquest."

"No, as far as I know she didn't. Louise is the daughter of my first wife."

Another ex wife? Where was she now? When Mavis went home, she felt all she was learning about Norman, was how little she knew of him.

Chapter 19

The morning before her next art class, Mavis had to look away for a moment as she pulled open the curtains to admit the bright sunshine. She blinked before gazing with pleasure at the rich colours in her garden. The grey misery of winter was over. Spring had arrived.

'You can't have a rainbow without the rain,' cautioned her calendar. Mavis didn't need the pretty colours of the rainbow to lift her spirits. She had her garden, the sunshine and her class. It would be good to see her new friends again and she was looking forward to improving her painting and drawing technique.

Nearly every class member returned for the second term. There was one new man. He was very dark. Mavis studied the colour and texture of his skin. What would it be like to paint him? Perhaps she would find out. Last term the class had voted to concentrate on still life and landscapes. Mr Bittern had promised to continue with those and to introduce them to portraits in the spring term.

"I'll arrange for a model, but first you'll practise on each other," he'd said.

If she had a choice, Mavis would choose to paint the new man. Looking at him, she thought of bright, bold paintings from the Caribbean. He took a seat near to Mavis and looked around.

"Don't worry, we were all new last term, so we know how you feel," Jenny said. "You'll soon get the hang of things."

"Thank you, I'm sure I shall. Actually, I was looking for my friend Angela. She recommended this course. She likes a laugh and said it was great fun."

"I don't remember anyone called Angela, do you?" Jenny said and looked enquiringly at her friends.

"Angela Nightingale?"

"You must mean Flo," Mavis said. "A colourful lady, with a distinct sense of humour?"

The new student laughed loudly, he laughed not just with his voice and face, but his entire body. Mavis smiled, it felt good to have caused such amusement. No wonder Flo was keen to practise her jokes; she doubted anyone could resist attempting to make the man smile.

"That's right, we use her real name at work, I'd forgotten she usually calls herself Flo elsewhere." He held his hand out to Mavis, "Robert Thursday."

Mavis shook his hand, as did Jenny and Vera.

"Pleased to meet you," Vera said.

"Well, well! If it isn't Mr Thursday," said Flo as she walked in. "Am I late or are you a day early?"

Robert's face suggested he'd heard that one before, but he didn't seem to mind.

"Don't tell me," Flo continued, "I know I'm late. Sorry about that. Just been having a barney with the Tate Modern. Said they wanted to put up me picture, then it turned out it was the rag I clean me brushes with they wanted."

"I hope you haven't sold them your homework before we've had a chance to see it?" Mr Bittern teased.

Mavis guessed the woman would soon think of an improbable story to explain why she'd arrived empty handed. Tim didn't wait to hear it; he took the register and began the lesson. Soon they were all dutifully sketching vaguely face shaped marks into their books, according to the proportions Mr Bittern noted on his board.

"Robert, I don't know if Flo has mentioned the trip to London, but you are very welcome to join us," Tim said during the break. "I'll be travelling on the train that leaves Portsmouth Harbour at nine forty seven. I'll be joining at Havant."

Mr Bittern had printed train timetables from the internet and he handed them round.

Once they'd got used to positioning the eyes a third of the way down the face and knew where to draw ears in relation to the mouth, Tim decided they could try to draw a real face.

"You can start on me. Don't worry, I won't mind if you give me a big nose or a squint," he assured them.

Leo produced the best portrait. It honestly did look very like the teacher. Most of the others got one or two features something like right. Although no one said so, Mavis could see neither she nor Jenny had any aptitude for portraits. Vera's attempt did look like a person, but it could have been anyone. Robert's drawing was really a caricature, the features were not in the correct proportions, but the expression on the face was clearly that of Tim Bittern.

"You have all done very well for a first attempt," Tim said. He discussed each drawing in turn and found something positive to say in each case. He offered suggestions for improvement.

"How much drawing have you done before?" he asked Robert.

"I haven't. I guess that shows?"

"So does your talent," Leo told him. "I really think he's got something there, don't you?"

"Indeed," Tim agreed.

"Well thanks," Robert said. He looked uncomfortable.

"Practise, that's my advice," Leo said.

"I will, thanks."

"Is that our homework?" Mavis asked.

"It could be, if that's what you'd like to do?"

"I think I would prefer to continue with landscapes."

"That's fine. That's what I intended. Remember those seascapes we did on the first lesson? Well, I'd like you to have another go. Robert, these were really simply a line of colour to mark the horizon."

"I have mine here," Geoff the quiet man said. He briefly held it up for Robert to see.

"Thanks. Think I get the idea."

Mr Bittern continued, "Think about the weather. Is it hot or cold, stormy or calm? Try to make this clear in the picture. Don't worry so much about a real location, although you can use one if you like, but get the feelings in. Make the viewer experience that weather. Will they want to put on a bikini or a Sou'wester? If you'd prefer to try a portrait then do. Paint or draw the person looking out to sea. Show us if they are happy or bored, cold, sunbathing. Whatever you like."

Mavis was reminded of the painting Jenny had done of Southsea beach.

"The figures in that were quite accurate, Jenny. It surprises me that your portrait today was, er, less so."

"Don't tell on me?" Jenny whispered.

"What do you mean?" Vera asked moving closer.

"I cheated. I traced it from a postcard."

Vera laughed and slapped her hand on the desk. "Oh Jenny, you're funny."

"You must think I'm terrible?"

"No, just enterprising. I wouldn't have thought of that," Vera said.

Mavis shook her head. Jenny had cheated; yet it didn't seem to matter.

Vera was very pleased to accept the invitation to look at Mavis's garden.

"I'll come tomorrow; if that's convenient?"

Mavis agreed. She would have preferred more notice, but if she put Vera off, when would she come? It was good in a way. At short notice, Vera wouldn't expect an elaborate meal. Mavis could buy something on the way home from work. Fortunately, Mother had trained her to always keep the house tidy; apart from buying food, there was little to do to prepare for the visit.

"I better take your telephone number, in case I can't find the house."

Mavis gave her the number. She was pleased to see that rather than use a scrap of paper, Vera wrote her number in a proper address book.

"See you tomorrow, then," Vera called as they walked out of college.

Mavis no longer saw Norman on Wednesday evenings. It took her class longer to pack up their painting equipment and to clean brushes and tables than for his group to close their text books. He didn't wait around afterwards. Mavis wondered if he was avoiding Vera, or if he waited in the car park and gave her a lift home. It was not the sort of thing she could have asked, even if she'd been interested in the answer.

Thursday was another clear bright day. Vera would be able to see the garden looking its best. The evening sunlight would make the brightest colours luminous and reveal the full subtlety of the softer shades. There would be over an hour of daylight left, when her guest was due to arrive. That gave plenty of time to walk around the garden.

'You can't have your cake and eat it', was the phrase on her calendar. Silly; no one would want a cake they couldn't eat, that would be no better than no cake at all. Did people actually think before writing such nonsense? Mavis needed more than a slice of cake for Vera's supper. What would be suitable? It had been a long time since Mavis had cooked for anyone except Mother and towards the end, there'd been little variety. Mother had been limited in what she could eat. She would ask at work for advice.

"I have a friend coming to supper tonight," she mentioned as casually as she could.

"That's nice; I hope he's good looking?" Janice said.

"It's a lady from my art class."

"Oh, well that's nice too," Lucy said.

"I'm not sure what to provide for the meal."

"Maybe you'd better get a selection of things, in case she doesn't eat something." Nicola suggested.

Lucy asked, "What would you normally have?"

"Bread and soup, perhaps salad."

"That would work. If you had a choice of soup, you could heat up which one she liked. Then have everything separate for the salad and she can just pick what she likes," Lucy said.

"That's a good idea and anything left will be tomorrow's meal," Mavis said.

"They've got a good selection of sliced meat at Tesco," Lucy said.

"Good pâté too," Nicola said.

Mavis bought the food at lunchtime. Lucy and Nicola had been correct, a wide choice was available. Mavis wasn't sure what salami and haslet were, but was interested to find out. Pickle was added to the basket too; anything not so good could be disguised in sandwiches for work. She'd never tried pâté, but as Nicola mentioned it, she bought small pieces of two different types. Intrigued by a cut 'n' grow salad she bought that too. The fresh breads smelt wonderful. She bought another loaf containing sunflower seeds. One loaf, labelled 'tiger bread', had an attractively marbled crust. It was too pretty to resist. Should she get wine, she wondered. No, she had no idea what to choose. Vera will be driving, so wine wouldn't be expected. What if Vera didn't drink tea? Mavis bought coffee; that seemed more daring than the unusual foods.

At home, she washed the best plates. Weeks had passed since she'd washed them last and years since they'd been used. She put food onto plates and covered them in cling film. What did people do before it was invented, she wondered. They couldn't have prepared anything in advance. They did; she remembered sandwiches prepared and draped with damp tea towels. How unhygienic!

Mavis checked her watch. Would Vera really come? Would she regret her ready acceptance? She might be disappointed with the garden; perhaps she would be expecting something large and impressive. Mavis shouldn't have invited her, but it was too late.

The doorbell rang, precisely on time. Vera handed Mavis something covered in silver foil.

"I didn't like to come empty handed. Normally I'd bring flowers, but that seemed a bit silly today, so I've brought a cake."

"Oh, thank you. Please, come in."

There was not enough room in the fridge for the cake.

"It'll be all right on the side for a bit, I only made it this afternoon, so it's nice and fresh."

The cake looked well wrapped, the edges folded over tightly and the foil extending under the plate.

"Would you like a cup of tea? Or shall we look at the garden first?" Mavis asked.

"Yes, let's see those flowers of yours while it's still light."

Mavis unlocked the back door and opened it for Vera.

"Oh my, it's really lovely. What a lot you've packed in. Looks just like the gardens you see at Chelsea. I don't mean the silly modern ones, the proper ones with lots of flowers. I always thought they were too good to be true, but …"

"Thank you. I do spend quite a lot of time in the garden."

"I never had much time for gardening and then when my late husband became ill we moved into the flat. Funny thing is that's when we started watching the gardening programmes on telly. I hadn't realised how many different plants there were. I've noticed different flowers of course, but just thought of them as all the same except different sizes and colours."

"I expect you know some varieties?"

"You'd think that Alan Titchmarsh would have taught me something wouldn't you? Hmm, let's see. Those must be daffodils I think?"

"Yes, that's right. Tête á Tête. The ones in that corner with the orange trumpets are Jetfire, and those cream ones are WP Milner."

"Crikey, you do know a lot about them."

"I do have an advantage; I chose them all, so I know them well."

"What are those dark purple ones? They look just like the hyacinths you can buy in bowls at Christmas. I always get some; for the scent."

"Smell them."

Vera bent as low as she could and breathed deeply.

"They are. They're hyacinths. I'm not so bad at this as I thought then. Those big bowl shaped ones, are they tulips?"

"Yes, Purple Prince."

"No, I meant the white ones, behind."

"You're right, they're tulips too. That one is White Emperor. I'm especially pleased with my tulips this year. I planted quite a lot of new ones last autumn."

"Is that another one?"

"Yes, Shirley and those small ones are Persian Pearl."

"Good name for it, it really does look exotic and jewel like."

They walked slowly around the garden. Vera asked Mavis the name of every flower that caught her eye. Mavis cheerfully answered every question.

"Now how about that cup of tea?" Vera asked when it grew too dark to distinguish the colours.

Vera took her coat and her shoes off, before asking if she could wash her hands. Mavis started to remove food from her fridge and take it into the dining room.

"I'd love to paint some of those tulips, they're just superb," Vera said as she helped Mavis carry in the food.

"You'll have to do it soon. They go over quite quickly," Mavis said.

"Do you think we'd get into trouble from Sir if we did the wrong homework?"

"Perhaps we could claim they were flower portraits?" Mavis suggested.

"I think we would get away with that," Vera agreed laughing. "How about if I come on Sunday? We could pick a vase of tulips, I could take us out to lunch somewhere then we can both have a go at painting them. That's if you'd like?"

"I would like that very much."

Vera unwrapped her cake. When Mavis saw her fold the foil instead of screwing it into a ball, she knew the cake would be all right to eat. When she smelt the sweet, rich aroma, she knew it would be better than all right.

"What a lot of interesting things you've got for me to try," Vera said as they sat down.

"I wasn't sure what you would like."

As Vera selected meat and salad, Mavis realised she'd forgotten the soup. It didn't matter, there was enough without.

They chatted as they ate. Mavis was surprised how easy it was to talk about personal matters with Vera.

"What's that?" Vera asked gesturing to the plate of meat. "Corned beef?"

"Something called haslet."

Vera helped herself to a slice. "Do you know I still only eat the foods my husband liked? I can't seem to get out the habit of buying and cooking the same things," Vera said.

"I know what you mean. I bought coffee for the first time today. It seemed almost wrong."

"Oh don't worry about what seems wrong, just what actually is wrong."

"Sometimes, it's difficult to know."

"True." Vera said "I've made some mistakes. I rushed into trying to make up for lost time after my husband died. I tried too hard to make friends and scared some people off and gave completely the wrong impression to others."

After cutting a generous piece of duck and orange pâté, Vera confided her husband had been ill for years. Her time had been taken up with nursing him; she'd made no friends after they moved. She spread the pâté onto a chunk of tiger bread as she spoke.

"Once he was dead, I didn't really know what to do with myself."

"I experienced a similar situation with Mother. She was ill too. Towards the end, I spent a great deal of time with her. She didn't like me to be away from her. After her death, I felt such terrible loneliness."

Vera nodded. "You feel you'll never be cheerful again, don't you?"

"I felt there was nothing but unhappiness. I wanted to die, I tried to …"

"Oh, Mavis that's awful." Vera reached over the table and squeezed Mavis's arm. "I was never as bad as that, but I haven't picked myself up so well since."

"I don't know what you mean?"

"Well, I've just carried on the same, except without Doug. You got training and then a job. That was brave."

Mavis said, "I had no choice."

"Yes you did. Some people would have relied on benefits."

"I prefer to work."

"Of course you do. You're a sensible woman, Mavis."

After Vera had left, Mavis stood facing her now dark garden, seeing nothing but her own face reflected in the glass. She smiled; Vera admired her.

'Look before you leap,' was on her calendar, Friday morning. Mavis had almost done that once. She'd looked over the edge of the Round Tower; but not leapt to her death. Hastiness then would have been a mistake, but Mavis was tired of being cautious. Maybe she should try leaping instead of just looking; leap into life, not death. There were so many things she'd like to do. Norman had suggested the theatre. It had never before occurred to her to go, but there was no reason why she shouldn't. The cinema too, and looking round stately homes and visiting gardens and who knew, maybe even going on a holiday? All those things she'd thought of, but never done. She would start doing them. Maybe Vera would come with her? Mavis was sure she would. Only last night, she'd enthused over the art galleries they'd see in London.

"What a shame we won't have time to visit the museums and cathedrals," she'd said.

They could go on other weekends, it would soon be summer. It needn't be too expensive; museums were free and so were other attractions.

Mavis made her lunchtime sandwiches from leftover haslet and spicy pickle. She picked a few leaves from the tub of salad leaves growing on her window sill, wrapping them separately to ensure they didn't make the bread soggy. In a plastic tub, she placed a large wedge of Vera's delicious cake. She'd share it with her colleagues. Vera wouldn't mind. She'd mentioned that a whole cake was far too much for one person and they'd eaten very little of it yesterday.

There remained enough pâté, salad and tiger bread for Mavis to prepare an ample supper. It'd seemed extravagant buying the different items, but she'd made three meals and there was still some left. There were many things she'd never tasted; curry, Chinese food, pizza. She must work up the courage to try more. Despite her recent experiments, the worst she'd faced was a bland quiche and that had been perfectly edible. Even if one or two items were so unappetising she couldn't eat them, would that be such a problem? The money spent would be worth it for the experience, and she might be able to give it to the birds. Perhaps she could take a cookery course? A good idea if she might be entertaining guests regularly. The cost of eating out was high, she felt more relaxed at home and, more importantly, she would know everything was properly clean.

Mavis rang Linda. Her cousin had tried to help her make a fresh start after Mother died. Mavis wanted to tell her she'd found the courage to begin living her own life.

"You deserve a bit of fun, Mavis. Everyone deserves some fun."

"It doesn't sound as if you're having fun from the way you said that," Mavis said.

"Oh, I'm all right. I just feel a bit taken for granted. The kids expect me to baby-sit at the drop of a hat. They think, because I have no job now, that I have no life. Trouble is they're right. Phil's not much better, as long as there are clean clothes to put on for golf and a meal waiting after his game he doesn't seem to notice me."

"Oh dear. I'm just as bad; I ring up for advice but never ask how you are. You always seem so cheerful, I assumed you were happy," Mavis said.

"I am really. I could just do with a change."

"Come and stay with me. We could go out somewhere and have some fun."

"My, Mavis, you have changed. Going out with men, gadding off to London, planning house parties."

"I don't know about a party, but we could have a nice meal, look at gardens, things like that. You have done a lot for me since Mother died. I value your support and would like to do something for you."

"That's nice of you."

"I did invite you before, but not for your benefit, it was because it suited me. Please come."

"I'd love to. I've already promised to do something next week, but I'm not yet committed to anything the week after. Is that any good for you?"

"Perfect. I will find out what we can do and let you know."

"Deal; now tell me about your man friend."

"He is kind and generous. He brought me flowers the day after my neighbour was killed, just to cheer me up."

"That was sweet of him. How did he hear about it?"

"He said he heard about it on the news. I hadn't thought of that, what a terrible shock it must have been for him."

"For him, why?"

"He used to be married to her."

"Crikey Mavis, that's a coincidence isn't it?"

"I was surprised to see him at the inquest."

"I didn't know ex-husbands had to turn up."

"I think it was just because he'd seen her a few days beforehand."

"He didn't push her did he?" Linda asked.

"No, no. It wasn't at her house. They went for a drink to talk about money, I think."

"Hmm and now he's taking you out. You'd better make sure you pay half."

"I think you're teasing me, Linda. Norman is not like that. I told you he's very generous. He always was."

"Always? I thought you'd just met him, at your art class?"

"That's where I saw him again yes. I knew him before. You met him, but perhaps you don't remember? Norman Merlin?"

"Oh, yes. I remember him. I hadn't realised this was the same man. Has he changed much?"

"Yes, I suppose we both have."

"Yes. Sorry, Mavis, I'd better dash. I'll give you a call in a few days to make arrangements for my visit."

Mavis thought over Linda's remarks on paying her share. When Norman had taken her out, he'd paid for everything. She liked that, it seemed the proper thing; although she was aware Janice paid her share with her boyfriend. That appeared to be what people did now. Norman hadn't expected her to pay and she wouldn't know how to raise the subject. Perhaps she could offer to cook him a meal?

Chapter 20

On the day of the trip to London, Mavis opened her curtains to let in the hazy sunlight. The misty clouds would soon clear; it would be a good day.

After checking her bag was packed with everything she needed and nothing else, she placed it by the front door. Without her packed lunch, library book and dictionary it felt very light. She prepared her breakfast. It would be a long and tiring day, a bowl of cereal might be insufficient to sustain her. Scrambled eggs on lightly buttered wholemeal toast were followed by orange juice and a small pot of apricot yoghurt.

As she walked to the bus stop, Mavis remembered her calendar. She hadn't read the quotation after hastily removing the old sheet. She didn't pause to wonder what it had said; she had more interesting things on her mind.

Perhaps she would see the boy. When she thought they were going to go by coach, he'd mentioned it. He'd said he fancied a day out in London, might see if there was a spare seat. He had a friend, in the college office, who'd do him a favour if he smiled nicely. He wasn't on the bus or ferry and she didn't see him on the train.

Mavis met Vera at Portsmouth Harbour station. They saw a small group waiting outside the station and wondered if they were from the other class. When Norman arrived, their guess was proved to be correct. He introduced both women to the members of his class. Jenny and several others joined the train at Portsmouth and Southsea station. A fuss was made over finding friends and saving seats for those yet to join. More people, including Norman's teacher and Robert Thursday, got on at Fratton.

Robert looked unsure where he should sit.

"There is a space here," Mavis said as she moved her bag.

"Thanks."

"Is Flo coming?" Jenny asked.

"Doesn't look like it," Robert said. "She wasn't sure; I think it depended on her daughter."

Mr Bittern joined at Havant.

"I'm glad so many of you could make it. I don't know if people have made their own arrangements, but I thought it might be nice to go to the National first, then after lunch there's the choice of the Tate Modern, National Portrait or a museum or something else if anyone's had too much art."

Norman pointed out it would be easy for people to get lost. Tim said although it wasn't an official college trip, he'd be happy to act as a point of contact for anyone who became separated and wanted to find the others.

"Of course, if anyone wants to go off and do their own thing, then that's up to them. I won't be checking up on people, so feel free to go shopping or whatever if you've had enough art for one day."

He gave his class members his mobile number. The other teacher did the same for his group. Mavis had Norman's number written in her note book, she added Tim's.

"Do you have plans for lunch?" Robert asked.

"I've brought sandwiches," Vera said. "London prices are often ridiculously high. It's a nice day; I thought we'd enjoy a picnic in a park, or by the river."

"Oh, I didn't think of bringing anything," Jenny said. "A picnic sounds fun though. Perhaps I could buy sandwiches somewhere?"

"Yes, we'll find you something, I'm sure," Vera said.

Mavis hadn't invited Vera to lunch with herself and Norman. She hadn't felt it was her place to do so. She thought Norman would have done that, but no. He'd said she'd misinterpreted his friendship before, perhaps he hadn't liked to, for fear of encouraging her. Vera was assuming Mavis would join her and Jenny. She was trying to think of a suitable remark, when a woman opposite leant over.

"Excuse me, but Sally and I have brought our lunch too. Could we join you?"

"Yes, of course," Vera said. "How about you?" she asked Robert.

"I've got some vouchers for half priced meals and a free drink at Pizza Hut, that's why I asked. If anyone would like one?" He looked around.

"Yes please, if you have a spare," a man from Norman's class said.

"Plenty."

"Might I be so bold as to request that I join your jolly little party?" Leo asked.

"Please do," Robert replied, grinning.

Robert soon had a group of people arranging to eat with him.

Norman, who sat immediately behind Mavis, said, "Just you and I for the restaurant then?"

Mavis enjoyed the journey. Discussing all they'd see and do was exciting. Robert Thursday was an amusing companion. When he saw Mavis was interested in the glimpses of the passing gardens, he pointed out incongruous items to her.

"Was that a train carriage?" he asked. "Did you see that polar bear?"

She'd seen something she'd guessed was an artificial snowman. Mavis joined in, looking for unusual items and guessing at their purpose.

"I'm almost sure I saw a giraffe."

"You did," Robert assured her. "It looked like it might have been one of those children's slides they sometimes have in pub gardens."

As they neared Waterloo, Mavis saw the London Eye. She'd heard you could see the whole of London from there. As exciting an idea as peeking into people's lives on the train, but slower; she could take in details, have time to consider what she saw.

"Is that the London Eye?" Jenny asked.

"It's bigger than I imagined," Vera said. "I'm not sure I'd want to go up there."

"I wouldn't. I don't like heights," Jenny said.

The entire group went together towards the National Gallery.

"At the risk of sounding like a teacher," Tim said. "I have a suggestion. Before we go to the gallery, there's something I'd like you to see."

Everyone agreed to a short detour.

Tim led them, along the embankment, to the sculptures commemorating the Battle of Britain. Mavis and many of the others, ran their hands over the aeroplanes, faces in gasmasks, the women loading munitions, the airmen running out into an uncertain future, the names of the dead.

"There's something else," Tim said. They walked on for a hundred yards and he indicated the Houses of Parliament.

"It really is a magnificent building," Leo said.

"Art isn't always a pretty picture in a frame; I just wanted to show you that."

Jenny clung on to Vera from the moment they alighted in Waterloo until they were inside the National Gallery.

It was as Mavis had hoped, they shared ideas and opinions. Part of the time, she walked and talked with Vera and Jenny; sometimes, Norman was by her side.

Vera and Mavis particularly admired Van Gogh's *Sunflowers*.

"I've seen it on posters, but they just don't do justice to the real thing," Vera said. "How I'd love to paint something so incredibly alive as that."

"It's very pretty," was Jenny's impression.

Mavis approached the picture. "I admire the way he's used his brush strokes, the texture of the paint suggests the formation of the seeds, do you see?"

Her two friends came closer.

"That's very clever. You could try that with your acrylics Mavis, I'm sure you could do it," Jenny said.

"I shall certainly try."

Mavis moved away from the painting until she could see it in its entirety. She knew the texture of the flowers would be felt by her finger tips if she ran them over the surface. She felt she'd also feel the warmth of the sun as it streamed through Van Gogh's window. If she waited long enough she would surely see a petal drop or hear a bee fly in to collect pollen. There was no scent from the flowers. The leaves and stems would smell though. If she were to reach out and crush one in her hand, the fresh vegetable aroma of the growing plants would be released on her skin. Mavis rubbed her palms together as though the rough stalks had scratched her hands.

She moved closer again, to look at the colours. At first glance, they seemed crude, daubed on with no subtlety. Careful study revealed progressive blending of shades. Yellow on brighter yellow, streaked with cream, enriched with red.

"There you are, Mavis," Jenny said.

"Yes."

"We thought we'd lost you."

What did Jenny mean?

"We'd gone on and when I looked back we couldn't see you."

"I was here."

"Come along, Mavis," Vera said. "We'll have to move quickly if we hope to see everything. Jenny wishes to see Constable's *Hay Wain*, we were looking for it."

"Mum has a print; she'll be thrilled if I can tell her I've seen the real thing."

They were unable to locate it. They asked Tim.

"Not all the paintings are on display at any one time. Some are lent out to other galleries; some are put in storage to await their turn for display. The collection is vast; there's not room for all of them to go on show. Have you seen Turner's *The Fighting Temeraire*? It's been voted as the greatest painting in the country."

"Is that anything to do with the sports ground?" Jenny asked.

"I'm sure it must be," Mavis said. "The Royal Navy name establishments after famous ships. I should like to see it; I walk past HMS Temeraire every day on my way to work."

"Oh yes, let's. My mum worked there for a while, in the office. She'll be chuffed if I can tell her about that," Jenny answered.

Mavis caught Vera's look as they both smiled at Jenny. She was so easily distracted and as easily pleased. Her cheerful enthusiasm was infectious.

"I'll come with you, if I may, to hear what you think of it," Tim said as he led the way.

"I'd say the fight has gone out of it," was Vera's opinion.

"It seems almost a ghost ship," Mavis added.

"What a beautiful sunset," Jenny said. "Beautiful, but sort of sad."

"So, come on, Tim," Vera demanded. "What do you think, is that really the greatest painting, or did it win the vote because of what it represents?"

"Maybe both, you see it is a ghost ship in a way. This is the scene more than thirty years after the battle of Trafalgar. Temeraire was being towed away for scrap. Turner deliberately pictured her as a ghostly shape in contrast to the more solid tug. The sunset is to represent the sun setting on that particular age of warship."

They all looked again at the painting.

"It works," Vera decided. No one contradicted her.

They divided into groups for lunch. Jenny clung on to Vera's arm, as those who planned to picnic, walked away from the museum. Norman offered his arm to Mavis. Mavis didn't take it; she moved her shoulder bag so it hung between them.

She said, "I understand Jenny's concern. I too feel as though I might be swept away with the crowds."

"Well, just in case we should get separated, I'll give you directions. We're going down here," Norman led her down the steps into Charing Cross station. "We'll go on the Northern line to Tottenham Court Road, then on the Central line to St Paul's. If you lose sight of me, go there and I'll find you."

They put their tickets into the barriers. Mavis's didn't open. A member of staff came swiftly to her assistance, but not before Norman had walked forward a few paces. She hurried after him, people pushed between them. Mavis panicked, feeling she was being dragged along against her will. She made her way through the crowds into a space where she could stand still. After a few deep breaths, she felt calmer and began walking again. Norman had gone.

Mavis looked at the faces rushing by. She didn't know these people, what they wanted, where they were going. She thought of the weight of the earth, people, escalators and perhaps the Thames above her. She must look for the exit; get out. There were signs, there must be signs. She saw one for the Northern line. That was the one Norman had mentioned: she was going the right way. Then she saw and heard buskers; the music soothed her. She stopped to listen for a moment. They were good, one on a fiddle and one with a flute. She'd heard snatches of music, but hadn't realised it was from buskers. Mother would have called them filthy beggars and dragged her away. Mavis was no longer Mother's little girl; she was a grown woman travelling across London to have lunch with a man Mother hadn't approved of. She dropped a few coins into the music case, open in front of the men. The one playing the flute winked at her. She continued walking.

At Tottenham Court, she followed signs for the Central line, arriving at the platform just as a train did. Passengers got off, their positions quickly filled by those on the platform. Mavis saw Norman board and followed him into a busy carriage. She clutched a pole as the train began to move. She opened her mouth to speak. It wasn't Norman; just a man wearing a similar coat.

A map of the line was pasted high on the wall. Mavis studied it. She saw the station where she'd boarded and St Paul's where she'd alight. There were two stops between them. Holburn was next. They reached Oxford Circus.

"Oh!" She'd gone wrong somewhere.

A woman, well covered with black trousers, long tunic and headscarf, asked, "Is something wrong?"

"I think I must be on the wrong train. I wish to reach St Paul's."

"Ah, you're going the wrong way. Never mind, get off at Bond Street and go back the other way."

"Thank you."

"And if you get lost again, head for an exit and ask one of the guards there. They'll help you."

When Mavis reached St Paul's, she stood near the exit trying to work out where she should go. Had Norman meant to wait at the station, or the cathedral? She'd wait where she was; he'd said he'd find her. The station entrance made a draughty, uncomfortable place to wait. She checked her watch; if he didn't find her soon it would be too late for lunch. She was cold and hungry.

"Found you at last, Mavis," Norman called as he strode towards her. "Are you ready to eat?"

She nodded.

"I wonder if you can guess where we're going?"

"No. You said St Paul's, but of course we can't eat in the cathedral."

"Oh but we can. In the crypt."

"The crypt?"

"Yes. Under the cathedral, where Nelson and Winston Churchill's tombs are, there's a café and a refectory. I've heard the food is very good there."

Mavis wondered if he were teasing her. He wasn't. They walked to the cathedral, down the steps, past stone statues of angels and carved wooden pews and into a large lobby. Norman showed her to the intricate gates of the crypt, erected in memory of Winston Churchill. He told her the tombs were behind it and then excused himself. Whilst he visited the toilet, Mavis read the information board. When Norman returned, she made no mention of what she had learnt. He guided her to the refectory and selected a table.

Before Norman had a chance to suggest the roast chicken, Mavis requested the fisherman's pie. He ordered a glass of wine for each of them. As they ate, Norman told her about the cathedral's history. Mavis enjoyed her food. Crispy potatoes topped a rich sauce, containing chunks of salmon, smoked haddock and succulent prawns.

"That was delicious, Norman. Thank you."

"Would you like dessert, another glass of wine?"

"No thank you, not just yet."

He smiled. "Maybe later?"

Norman continued talking about places of interest in London, until they were the only diners left and the tables around them had been cleared.

"So, Mavis, what would you like to do now?"

"Are we not meeting the others in the Portrait Gallery?"

"Yes of course, if you wish. I thought perhaps we could do something else."

"Will there be time? I imagine we will be the last to arrive."

"We could go afterwards. There is no need to rush straight back home."

"I suppose not."

"There are so many other things to see. It would be a shame to visit just two galleries and waste the opportunity. We could stay into the evening, perhaps have another meal."

"The Tate Modern is said to be interesting," Mavis said, without enthusiasm.

"Yes, although I feel there are only so many paintings I can look at in one day. We can go anywhere you like, do whatever you want."

Could that be right? If she named her wish, it would be granted.

"Norman, I should like to go on the London Eye."

Norman said nothing. She looked at him.

"What a lovely idea, Mavis. We'll see the lights of London from the sky."

As they travelled back to Trafalgar Square, Mavis accepted Norman's offered arm and they didn't become separated again.

Vera and Jenny were not in the Portrait Gallery.

"Perhaps they've already been and gone?" Norman suggested.

"I suppose they may have done. It's not very warm so they wouldn't have lingered over their picnic."

"Your teacher isn't here either, Mavis. I expect he's taken them somewhere," Norman said.

"Yes, that seems likely."

Jenny would be all right; Vera would look after her.

Mavis admired the skill of the portrait painters, but did not enjoy the pictures as much the ones she'd seen in the morning.

"Pictures of people are only interesting if you know the person. Otherwise, it's difficult to judge if the artist has captured their personality," she said.

"Does that apply to landscapes too; do you prefer those where you recognise the view?" Norman asked.

"No, it's not the same. With a place, it can mean different things to different people. With people, it's different. It doesn't matter how they're painted, or how you feel; good people are good, bad people are bad."

"Doesn't it depend on how they treat you? A person could have done something bad, but if they were good to you …"

"No, Norman."

They moved on to another painting and then another, without speaking.

"Would you prefer to return to the National?" Norman asked.

"No, it was very interesting, but I agree; there are only so many pictures you can appreciate at one time."

When they reached the London Eye, they saw people queuing.

"I'll see how long the wait is," Norman said.

This time Mavis didn't have to stand for long, alone, in the cold wind, before he returned.

"The wait will be quite some time; perhaps we should take a river cruise instead? Most of the places of interest have been built along the Thames, so we will still see most of the city."

She agreed and they walked over Westminster Bridge and on until they found a landing stage.

Mavis enjoyed the trip and asked Norman to point out the famous landmarks. After the hour long boat ride, she agreed she'd seen the entire City. She felt as though she'd walked around every place of interest.

"Supper?" Norman asked as they stepped out of the boat.

"I'm not terribly hungry; I would like a drink though."

"Me too."

"Tea or coffee, I mean, not wine."

"You shall have whatever you like," Norman assured her.

After a clotted cream tea, complete with fresh strawberries, Mavis felt ready to go home.

They reached Waterloo a few minutes before the Portsmouth train was due to leave. Mavis relaxed into the seat; she need do nothing more than sit still for an hour and a half. Her feet didn't hurt, but she felt tired all over. Even the muscles of her cheeks were sore from holding her face in a near permanent smile.

"Had a good day?" Norman asked.

"Very good. Thank you, Norman."

She couldn't help yawning.

"Tired?"

She nodded.

"Well, you just relax. I'll see you get safely home."

"Just as long as there is a ferry, I'll be fine."

"No, don't worry about that, I'll drive you. I don't want you have to catch the ferry on your own late at night and then hang about for the bus."

Catching the last bus would have meant she arrived home only an hour later than from her art classes. She could manage the journey well enough.

"Thank you." It would be warmer and more comfortable in Norman's car.

Norman put his arm around her shoulders. Mavis sat very still.

"Did you have a favourite painting?" Norman asked.

Mavis thought of *Sunflowers*. How could she explain her feelings for something that had impressed her so deeply?

"There were many I admired."

214

"I know what you mean. There were so many it was a job to take it all in. They are so much more impressive when you see them for real aren't they?"

"Yes, yes they are. I feel so privileged to have seen such works for myself."

"Privileged? I don't know about that. The amount of tax the government takes off us, it's only right we get something back for it. Don't you think so?"

Mavis didn't want to think of politics. She wanted to close her eyes and picture bold brushstrokes in burnt umber and yellow ochre.

"Did you see *The Fighting Temeraire*?" she asked.

"Yes, I did. That was an interesting work. I particularly liked the use of the setting sun as a representation of the end of a golden era."

Norman continued to talk about the paintings he'd seen and to give his opinion of their historic significance. Each time he paused to select another painting to describe, Mavis thought of a page in a guidebook being turned. She relaxed against Norman, allowing her head to rest on his shoulder. She murmured an agreement each time his voice rose and then stopped to indicate a question.

The night air as she walked, still sleepy, from the station to Norman's car felt as hard and cold as Mother's words. She was not with Mother, she was with Norman and he was holding the door open for her.

"I'll put the heater on, soon have you warm."

"Is this a different car, Norman?"

"It's a courtesy car," he told her. "Mine is in for repair, so the garage have loaned me this one"

"Oh dear, did you have an accident?" Mavis asked.

"No it wasn't an accident," Norman said.

What would the neighbours think, if she invited him in? Of course, Marie French was long past thinking anything and when alive hardly in a position to judge others. The other neighbours might wonder. Let them; if they had nothing more interesting than her business to consider, they would appreciate her providing an excuse for gossip. It had been a long day and he must still drive home, but it wasn't really late. Late to be getting the bus home, but not yet bedtime.

"I have coffee; would you like some?"

They sat together on her sofa. The same sofa they'd been on when Mother had come back and said those awful things. It felt awkward for a moment and then he asked to see her paintings. She took him into the dining room and spread out those he hadn't yet seen.

"Nothing like we've seen today," Mavis said.

"Well, no, but you are just learning. You wouldn't expect them to equal grand masters. I like them though," Norman said. "I like them much more than some of the modern ones, at least I can tell what yours are supposed to be."

A tactful, but honest, answer. She wouldn't have liked him to criticise and wouldn't have trusted lavish praise. Mother had been wrong about Norman; he was kind, generous and honest.

Chapter 21

Mavis still had half a weekend to enjoy. A whole day with Vera; picking flowers, talking, painting and eating. She'd eaten out more in the last few weeks than in the rest of her life, but not so often she wasn't looking forward to the pub lunch Vera had promised. They could have tea at home; she would buy cakes. It would be strange to shop on a Sunday, but the Co-op would be open. If other people shopped then, why shouldn't she? There wasn't time to lie in bed making plans; she got up, eager to start the day.

On Saturday, she had not stopped to read the quote after quickly and carelessly removing Friday's sheet. She read, 'Pride comes before a fall' and then tore off the page and folded it in four. Had she been proud yesterday? A little perhaps; of her ability to make her own way on the underground, after losing sight of Norman. There had been no fall though; the day had been thoroughly enjoyable.

'Home is where the heart is,' was Sunday's message. The house, once Mother's, was beginning to feel like Mavis's home. Mavis looked after the house and paid the bills; she'd done the work for Mother, now she did it for herself. Mavis didn't clean because she had to; she did it because she wanted her home to be nice. It was nice. Mavis hadn't considered if it was all right to invite Vera. Of course, it was all right for her to invite a friend to her home for the day, or her cousin for a weekend. Or a man, if she wished.

Mavis now often picked flowers to arrange in the house. Mother wouldn't have liked that, wouldn't have allowed it. Mother was no longer there. Mavis wasn't doing it to spite her dead mother or just because she could. She was doing it because she wanted to. Things had changed, Mavis had changed.

She tidied up and cleaned the crockery and glasses they would use. She didn't know which vase would be best; perhaps

Vera would like to choose? To ensure there was plenty of choice, Mavis washed and polished them all so they were ready for use. It must have been weeks since they were last cleaned, she could feel particles of dust on the surface of some. Mavis wondered why her mother, who couldn't bear the sight of flowers in the house, had owned so many vases. There were things about Mother she would never know. She'd heard people say they wished they'd talked to someone more in life, how they wished they'd asked questions. Mavis had no such regret; Mother would never have answered the questions.

Once the house was tidy, she cleaned the bird table and scrubbed the birdbath then replenished the food and water. She emptied the seeds and nuts from the hanging feeders, shaking them over the grass. Then she filled and re-hung them. After each item had been cleaned, she scrubbed her hands with a brush, ensuring no trace of dirt remained under her nails and in the cracks in her skin. E45 cream was applied. Her hands were still chapped and sore, despite her care to keep them clean and to dry them thoroughly.

She didn't know when the shops opened on a Sunday, probably later than usual. She had a cup of tea and then a stroll around the garden. There was no rush to buy the food; there would be little preparation required, other than to put the items on plates. Vera would excuse her whilst she did that, or perhaps would come into the kitchen and talk whilst she worked.

The weather had been calm and cool. The tulips Vera had admired during her brief glimpse on Thursday evening were still in perfect condition. There were later sorts still in bud. She'd allow Vera to make the choices. If Mavis was pleased with her own attempt to paint the flowers, she would repeat the process in a few weeks, with other flowers and different colour combinations. Would Vera want just tulips or prefer to add other things? Mavis couldn't decide what would be best. There were so many plants looking good. Any combination would be successful. Mavis always took care to ensure each plant in her garden worked well with its neighbours. For summer, that was a challenge. The multitude of blues and pinks competed with, rather than enhanced, each other. Mavis had studied each plant and thought carefully before making her purchases.

There were no such problems in spring. Although many of the colours were rich and bright, they seemed to work together to create a cheerful whole. Each colour added depth and emphasis to those beside it. The foliage too, lush and fresh, added life to the scene. However vivid a spring bloom it always looked good in her garden. Something to do with the light at that time of year and a reaction to the grey darkness of winter, her gardening books informed her.

At the Co-op, Mavis chose a selection of items. First, she picked out a chocolate sponge, the kind that could be sliced into wedges. She bought scones and clotted cream. There was a 'buy one get one free' promotion on jam, she selected both raspberry and strawberry. She added a pack of chocolate cup cakes and a Battenberg to her basket. There were far more cakes than the two women would consume in an afternoon, but they'd keep fresh sealed in plastic containers and placed in the fridge, for as long as it took Mavis to eat them.

The cakes were put away in cupboards, the cream in the fridge. She looked at her watch; quarter to eleven. Vera would be there any moment. Mavis walked around the house, ensuring everything was in order.

At eleven, Vera hadn't arrived. Mavis stood in the dining room, looking onto the street. She saw several cars approach, but none were Vera's. None stopped.

At quarter past, she hoped Vera hadn't had a problem with her car.

Twenty past. There must be a reason for Vera's absence. She wouldn't be so rude as to be so late. That loud woman, Flo, with the colourful dresses, always arrived late to art classes. Jenny had said perhaps she didn't finish work until late, or had a long journey. Mavis had said she thought it rude to arrive late and disrupt the others. Vera had agreed, saying Flo should organise her life better. Vera was not late unless an unforeseen problem arose; if Flo's problems arose every week then she should be predicting them.

Vera wouldn't be late without reason. Perhaps she wasn't coming. Perhaps she'd taken offence because Mavis had spent yesterday afternoon with Norman and not her? No, that didn't seem likely. Vera had been perfectly happy bossing Jenny and telling her what opinion to form of each painting. Mavis remembered Vera's words as they'd separated for lunch, "Enjoy your meal and we'll probably see you later. If not, have a good afternoon and journey back." That hadn't implied Mavis should be with them later in the day. She smiled to herself, recalling she'd done exactly as Vera ordered and had indeed enjoyed lunch and the afternoon. Vera hadn't said, "See you tomorrow." Did that mean anything? Probably not.

Was it possible Mavis had made a mistake and Vera wasn't coming today? She'd said eleven and mentioned that would give them time to pick flowers, have a meal at twelve and then paint. Vera had certainly said Sunday and had talked of a roast lunch, there was no mistaking the day, but could she have meant next week?

Half past eleven. Mavis knew then that Vera wouldn't come. There must have been a misunderstanding over the date for Vera had her telephone number and would surely have called otherwise. Mavis felt disappointed she wouldn't have a roast meal. She could, of course, walk to The Wyvern. The distance was no further than her morning journey to the bus stop, but although she could board a bus alone, she couldn't enter a pub and order a meal alone. Other women might, but Mavis didn't feel she could.

Ham and cheese were in the fridge. There was bread too; for the sandwiches in the week ahead. She didn't need a large lunch; she would indulge in an extravagant tea to compensate for the day's disappointments. A cheese or ham sandwich didn't appeal; could she make it more interesting? In the cupboard, she had a jar of pickle. She remembered Janice describing a toasty machine she'd bought. She'd mentioned putting in too much pickle. It had spurted out, red hot, as she bit into the sandwich. Mavis had been reminded of the panini she'd eaten in the Discovery Centre. Mavis didn't have a special machine. She did have a perfectly serviceable grill on her cooker. She'd make a sandwich with both cheese and ham, add a scrape of pickle and then toast it.

First though, she'd have her customary glass of sherry. The bottle and two glasses were in the dining room, ready to offer Vera a drink before lunch. As she went to fetch them, she saw the vases and the dining table draped with paper ready for painting. She must put everything away before lunch. What a shame, with no afternoon of painting she had little to do. She could still pick flowers and paint them. That would mean she couldn't have lunch at the dining room table.

Mavis looked at the table for a moment. She cleared the half where Vera would have worked. The flowers should be picked before lunch, to allow them to absorb water and settle into position before she began to paint. She could place the flowers on the other side and move them back into the centre once she'd eaten.

She picked a variety of different tulips, selecting carefully so as not to spoil the garden's display. She arranged them in her hand as she gathered them. It didn't take long for her to have enough for a vase of colour.

Mavis poured her sherry and sipped it whilst admiring the flowers. So many colours; not just in the various individuals, but in each petal. The flowers were very detailed, incredibly intricate. The textures varied. Each bloom reacted differently to the light; some reflected it, in others it shone through as though the blooms were lit from within. It would be a challenge to reproduce the effects, a challenge she was eager to begin.

The toasted sandwich smelt delicious. The cheese bubbled out the sides oozing onto the plate as she cut it into quarters. She carried the plate into the dining room and set it down near the bottle of sherry. She hesitated only a moment before refilling her glass. The meal was very pleasant.

After washing and drying her plate, she began to sketch the flowers. There were too many. It was difficult to clearly see all the shapes. Mavis filled another, simpler, vase and put in just five stems. Another sketch was begun. When she was happy with the rough outline, she began to paint. The colours were mixed and re-mixed to get them perfect. The flowers came to life as she added paint. Just as the real ones had expanded with the water and warmth of the house, those on her page expanded with the touch of her brush. They grew larger as she applied more colour. They changed from the original, reasonably accurate sketch. The shapes became more pronounced, the colours extreme. The petals on Maytime, already elegantly pointed, became stretched and twirled, not out of recognition, but away from reality. The true colour, a rich pink, was on her page even brighter. The blending of shades was less gradual, more dramatic. The Black Parrot became so convincingly feathered it might have fluttered its wings and risen from the vase. Shirley no longer blushed sweetly under a dusting of lilac freckles; she flaunted her speckled decorations. White Emperor and Purple Prince seemed on the verge of a duel to decide their supremacy. The one, glowing in regal majesty; the other, icily magnificent. The flowers she created were not identical to the ones she'd grown. They were beautiful. They were not growing, living things, but they were as alive as those whose roots still quested through the borders of her garden.

At last, Mavis felt she could do no more to improve her painting and stopped. The moment she'd done so she felt hungry. She tidied up and was surprised to find her empty sherry glass on the dining room table. She'd become so absorbed she hadn't noticed she'd drained and discarded the glass. Mavis had forgotten about Vera too. She must have meant she would visit next week. Mavis was pleased she didn't have Vera's telephone number, what a fool she would have looked had she called to ask why she hadn't arrived. She would have appeared too eager to develop the friendship; would have revealed her true feelings.

Chapter 22

Mavis chewed her breakfast cereal and pondered the words on her calendar. 'There's always more fish in the sea', that was usually the expression used when a relationship broke down, to suggest the broken hearted would find another lover. Most of them did she supposed. From what Linda had told her of her children, it was true. They seemed to have found new boyfriends every month until they'd met the men they'd married. Mavis hoped they wouldn't need to go fishing. The sea was no place to find love.

Linda would provide all the details of her family when she came. She'd probably bring photos too. All Mavis really knew of her cousin, was how she felt about her family. She'd been surprised to learn Linda wasn't happy. Silly to think Mavis could be the only one to feel that way.

"Lovely weather," Janice said at lunchtime. "It's a shame not to go out; do you need to go into town, Mavis?"

"No, I have my sandwiches."

"I've got my lunch too."

Mavis looked through the window. The sky was very blue, the tiny wisps of cloud simply emphasised the clear sky around them. As Janice said, it was far too nice to sit inside at their desks. She would like to take her lunch to the park, but it would be rude to leave Janice alone.

Janice said, "We could go for a walk, take our lunch down to the sea and have a sort of picnic and a wander round?"

Mavis remembered she'd planned to do that, go and look at the cathedral and other places of interest. There were still many places in Portsmouth she'd not visited.

223

"A good idea. I'd like that."

They were leaving when Sandra asked if they were going shopping.

"No, down towards the beach," said Janice.

"That sounds like fun," Sandra said.

Janice looked at Mavis, who nodded her head.

"Would you like to come with us?" Janice asked.

"I don't want to be in the way."

"We're just going for a walk. It's up to you," Janice said.

Sandra went with them. They walked down Cambridge Road towards the seafront in Old Portsmouth. They climbed up on the sea wall and looked out to the Isle of Wight.

"It's closer than I thought," Janice said as she opened her lunch box and squeezed a sachet of salad cream onto her salad.

"I don't know how far it is. A mile or so I suppose. It doesn't take long on the hovercraft," Sandra said.

"Eh? Oh, no, I meant the walk down here."

Sandra looked at her watch. "It's only quarter past twelve."

"Really? We should come down here in the summer. We'd easily get half an hour on the beach after we'd eaten lunch."

"Yes, Janice we should," Sandra agreed. "It's a shame to spend all day so close and then never come down here."

"I've often intended to walk down, or look in the cathedral or visit the parks," Mavis said.

"We will when it's warmer then," Janice said. She shivered.

"It is cold, despite the sunshine," Mavis said.

"Let's get moving then," Sandra suggested.

As they turned to leave, Janice indicated the ruined Garrison church.

"What's that? There's a sign outside."

They walked closer.

"The church is open. I've never seen inside," Mavis said.

"Neither have I," Sandra said.

224

"Nor me," Janice said. "We've got time for a quick look if you fancy it?"

They read a plaque that stated the church had been bombed in the war. The damage was obvious; half the church had no roof. More plaques announced the undamaged part was still used for special occasions. They admired the lovely stained glass windows. One had aeroplanes on it, could that be right? Yet another plaque informed them the original window had been damaged during the war and a replacement made to reflect that. They looked at the gothic mediaeval font cover; that too had a plaque to explain its history.

On the way back to the office, they were passed by Norman. He gave them a lift and was introduced. Mavis felt pleased to be the one introducing her friends to each other. When they returned, Sandra took painkillers. There was gentle teasing over Mavis's distinguished boyfriend. Nicola and Lucy wanted to know all the details. Janice described Norman, "Smart suit, nice hair, not at all bald. Neat moustache, very swish car."

"What sort?" Lucy asked.

"A Jaguar," said Mavis at the same time as Sandra said, "BMW 3 series with leather seats."

"Well, which? There's quite a difference," Lucy said.

"I expect Sandra is right, I know very little about cars."

"Obviously," said Sandra.

"I remember now. He told me his car is a Jaguar, but this is a different one."

Later, Nicola asked Mavis about Sandra.

"How does she seem to you?"

"Sometimes, she is a bit abrupt, but today she asked to come when we went for a walk and was quite pleasant."

"Oh, good. I've been worried about her."

"Why?" Mavis asked.

"Probably nothing."

On the way home, Mavis went to Lee-on-the-Solent library and borrowed a copy of Christopher Lloyd's, *Colour for Adventurous Gardeners*. She'd borrowed it last autumn and, along with other works by the same author, it had been the inspiration for her superb display of tulips. She wished the garden would retain its mid-spring glory for more than a month or two. This year, she would be braver and make more effort. She would buy more of Christopher Lloyd's books too. Occasionally, she looked in bookstores and the charity shops, but did nothing more. Perhaps if she asked, a shop could order them, or maybe Janice would show her how to look for them on the internet. She'd heard the girls in the office say you could buy anything that way and often at very reasonable prices.

She gazed at the vases of tulips as she drank her tea. She studied the paintings she'd done on Sunday. They were not good technically, but the flowers in the second one were quite pleasing. The vase wasn't right. It didn't look at all like clear glass with water in. It looked grey and wrong. Perhaps she could ask Tim for advice.

Mavis felt she'd made a better job of the vase in the preliminary sketch for the larger bunch of tulips. They were displayed in a china vase. Perhaps she should transfer the five stems to another vase and try that? She did. They looked much better, the plain white with its straight sides would be easier to draw and the simple shape didn't detract from the flowers. She was sure she could do an even better painting. Perhaps once she'd eaten she would try sketching it?

There was the gardening book too; she was keen to read it again. She wished to compare the words that had inspired her, with the effect she'd created and work out how to extend and improve it. She would read whilst her pie heated in the oven.

The ping of her timer was almost drowned out by the ringing of the doorbell. It was probably Norman. She'd tried to hint he should call first. She didn't like being taken for granted. She'd heard the advice Lucy gave Janice on the new boyfriend; to start as she meant to go on and not put up with treatment that would later annoy her.

Mavis switched off the oven and went to the door. Norman stood on her front step. Mavis had plans for her evening; she unlocked the door and told him so. He looked unhappy at the news. Mavis didn't feel the need to explain. She didn't wish to live her life at his convenience; neither did she wish to upset him.

"Perhaps we could do something together another day?" she suggested.

"Are you busy tomorrow?"

"No."

"I'll come and pick you up then, about seven?"

"I shall look forward to it."

He kissed her cheek and left.

Mavis carried out her plans for the evening. She was pleased with the new painting. She would take it to her evening class. Mavis wondered what Vera would say when she saw Mavis had done alone, what they were going to do together. She would explain she couldn't wait to start. They would still have the Sunday together exactly as planned and would benefit from Timothy Bittern's advice in light of her first efforts.

She read for longer than she intended. Her eyes felt heavy as she put the book on the shelf.

Mavis slept well and didn't wake until the alarm sounded. No banging gates or unpleasant dreams spoiled her rest. She wondered where Norman would take her that night. As he wasn't collecting her until seven, she would be eating later than her usual suppertime. She'd better pack herself a substantial lunch.

'You get nothing for free', she read as she buttered bread and sliced cheese. She put a packet of instant soup into the bag that held her lunchbox and added a wrapped apple. Her lunch was inexpensive, but not free.

The crumbled end of the loaf and a scoop of mixed seeds were put out for the birds. They didn't get something for nothing, it might appear that way but she gained great pleasure from watching them and felt as if they were her friends. It was her choice to feed them. They took what she freely gave; they didn't make demands.

At work, Mavis made the mid-morning drinks for her colleagues. Sandra looked up as she carried in the laden tray.

"St Vincent College just phoned for you. Rita someone? I couldn't understand very well."

"I don't know anyone named Rita."

"It was something about cancelling the visit on Saturday. I've written the number and name, I said you'd call back."

Sandra handed Mavis a note, 'Rita Lagopus' was printed, followed by the college's phone number.

Mavis rang back but Rita was on another call.

"Would you like to hold?"

Mavis waited.

"Hello, caller? Sorry, Ms Lagopus is still on her call. Would you like to continue holding?"

"No, thank you. I will call later."

She tried again after lunch. Rita Lagopus was unavailable.

"I believe she was calling about my evening class. Do you know if it has been cancelled?"

"None of the classes have been cancelled," she was assured.

A copy of the *Portsmouth News* had been left on a seat in the bus station. Mavis sat next to it. When her bus arrived, she picked up the paper and took it with her. She skimmed through, reading the headlines in search of something of interest. A loud blast from a car's horn caused her to look out.

A fellow passenger muttered, "Bloomin' BMW drivers think they own the road."

Although she could see several cars, Mavis didn't know which one was a BMW. She wondered if the driver had been at fault, or of he'd been beeping at some obstacle in his path. She looked back to the paper and the headline 'Woman killed in car crash' caught her eye. She didn't usually read the reports of accidents, and probably only noticed this one because Janice had recently been hit by a car. Someone had been run over and killed, she read. A woman who'd left a daughter. The woman wasn't named; Mavis thought of people she knew who had daughters. That was silly. Many people died in accidents every day, it wasn't likely to be anyone she knew.

Norman arrived promptly at seven, sporting enough colour for two people. His pale grey suit was similar to the one he'd worn to London, but the lime green shirt and turquoise tie combination was something new. Mavis was pleased she'd chosen to wear a charcoal two piece and cream blouse. She wondered if

Norman was colour blind, or if something had happened to either the shirt or tie he'd intended to wear. He took her to the pictures; a historical romance. Mavis considered the heroine to be foolish and shallow. She appeared to want nothing more than a handsome husband, caring not that he was unsuitable. The film did have something to interest her; many of the scenes were set in and around a stately home. The house was magnificent and the gardens were superb. Afterwards they went for another meal at The Alverstoke.

As they sat down, Mavis said, "I enjoyed the chicken very much last time and am looking forward to trying something different this time."

She ordered a medley of melon to begin and cutlets of lamb in a herb crust as her main course. After enquiring into the flavour of the soup of the day, Norman ordered that and a steak. He told her he did not eat at home much; his small rented flat wasn't all that inviting.

"If that is the case, why do you not live somewhere else?"

"Until recently, I've been away with work for a large proportion of my time, so I haven't had a great deal of opportunity to look for something suitable. I intend to wait until I see somewhere perfect. Somewhere like you live would be ideal. Good size rooms, well constructed, comfortable, good location."

Mavis agreed her house was nice.

Norman said, "You look after it well too, care for it. I don't suppose you would want to move?"

"Oh no. I shall stay there. I think I might redecorate."

"Good idea, you could have some lighter colours, brighten the place up a bit. Maybe get some of that laminate flooring, things like that can really improve the value of a property. I could help you."

Mavis didn't want to improve the value of her property by decorating it in someone else's choice of colours. She wanted her home to suit her, reflect her taste. The arrival of the main course came after a pause in their conversation. Mavis concentrated on her lamb; it was as delicious as it had sounded on the menu.

"I saw a great offer for this weekend, two nights with dinner in Oxford. I've made a provisional booking for us," Norman said.

229

"No," Mavis said. What did he have in mind? Would he expect them to share a room? She imagined Norman watching her as she climbed into a bed, just feet from where he lay. The idea was unacceptable.

"What do you mean? Don't you like Oxford?" he asked.

"I mean that I have made plans for this weekend."

"Plans?"

"Yes, a friend is visiting me."

"Who? All weekend?"

Mavis didn't wish to explain about Vera who was visiting for an afternoon. She didn't need someone else to make plans for her. She had a great deal she wanted to get done in the garden. Shrubs needed pruning and it was warm enough to sow seeds. Next weekend, Cousin Linda would be staying; she couldn't garden then.

"Sorry, Norman, but I've made arrangements for both this weekend and next."

"Pity, maybe the one after that?"

"We'll see," she said.

He took her home. She did not invite him in for coffee.

When Mavis woke, she was still thinking of the things Norman had said the previous evening. Mavis didn't wish to share a bedroom with Norman. She wasn't sure she wanted to spend an entire weekend with him, regardless of the sleeping arrangements. She enjoyed his company, but she had other friends and things she wanted to do. It was all moving too fast. She'd not seen him for years and now he seemed to think that after a couple of weeks he had the right to progress the relationship towards a level of intimacy she didn't desire.

Her calendar suggested, 'It is better to have loved and lost than to never have loved at all.' She supposed she had loved him once, but that was a long time ago. She'd lost him temporarily when Mother had thrown him out. Her love hadn't endured.

She packed her sketches and the painting of the tulips into her portfolio. It hung on a coat peg at work and later, rested on the garish orange sofa in the discovery centre as she ate her early supper. Mavis carried it into the college classroom. She hadn't put it down before Jenny clung to her and started babbling.

"I didn't know if it was right to come, but the counsellor said that it would be best. Anyway I wanted to talk to you about the funeral and …" She started crying. Mavis felt uncomfortable, but let Jenny hold on to her. Mavis slid the straps off her shoulders and eased the portfolio case and her bag on to the floor.

Jenny continued to speak, but her sobs made the words incomprehensible. Mavis put her arm around Jenny; Nicola had done that to her when she'd been upset. It had made her feel less alone.

Tim arrived. "Mavis, Jenny, I'm pleased that you both felt able to come."

Mavis said, "Hello." She gestured to Jenny, "I am afraid she is rather upset."

"Not surprising, considering what happened. Rita Lagopus has done what she can to help of course, but it will take a long time to get over the shock; if she ever does."

"Yes."

The message from the college must have been to prepare her for whatever was happening.

"Rita will be here in a moment. She wasn't able to speak to everyone personally and wants to update people with the information we now have."

"Good," said Mavis; she would soon be given an explanation.

"Are you all right Mavis? It must have been an unpleasant shock for you. You and Vera were friendly weren't you? I know you were in class, but I believe that on Saturday she mentioned going to your house?"

"Yes."

Vera? Something had happened to Vera.

Other students began to arrive. Vera and Flo were absent. There was none of the usual chatter and teasing. A short, plump, dark haired woman knocked on the doorframe and walked in. She stood next to Tim.

"Hello everyone. I am Rita Lapogus; the college counsellor. I'm sorry to be meeting you all under such tragic circumstances."

Chapter 23

Rita told the class that Vera had died as a result of the injuries she'd sustained on Saturday. She'd come into contact with the underground track and been electrocuted.

"How did it happen?" asked someone who hadn't gone on the trip.

"She was trying to get my handbag back," Jenny said and began crying. Rita comforted her.

Tim explained there would be an inquest, but it appeared Jenny had been mugged and Vera had chased after the muggers. Jenny had then lost sight of her in the crowds. Although the station was crowded, no one seemed to know how she had got onto the electrified rail.

"No, no. She can't be dead. She was going to come to my house. She was going to be my friend," Mavis stuttered.

Rita tried to comfort her too, but Mavis didn't want the woman to touch her. Realising she was making an exhibition of herself, she tried to calm down.

"It has been a terrible shock. If anyone would like to talk, then I can take them somewhere private," Rita offered.

No one accepted.

"I'll leave some cards, please feel free to call me." She left.

Jenny said, "Rita was very kind. If you want to talk, Mavis, Rita will help. I've talked to her a lot and the police too of course."

"Mavis, I'm so sorry," Tim said. "I thought you knew."

Mavis said nothing; felt nothing.

"Perhaps you should speak to Rita," Tim said.

Mavis said, "I am too shocked now to take it in. Perhaps I will speak to her tomorrow."

"Oh, yes, good idea," Jenny said.

Tim suggested, "Perhaps concentrating on our painting will help," and they started the lesson.

Because of the trip to London, hardly anyone had done the seascape homework. Those who had were happy to have another go in class. They all worked on the idea of a calm sea or rough weather. Mavis painted, but couldn't concentrate on the task and his words. She thought of Vera and how she would never be her friend.

She was reluctant to produce her flower pictures. It didn't seem right; she'd painted them whilst waiting for Vera. Vera, who was dead as Mavis blended the green for the stems. Did Vera die quickly? They would know at the inquest. Mavis didn't want to go to another inquest. It had been interesting last time, but it wouldn't be so interesting again and she didn't want to hear if Vera had been in pain, if she'd suffered, if she'd known she was dying. Why had she chased the muggers? Just to get Jenny's bag, what was special about Jenny's bag? Did Jenny get it back? Vera was to be her friend; not Jenny's. Why risk her life for a bag, when Mavis needed her. Vera shouldn't have done that. Vera shouldn't have died, it wasn't right. Something wasn't right. Vera shouldn't be dead.

Jenny spoke of a funeral. Vera's funeral.

"Will you be going, Mavis?"

"When is it?"

"Friday, in St Thomas's, would you be able to get time off from work?"

"I expect so."

Nicola would be pleased she wished to take leave, yes that would be all right.

"Can we meet somewhere first? I don't really want to go on my own," Jenny asked.

"Yes, of course. Where is St Thomas's church?"

"It's the cathedral, Mavis. I didn't know ordinary people could be buried there, but her daughter, Alice, said that's where it is. Vera went there regularly. I didn't know that either."

"We didn't know her very well," Mavis said.

"No, but she was our friend, wasn't she?"

"Yes, she was."

They arranged to meet outside the school close to where Mavis worked.

The boy waited in the lobby, after the class. As people came out, they were discussing the funeral.

The boy asked, "Whose funeral?"

As they walked to the bus stop, she told him it had been her friend who'd died.

"What a horrible shock."

"Yes it was."

"Worse than finding, sorry I ..."

"Worse than finding the body of my neighbour do you mean?" Mavis asked.

"Something like that."

"Yes, worse. Not more of a shock I suppose, but it feels worse."

"Losing a friend would be worse than losing a neighbour or just someone you knew."

"Like the pale girl?" Mavis asked.

"Who?"

"The girl with the headphones at the bus stop who ..."

"Oh yes, I know who you mean. I didn't like her much, but you aren't supposed to say that," the boy said.

Mavis looked at him.

"You're supposed to be nice about dead people, but I don't think that's right. I think you should be honest. I think you should always be honest."

"So do I. I didn't like her either," Mavis said.

"I'm not surprised. She was rude," the boy, Jake, said.

"She was rude to you?"

"No, to you."

"Yes she was," Mavis agreed.

"What about Ms French, did you like her?"

"No."

They reached to bus stop and sat together on a bench.

"People die all the time. It's better when it's someone you don't like," Jake said.

"I liked Vera."

"Your friend from the class?"

"Yes. I know people die, but why did she have to die now when she was going to be my friend? It wasn't time for her to die, it wasn't right."

"No, if she was your friend she shouldn't have died."

"Everyone does die though. Eventually they die and leave you," Mavis told him.

"Someone else has died?"

"I was thinking of my father. He died when I was a little girl. I loved him but he left me and died."

"That's sad, but you still had your mum."

"Yes, but she's dead now," Mavis said.

"Recently?"

"Last year. That wasn't so sad."

"You didn't like her as much as your father? I'd have thought you would love a mum more. I'd love my mum, if I could get to know her. My real mum I mean."

"Do you know anything about your parents?" Mavis asked.

"Not much. I used to think they must be dead, why else would they abandon me?"

"But they're not?"

"I don't think so. All I have is her name on my original birth certificate. There's no father, so I think she gave me up because she couldn't look after me on her own. That seems more likely doesn't it?"

"Yes. Can you trace her?"

"I've asked the social worker to try. Sometimes, people want to be contacted and leave details."

"Not this time?" Mavis asked.

"No. The social worker said that often the mum feels bad, doesn't think the child will want to know them. I would though, I'd want to know. I wouldn't be angry, not if it wasn't her fault, if she had no choice." The boy looked at Mavis, as though pleading with her to understand.

"Yes, I see. What about your adoptive family?"

"They've been great, looked after me well and everything. I'd want her to know that I've been happy, that maybe she made the right choice. I've been happy with them, but it's not the same as a blood relation is it?"

"No, I suppose not."

Once home, Mavis put her flower paintings away. They made her think of Vera. Knowing she'd be unable to sleep she retrieved the sleeping pills from their hiding place at the back of the corner cupboard. They worked after Mother's death when she'd been agitated over having to get training for work and pay the bills. She shook some out on to her hand; six, seven, eight.

She put them all back in and read the label. The tablets were still in date and the dosage was two with a glass of water. She selected a glass, ran the tap and then filled it. Again, she shook out a handful of tablets. Her friend was dead, she could be too.

Mavis returned all but two tablets to the bottle. She swallowed the two, drank the water, washed the glass and went to bed.

She slept and dreamed. Dreamed of her dead neighbour sending her cat over the fence and then laughing so hard she fell and died. Dreamed of finding Mother dead, instead of calling the undertaker and doctor she put on her coat and went to work. Dreamed of the underground station and Vera falling on the track. As she landed, her body turned over and it wasn't Vera, it was Sandra who lay there charred and dead.

Mavis woke and remembered; yes, that was better, it should have been Sandra whom she didn't like, not her friend Vera. Mavis woke fully, it was too late now. Vera was dead. Sandra lived and Vera did not.

For the rest of the night, Mavis drifted between unpleasant thoughts and disturbing dreams. Sleep brought little rest, waking gave no relief.

'Tomorrow is another day,' was the phrase revealed when she removed yesterday's sheet from her calendar. Mavis had to get through today before she could face tomorrow.

She looked out on her sunlit garden. The tulips Vera had admired were almost gone now. The faded petals carpeted the ground. No tears fell from Mavis's red-rimmed eyes. Mavis spilt the milk; a few drops ran down the side of the kitchen unit. She wiped it up. Although she thought she'd got it all, she had to be sure none had dripped under the fridge. It was heavy and awkward to move, she trapped her toe under a corner as she tried to manoeuvre it. She scuffed her shoe and bruised her skin as she dragged the fridge off her foot. There was no milk on the floor, but it was dusty. Of course it was; she hadn't moved the appliance for months. She couldn't possibly leave it like that. She vacuumed the vinyl flooring then cleaned it with a cloth moistened with disinfectant. The work had to be done quickly or she would be late for work. The fridge seemed to resist as she edged it back into position. It would not go close enough to the wall. She pinched the tip of a finger between the fridge and the work top. Her tears fell; it wasn't fair, nothing was fair.

When she reached the bus stop, Bert's wife chatted away to her. Mavis didn't listen, but Bert's wife was undeterred.

At work, Janice tried to talk to Mavis about the book she was reading. Mavis didn't want to listen; she didn't want someone else to appear to be her friend, not if they might go, not if they might die.

Her head throbbed, she was tired and her unhappy thoughts tumbled over and over each other, trying to force her to acknowledge her grief. She rested her elbows on the desk and held her head steady. She closed her eyes. If she concentrated on nothing, she could stop thinking.

"Are you OK?" Sandra asked.

Mavis looked at her. Why was the woman speaking to her?

"Do you want some aspirin?"

Sandra wanted to give her pills. Mavis didn't want them; if she were to end her life, she would do it the way she'd planned. She wasn't sure that's what she wanted. She wasn't sure of anything except the need to stop thinking.

"No, go away."

"You look as though you've got a headache."

Why had Sandra said that? You can't see a headache; it was to confuse her, to make her take the pills.

"Go away, why can't you leave me alone?" Mavis shouted.

Sandra left her alone. Janice and Lucy left her alone. Mavis held her head still and concentrated on nothing. No one spoke for half an hour, until Nicola came out of her office.

"What's up with you lot? Has someone died or something?"

Mavis felt her fingers grow wet against her face. Her head wouldn't stay still, nor her shoulders. She cried noisily. She continued to cry until she became aware of the gentle pressure of arms holding her close. A head of dark silky hair was next to hers. One of her hands was held firmly. A gentle voice told her over and over that it would be all right.

"It'll be all right, Mavis. Just let it all out, then you'll feel better. It'll be all right," Janice said.

Nicola was holding her hand. Janice had her arms around her. When she stopped crying, they let go of her. They stayed close and spoke kindly. Sandra brought tea, Lucy gave her tissues. Mavis told them her friend had died, explaining when and how. She blew her nose and drank the tea.

"I am sorry, I have done no work and I don't think I can."

"That's all right, Mavis. Would you like to go home? I could drive you," Nicola said.

"No, I don't want to go home. I think I would like to go for a walk."

"Well, OK, if you want to, that's fine."

Mavis walked towards the cloakroom.

"I'll come with you," said Janice.

"No. No, thank you, Janice. I would like to be on my own." Mavis took off her shoes and pulled on her boots.

"You're upset; you shouldn't be on your own."

"I just want to walk on my own for a little while."

"Mavis, you're my friend, I don't want …" Janice stopped talking and watched Mavis button her coat.

"I am just going for a walk. I won't be long."

"You'll be all right? You're sure?"

"The fresh air will do me good. I didn't make myself any lunch today, so perhaps when I get back, you will come with me to the sandwich shop and advise me on what to try?"

"Yes, of course. See you later then."

Mavis turned right out of the office. She walked briskly to Cambridge Junction, past the Duke of Buckingham. Her pace slowed as she reached the cathedral. She'd still never been inside. Soon she would get her chance; at the funeral of her friend. As Mavis turned at the sea wall, she glanced to the left; that was the way she and Janice and Nicola had walked when they'd visited the Garrison church. Mavis turned right and walked, in the shadow of the high stone wall, towards the Round Tower.

A man, huddled in a filthy anorak was slumped in the entrance to Victoria pier. Three empty beer cans were at his side. A fourth was in his hand. Mavis remembered the man she'd bought a pie for. She'd thought he wanted drink when he'd asked for money to buy food. She tried to help him by giving food and advice. Had it done no good? Did nothing ever change?

"What're yous lookin' at?" the drunk snarled.

It wasn't the same man.

Chapter 24

Mavis climbed the steps of the sea wall. She walked along the top, looking neither out to sea, nor over old Portsmouth. She looked where she was headed; the tower. The gin and sleeping tablets were at home; that didn't matter. People sat, enjoying the sun and the view, on top of the tower. That didn't matter, she wasn't going to jump; not now.

A man with a large canvas bag climbed the steps behind her.

"Hi, Richard," he greeted a thin fair man who was looking out to sea.

Richard's friend unzipped his bag, revealing cameras and lenses. The man had a radio device. Each time it crackled into life, Mavis heard voices request permission to cross the harbour. Other men arrived, greeting each other as they took up their positions. They too had camera equipment. One man had five cameras slung around his neck. Another, twice the size of his friends, wore postal uniform.

Richard gestured to the radio, "Heard anything?"

"Nothing yet."

"Excuse me," a woman said the man with the radio. "Are you waiting for HMS Kent?"

"Yes," the photographer confirmed.

"My son is on her."

"You'll see him soon then."

"Have you heard something on your radio?"

"No, but the ship's out there." He pointed to a dark speck on the horizon. The woman, the men and Mavis looked.

"Are you sure that's it?"

"He's sure," the postal worker told her. "If you can see a smudge, he can see a ship."

The radio crackled again. Male voices spoke.

"Was that it?" the woman asked.

"Yes," the postal worker said. "That was the captain giving QHM, that's the Queen's Harbour Master, his position. The ship should be in, right on time."

"Thank you. I can relax now; I've been so worried about him."

Mavis climbed down from the tower. She must get back to the office; if she were gone too long Janice would worry.

She was expected, and wanted, at work. She would be welcomed too, at her art class. Cousin Linda had travelled hundreds of miles, and would do so again, in order to visit her. She was supposed to be on land, at her job, in her home; not floating in the Solent.

Before lunch, she asked Nicola for time off to go to the funeral. Nicola said, "Of course you can. That's not a problem."

"Thank you." Mavis turned to leave Nicola's office.

"I'm really sorry about your friend, Mavis."

"Why?"

"Well, because her death has upset you."

Mavis didn't know how to reply.

Norman phoned her after six. She asked if he were going to the funeral. He wanted to come round. She said, "No, it would not be right the night before Vera's funeral."

"Mavis you're upset, let me come. I could help."

"No, Norman." She replaced the receiver. He couldn't ease her grief and she didn't want him to try. She didn't want to be cheered up. Her chance of having a friend had been lost. It was right she should be sad. Norman wasn't mourning Vera. He was using her death as an excuse to appear kind and to get close to Mavis. She didn't know what he wanted, but he wasn't going to get it.

She pulled the fridge away from the wall and cleaned properly beneath and behind it. The task had been rushed that morning. She removed every trace of dust from the back of the appliance. The washing machine was next. Fortunately, that had wheels, so was easier to move. She cleaned the machine and the newly exposed floor and walls. Once she'd put it back in its place, she removed the detergent drawer and scrubbed it. The filter too was cleaned. Next, she washed the kitchen floor. The cleanliness of the kitchen comforted her very little.

The bathroom was tackled next. Not until she was sure no trace of limescale, nor smear of soap remained, did she stop. Mavis drank a cup of tea before she cleaned the insides of her windows. She used a weak solution of sugar soap to wash the doors and their frames and the skirting boards. Then she had to stop, she'd become too tired to continue.

Her hands were cracked and bleeding. She put disinfectant on them; the cracks might attract dirt and infection. It stung, but at least they were clean.

The overcast sky on Friday morning suited her mood. It was as if the clouds had worn dark clothes and gathered to help her mourn her dead friend.

Only her calendar seemed unaware of the funeral. 'Always look on the bright sight of life,' it urged. Mavis would if there were one. There was no bright side to burying a friend before the friendship had developed.

Mavis left the office at midday to meet Jenny. Jenny was protected from the drizzle under the bus shelter. She sat on the bench holding a wreath. Mavis hadn't thought to buy flowers. She should have done so; Vera liked flowers.

Jenny said, "I guessed you wouldn't have time, so I haven't written on the card yet. Shall we put just our names, or have it from the whole art class?"

"Sign it, 'from your painting friends'," Mavis suggested.

Norman sat next to Mavis during the service. The rain had almost stopped when Vera's coffin was carried out and returned to the hearse to be taken for burial.

Mavis looked for Norman; he would have room in his car for herself and Jenny. She couldn't see him.

"Do you need a lift?" a lady asked. "I've got room for two more."

Mavis and Jenny were driven to the graveyard. The other ladies in the car discussed the hymns during the drive. Mavis looked out of the window. Every few yards there was a sign advertising a film or a show; entertainments she would never attend with Vera.

The ground was wet. Someone slipped as they walked to the graveside and was forced to step onto the pile of freshly dug soil to regain their balance. The ground was heavy clay; it must have been difficult for the grave diggers. What a sad job. Mavis found digging hard enough work in her own garden; she didn't have to go down six feet into the subsoil. She planted seeds and bulbs. For her, the task symbolised the beginning of a life cycle. Here it was the opposite. Even the beauty of the flowers was spoilt; they would be left to wither unseen on the grave.

Vera's daughter spoke to her and Jenny. She told Mavis her mother had been pleased to have met her, "She'd phoned me to say she was enjoying the art class and she sounded quite excited that she'd found a new friend."

She turned to Jenny, "Hello again, I'm glad you could come, especially as you were with her ..." She stopped talking and began to cry. Soon she blew her nose and apologised.

Jenny patted her arm. "It's OK, Alice, we quite understand."

Alice asked, "Will you both come back to the house? I'm afraid I haven't arranged much of a wake, but..."

"Oh no, we wouldn't want to put you to any trouble," Jenny said.

"It wouldn't be any trouble. Please come I ..."

"You would like to talk about your mother?" Mavis guessed.

"Yes, yes I would."

"Then we will come."

"Yes, of course," Jenny agreed.

Mavis again looked for Norman. He was sure to wait and offer to drive her home; possibly to take her for a drink too, in an effort to cheer her up. Norman had gone; Mavis couldn't remember seeing him since they were in the cathedral.

They were taken back to the house. Tea and cakes were provided by Alice and her husband. The arrival of a neighbour with Vera's granddaughter helped lighten the sombre mood. The guests took turns in holding the child or cooing over her. Most people had one cup of tea and left. Jenny thought they should leave too, but Vera's daughter asked them to stay. The three of them discussed Vera. They all cried. Mavis found sharing her grief to be therapeutic. She felt sad, but not inconsolable. She took comfort in being with people who'd known Vera and missed her. Maybe her presence helped them? Alice's husband brought them more tea. When there was no more to say, no tears left to shed together, Jenny and Mavis were driven home by Alice's husband.

Mavis washed her face and changed her clothes. What should she do? Could she paint, would that be appropriate, or would it make her too sad? The phone rang. It might be Norman, she didn't want to speak to him. She picked up, but didn't speak.

"Hello, Mavis? Can you hear me?"

"Hello, Linda. Yes, I can hear you."

"Oh good, I tried calling earlier, but you must have still been at work, I suppose. I'm at Bracknell now, so I should be with you in about an hour. Maybe a bit more, the traffic's quite heavy."

How could she have forgotten Linda's visit? "Drive carefully, I'll see you soon."

There was not time to get things ready for a meal. Linda would need to eat. A bought meal would be a poor substitute for one she planned and prepared herself. She rang The Wyvern and asked if it would be possible to have a meal there. The landlord sounded very friendly,

"No problem at all, what time would you like to come?"

Mavis booked for eight o'clock. That was late for dinner, but it would allow time for Linda to arrive and settle in. Mavis went to the Co-op and bought more milk, fruit juice, cereal and eggs. She hadn't prepared dinner, but at least she would be able to offer Linda a good breakfast tomorrow. Croissants were on special offer; she bought them too. She picked flowers to put in Linda's

245

room. She made the bed and vacuumed all the carpets. There was no time to do more before the doorbell sounded.

Norman, not Linda, stood on her step.

"Hello, Mavis. I couldn't bear to think of you all alone and upset, so I've booked a table for us at The Alverstoke."

"You should not have done that, Norman."

"Of course I should. It's my job to take care of you."

"No, Norman. It isn't."

"Well, I hope that at some point in time you will feel …" He paused as Linda's car pulled onto the drive. "Who's that? Bit of a cheek using your driveway, Mavis."

"Why should she not use it?" Mavis didn't wait for an answer, she hugged her cousin. "I'm so pleased to see you. Shall I take a bag?"

Norman still waited on the doorstep.

"I don't know if you remember Norman? Norman, this is my Cousin Linda."

"Hello, Linda. Of course I remember you, how nice to see you again."

"Hello, Norman." Linda shook his hand.

"Well, goodbye, Norman," Mavis said. "I shall be busy this weekend. You may telephone me on Monday, if you wish."

The two women went inside without waiting for a response. Linda was impressed with Mavis's handling of him.

"Reminds me of something my daughter said once, 'treat 'em mean, keep 'em keen'."

"He is quite keen enough, I think."

Linda laughed. "Oh, Mavis, you do make me laugh. So what's been happening with you?"

"My friend Vera died. It was her funeral today."

"Mavis! Oh, Mavis; no."

"I'm sorry. I was upset; I'd forgotten that you were coming. I only learnt of her death on Wednesday and it upset me and …"

"Well, of course it did. Oh, Mavis." Linda held Mavis close, until her sobs subsided.

"I'm sorry, Linda. I haven't prepared a meal. I should have got things ready for you. I couldn't keep my friend and I'm treating you badly."

"Don't be silly. I'm fine, don't worry about me. Now just let me put my case in my room and freshen up. Then we can talk properly."

"Yes, of course."

"I'm in my usual room?"

Mavis nodded.

"If you still have any sherry, how about a glass before we think about dinner?"

Linda soon came back downstairs. Mavis had taken sherry, glasses and coasters into the living room. She poured them a small glass each.

"Cheers," Linda said and took a sip.

"I'm glad you're here, Linda. I felt much better after the funeral. Vera's daughter invited Jenny and I to her house. We talked about Vera, it upset us, but it also helped. Does that make sense?"

"Yes, it does."

Mavis drank some sherry.

Linda asked if Mavis had eggs. "I could do us an omelette."

"I've booked a table at The Wyvern; I've heard it's very good. More like a restaurant than a pub."

"Oh that sounds wonderful, Mavis. What a good idea." Linda put down her unfinished drink. "I'll save the rest for later if you don't mind. I'd like a glass of wine with my meal and any more might put me over the limit."

"You won't need to drive, it's just a few minutes walk away."

They were shown to a table and asked if they would like drinks.

"A glass of white wine for me. What would you like, Linda?"

247

"The same please, not too dry."

"Two medium white wines coming up."

They looked at the menus and read the specials board.

"I think I shall have Red Mullet," Mavis said, after a few minutes.

"What's that like?"

"Actually, I don't know, but I do like fish, so I expect I shall enjoy it."

"You are being brave. I can't decide. It's such a treat not to have to cook it that I'd be pleased with anything."

Mavis looked at her cousin. Linda didn't seem annoyed Mavis hadn't cooked for her. Perhaps Linda enjoyed being taken out for a meal as much as Mavis had when Norman had done the same for her?

"Please have whatever you would like. I've earned the money and can spend it how I choose."

Linda grinned. Although her smile emphasised the lines in her face, the soft lighting in the pub was flattering. The candlelight was reflected in her eyes and her brown hair looked rich and glossy in contrast to the pale wooden panelling.

"That's nice of you, Mavis. I'm tempted to be adventurous myself."

"There is a starter of grilled goat's cheese, with caramelised shallots and cranberry glaze."

"Sounds nice. Are we having starters? If you don't mind, I think I'd prefer to have a dessert. We don't often bother at home and I rather fancy something rich and gooey."

Mavis remembered the cheesecake she'd once shared with Lucy.

"Shall we share the starter? We could still have dessert."

"Yes, let's. Oh, here's the waitress and I still haven't decided."

"I can give you a few more minutes if you like?"

"No, no, I'm too hungry to wait. You go first, Mavis."

Mavis ordered then looked at Linda.

"I think I will have some kind of fish too."

"The swordfish is nice," the waitress said. "I'd never had it, so the boss let me try a piece. It's good, quite meaty if you know what I mean and the lime sauce on it, that's really scrummy. It comes with sautéed new potatoes and…"

"Stop. Yes, I'll have that."

"I'll ask chef to be quick with your starter."

"Thank you."

"How are you, Linda?" Mavis asked when the girl had left. "You sounded unhappy when I spoke to you last. I am sorry, I had forgotten."

"Oh, I'm all right. I was just a bit fed up. Don't worry about me."

"And your family? The children?"

"All in good health, I'm pleased to say. And you, Mavis?"

Mavis told Linda she'd thought Vera would be a proper friend, but of course, she had a proper friend in Linda.

Their starter arrived. The waitress brought a spare plate and two sets of cutlery.

"I almost don't want to spoil it, it looks so pretty," Linda said. That didn't prevent her from handing Mavis a knife and holding the empty plate ready to receive her share. The creamy cheese, sweet onions and tangy sauce were soon gone.

"Linda, I gave away the copy of *1984* to Janice at work. I'd already offered it to her before I remembered you gave it to me."

"Oh, that doesn't matter; I hope she's enjoying it?"

"Yes, well I am not sure she actually enjoyed it as such, but she enjoyed having the opportunity to do so. She has finished it now. She saw that it had been a gift and returned it to me. It helped her stand up to her mum."

"Always a good thing." Linda smiled as she spoke.

"It wasn't until I was about to part with it, that I understood the inscription you had written."

"I don't remember?"

"You told me to escape the thought police. You meant me to escape Mother's influence occasionally."

"Yes, I did hope you'd do that. She seemed to be holding you back, almost suffocating you after your father left."

"Don't say left." Mavis drank more wine; she didn't put her glass down.

"Sorry, I didn't mean to bring back unhappy memories."

"It's not that, it was sad of course, Daddy was wonderful, but it was a long time ago. It's the euphemisms. It infuriated me when Mother died. 'Passed away' 'at peace' that's the kind of thing people say when what they mean is dead. Death is final, it's better to accept that."

"I didn't mean when he died, she stopped smothering you then and withdrew so much she practically neglected you."

"She did change, but that was later. Daddy died when I was a little girl. I heard people talking once, they said things about Mother and Daddy that I didn't understand."

"You never knew?"

"Knew what?" Mavis took another gulp of wine.

Chapter 25

"Your father left your mother when you were about six. He didn't die until about fifteen years later," Linda said.

"He left us?" Mavis asked.

"Left her is more accurate. I believe she smothered him in the way she smothered you after he left. He was an outgoing lively man, but she didn't like him having any friends or interests away from home. She killed their relationship."

Their meals were placed in front of them. "Can I get you any sauces?"

They declined and began to eat.

"Your father wanted to migrate to South Africa. He did in the end. He wanted you and your mother to go with him. She thought it would be dangerous for you. They argued. I didn't know anything about it at the time of course, but he wrote to my mum for news of you."

"I thought I remembered days out with Daddy after he was dead. No, that's not right."

"I know what you mean. It must have been a confusing time. After they split up your dad tried to get custody of you. He didn't want to leave you behind."

"I don't remember much. Mother rarely spoke of him."

"Apparently she was very upset. I think you might have been ill or something at the time. I'm not sure about that, but I do know she was sure it wasn't in your best interests to go. She didn't want him to go either; she thought he would come back to her. She loved him and he loved you."

"She gave up the man she loved to protect me?"

"Yes. He later died out there."

Mother had made sacrifices in order to bring up Mavis in the manner she'd felt best. No wonder she'd been bitter. Mavis had repaid that sacrifice though, at the end. Mother had done her best for Mavis and Mavis had done all she could for Mother.

"Shall we have another glass of wine?" Linda asked.

Mavis looked at her glass. It was empty.

"Might it not make us silly if we have too much?"

"It might; would that be such a bad thing?"

The waitress approached. "Is everything all right with your meals?"

"Yes, very nice thank you," Mavis said. She'd eaten little because they'd been talking, but she intended to eat every scrap.

"Delicious," Linda agreed.

"Can I get you any more drinks?"

"Yes," Mavis said.

"Two white wines?"

They nodded.

 Would that be large or small?"

"Large, please," Mavis said. It was probably more economical to buy the larger size.

When the wine came, the glasses where indeed very large. None was wasted.

The next morning, Linda watched Mavis remove the sheet of paper from the calendar, fold it and put it in the bin.

"Do you always do that?"

"Yes, there is a separate sheet for each day. Today it says, 'One step at a time.' I believe they are supposed to be motivating."

"That's not quite what I meant."

Mavis emptied the kettle, rinsed it out and added fresh water. She fitted in the lead and switched it on.

"Mavis, I hope you're not going to be offended, but …"

"Yes?" Mavis lit the oven to heat the croissants and poured glasses of fruit juice.

"Well you seem a bit compulsive. It's good that you're clean and tidy of course, but you overdo it a bit."

"You think I am doing things wrong?" Mavis asked as she set out cups and bowls.

"Not exactly. It's more that you do too much."

"I like to keep things clean. Mother insisted on it and I think she was right." Mavis filled the tea pot and milk jug.

"Yes of course. Sorry, I didn't really mean to criticise. It's just that you seem to spend so much time cleaning you don't have much time left for anything else. Look at your hands, all the detergent has made them sore."

Mavis looked at her ragged cuticles.

"I like to keep things clean."

As they cleared up after breakfast, Linda said, "What's the plan today?"

"I thought perhaps you would like to look round some gardens?"

"Yes, that would be nice. Exbury is good at this time of year I think?"

"Yes, yes it would be."

"You were thinking of somewhere else?"

"I'm sure that Exbury will be very nice," Mavis said.

"Mavis, where were you thinking of?"

"There are some small gardens in Gosport. The Crescent garden, Anglesey gardens and Stanley Park, I have not been to them, but I know where they are. I can go myself another time."

"We could do both couldn't we? How about we go to Gosport today? We can get some lunch while we're out, or buy something to cook here later. It would be fun to explore."

They went to Stanley Park first. They looked at the bedding displays, mostly tulip stalks, almost over wallflowers and gaudy polyanthus. They decided the delicious scent of the wallflowers compensated for their disreputable appearance and the tulips must have been lovely.

"I don't know as I like the mixed polyanthus though. They're certainly colourful, but perhaps too much of a good thing?" Linda said.

"I agree. A single colour, with an underplanting of forget-me-nots or double daisies would have been better."

As they walked through the park and up towards Anglesey gardens, Linda told her that she and her husband were bored with each other.

"I'm sorry, I had no idea you were unhappy."

"We're not really unhappy, we just have no conversation. We're not going to split up, or anything. It's good for me to get away for a while, have a break and someone else to talk to. If you would like, I could come down for more weekends or we could go somewhere together?"

"What about your grandchildren?"

"I'll still see them, but I'm fed up with being an on demand babysitter. The children are never brought to visit me, they're just dumped by their parents while they go out and I'm expected to be grateful."

"Oh."

Linda laughed. "I sound as though I'm getting old and miserable don't I? Sorry, Mavis. Just saying it has made me feel better. It would be good to see more of you though. I'm enjoying this weekend. Maybe you could come and stay with us too?"

They reached the road.

"I would like that, Linda. Thank you. The garden is just across there."

Linda admired the huge pergola. "This is really impressive. You wouldn't know it was here would you?"

"No, in fact I didn't realise it was a public garden until last week, when I asked about places to visit. The tourist information office told me."

"I wouldn't have thought of doing that. I'll do that for when you come to stay with me. We can go to Beth Chatto's place too."

"Is that near you? I didn't realise. I have several of her books; it would be lovely to see the gardens for myself."

"If you like her books you should read Christopher Lloyd's."

"I do, he's very good. Well, was."

"We could go to Great Dixter. I'm not quite sure where it is, to be honest, but I can find out. If it's too far to go in a day we could stay in a hotel for a weekend."

"A hotel? I've never stayed anywhere except with family."

"It would be fun, Mavis. Someone to cook and clean for us. Nothing we need do except eat, drink and at look at gorgeous flowers. We could go in the summer. Say you'll come?"

"Yes, yes I will."

"Well, that's assuming you're not whisked off somewhere by that man of yours. If he gets keen, you won't want to spend all your weekends with me."

They looked at the beds of mauve pansies, aubretia, dazzling arabis, and fat clumps of dicentra and aquilegia just showing colour. Mavis told Linda she wasn't sure if she wanted to get involved with Norman.

Linda advised her to think carefully about committing herself to anything, "Have fun, but don't get tied down. It's not just your mother who wasn't sure about him."

"I have some doubts too, but I'm sure it's just because of all the accidents, that and re-reading all the Agatha Christie's from the library."

"Fancy yourself as Miss Marple, do you?"

"I'm sure I'm being melodramatic."

"I've always fancied one of those murder mystery weekends. You tell me what's been going on and we'll exaggerate it out of all proportion and then work out 'who dunnit'."

"You know about my neighbour, the one who fell?"

"Yes, I still don't understand about that."

"The inquest showed she'd been drinking, that's why she fell."

"Yes, but why was the silly woman up the ladder to start with?"

"She was putting up one of those awful satellite dishes."

"That doesn't help. Who benefited from her death?"

"Oh, I see ... Well, I did for one. Once she was dead her cat was taken away and it stopped chasing the birds and messing in the garden."

"Well, if you tell me the cat is dead, you'll be my number one suspect."

"You don't think I killed her then?"

"It seems unlikely. Are there any other suspects?"

"Norman perhaps? He was married to her," Mavis said as they crossed the road back into Stanley Park.

"Did she leave him some money?"

"Not as far as I know. He said there was some irregularity over investments, but I gather that money was already his. He might have been paying maintenance?"

"Would that be enough?"

"He seems to be rather fond of money."

"Oh?"

"Yes, he is often recommending ways for me to invest or …"

"Mavis, you won't will you? Not without checking with someone else?"

"No, I won't be following his financial advice. For all his interest in the subject, he doesn't seem to be terribly good with money. He lives in a rented flat; I have always understood renting to be a waste of money."

"Yes, if you can afford to buy I think that's most sensible. Perhaps he can't?"

"Then he cannot have spent his wages well."

"OK then. Norman is chief suspect for her death. If only we could find links between him and the other people."

"We can. He knew Vera and he had another wife and a daughter. A mother was run over in Fareham."

"He really doesn't like paying maintenance does he? Mind you, there's someone else with a link between them. Maybe I'd better cook supper tonight."

"I don't understand."

"Well, you are a poisoner, Mavis."

"Me?"

"Cousin Lilly?"

"Oh, yes, but that was an accident and she didn't die."

"I know, sorry that was a silly thing to say. I've always felt bad about that," Linda said.

"You, why?"

"Well, you remember how greedy she was?"

"Yes. Every time I asked for cake and biscuits, Mother told me to be careful or I'd end up like Lilly."

"Yes, mine too. Well, when she came to stay, she'd eat all my sweets and anything she could get her hands on. I got annoyed with her, so I started telling her that all the cakes and sweets had peanuts in. She didn't believe me and started breaking things in half to check."

"She really was very unpleasant."

"Yes," Linda agreed. "I'm afraid I laughed when I heard how ill she'd been after eating the biscuits you made."

"You wouldn't have laughed if you'd seen her. The noise she made, as she tried to breathe, was awful."

They didn't speak again until they reached the car park.

"So, where to next?"

"The Crescent, I think. Then we could have a quick walk round the Ferry gardens before we go to the supermarket."

They talked about Linda's family as they walked round the Crescent garden, admiring the specimen trees and attractive perennials. Rain threatened when they reached the Ferry Gardens. They walked quickly through, not bothering to go down to the sundial.

"It's cold when the sun's gone in, isn't it?"

"It's lovely here in the summer; shall we come back then?" Mavis suggested.

"Yes, I'd like that, and to the other gardens too. Perhaps we could take a picnic. Talking of which, what shall we eat tonight?" Linda said as they got into the car for the short drive to the supermarket.

"You mentioned an omelette last night. I have some eggs, so we would just need a filling and maybe some salad and fresh bread to go with it."

"Good idea, how about a Spanish omelette?" Linda said.

"I'm not sure how that differs from an ordinary one?"

"It's a bit more substantial, it has potatoes, onions, bacon and other things mixed in."

They bought the ingredients Mavis didn't already have and a bottle of Rioja to drink with it.

Linda peeled and chopped a large potato and added it to a pan of simmering water. Mavis cleaned the chopping board and knife. Linda heated olive oil in a frying pan and chopped the bacon. Mavis took away the chopping board and knife, washed and dried them, wiped the work surface with a disinfectant wipe and replaced the board. Linda chopped an onion. When she added it to the sizzling bacon, Mavis picked up the board and put it in the sink.

"No wonder your hands are so sore, Mavis, you never have them out of the hot water and detergent."

"I like things to be clean."

"Yes, I know that. Clean is good, but honestly you're overdoing it."

Mavis wiped the work surface.

"You don't think so?" Linda asked. "I'm going to chop the red pepper next, then the green. Do you intend to wash the board between each of them?"

Mavis dried the board and handed it back.

"You wiped all the vegetables clean before I started. They won't contaminate each other," Linda said.

"No, I suppose you're right."

"Don't look like that. I guess you've just got into the habit and you don't think about it."

"It seems wrong to just watch you cook for me," Mavis said.

"You could open the wine."

"Perhaps a sherry first? That's Spanish."

"Now, that's a very good suggestion."

"What does your calendar have to say for itself today, then?" Linda asked on Sunday morning.

"Laughter is the best medicine."

"Well, I agree with that. You've really cheered me up this weekend, Mavis. Thank you."

"I have?"

"Yes, it's been lovely talking to you and going to the pub for that delicious meal and the gardens and everything."

"I'm sure we shall enjoy today too."

The weather seemed to echo their mood. When they arrived at Exbury, the sun was so hot, the sky so blue and the air so still they left their coats in the car. The scent of the azaleas, clematis Montana and bluebells was trapped under the tree canopies. Each time they saw a bench, they sat for a minute to enjoy the fragrance and the spectacular show of flowers. The rhododendrons were superb, their bright colours highlighted by the fresh greens of oak trees, new hydrangea leaves and unfurling ferns.

"The colours really are vivid aren't they?" Linda said. "Rhodies do put on a magnificent show."

"They do when grown on this scale."

"Yes, that's the trouble with them. You need enormous banks of them in a few acres of woodland to look good."

"And acid soil," Mavis said.

"True, they're not for us then. How about black swans, do you fancy digging a pond for some of them?"

"No, I don't. I would like to see them though. Do you think we shall?"

"I hope so," Linda said.

They did see the swans, but not until they'd been for a trip on the steam train. They crossed the Japanese bridge and walked down to where the River Beaulieu flowed into the sea. Linda was surprised to be able to see the Isle of Wight.

"I didn't realise it was so big. I've never been over there, have you?"

"Yes, it was on a school trip. I would like to go again."

"Shall we add it to the list of things to do on one of my visits?"

"Yes, that will mean you need to visit quite often," Mavis said.

"Not a problem for me."

They grinned at each other.

They went in search of lunch; on the way to the tea rooms they finally saw the swans.

Chapter 26

Mavis felt reluctant to get up on Monday. Not because she didn't want to face another day; because she was tired. She'd spent hours walking with Linda and then sat up late, talking and drinking on two evenings. She'd enjoyed herself and was delighted to know Linda felt the same way. On Sunday evening, the house had seemed quiet without her cousin's chatter. She'd put the sheets Linda had used in to wash and vacuumed the floors but felt reluctant to do more. The colours of the flowers and the calm beauty of the swans were difficult to forget. Perhaps she could capture them in a painting? Such a big scene really needed a much bigger canvas than the sheets in her book.

With an effort, she pushed away thoughts of the weekend and the warm blankets. 'Time and tide wait for no man' she read. That was true; it was also true that the bus would not wait for Mavis. She barely had time to feed the birds, prepare her lunch, eat breakfast and wash up and dust around the house. She remembered Linda's remarks about her cleaning routines, was it possible she did too much?

Rushing to the bus stop, she considered another of Linda's suggestions; driving lessons. She'd learnt to use a computer; she could probably learn to drive a car. She could certainly afford to do so. It would be nice to have the freedom to visit gardens that were not on a bus route and to go and stay with Linda. She wouldn't waste so much time at bus stops either. Maybe she would try. Perhaps Norman would again allow her to practise in his car. She would ask him.

At the bus stop, she mentioned the idea to Bert's wife.

"Ooh you're braver than me. I wouldn't want to try it. You hear of so many terrible accidents and then there's all them cyclists with no lights, shouldn't be on the road they shouldn't, but still you'd never forgive yourself if you hurt one would you?"

Mavis thought she probably could forgive herself, but didn't say so.

Sandra was absent from work. She didn't even call to say she was unwell. Nicola called her house; she got no reply.

Lucy said, "I wasn't expecting to see her anyway because of something she said on Friday."

"I haven't written in the diary that she was to be away," Nicola said.

"I can't remember exactly what she said now, but when I said, 'see you Monday' she said something. Sorry, I wasn't really listening."

"Maybe she meant to ask for the day off and forgot, or perhaps she asked ages ago and I didn't write it down. Never mind, she's not one to just skive off and we'll find out about it tomorrow," Nicola said.

"I hope she's gone somewhere nice," Janice said. "She needs cheering up a bit."

Mavis and Janice walked down to the beach at lunchtime. They talked about books on the way. Janice had just finished reading, *The Secret Adversary* and loved the idea of working as a private detective.

"My cousin Linda and I were just saying the same thing this weekend."

"I don't suppose it would be as much fun as it sounds, probably just a lot of hanging about watching people."

"I think I'd prefer that to anything more exciting, and of course I could use my little grey cells and deduce things." Mavis tapped her head and smiled as she spoke.

"You'd be good at that. You're observant."

"Thank you, Janice. You would be more suited to the action tasks I imagine. You are always eager to get on with things."

"Yes I am, aren't I? Let's start our agency, what shall we can ourselves?"

"Quicke and Forthright?"

"Brilliant! And our first case?"

"I was not aware that we had a client?"

"Well, no we haven't. I reckon we'd need to solve something first. Then we'll get a reputation and people will come to us."

"I see. Do you know anyone who has lost a priceless jewel?"

"No, sorry I don't," Janice said sadly. "Hey, hang on, you're teasing me aren't you?"

"Yes, Janice, I am. Sorry, but your eagerness amused me."

"Oh, really?" Janice pretended to be annoyed. "So come on then, what were you and your Cousin Linda going to investigate?"

"Murder."

"Murder? Who's dead?"

"Several people."

"Who? Are they linked? Do you suspect anyone?"

Mavis told Janice about her neighbour, Vera, the pale girl, the woman from the newspaper. They decided Norman had killed them all. His ex-wife was insured, with him as beneficiary. The woman in the paper was another ex-wife, also insured.

"The pale girl, she saw him do it, so he killed her too. He'd seduced your friend Vera and persuaded her to leave him her money. Oooh, you'd better be careful, Mavis. Unless you like dangerous men?"

"Sorry, Janice; Norman didn't kill Vera. I was with him the whole day."

There was no time for them to find the 'real villain,' they were due back at work. They had a lot to do that afternoon and as they were a person short, there wasn't time for speculation.

Jake was on the bus. Mavis mentioned driving lessons. The boy was learning to drive.

"I can drive. I've driven my cousin's car, but I need proper lessons before the test."

He told her about the theory test and the book to learn from. She could borrow his when he'd finished with it.

"That might be a while, the lessons are quite expensive. I'm hoping I'll be given some for my birthday. I'll be eighteen soon. Things happen when you're eighteen. You find out things."

Mavis agreed, but believed this boy and most of his contemporaries were more aware at sixteen than she had been at twenty one.

Norman called and asked if it would be convenient for him to visit. She said it was and he admitted he was just round the corner. Mavis was pleased. Although obviously keen to see her, which was flattering, he'd accepted her instruction to phone first.

They went for a meal.

"Did you enjoy your weekend with your cousin?"

"Yes, very much. Linda is interested in gardening, so we visited The Crescent and Stanley Park. She taught me to make a Spanish omelette. It was delicious. Perhaps I could cook it for you, one day."

"I would like that. I'm sure you're a very good cook."

Norman told her he would take her to visit gardens, was there anywhere in particular, she would like to go?

Mavis named Hyde Hall and Harlow Carr, but admitted she didn't know how far away they were. She told him that as she was a Royal Horticultural Society member they would get in for free. "I'd enjoy visiting one of the big flower shows, at Chelsea or Hampton Court perhaps."

"We should join the National Trust too, if you like looking at gardens. You like old buildings too, don't you? You and your friends visited the Garrison Church in Southsea. I imagine that was your idea."

Mavis agreed, but wasn't sure what she'd agreed to. She disliked his possessive tone and presumption with the 'we'. "I have been thinking of learning to drive."

"You were learning years ago. You didn't take your test?"

"No. Mother was ill and I had to stop the lessons."

"I can teach you again; lessons are expensive."

"Yes, I know. At least £20 I believe. I don't know how many I would need?"

"Not so many if you get some practise in my car first."

Mavis was sure he was right, she'd suggested the idea to Linda, but she didn't like how Norman seemed to be trying to take over her life. Perhaps she was being silly, she was used to being on her own and he was just being kind.

She told him she could afford lessons.

He said, "Save the money for a car. I'll help you find something suitable."

As she got ready for bed, she remembered Janice casting him as the murderer. He certainly had the charm and confidence to persuade women to turn over their money. That didn't make him a murderer. Of course, he wasn't; there was not really a murderer at all. He couldn't have killed Vera even if there were. He'd been with her the whole day. Well, except for when she got lost in the underground, but he couldn't have known that would happen and it was in a different station. As she switched off the bedside lamp, she pictured him after she'd found her way to St Paul's station and waited for him. He'd smiled as he'd walked towards her. He'd walked from the opposite direction to which the cathedral lay. She began to wonder where he had been whilst she'd taken the wrong tube, and then she slept.

'Beauty is in the eye of the beholder,' Mavis's calendar informed her. She was well aware no one beholding her would find any beauty. 'A face only a mother could love,' that was the expression she'd heard in connection with other ugly people. Mother had loved neither her face nor anything else. No, that wasn't right; Mother had loved her enough to end her marriage in order to protect Mavis. Mother had never told her she was pretty. Other people had told her she was attractive, Daddy and Norman amongst them. She didn't believe them.

Mavis's lack of personal beauty didn't mean she despised the quality. As a child, she'd hoarded feathers, ribbons, birthday cards. Anything pretty was kept safely in a special wooden box that she locked and stored in the cupboard beside her bed. Those trinkets comforted the lonely girl she had once been.

Daddy had given her pretty things, the father who hadn't died, but had gone away. He'd come back to see her though, he must have done. She remembered those visits only vaguely, her mind had always refused to clarify the order of events. Now she knew the truth, she was free to remember without fear of fresh

265

pain. Mother hadn't been there, not the later times. It had just been Mavis and Daddy that day on the Round Tower. He'd pointed out to sea and told her there was a world and a future waiting for her. She had to have dreams and make them come true.

"What dreams, Daddy?" she'd asked.

He'd laughed. "I can't tell you what to dream, Mavis my love. I can't write it down or paint you a picture. You make your own dreams."

Daddy had left, but he'd come back sometimes and brought beautiful gifts. As she got older, the trinkets became proper jewellery. Mavis never wore it. That was a silly waste. She checked her watch, yes, she had time. She went upstairs and opened her box. Nestling on the velvet lined drawers were a mixture of the simple treasures of childhood and real jewels. She spotted the item she wanted; a brooch shaped like a bird, the plumage glittering with semi-precious stones. She pinned it to her jacket and left for work.

The boy was on the bus, he noticed the brooch.

"Is that new?"

"No, my father gave it to me, when I was a girl."

"Definitely not new then. Oh, sorry, I didn't mean ..."

"You needn't worry, I'm perfectly aware that I'm no longer a girl."

"How old were you when he gave it to you then?" Jake asked.

"It's difficult to remember." She smiled, "Not because I am so terribly old, but because he left when I was very young. I thought he'd died then, although I have memories of him after that. I thought I'd imagined him, to comfort myself, but I've since learnt he didn't die. He left us, well left my mother. He came back to visit me."

"I'm glad he came back to see you. It's hard not to see your parents. You know there must be a good reason, they wouldn't just leave you, but a kid doesn't always understand. It's great when you see them, when you can talk."

Mavis felt uncomfortable, what did he mean? He was adopted, the pain of separation made sense, but how could he be talking to his parents? She had done it again, said too much to someone. She thought she'd got better at conversations in the last few months, but she still had trouble stopping talking once she'd begun.

"Maybe we shouldn't talk about this now?"

"No? I suppose it can wait. I'll be eighteen soon, it will all be different then."

What would? Mavis wondered, but didn't ask.

At work Sandra's daughter phoned in, Mavis answered the call. Sandra was ill and would not be at work. Her daughter sounded upset. Mavis remembered the constant, draining demands of her own sick mother and tried to be kind.

"Thank you for letting us know, are you with her now?"

"I'm just on my way to see her."

Mavis reported to Nicola.

"Oh well, that solves that mystery. I wonder why she didn't call us herself yesterday? Still if her daughter's popping in to keep an eye on her, she'll be fine."

At lunchtime, Janice suggested Sandra was the killer. She was pretending to be ill so she could kill again and have an alibi.

"Why would she do that?"

"She heard us talking and wants to throw us off the scent?"

Mavis wasn't convinced. Keeping an open mind was one thing, but Janice's ideas didn't seem very realistic.

"Why has she killed the other people?"

"Jealousy. She's after your boyfriend. The other people are his ex-wives, she's eliminating the competition, watch out, you'll be next."

"The pale girl was too young to be his wife."

"His daughter?"

"I don't think so. Norman himself is more likely to be the killer."

"Yes, that's true. The girl could still be his daughter; maybe she demanded he support her through college? His ex-wives were all claiming maintenance, so they had to go. Your friend Vera had seen through him and wouldn't sign her money over to him and he was afraid she'd warn you. I expect it was him

267

who pushed me into the traffic too; he could tell I'd work it all out."

"Maybe."

Mavis wasn't convinced Norman was a serial killer, although if he were she guessed money would be the motive. What an idea! The man did seem overly interested in financial matters, but that didn't mean he might try to cheat people out of their savings.

Mavis didn't go straight home; instead she walked up to Commercial Road with Janice. Mavis bought new paints, but not until after they'd been met by Janice's boyfriend. The boy had hair that wanted cutting and trousers that needed pulling up and fixing into place with a belt, but he had a kind face.

"It is a pleasure to meet you, Janice has talked a lot about you," he said after they were introduced.

Mavis was impressed with him. Mother wouldn't have approved, but Mavis was beginning to see beyond first impressions. He wouldn't try to take her money. He didn't embarrass Mavis by any display of affection toward Janice, although he seemed to care. This boy wouldn't run after one harsh word from Janice's mum.

She went straight to art class as it wasn't worth going to the library first. The class were subdued. Leo and Robert did their best to keep the atmosphere light hearted, but they were no substitute for Vera and Flo.

"Is Flo unwell?" Jenny asked Robert.

"I don't know, I haven't seen her at work the last few days. Come to think of it, I haven't seen her since the last time she was at this class."

Jenny began stroking her hands across each other. Mavis tried not to watch, she found the repeated gesture unsettling.

Tim showed Mavis the picture she'd painted the night she'd heard Vera was dead. It showed a stormy sea; an angry scene, dark clouds, huge cold waves. A storm where those who set sail might never be seen again.

He said, "It's very powerful, Mavis; very expressive. You were very upset when you painted it; that's why it's so good. A painter needs to let themself go, in order to be truly expressive. You shouldn't paint what you think others might wish to see, only what you feel."

That night, Mavis dreamt of painting her emotions. She layered on thick wodges of vibrant oils, yet produced nothing but a weak, grey water colour.

Chapter 27

'It's all part of life's rich pattern,' the calendar informed Mavis the next day. She doubted there was a pattern to life. If there were, she couldn't see it.

The boy waited at the bus stop. She greeted him, "Good morning …Jacob." She was pleased to have remembered his name. He simply nodded without looking at her. He didn't seem happy; could she have got the name wrong? She was sure she hadn't. She remembered because of the Jacob sheep with four horns she'd seen once on a school trip. There had been a teacher called Mr Jacobs and some of the boys had found this amusing. Mavis remembered that when the boy told her his name, she'd wondered if he'd ever seen the sheep and other boys had teased him. Perhaps he just preferred to be called Jake?

She didn't have time to worry about it, because Bert and his wife arrived to give her news of Lauren. Some bigger children had been showing off by standing up on the swings. They'd persuaded Lauren to try.

"And they pushed her higher and higher. Poor little mite lost her grip and went flying. Only broke her arm didn't she? Her poor mum felt that bad. She'd been talking to a friend, the mother of one of the kids doing the pushing as it happens. Had her back to the swings like, but could hear little Lauren and the others laughing. That's 'til there were shouts and then it went quiet."

"The poor girl."

"Brave as anything she was. Hardly even cried, so Karen said."

Sandra was still absent from work.

"All I know is what her daughter told me this morning," Nicola told them. "She sounded upset; all I really understood was that she's in hospital and expected to be there for the next week or so and that there's been some kind of trauma or injury to her brain."

"That's what The Hamster had isn't it?" Janice asked.

"What do you mean?" Lucy asked.

"Richard Hammond, the guy who does that Brainiac thing and presents Top Gear."

"Oh yes, I know, he had that awful car crash a few years back, didn't he?"

Mavis made tea, whilst the others discussed the medical history of a man she'd never heard of. Had Sandra been driving? Was the accident her fault? When the tea was ready, the conversation had moved on to the drinking habits of another celebrity whose name was unfamiliar to her.

Mavis wondered what was wrong with the people around her. Everyone she knew was dead, ill or injured. That night, she dreamt of pushing Sandra under the wheels of a speeding car. She felt the soft material of Sandra's new jacket under her chapped hands. She had time to contrast the sheen of the beautifully coloured material with her cracked and mottled skin before Sandra's head connected with the vehicle. The brain injuring thud followed by a squeal of brakes sounded so clear that, as she woke, she wondered if a real car crash had happened outside her house. For a minute, there were no further sounds other than the usual nocturnal creakings. Then, there was another thud. Mavis recognised the sound; her neighbour's gate banging in the wind. It no longer squeaked, someone, perhaps the estate agents, had cured that. Still the sound was associated in her mind with death. Perhaps the gate banging in the night had caused her bad dream? It had been nothing more than a dream, Mavis tried to comfort herself.

Sleep didn't return; memories did. She thought of Marie French falling to her death. 'Did she fall or was she pushed?' people always asked. Well, some people asked and a small sing song voice inside her head repeatedly asked Mavis. Vera didn't fall onto that railway track, she didn't jump either. Mavis hadn't jumped from the Round Tower on the day she'd planned to. She hadn't allowed her body to drop into the water, to fall to its death. Since then others had fallen, or were pushed. They were dead. Sandra wasn't dead, not yet anyway. The pale girl was. She'd fallen into the High Street hadn't she? Was that a memory or a dream? The woman from Fareham, did she fall, was she pushed? Mavis couldn't remember. Janice had been pushed.

Mavis had lived, but others had died, or were dying now. Why was it happening to people around her?

Her calendar didn't have the answer. 'Practise makes perfect,' was all she learned from it that Saturday. Mavis didn't think many people practised anything, or cared to reach decent standards. They certainly didn't aim for perfection. She tore off the tiny sheet of paper; as she did so, it resisted. She was careful not to tug; to do that would have caused it to rip. After folding it upwards she ran her thumbnail over the perforations, then resumed tearing the small sheet from the stub. She folded it in half, then into quarters. As she did, the corner buckled. She should have taken more care. It had happened before when she had been hasty; not ensuring the first fold was completely flat before making the second. She unfolded the sheet and tried again. No crease the second time, but the edges were not as crisp as they would have been if she'd got it right at the first attempt. She pushed away the memory of the last time she'd folded one of the pages untidily. That had been the morning she wasn't paying attention because of the excitement over the trip to London. It had been the morning of the day Vera had died. It was silly to be superstitious. She shouldn't pay too much attention to a tiny piece of paper. She dropped it into the recycling bin, determined to forget it.

Sunday's quote read, 'The future will look better tomorrow'. That was easy to forget. Why would she remember something that made no sense? Tomorrow, the future will be the present. It is unlikely to look better than the past.

That night, Mavis woke several times to the sound of bins and patio furniture blowing around in the wind. Tomorrow things would not look better. Her precious flowers would be tattered and unsightly. Tender new growth on shrubs and perennials would be damaged. The garden and street would be littered with debris. It was possible that fence panels would have been blown down.

As soon as she woke on Monday morning, Mavis looked out to assess the damage.

"No, no," she heard herself cry. The mulberry tree was destroyed. Where once its beautiful crown had been joined to the trunk, there was a jagged ugly amputation. Branches, with their infant leaves, lay on beds and shrubs. Mavis pulled the curtains shut. She wouldn't see the devastation. Her tree, her beautiful tree, could not have been destroyed.

In the kitchen, she kept her back to the window. She made breakfast and read the calendar quote, 'Every problem has a different solution'. Mavis had thought her problems were loneliness and boredom. She'd thought her death was the solution. Now she didn't know what was wrong. Everything was wrong; out of control, impossible to understand.

At lunchtime, as she walked to town, it rained. People around her put up umbrellas, intent only on sheltering themselves and oblivious to those around them. A man accidentally jabbed Mavis with his gaudily striped brolly. Later she saw him again, waiting with a group of people to cross the busy road. He was leaning forward, looking she supposed for a break in the traffic. How easy it would be to bump into him, give a shove and send him sprawling into the road. With hoods and umbrellas raised and the drizzling rain obscuring vision there was little chance of anyone noticing her stumble wasn't accidental. She could easily have ensured he never caused her discomfort again. Mavis stepped forward. She walked past him and back to work.

No. It could not have been her. Mavis could not have pushed those people to their deaths. Surely, she could not have done that?

When she got home, Mavis looked out again at her garden. She looked through the window; she couldn't bear to go out, to touch the rough bark and shredded leaves. The tree was lost; there was nothing she could do about that. Branches lay on other treasured plants. They would cause damage if left where they were, more if the wind rose again and tossed them from where they rested on living, vulnerable treasures. She must clear up.

The tree was too big, too heavy for her to tackle alone. Mavis looked through the yellow pages. Searching for a company to remove the remains of the mulberry reminded her of looking for a firm of undertakers who would remove Mother's body. Her own body shook and her face was wet with tears.

After a glass of sherry, Mavis felt braver. She rang a tree surgeon, who agreed to help, but warned the storm had covered a large area.

"Is the tree likely to cause injury to anyone, or damage to property?" he asked as though that were of more concern than its loss.

"No, it is all on the ground in my garden. Unless there is further strong wind, then I imagine it will stay where it is."

"Good. I've had calls from where large branches are damaged but still attached on a tree near a school. You'll understand I have to deal with stuff like that as a priority?"

Mavis did understand. The man took her details and promised to visit on Saturday, to assess what needed to be done and he hoped, to remove the fallen tree.

The next morning, she found an envelope dangling from her letterbox. Not the post, it was too early and there was no stamp. It had her name on it; the surname was spelt incorrectly, but it must surely be meant for her? The name was handwritten, there was no address. Those things suggested this was no official communication. What else could it be? It wasn't a rude, scruffy note from Marie French. Something from Norman perhaps? What could he wish to write, that he couldn't say to her face? It felt as though it contained a card. She received Christmas cards from some neighbours, but not of course in the spring. It was not her birthday and even if it had been, she wouldn't have expected to receive a card in such a manner.

She didn't receive mail regularly enough for the opening of unexpected cards to have a proper place in her routine. Mavis propped the card up on the table and began making breakfast.

The calendar quoted, 'It's an ill wind that blows no good'. She had to swallow hard to prevent herself crying again over the loss of her tree, as she thought of the ill wind that had destroyed it. The wind referred to was not real, she must think of the meaning behind the words; and not look outside.

If people were being killed, then there must be a reason for it. The people who were dead were all connected to her; her neighbour, her friend, her colleague. Would everyone she knew be killed? She must not allow that to happen. There were people who didn't deserve to die. Cousin Linda for one. There were others. There were good people; people who'd been kind to her. They didn't deserve to be pushed to their deaths. Sandra wasn't dead yet, but that was unimportant. What mattered was the intent behind the actions. Whoever had caused the deaths and injuries had done so for a particular purpose. She must discover that purpose. Mavis herself must be pivotal. Perhaps someone was killing people close to her in order that she might be considered the guilty party. Why would they do that? She could understand a killer not wishing to accept his punishment, but why did he kill them all? Perhaps one was killed for his benefit, the rest selected to incriminate Mavis. Perhaps; but she must consider other possibilities.

She washed up the breakfast bowl and cup before opening the envelope. It was an invitation to attend the 18th birthday party of Jake Riley. The party would start at 7.30 on Friday 22nd May and be held in the Lee-on-the-Solent community centre. A mistake after all, Mavis was hardly the person to attend a teenager's party. She didn't know any teenagers except Jacob and Karen. Jacob? Of course! The invitation was from him. How very odd. He spoke pleasantly to her, but they didn't know each other well. Why ask her? He must have plenty of friends his own age. She recalled he'd mentioned his forthcoming birthday; perhaps he thought, having done so, it would be rude not to ask her? Mavis noted the date in her diary.

Excepting Vera, all those who were killed were people Mavis had disliked. Could the killer be trying to help her? Mavis wasn't able to solve this alone, she needed help, but who could she trust? Cousin Linda. Mavis felt she could trust her. She wanted to trust her, but must think clearly. Living some distance away made her an unlikely suspect. Not impossible though, she could drive. Had Mavis called her at home when any incidents happened? Yes, Linda had been at home the evening the pale girl had been run over. She'd telephoned Mavis several times, because she'd rung the first time to warn her of the dangers of icy paths. On getting no response, she'd become concerned and called again and yet again until Mavis arrived home. She wouldn't have known Mavis was not home, had she not called.

Was there anyone else? She would like to be able to talk things through with Janice. The girl would see things from a different perspective. Janice said she was pushed, if she was a victim then she couldn't be the killer. Janice was pushed, those bruises had been real. Perhaps that was a warning? One of her friends was injured then another killed. She could trust Linda and Janice; no one else.

At work, Mavis made the mid-morning coffee. As she waited for the water to boil, she noticed dull white marks on the sink where water had splashed and dried. Was it clean water? There was no way to know.

Mavis began to remove items from the work surface and place them on the table where Sandra frequently ate her lunch. Under the tray that held the plastic containers filled with tea, coffee and sugar were grains of sugar and a dirty brown mark. The area had obviously not been cleaned for several days. Mavis began to scrub, using almost boiling water and bleach. She was furiously scrubbing when Lucy arrived.

"Steady on Mavis, or you'll wear the pattern away."

"What does that matter so long as I remove the germs?"

"What germs?"

"How would I know? I really don't like to consider what such a dirty surface might harbour."

Lucy left and Mavis kept scrubbing. Nicola came into kitchen.

"Mavis, are you all right?"

"Yes, I'm just getting this surface clean then I'll get back to work. Things need to be clean."

"Well, of course they do. That's why we all clear up after ourselves and expect those who share the kitchen to do the same. Has someone been leaving it in a poor condition?"

"Everyone."

"What's happened?"

"Happened? Many things have happened."

"In the kitchen?" Nicola asked.

"No, not here. It just needed cleaning."

"Mavis, was it worse than usual?"

"No, no I suppose it wasn't."

"Then it's clean enough."

"Almost."

"No Mavis," Nicola put a hand on Mavis's arm and removed the scouring pad from her hand. "It's clean enough now."

Nicola took Mavis out of the kitchen and sat her down in her office.

"You're clearly worried about something, Mavis. Would you like to talk about it?"

Mavis shook her head. She was almost sure she could trust Nicola, but how could she know?

"You like things to be very clean, don't you?"

"Yes."

"Are you the same at home?"

"Of course."

"Mavis, your hands look very sore. The cleaning fluids must sting."

"Yes they do. That worries me. I don't wish to get an infection from the cracks."

"No, of course not. Perhaps you should see your doctor about them?"

"Do you think he would give me antiseptic cream to help keep them clean?"

"I'm sure he would be able to help you. Make sure you tell him that all the different cleaning fluids you use sting your hands and how often that happens, I think that might be important."

"Thank you, yes I shall."

"Why not ring for an appointment now?"

Mavis did as Nicola requested. As she wrote down the details of her appointment in her diary, she saw the entry for the boy's birthday party.

It was a strange idea to ask her, but then he was a strange boy. He occasionally said peculiar things. Maybe he did peculiar things, too. Mavis had spoken to him shortly after meeting Vera, before she'd the opportunity to get to know her. Mavis's initial impressions of Vera hadn't been favourable and she'd shared those opinions with the boy. He wouldn't have known she'd changed her mind. He seemed attached to her. It was he who'd walked with her from college the night she'd considered climbing up the Round

Tower. He'd walked with her and she hadn't jumped to her death. He'd spoken to her when she'd been unhappy. He'd moved other boys, so she might shelter from the rain. He'd been kind to her; perhaps he thought he was helping her by removing those she disliked.

One of the people who'd died was Norman's ex-wife. Mavis didn't know if Norman had to pay her maintenance, but knew he wouldn't like it if he did. Norman was fond of money and would not like to have to give any to a woman he no longer cared for. Of course, he wouldn't have to pay it to a dead wife. Perhaps the woman from Fareham had been his wife too? Norman had another wife and a child; the dead woman had left a daughter. Vera lived near to Norman, perhaps she'd known something? What about Sandra and the pale girl, she could see no motive there. It would be money, if Norman were the killer the motive would be money. Did that mean he wanted her money? She didn't have much; there was the house though.

Norman rang on the Friday evening to ask if she'd like to go away for the weekend. She didn't; the tree surgeon was to remove her tree and she had the garden to clear.

"No thank you."

"We could look at gardens, or perhaps visit a stately home."

"I said no, Norman."

"Yes, but I hadn't said where we were going …"

"I said no, because I don't wish to spend the weekend with you."

That was true.

She would have enjoyed going for a meal and some pleasant company after the hard work and distress of dealing with the aftermath of the storm; but he hadn't offered that. It seemed she must do whatever he wanted or manage without him. She'd adapted her life to fit in with Mother; she would not do the same with him. She'd been right to be firm with Norman.

Chapter 28

'You can't depend on your eyes when your imagination is out of focus', Mavis read on Saturday. She wasn't sure her imagination was out of focus, there did seem to be a problem with it however; it simply wasn't working. Her mind was full of dead people and dead trees. There was no room for anything else. Mavis tried to think of something pleasant whilst she waited for the tree surgeon. She considered her art homework, but could think of no familiar object she could paint in an unusual situation. She should have asked Tim to explain the assignment. When he'd suggested it, she'd found the idea intriguing. Art, she felt, should make a person look at things afresh. That perhaps was his intention, to make them look more closely at familiar objects and see them differently. But which object? Should it be something familiar to her, or to the viewer?

Mavis was pleased the weekend was extended by the bank holiday. The extra time would be needed for tidying the garden and the thinking she had to do. The tree surgeon arrived on time. He brought tools and two assistants.

"Let's take a look then," Roger said as soon he'd introduced himself.

Mavis opened the side gate, to allow the men into her garden.

"Don't worry, Miss Forthright. I know it looks bad now, but we'll soon clear the branches for you and you'll get your lovely garden back." Roger studied the broken stump.

"Do you want this out, or left to regrow?"

"Is that possible?" Mavis asked.

"With mulberries, yes. Not guaranteed, but possible. It won't be the same shape again, of course; more like a big bush."

Mavis wasn't sure. She explained she'd like the tree to be saved, but didn't want an ugly stump left to remind her of what she'd lost.

"We'd cut it so it's tidy. It'd be cheaper and quicker to leave it, but it's up to you."

"Please leave it." The tree deserved another chance. If it failed to regrow, she could plant a clematis to cover the trunk.

"Righto then. Should have this done by lunchtime."

Roger was as good as his word. The trunk was tidied, the branches cut and removed and the men paid by a quarter to twelve.

Mavis surveyed the damage. There was less than she had feared. She would fetch her secataurs, trim back those plants which were damaged and compost the pieces. She could sprinkle around some Growmore, water well. Within a week or so all would look much as before. All except the tree.

She removed her gardening clogs and went inside. She washed her hands and washed and dried the cups that she and the workmen had used. She fetched her secateurs, wiped the protective oil from them and went out to start work. As she stepped into the area that had previously been under the tree canopy she marvelled at the difference the extra light made to the scene before her. As she trimmed the crushed geraniums, heucheras and the golden choisya she knew they would grow back better than they'd been before. The choisya was straggly. Had the fallen mulberry not snapped some branches she would still have cut it back. It was probably good that she would now, in order to create a pleasing shape, have to cut severely. Often she lacked the courage to prune as hard as was required. There would be no fragrant blooms this autumn, but then there never had been. There had been precious few in recent springs, none at all the last two. The plant would have time to produce new growth before the winter. It would bloom next year.

She slashed the geraniums back almost to the ground. She knew from experience that fresh new leaves would soon appear. With the encouragement of food and water, she might soon be rewarded with blue flowers. The heucharas needed more care than a few kindly meant cuts. The plants were too sprawling and gappy to look attractive. She dug at the edge of the clumps and removed some of the better pieces for propagation. The remainder were fed and watered; she would allow them the same chance as the others to prove their worth. If they improved sufficiently they could stay; if not, they would be replaced by the new plants.

Fresh territory had been revealed to Mavis. Perhaps she would not just fill it with more of the same. There was the Brunnera *Jack Frost* that she'd admired on the visit to Exbury with Linda. The silvery foliage would look good amongst the other plants. There were other things she could try too. It would be pleasant to study her books and contemplate changes.

Mavis looked at the stems she'd cut. She'd severed all that was damaged, all the pieces that had grown weak and ugly in the shade of the tree. Mavis empathised with the plants. She too had lived her life in the shade. Her years had been one gloomy season in the cycle of life.

First, as a baby, she'd needed the care of her parents, the shelter of the tree. The bare branches of the tree had kept the worst of the world away from her. As she'd grown stronger and reached for the light, the buds of the tree began to expand. Her protection changed. Daddy left, but the shelter did not lessen. As the canopy overhead became denser, it no longer protected, but smothered. She'd tried to reach out from the dark shadows, but had not grown enough, she lacked the courage.

Mother had died; the leaves fell. She had, at first, been weighed down by the dying leaves. She'd almost been lost beneath the accumulating mulch. A gentle breeze had sprung up, perhaps the wind of change. She'd seen through all that pressed her down. She had begun to expand and grow.

It was not too late to hope for a late flowering. It would not be the drama of spring tulips, nor the voluptuous plenty of summer roses. Mavis's blooming would be subtle. Only those close to her would notice it.

On the Sunday, her calendar suggested she should, 'Be prepared'. Mavis's house was perfectly clean. She had tea and coffee and biscuits, but no friends who might call round for a chat. The spare room was made ready for a guest who would not come. Her garden was tidy, the paths swept, yet no one would walk round with her to admire the bright flowers and neatly trimmed shrubs.

No one to notice the changes made by the absence of the mulberry. How could something so important to her not matter to anyone else? She read interesting books, but there was no one with whom she could share the opinions she formed. Why had she been so abrupt with Norman? If she'd been kinder, had taken the trouble to explain her feelings to him, he would have spent time with her over the weekend. Perhaps she could ring him tomorrow and say she had been busy for the weekend, or she was sorry, or … She didn't know what she could say; not the truth. She couldn't ring and say that though she didn't trust him, she was lonely and his company would be better than none.

On Monday she was cautioned, 'Be careful what you wish for'. Mavis didn't wish for her happiness to be dependent on Norman. She didn't call him. She searched for books to lend to Janice. As she rearranged the remaining books to create a balanced look, she took a cookery book from its usual position. It was a long time since she'd used it. When had been the last time? Leafing through to see if a recipe would spark a memory, she saw one for rhubarb tart. There was a great deal of rhubarb in the garden. Making a tart would give her something to do. It need not be wasted; she could take it to work and share it. Her colleagues sometimes brought cakes or other treats. Mavis rarely thought to do the same. She could take custard powder too; there would be milk and sugar at work. The pie could be heated in the microwave. It would not be quite so good as it would be fresh from the oven, but covered in hot custard it would surely be enjoyable.

On Tuesday morning she learnt, 'Not all advice is good advice'. That was true; she must make her own choices. If she was to have any happiness, she must make that for herself too. Bert and his wife would not be on the bus; they never were on Tuesdays. Mavis would have no one to talk to until she got to work. Packed in her bag were two books for Janice, her lunch, the carefully wrapped rhubarb tart and custard powder. There was no room for her to carry a book to read. She would re-read a little of one of those intended for Janice. Once the girl had read it, they would be able to discuss it. Janice had wanted to talk about *1984*, but Mavis's memory had proved insufficient. She would read it again, now Janice had persuaded her to take it back.

Janice seemed pleased with the suggestion.

"That'd be cool. You could help me with the bits I don't get. Actually, I was thinking of something else we could do, if you like. I noticed that the library often have more than one copy of the same book, that's what gave me the idea."

"Oh?"

"I was thinking, we could both get out the same book. A mystery one, you know with clues and that. We could agree only to read the same amount at a time and then see if we can work out who did it. We can talk about it and that, then see if we both think it's the same person and if we're right."

"That is an excellent idea Janice. I should like to do that. We must look for a suitable book."

'Cut your coat to suit your cloth,' Mavis was instructed on the Wednesday.

Mavis had nothing to hide. If a misguided person killed people for a reason connected with her, that didn't make her guilty of anything. It was hardly her concern, except people close to her were dying. There were people she wished to protect. The only way of doing that was to discover the identity of the killer and to provide the police with the evidence to stop him.

Janice was one of those who must be protected. She was also the person who would be of most assistance to Mavis as she searched for the truth. It was right Janice should help, as it would ensure her safety. Besides, she'd professed herself eager to commence detective work. Should she tell the girl she may be a potential victim? Perhaps not. It might frighten her and cloud her judgement.

Mavis went into a shop after work and saw a coat very like Sandra's new one. She would have liked to own something like that. Although she had imagined it to be expensive, the one Sandra had was obviously of good quality. It would last a long time and therefore be value for money. The colours were lovely, warm and cheerful without being gaudy or attention seeking. Perhaps she would try it on. Tweed was a classic; to purchase such a garment would be an investment. Mavis reached out to take a coat from the rack. It was not the roughly textured tweed she had expected, the material was soft and silky, just as it had been in her dream of pushing Sandra into the road. How could she have known that?

Mavis ran through the shop. The coat was still in her hand. She dropped it. The garment did not fall away, but caught against her body as she ran. She threw it free; escaping it and the shop.

When she stopped running, she was in the bus station. There was a bus with its engine running and a passenger showing a pass. Mavis climbed on behind him and reached for her purse.

"Just made it, didn't you?" the driver remarked.

Mavis was breathing too heavily to reply. She took two pounds from her purse and put them down next to the ticket machine.

"Hospital is it, love?" the driver guessed.

She nodded, accepted the coin he gave as change, took her ticket and sat down.

Mavis didn't understand about the coat. She'd never touched it in the office. How could she have known how it felt? The bus was going to the hospital; that was good. Sandra was at the hospital. She must get to Sandra. Could Sandra provide an explanation, or would she ask for one? Could Sandra talk, would she talk, did she know what happened?

Mavis read the names of the departments. She went to the Critical Care ward. A woman in nursing uniform stopped Mavis and asked who she had come to see.

"Sandra Rooke."

"I think she's asleep, but if you would like to follow me, you can see for yourself."

The nurse led the way to a small room containing a single bed, wheeled cupboard and some medical equipment Mavis was unable to identify. Sandra was there. Her head had been shaved and there were tubes connected to her. A drip of clear liquid was attached to her arm. The nurse bent over Sandra.

"Sandra, there is a visitor for you."

There was no response from the bed.

"Are you a friend, or relative?" the nurse asked.

"I work with Sandra."

"Your name?"

"Mavis."

"Sandra, it's your friend Mavis from work. She's come to see you."

Still no response.

"Sorry." The nurse shrugged and walked away.

Mavis looked at Sandra. She barely seemed alive. Mavis didn't know if Sandra was sleeping, or if the nurse had employed 'asleep' as a euphemism for coma or other non-conscious state. Mavis watched the slight rise and fall of Sandra's chest. She stared at the tube taped under her nose, then allowed her gaze to follow it until it connected to a cylinder. 'O2' was stencilled on the side. Sandra was being supplied with oxygen to help her breathe.

Fluids dripped hypnotically into a valve in her arm. Mavis had heard the term drip before, but hadn't realised the medication or plasma really did drip, drip, drip, slowly into the patient. She watched the life sustaining liquid fall slowly and regularly into the tube in Sandra's arm; each drop as faint and continuous as a reliable clock. As the seconds passed, it became possible to imagine Sandra growing stronger. Stronger; but not strong. She looked weak and vulnerable. The tubes that kept her alive were thin, pliable. It would be easy to pinch one between finger and thumb and stop the flow. A single sharp tug would cause the straw coloured liquid to dribble slowly onto the floor.

Mavis couldn't hear the oxygen as it seeped from the tube into Sandra's airway. There was no hiss to indicate the assistance her lungs received. Perhaps there would be a gentle sound of escaping gas if the small piece of tape holding the tube in place were to become dislodged. Mavis felt sure there would be a hiss if someone were to wrench the rubber seal that connected cylinder and tube.

The quiet of the room soothed her. The blanket that covered Sandra was rucked up. Mavis smoothed it flat. She wondered at her panicked journey there. She looked at her watch. Her art class began in just over an hour; she didn't have much time. Sandra was still resting peacefully, exactly, or almost exactly as when Mavis had arrived; there was no need for panic.

Mavis arrived only slightly late at her art class. She painted without concentrating and used a large quantity of paint.

At home, Mavis felt shivery. Sherry might help. Her hands shook as she splashed some into the glass. She gulped it down and although she spluttered, immediately she felt warmer, calmer. She poured more and sipped it. She knew something was wrong. She knew things about the people who had died. She remembered things, or had she dreamed them?

Perhaps she should call Constable Martins. The officer had asked her to call if she remembered anything. Was that about Marie French? Yes, it probably was, but that didn't matter. Constable Martins would hear her confession. Mavis called the number; there was an answerphone message. Mavis began to speak then abruptly hung up.

She didn't know for sure if she'd pushed Sandra. Could a person really do such a thing and not remember? She did remember how the coat felt. Mavis remembered the pale girl's face as she'd fallen. She didn't want to remember more. She didn't want the people close to her to die. She had been going to die, to kill herself. That hadn't happened and now other people had died. If she were dead, the pattern would be broken. There were still the tablets; she would take them.

She took two with a sip of water; shook out more, was about to take them when she noticed her painting bag. It had been discarded as she came in. It couldn't be left; she must put the contents away and return the bag to the cupboard.

The paint box slipped from her grasp, spilling its contents. Brushes rolled away and a tube of paint skidded under the sideboard. Slowly everything was retrieved and put in its proper place. When she'd finished, she saw the sherry bottle and the glass she'd drunk from were still on the dining room table. She felt so tired; her limbs were heavy and her eyes sore; she must sleep. She put the bottle away and washed and dried the glass. Mavis went to bed.

The sun shone too brightly in the morning. It hurt her head and forced her eyes to squint. She pulled the bedroom curtains closed again until she was ready to go downstairs. Before filling the kettle, she closed the blind and swallowed two paracetamol.

The bottle of sleeping pills sat on the worktop. Why had she had left them there? She must have taken some last night. How many? Too many or not enough. She'd been confused, frightened and had wanted that to end. Was there a way to end the torment without ending her life? Could she really have killed all those people and repressed the memory, as she repressed the memory of her father's abandonment of her? No, that was wrong. Daddy had left Mother; he'd come back to visit her. That was a different issue. The past was no excuse for present actions. If the dreams were reality, then she was ill. If she was ill then she could be treated. If. First, she must learn the truth.

She had a doctor's appointment booked. That was good; if she needed treatment, she would seek it. Should she go to work? She might hurt someone, but at least there, people would keep an eye on her.

The computer screen was too bright, the words out of focus. After admitting to Nicola she felt unwell, most of Mavis's morning was spent in the dimly lit stationery store. Once the shelves were dust free, the envelopes tidily stacked according to size and everything neatly labelled, she felt better. A lunchtime walk with Janice further restored her health and cleared her head.

"I visited Sandra yesterday," Mavis said.

"Really, why?"

"I had time before my class. I normally go to the library, but as I went through the bus station I saw a bus just about to leave for the hospital."

"Oh, right. How was she, oh dear, I suppose I should have asked that first. It just seemed odd you going to see her."

"She was asleep."

"Oh. Oh well, it's the thought that counts."

Could Janice know what her thoughts had been?

"Which thought?" Mavis asked.

"Going to see her. It was nice of you, especially as she's sometimes not that nice to you. She won't know you were there though. Not if she didn't wake up."

"No, she didn't wake up."

In the evening, Mavis had a visitor.

"Hello. Mrs Forthright?"

"Miss," Mavis corrected.

"Sorry. Um sorry, to trouble you, but I'm Mrs Riley; Jake's mother. Could I come in for a moment?"

Mavis showed Mrs Riley into the lounge.

"I don't really know how to begin."

Mavis waited. Her visitor tried to smile. Mavis felt uncomfortable.

"Have you come to talk about Jacob?" Mavis guessed.

"Yes, it's a bit difficult to know …Perhaps I, well it's Jake. I think he told you he was adopted?"

"Yes."

"He got the idea that you're his birth mother."

"His mother! Why would he think such a thing?"

"He has his original birth certificate. Her name is Margaret, her surname is the same as yours, although I think it's spelt differently. Hers has a W."

"I see."

"I know, of course, that it's not the case and have told Jake so. He is now very embarrassed that he behaved inappropriately."

"There is no need for him to be. It is true that he has said things that I didn't understand."

"He has been horribly confused. I suppose it's our fault for keeping the truth from him."

"He didn't know he was adopted?"

"Yes, he knew that, but we didn't tell him why. One day he heard us talking about her, his birth mother. He naturally assumed she must live locally."

"At least I now know why he invited me to his birthday party."

"Please do come if you would like to. It would be good for him to see you there and know you're not upset about the misunderstanding. He's very upset and confused right now."

Mavis noticed the woman shaking. It wasn't only Jacob who was upset. Mavis led the boy's mother to the living room and guided her into a chair.

"I do understand."

"Thank you, I had a feeling you would. Jake has told me quite a bit about you. It's a shame he wasn't right."

"You wish I was his mother?" Mavis asked as she placed the crocheted throw over her guest.

"Well, sort of. I suppose it's more that I wish she wasn't. I'm sorry, I know my son confides in you. I can see why. You're easy to talk to. I think it might be best if I tell you the truth."

"The truth is always best, but not always easy."

The woman nodded, but made no effort to explain. Mavis offered tea, "Or perhaps you would prefer sherry?"

"You're very kind."

Mavis didn't know what the woman wanted to drink. Sherry would be quicker; she brought a glass. The woman drank some.

"You must think I'm terrible," she said after she'd taken a few sips and some colour had appeared on her face.

"No, I don't think that."

"She is. Jake's birth mother is in a secure institution. She'll be there for life I think. She was violent, still is I suppose. They couldn't seem to cure her. We fostered Jake when she began treatment. When it became clear she'd never be able to care for him, we applied to adopt him."

Mavis poured herself some sherry and topped up Mrs Riley's glass.

"How old was he?"

"He was seven when we adopted him, but less than a year old when he first came to us."

Mavis encouraged Jacob's mother to talk about the boy, by asking about his childhood. Mavis recalled conversations with Linda about her grandchildren and repeated the questions that had provoked the happiest memories. Talking about his pet rabbit, earlier birthday parties and his schooling calmed his mother. Mrs Riley urged Mavis to attend the party. She seemed quite cheerful when she left.

The boy must be the one killing people. He'd thought she was his mother and wanted to help her and he had the hereditary tendency to unstable behaviour. What he'd done was wrong; very wrong, but he'd done it for her. She must calm down and think how to help him.

The phone rang; it was Constable Martins asking if anything was wrong. Mavis had intended to confess. How foolish she would have appeared had she done so. She knew the truth now, but this time she wouldn't act without thinking.

"It was nothing urgent, I just wanted to talk. I'm sorry to have bothered you."

"It's no trouble, don't worry. Look, I'm due in court over the next few days and I've got a ton of paperwork. I could still make time if you need to speak to me, but if it can wait for a few days, I'd have much more time. We could have a proper chat?"

"I think that is an excellent idea."

"See you soon then."

Mavis had missed a person on her list of people to be trusted. The young policewoman was honest and sensible. Mavis knew that when the time came to tell what she must, it was to Tanya Martins she would speak.

What must she say though? Of course she must first find out the truth; what exactly had been done and how. Mavis realised she'd made some assumptions. She'd taken for granted all the incidents were connected. They might not be. She must learn more before she could act. There was the motive of course, she must establish that. Would it help the boy's case that he'd done what he had, not for his own benefit, but to ease her life? He'd thought she was his mother and had wanted to please her. Mavis would like a son like him, if only he didn't kill good people like Vera. Of course, he hadn't known her, was unaware Mavis's initial impression was wrong. He shouldn't have killed her without knowing the truth. Jacob was so young, so full of plans. How could he learn from his mistake if he was locked up for the whole of his youth? Mavis was older; had less to live for. He'd wanted to help her; now she must think of a way to help him.

Mavis was relieved; Janice and Cousin Linda were safe now. The boy wouldn't wish to harm either of them. She supposed that now he knew she wasn't his mother he would no longer wish to kill those she disliked either. That was probably just as well; it wasn't right. If the killing had stopped what good could she do? It was too late for Vera. Not too late for her daughter though, or Sandra's daughter. They deserved to know the truth. Children deserved to know the truth about their parents. It was difficult to know the right thing to do. She needed to gather evidence before she could decide.

Chapter 29

The sun was bright and cheerful. Mavis opened her bedroom window to feel the warmth on her face and smell the sweet scent of the viburnum. She dressed quickly, eager to make herself a cup of tea to drink in the garden. Knowing if she were to walk round she'd become absorbed in admiring the fresh new growth and risk being late for work, she sat still. If the weather remained fine, she would indulge in leisurely al fresco breakfasts over the weekend.

'One step at a time,' the calendar cautioned. Good advice; if something was rushed then it wasn't done correctly. Mavis washed and dried the breakfast things properly. She didn't give them a quick rinse and leave them to drip, in the manner of the people she worked with. That wasn't washing up. The same principle applied to other matters too. Before she decided what must be done about the boy's behaviour, she must establish the facts.

The boy got on the bus. Mavis smiled at him and said good morning. He looked embarrassed, but returned her greeting. Bert and his wife were there and Bert's wife chattered to her all the way, telling her of a lovely picture Lauren had drawn.

"Very artistic she is. Bit like you, I hear?"

Mavis was surprised by the remark.

"Karen told us you go to art classes, isn't that right? I do get things wrong sometimes, don't I Bert?"

She elbowed Bert.

"Eh?"

"Get things wrong sometimes, don't I?"

"What's wrong?" he asked.

"I thought Mavis here did art."

"Yes, dear."

"What do you mean by that? Yes she does, or yes I'm wrong?"

"You're right dear, she does them classes. Karen was telling us."

"There you go then."

Faced with such compelling evidence, Mavis was forced to admit she did indeed, 'do art'.

"Proper paintings is it, or that modern art?"

"I paint pictures of flowers, and seascapes."

"Seascapes, what's that then?"

Mavis didn't reply as another jab from his wife's elbow indicated that Bert should answer.

"Landscapes, but with the sea instead of trees and that," he said.

"Oooh, lovely, I like a nice landscape I do."

Mavis returned the conversation to Lauren; she was then able to listen to a flow of chatter, with no further risk to Bert's ribs.

At work, there was a call from Sandra's daughter. Sandra was conscious and expected to make a good recovery in time, Nicola told them.

"Apparently, she had some kind of abscess on her brain."

"A growth?" Lucy asked.

"I don't think so; her daughter spoke of it being drained. Anyway, her brain wasn't really damaged, not permanently at least. Pressure built up and eventually it caused her to become unconscious. The important thing is that she'll be OK."

"Poor woman, that explains all the pills she took. She must have had terrible headaches," Lucy said.

"It explains her filthy temper too," Janice said.

"Janice!" Lucy said.

"Well, it's true. She was always snapping at people for no reason. You never knew where you were with her. Nice one minute; bite your head off the next."

"Yes, but …"

"Yeah, I know what you mean, Lucy. It doesn't seem right to moan about her now, not if she's really ill. Perhaps it wasn't really her fault," Janice said.

"I'm sure that if I had constant headaches I'd be pretty moody," Nicola said. "If it was bad enough to knock her out, well, it must have been awful. I don't like to think about it."

"She must have been in agony," Lucy added.

"She seemed peaceful on Wednesday."

Nicola and Lucy stared at Mavis.

"Mavis visited her before her art class," Janice explained. "I think we should all go, if she's OK for visitors now."

"That's a good idea, Janice. I'll phone her daughter back and see when the best times would be."

Mavis had been wrong about Sandra, the boy hadn't pushed her; no one had. Her dream had been a dream, nothing more. If she'd been wrong about Sandra, what did that mean? She couldn't concentrate with all the chatter, she had to think. She went to make drinks. On the way to the kitchen, she knocked the back of her hand on Sandra's chair. No one was sitting in it and no tweed jacket was draped over it, but that hadn't always been the case. Perhaps she'd touched Sandra's jacket without realising it? Her hand was very painful; the knocked vein began to throb. She made the drinks and took them back in.

Nicola, Janice, Lucy and Mavis visited Sandra in turn over the next few days. Nicola went first, taking a bunch of flowers, paid for by them all. She reported Sandra was drowsy, but conscious and able to recognise her and say a few words. Janice and Lucy's visits revealed steady progress in their colleague's condition. By the time Mavis went to see Sandra again, she was sitting in a chair and eager to talk.

"I'm very pleased to see you, Mavis. I heard you came before. That was nice of you, especially as I've not always been very friendly towards you. Sorry, I'm not usually so bitchy. It was the headaches."

"Yes, I know."

"It's a huge relief to know what caused them. I knew something was wrong you see and it scared me. I didn't go to the doctors in case it was cancer. It isn't, but I'm lucky I was found just after I passed out. If my daughter hadn't got worried and come round ..."

"You are better now?"

"Much better, thank you. I'm going to be fine."

"Good."

They didn't speak for a short time.

"I know I shouldn't complain, but I'm so bored in hospital," Sandra said.

Mavis took a book from her bag.

"I brought you a book. Reading helps to pass the time."

"Is that what you do?" Sandra asked.

"Fortunately, I have not needed to stay in hospital since I was a child."

"I didn't mean that. I meant to fill in the time when you're not at work. I know you're not keen on the telly and you haven't got any family, but I don't know what you do. I suppose I've never bothered to ask."

It was true, Sandra hadn't asked. It was also true that Mavis hadn't volunteered information or made similar enquiries about Sandra's life.

"Yes, I do read quite a lot. Detective fiction mostly. I am also a keen gardener."

"Oh, I didn't know that. I like growing things. I live in a flat, but I've got a biggish balcony and it's full of pots. I even grow vegetables in the summer. Have you got a big garden with flower beds and a lawn and trees?"

"Yes, well, I ..."

"Something wrong?"

How could she explain her loss to Sandra? Her intention had been to offer sympathy, not to seek it.

"A tree was damaged in the strong winds."

"Oh, what a shame. Is it bad?"

"The tree surgeon cleared away the branches and neatly trimmed the remains. He thinks it may grow again, in a different shape."

"I hope so. That would be good wouldn't it? Like having a new tree really?"

"Yes, I suppose so," Mavis said.

"That's what I like about my pots. I don't mean I wouldn't like a proper garden, but pots do have some advantages. It's easy to change things if you want. Just empty one out and start again."

"Yes, that's true. I intend to make a new planting underneath the tree. Originally, there were sun-lovers there, but as the tree grew, it shaded them out. I shall make a new garden, with suitable plants."

"Good idea, what will you plant?"

They discussed plans for Mavis's garden, and the vegetables Sandra intended to plant as soon as she was well enough. When that topic was exhausted, Sandra asked for office gossip. Mavis enjoyed being the one who knew things and had interesting things to say, rather than being the bored person.

Sandra thanked her for coming, "It's very kind of you to take the trouble, especially as we haven't always been the greatest of friends."

Mavis realised she had the power to make people happy.

Mavis's visit to Sandra was followed by a visit to her from Tanya Martins. Mavis made tea and offered cake. She placed a tea towel over her guest's knees, "For the crumbs."

"Oh yes, I remember. You like to save them all for the birds. I think it's a great idea; in fact, I've started doing the same thing when I remember. Do you know, it really helps keep the kitchen floor clean?"

"I imagine it would."

"So, what's been going on around here then?"

Mavis avoided mention of Jacob, but talked about the people who'd died.

"You make it sound as though there's been a string of murders."

"Has there not?"

"No, none at all, I'm pleased to say."

"But, my neighbour?"

"You went to the inquest; it was an accident."

The police were unaware of all the facts. Mavis should tell them, without vital evidence they couldn't learn the truth. She kept quiet, she might get arrested and then she'd never learn what had happened, and would be unable to help Jacob.

"The pale girl …"

"Who?"

Mavis explained.

"Suicide, we found a note, pressure of exams. It was in the paper and on South Today."

"The woman who was run over?"

"You will have to give me a bit more to go on, we don't get many murders around here, but we do have more than enough RTAs."

Mavis tried to work out her meaning.

"Road traffic accidents."

Mavis told the WPC all she could remember.

Constable Martins used her mobile phone to call the station.

"The lady in question was run over, by joy riders. They were caught and will be punished. That's not murder though, granted their stupidity caused her death, but that's not quite what you mean is it?"

"Perhaps someone pushed her in front of the stolen car. That would be murder."

"I suppose it would, but that wasn't what happened. She was riding a bike."

'That which does not kill us makes us stronger,' she was informed. Did that mean the same as learning from one's mistakes?

Mavis had made mistakes, how could she have imagined she'd killed people, or that the boy had done so? She'd been confused of course and there were the dreams. She hadn't been well, maybe the afternoon's doctor's appointment would provide some help.

At work, she told Janice about the real causes of death.

"That's a relief," Janice said. "When we first talked about it, I didn't really believe anyone had been murdered, I thought it was just a game. Then when other things happened and I remembered I was pushed, I got really frightened."

"You were pushed then? I'd begun to wonder if I'd imagined everything."

"I was, but I suppose it might have been accidental, somebody stumbling into me or something. That's what I tried to tell myself, that nobody really wanted to kill me."

"I expect that's what happened. Why would anyone want to hurt you?"

"Thanks, Mavis. It was awful to think that."

"It appears that I was wrong about everything. Perhaps we wouldn't have been very good detectives."

"Oh I don't know, at least we used our imaginations. Solving straightforward crimes is easy, I expect, and the police solve most things anyway, especially the serious stuff. I reckon we should go in for more unusual things, not murders and that, but puzzling things."

"That would be interesting Janice, I do like trying to work things out, but I'm not at all sure I'd be any good at that either. I'm never very good at solving murders and mysteries in books."

"Well, you were sort of right about Jacob. He was acting strangely. You just didn't know why. Seems like your instincts are right; it's just that you don't know much about teenage boys so you couldn't tell in what way his behaviour wasn't normal."

"Perhaps." Mavis didn't know much about any group of people other than fictional characters; no wonder her deductions had been wrong.

"Will you go to Jacob's party?"

"I don't know."

Another thing Mavis didn't know anything about was teenager's parties; maybe it was time to begin her education. Janice could be her teacher.

"What would you suggest?"

"Yes, go. If you don't he might be upset and it sounds like he's got enough problems with that terrible mother of his."

"Yes, that must be difficult for him."

That was something Mavis could sympathise with.

"I think you should go early, as soon as it starts. It'll be quieter then, his family will be there, but not all his mates. Talk to him and his mum, you know her now, don't you? If there are any neighbours you recognise, talk to them too. Then you can go as soon as you're fed up. People'll remember you were there, they won't know when you left. Don't tell them later. If they mention the party, say it was very nice. If it was, they'll think you stayed; if it was awful, they'll just think you're being polite."

Mavis was impressed with Janice's clever strategies.

"Should I take a card?"

"Depends, if it's not actually his birthday then send the card on the right day, especially if it's before. It's nice to get them on the day, isn't it? Same with the present. Mind you if the party is beforehand, you might want to take it. If everyone else is handing things over you might feel a bit awkward."

Clever Janice. Mavis wouldn't have thought to buy a gift, but of course, she must do so. She could easily imagine a scene where everyone else arrived with beautifully wrapped gifts and she came empty handed. She would indeed have felt awkward.

The doctor asked her how her hands had become so sore.

"From cleaning. My supervisor told me to tell you that bleach and other cleaning products sting."

"You clean at work?"

"Yes, and at home of course. I live alone."

"Ah, that explains it. Prolonged immersion in water and exposure to harsh chemicals has dried out your skin. I assume that you don't wear gloves?"

299

"No, I don't." Mavis had bought some once, but when she washed them out after use, she could not get the insides properly dry again. They were then clammy and, as her hands were no longer kept dry, there seemed little point in wearing them.

"Well, you should try to use them whenever you can. I'm going to prescribe some cream. Apply it before you put on the gloves. While you are working, the cream will be absorbed. Re-apply it each time you wash your hands and before you go out in the cold or do any gardening, anything that might get them wet and dirty."

"And this will keep them clean?"

"Yes, it acts as a barrier, preventing damage to your hands. If you apply it regularly, your hands should soon improve. It will help if you don't get them wet or expose them to chemicals more often than you need to. Perhaps there are other tasks you can do at work for a time?"

"Yes, thank you doctor."

Whilst Mavis waited for her prescription to be filled, she bought a pack of rubber gloves.

Norman rang, suggesting they went out. Mavis wondered if she'd been wrong about him. She seemed to have lived her life treating everyone as though they were a character in a book. She still believed he was overly interested in money, but he'd not killed her neighbour in order to keep it to himself and there was no evidence he was trying to cheat her out of hers. Perhaps his investment tips had been intended as helpful advice.

She agreed to go for a meal. Not having to wash up, after making her own, would be good for her hands. Mavis needed friends to teach her how to be happy. Mother had taught her to cook and clean and run the house. She got training for a job and had learnt to support herself. That meant she could cope with life. Well, it should have done, but it didn't; as the bottle of gin, sleeping tablets and visit to the Round Tower proved. She needed to learn to enjoy herself. She'd done that on occasions with Norman. There was no reason why she shouldn't continue to do so. She had fun with Linda too; there could be many repeat visits.

Janice, and others, will give her valuable advice on not being unhappy.

She had interests now, the birds and her garden. Over the winter they had become a chore. That was because they were her only interests, she expected too much of them by way of entertainment. Now, she had her painting, new friends, places to visit and the possibility of detecting things, real mysteries, with Janice.

Early on the morning of the party, she dropped a birthday card through the letter box of the boy's home. It contained a cheque. After consultation with Janice, she'd learnt that would be very acceptable.

At 7.15, she locked her front door and walked to the community centre.

"Thank you so much for coming," Mrs Riley said.

"Thank you for inviting me." Mavis smiled at Jake and his mother. "Happy birthday, Jacob."

"Hello, Mavis. Thanks for the cheque."

Bert and his wife were there. She told Mrs Riley she knew them and was taken over to their table.

"Minnie, Bert, I believe you know Mavis?"

"Oh hello, Mavis dear. You come and sit here with us. We picked this table because it's furthest from the disco. Nice to see the youngsters having fun, but it deafens us don't it, Bert?"

She nudged him.

"Eh?"

"I said it deafens us."

"No dear."

"No?"

"That's right, dear." He winked at Mavis and took a sip of his pint.

When Bert's wife learnt that Mavis lived on her own, she invited her round for a meal on Sunday.

"Nothing fancy, just what we'd be having ourselves."

Mavis hesitated.

"Please do come, it would make a nice change for us, someone different to talk to."

"Makes a smashing roast, my wife," Bert told her.

Mavis accepted.

Another couple joined the table; the lady from the library, and her husband. They had sat down before Mavis recognised the assistant librarian. A search in her shoulder bag for a tissue allowed Mavis to look under the table at the woman's feet. They were encased in shiny yellow plastic that extended to just below her knees. Above the high heeled boots, the woman wore a practical, high necked dress made from navy wool.

As Mavis sat upright again, the woman from the library smiled at her. Minnie introduced them.

"Lilly and Daniel is Jake's aunt and uncle. Mavis knows him from getting the bus to work and home from college and that."

Bert explained he was a friend of Jake's dad and used to give the boy a Saturday job. The group discussed Lee-on-the-Solent and how it had changed, then moved on to gardening. Lilly was a member of the horticultural society.

"Mavis, you're interested in gardening. I know that from the books you borrow. You really should think about joining."

Mavis had seen the leaflets slipped into some of her books but hadn't realised they were aimed at her; she'd thought it standard practice. Now she saw they'd been intended as a personal invitation to join.

"You've got an allotment haven't you, Bert? You should join too. We have interesting talks, lots of trips to gardens, three shows, there's the trading hut where you can buy everything you need compost, fertilisers all that. Quite cheap and no need to drive out to B&Q or one of those places."

Mavis mentioned she didn't drive.

"Be good for you then. You can just get small amounts you can carry, or often someone'll drop it round for you. The trips would be good too, we have a lot of them and don't worry about not knowing anyone who's going. You'll have a coach load of friends by the time you get back. There are plant sales too. Get some really good stuff there at bargain prices. Not bad for two quid a year. There's a newsletter too, with tips and all that."

Mavis said she would go along to the trading hut on Sunday to join up, on the way to lunch with her new friends.

Chapter 30

Mavis woke up to a strange sensation. As she washed and dressed she wondered what was different. She wasn't ill. In fact, she felt very well. There was no time to puzzle it out; she had a lot to do! Because of visits to Sandra, sowing flower seeds and Jacob's party, she hadn't done any painting the previous week. She was eager to do some that Saturday. A scene of her garden was almost complete and she wished to show it to Tim. She'd intended to work on it after returning from the party, but had in fact stayed very late; Bert and his wife had walked her home. Minnie had said what a lovely garden she had.

"Can't see it now, but I've often admired it. Always got cheerful flowers, haven't you? I love flowers."

Mavis intended to pick flowers for Minnie. It would be best to do that today and let them stand in water overnight so they would be ready for Bert's wife to arrange.

Perhaps the lady in the library would like some? She said she arranged flowers. It would be a nice gesture to take some next time she returned her library books.

There was gardening to do too. She wouldn't have much time on Sunday, not if she was to give the house its usual thorough weekend cleaning. Oh dear, she wouldn't be able to do that either, she was going out to lunch and didn't know how long she'd stay. It was likely she'd be taken to view Bert's allotment. She would enjoy that. She must clean extra thoroughly today then. There was the shopping to do though. Well, that could wait. There was ample in the fridge for Saturday, or would be once she picked some salad leaves. She needed nothing for Sunday. She could do the shopping for next week on Monday, on her way back from work. A change to her regular routine wouldn't be a problem. She could choose to make the change. Weekends were really too busy to get everything done. The shops were crowded too. She wondered why she'd always done it then. To fill in time, that was why. How odd, when there was so much to do. She'd better get up, not lie there thinking.

'No pain, no gain,' was printed on her calendar. Wasn't that what people said about exercise? Regular gentle exercise was all that was required, that and a modest diet, kept you fit and healthy. Mavis was lucky she enjoyed gardening. That was a great aid to maintaining her health. Perhaps that wasn't the meaning of the message? The others referred, she was sure, to life in general. That would mean to make gains in life you must do painful things. Surely that wasn't right? Mavis was happier than she'd ever been, but it wasn't through sacrifice. It was through luck partly and also through choosing to do things she enjoyed. She'd made friends and would make more. She had her painting, at which she was improving all the time, not by suffering but by practising doing the very thing she wanted to do; paint. There was the garden and soon she would be in a gardening club. She could visit gardens and talk to people, share experiences. She'd recently gained so much, but not through pain.

There had been pain in her life; Daddy leaving and Mother's coldness, the difficulty of Mother's final years and the terrible loneliness after her death. More recently she'd been hurt by the loss of her friend and the damage to her tree. Vera was lost forever, but the tree might survive. The injury to her garden would soon be covered by fresh new growth. Mavis would overcome sadness. She now had friends. Vera had shown her that was possible. She had plans and hopes; a future.

Mavis knew the name of the strange sensation she'd felt on waking; happiness. No longer was she disappointed on waking that she hadn't, like Mother, died in her sleep. She didn't leave her bed for fear of the dreams she would have if she lingered, but because she wanted to get up and start doing the things she'd planned for the day. She wanted to get on with living.

The bird table was empty, not a seed or crumb remained. It looked perfectly clean and dry. Mavis took out seed and the crust from her loaf and refilled the peanut feeders. There was very little water in the bird bath. She tipped out what there was, rinsed the bath clean and refilled it.

No new growth was yet visible on the mulberry. Mavis ran her hand over the bark. It didn't feel dead. She could see, or thought she could see, tiny swellings from which new buds might burst. The shrubs that had been crushed under fallen branches were already shooting fresh new leaves. In a week or two, the cuts she'd made would be hidden. Perennials too were proving she'd been right to cut them back hard. Their growth was astonishing, as was that of the weeds and seedlings.

When the compost bin was full and her back stiff, Mavis went inside for a cup of coffee. It was past her usual lunchtime. She ate quickly, thinking of her painting. The plate and cup she'd used were put in the sink. She'd want another drink soon as she'd only had one since breakfast; she'd wash up then, it would waste precious daylight to do it immediately.

Mavis covered the dining table and laid out her painting of the garden and equipment. As she opened up her painting equipment part of the cellophane wrap snagged on a crack in her skin. She must take better care of her hands. Without regular applications of cream the fissures on her finger joints were sore where they were stretched to hold the brush.

She couldn't decide why the painting didn't satisfy her. Still in her portfolio was another unfinished work. That was of a vase of flowers, it was simply incomplete, needing more work. It would be easier to continue with that one, but the garden scene was her homework. Tim's idea had appealed to her. The task had been something unfamiliar, painted in an unfamiliar way. That was the problem; there was no angle in which to view the garden that was not familiar to her. To others, it might appear she'd accomplished the aim, but she knew she hadn't. She saw the garden from below as she bent to weed, from above each morning as she admired it from the bedroom window. Each time she finished working, or stopped for a rest, she looked back on what she'd done. There was nothing in her garden with which she wasn't familiar.

She flipped through her sketch book for inspiration. There was a drawing of the mulberry tree. That was what she would paint; nothing. She'd paint the space where the tree had been. Jagged ends to the trunk would be shown as they'd been that first morning, to represent the violence and destruction. The rest of the garden would be shown as it was now, tidy and beginning to recover. She took her sketch book outside and began to draw.

Before going inside, she gathered some sprays of fresh new leaves and a few flowers. Having the plants before her as she worked aided in matching colours and accurately depicting textures. Painting occupied her for longer than she expected, although she should have learnt to expect that to happen; once she got absorbed in what she was doing she didn't notice time passing.

As she prepared her supper, Mavis marvelled at her new happiness. She'd been happy as a child, when Daddy was still at home, but had let her joy slip away. She wouldn't do that again.

Sandra, because of her illness, had lost friends. Mavis knew behaviour could do that. Her own had prevented her forming any; Sandra's had driven them away. Mavis would be Sandra's friend now, they could encourage each other to build new strong relationships.

The detective agency with Janice, could they really do that? No, they couldn't become private detectives. That was a silly idea, but they could act like Miss Marple and investigate things that interested them.

She had no time and no energy left to clean the house. She'd have to tidy away the painting items and wash up after supper, but anything else could wait. As she put on cream and gloves she was reminded of the doctor's advice. Perhaps it would not hurt, until her hands were better, to do less cleaning. She could leave the spare room until Cousin Linda was due and do it extra thoroughly then. She needn't wash the plates and glasses she hadn't used either.

Washing up after supper, she looked at the flowers she'd picked. The creamy white of the late tulips would be perfect in the vase of deep hued peonies she was painting. That was what the picture needed, some light to act as a contrast to the richer colours. Mavis placed a tulip in the vase; the effect was good. A single perfect cream tulip glowed against the massed darker colours. Their ragged outline, graduations in colour and variety of sizes emphasised the purity of the singleton. No, not purity that suggested good and bad, simplicity was a better word. The flowers were different, but one wasn't better or worse than the others.

On Sunday morning, she slept later than usual. Her plans for a thorough cleaning of the house were further delayed by a call from Norman.

"Mavis, I have just seen an advertisement for tickets to the Hampton Court Palace flower show in July. I believe you once told me you would like to see it?"

"Oh, yes."

"Really? Good, shall I see if there are tickets still available? I could drive us up there and back."

"Thank you, Norman. That is very kind of you."

There was no time to do more than vacuum the carpets and clean the kitchen and bathroom. As she walked to Bert and Minnie's, carrying the flowers, she felt troubled by leaving the house uncleaned.

Lilly from the library wasn't at the horticultural society's trading hut. That didn't mean Mavis wasn't warmly welcomed.

"Hello, hello. Don't be shy, come and take a look," an elderly man encouraged. Mavis stepped inside.

"Are you wanting something in particular, or just taking a look?" he asked.

"I just came to have a look, and to join the society."

"Oh, good we always like new members. Hang on a sec." The man turned and shouted, "Hazel, new member, love." He turned back to Mavis, "Hazel'll sort out your membership."

Hazel appeared and asked Mavis to write her name and address in a book.

"It's two pound for the year. For that you can use the shop here, come to all the social evenings and you get the newsletter delivered."

"Here's the latest newsletter," the man said, handing her a leaflet.

"That tells you about the meetings. I hope you'll come along to them and maybe on some trips. We've got one coming up, to the Water Perry gardens. Just give me a ring if you fancy it," Hazel said, indicating her details on the page.

The flowers were admired, "Did you grow them?" Mavis nodded. "Perhaps you would consider entering some in the show? The details of that are in the leaflet too."

"Thank you. I will read this, then," Mavis promised as she left.

Minnie had cooked a joint of beef for lunch. It was served with crunchy roast potatoes, fluffy Yorkshire puddings a selection of vegetables and a jug of rich gravy. She opened a bottle of red wine and poured them each a glass.

"Cheers," Bert said and raised his glass. They each took a sip and began to eat.

"Lovely Yorkshires, Min. You've done us proud."

"It is a delicious meal," Mavis agreed.

"The veg is all from Bert's allotment," Minnie said.

Mavis ate the broad beans, purple sprouting broccoli, braised leeks and mashed swede. "They are all delicious; I grow a few salad leaves myself, but have never attempted anything more adventurous."

"The beans are a darn sight easier to grow than lettuce," Bert said. "The other things are easy enough too. Perhaps you'd like to walk off your lunch with a walk down the site and I'll show you."

"Apple and blackberry pie for afters," Minnie told them. "Would you like custard or ice cream, Mavis?"

"I really don't mind. Either would be very nice."

"What about you, Bert?"

"What's that?"

"Ice cream or custard?"

"Yes please, Min."

Mavis was given a dish of pie and offered a jug of custard. Minnie placed a portion of pie at her own place and went back to the kitchen. She returned with two dishes for Bert. In one, the pie was topped with ice cream, the other surrounded by creamy custard.

Bert beamed at her then ate the lot.

The allotment site was busy with people working. Most people looked up and called greetings to Bert. Mavis had expected to see men cultivating vegetables and wasn't disappointed. She was surprised to see the men were not all old and they were outnumbered by women and children. In addition to neat rows of vegetables, there were flowers and herbs and fruit bushes.

Bert's plot was very neat and clearly productive. He showed her; carrots, peas, cabbages and onions in addition to the types of vegetable they'd eaten for lunch. The vegetables were in various stages of development. Bert explained his system.

"I like to have a choice of fresh veg all year. I've always got stuff ready to pick, things coming on and other things just sown. See them beans? They'll be over soon and I'll put tomatoes in their place. When the leeks are gone, I'll put in some peppers."

"We're never short of tasty veg. Proper spoiled for that I am," Minnie boasted.

Bert showed Mavis how he cared for the crops and told her how good for his health it was to work outside. Mavis noticed the allotment also had a beneficial effect on his hearing. He didn't miss a single word of her questions, nor any joking remarks from his friends. Some people teased him about the forthcoming show.

"The show is great fun, lots of rivalry of course, but it's all in fun. I put in veg and Min enters her cakes and jams. You should enter some of your flowers."

"The gentleman in the trading hut said the same thing."

"There you go then."

"Will you come back for tea?" Minnie asked.

"That's very kind of you, but I …"

"Karen is coming with little Lauren. I told her yesterday you were coming and they're looking forward to seeing you."

Mavis spent the remainder of the afternoon helping Lauren paint, but not until after wrapping the child's cast in a carrier bag to keep it clean.

On Tuesday, Janice told Mavis that her mum had lost her purse. There was very little money in it, and luckily not her credit card, but it did have other things she would like to get back.

"I said, 'Don't worry, we'll get Quicke and Forthright to investigate'," Janice said.

"That is an excellent idea, Janice," Mavis said. "That is just the sort of thing we could look into. Where did your mum have it last?"

"She took her credit card out in Debenhams, that's why it wasn't in there. She'd stuffed that in her bag along with a receipt, but that's not the point, Mavis. She asked about Quicke and Forthright."

"Well, that is good, we …"

"No, no, because of the name. It's my dad!"

"Your father took the purse?"

"No, he's Forthright. That's his name. I didn't know, it's not on my birth certificate. He wasn't around then."

"That's not your fault, Janice. I guessed that your mother was unmarried, but..."

"I'm not worried about all that, but don't you see we could be related? My dad could be your brother, or half brother or something. And it's not just that I never knew him, he didn't know about me, mum never knew till he'd gone."

"Then we have two things to investigate; your mother's missing purse and the identity of your father."

"Can we do that? Find out if we're related?"

"We can try, Janice. I know that people do research their family trees, so I imagine it will be possible."

As she'd planned, Mavis did her shopping on the way home. She was surprised that when she started cleaning the house, it was no worse than it would have been if it had received the regular weekend attention. Perhaps she really was doing more than she needed? She shook her head. Walking away from her house on Sunday, knowing the carpets were not vacuumed and the surfaces had not been dusted had made her feel uncomfortable. Such tasks could be left if completing them in accordance with her routine would cause her to miss something more interesting, but she had no intention of regularly neglecting the cleanliness of her home.

Her life was changing, she could, should, reassess much of what she previously took for granted. She might have a brother, although that seemed unlikely. Janice might find her father. She had much to look forward to, she had a future, but first she must say goodbye to the past.

Chapter 31

As she'd done at the beginning of the year, Mavis visited the tourist information offices to check on shipping movements. She noted down days when no unusual vessels were expected. She waited for such a day to coincide with inclement weather; she wished to be alone.

Mavis again climbed to the top of the Round Tower. It seemed so long ago that she'd been planning her death and planning to say goodbye to her life. Now, she was letting go of unhappiness and planning her future. It hadn't been long. A year ago, Mother had been alive. Mavis had not been happy, but her life had held some meaning. Her task had been to care for Mother. It hadn't been possible to please her, but Mavis had been able to satisfy Mother's physical needs. Mavis had thought she disliked Mother. Perhaps she had, but she'd loved her too. She'd not known Mother loved her. The knowledge would not have helped Mavis wash the soiled sheets. It wouldn't have helped her plan the funeral or face her life once she was alone. It would help her, in the future, to know that she had been loved. That she was a person it was possible to love.

A seagull flew by, screaming its harsh cry. Mavis watched it until her vision was blurred by tears and she too was making sounds of distress. She cried for a long time, mourning Mother. Tears fell for Daddy too and for all the years she'd been unhappy. When her tears were all shed the past, like the seagull, was gone.

She said goodbye to Mother, saying the words aloud. She'd not been perfect, but she was gone now and she had made Mavis the person she was. Next, she whispered a farewell to Daddy. She knew little about him; maybe he'd not been perfect either. Lastly, she said goodbye to the old, constantly unhappy, Mavis.

Mavis walked to the wall of the tower and leant out, looking down into the cold sea. The rocks were covered; the tide had turned. She shivered; her future was not down there, it was all around her. Mavis had choices; there were many things she could do. It had taken her a long time to discover herself, but Mavis was all right.

She drew a rough sketch and made sure she would remember the view and how she felt; maybe when her painting skills improved she would paint the scene and fill it with hope. In the meantime, she'd better go and catch the ferry; she had friends to meet, a class to attend and no good excuse for being late.

The End

Also by Patsy Collins -

Escape to the Country.

Leah is accused of a crime she didn't commit. Dumped by Adam, the man she planned to marry, she escapes to Aunt Jayne's smallholding in the Kent village of Winkleigh Marsh. Heartbroken and homeless, she strives to clear her name and deal with her emotions.

Jayne treats Leah's unhappiness with herbal remedies, cowslip wine and common sense in equal measure. In return Leah works hard for the delicious home-cooked meals they share. She wrestles with sheep, breaks nails and gets stuck in the mud - learning as much about herself as she does about farming. Soon Leah is happy milking cows, mucking out pigs and falling halfway in love with Duncan, a dishy tractor driver.

Back in London, steps are being taken to investigate what's happened to the missing money. It looks as though the real embezzler must soon be unmasked and Leah will have to choose between resuming her old life or starting a new one.

That's when her problems really start.

A Year and a Day

Despite Stella's misgivings her best friend Daphne persuades her to visit a fortune teller. Rosie-Lee promises both girls will live long and happy lives. For orphaned Stella, the fortune teller's claims include a tall, dark handsome man and the family she longs for. Stella doesn't believe a word, so Rosie-Lee produces a letter, to be read in a year's time, which will prove her predictions are true.

Stella remains sceptical but Daphne is totally convinced. She attempts to manipulate Stella's life, starting by introducing Stella to her new boss Luigi, who fits the romantic hero image perfectly. In complete contrast is Daphne's infuriating policeman brother John. Despite his childhood romance with Stella ending badly he still acts as though he has a right to be involved in her life.

Soon John is the least of her worries. Daphne's keeping a secret, Luigi can't be trusted, romantically or professionally and both girls' jobs are at risk. Worse still, John's concerns for their safety are proved to be justified.

John, and Rosie-Lee's letter, are all Stella has to help put things right.

Not a Drop to Drink (short story collection)

'They' say the human body is around 70% water. It's not true.

We could drink straight H20 of course. Usually we don't. More likely it's vitamin rich juice or teeth rotting cola. We like a nice cup of tea to calm us down or cheer us up. Perhaps a nice glass of wine to celebrate or drown our sorrows. Two glasses. Too many glasses.

Our bodies do contain liquid of course. Never just water though. What's in yours; acid and bile or the milk of human kindness? Blood, sweat and tears of joy or sorrow?

It's these waters I hope you'll find running through my stories. Cheers!

If you'd like to learn more about the author and her writing, please visit her blog - http://patsy-collins.blogspot.co.uk/ or her facebook author page - http://www.facebook.com/PatsyCollins.writer or find her on twitter @PatsyCollins

You can also read many of Patsy's short stories at www.alfiedog.com

3664142R00174

Printed in Great Britain
by Amazon.co.uk, Ltd.,
Marston Gate.